SEASIDE *Sunsets*

Seaside Summers, Book Three

Love in Bloom Series

Melissa Foster

ISBN-13: 978-1-941480-06-9
ISBN-10: 1941480063

This is a work of fiction. The events and characters described herein are imaginary and are not intended to refer to specific places or living persons. The opinions expressed in this manuscript are solely the opinions of the author and do not represent the opinions or thoughts of the publisher. The author has represented and warranted full ownership and/or legal right to publish all the materials in this book.

SEASIDE SUNSETS
All Rights Reserved.
Copyright © 2014 Melissa Foster
V1.0

This book may not be reproduced, transmitted, or stored in whole or in part by any means, including graphic, electronic, or mechanical without the express written consent of the publisher except in the case of brief quotations embodied in critical articles and reviews.

Cover Design: Natasha Brown

WORLD LITERARY PRESS
PRINTED IN THE UNITED STATES OF AMERICA

A Note to Readers

If this is your first Love in Bloom book, then you have many other characters to fall in love with, starting with the Snow Sisters, then moving on to the Bradens, the Remingtons, and the rest of the Seaside Summers gang. The Love in Bloom series follows several families, and characters from each subseries appear in future Love in Bloom novels.

Before I started writing this novel, I thought it was going to be difficult to find the perfect woman for Jamie Reed, but the minute I met Jessica Ayers, I realized that it wasn't going to be difficult at all. It was a sexy, fun ride. I hope you enjoy them as much as I do.

Seaside Sunsets is the third book in Seaside Summers series and the newest addition to the Love in Bloom series. While it may be read as a stand-alone novel, for even more enjoyment, you may want to read the rest of the Love in Bloom novels (Snow Sisters, The Bradens, The Remingtons, and Seaside Summers).

Melissa Foster

For Jon, who makes geekiness cool

PRAISE FOR MELISSA FOSTER

"Contemporary romance at its hottest. Each Braden sibling left me craving the next. Sensual, sexy, and satisfying, the Braden series is a captivating blend of the dance between lust, love, and life."
—Bestselling author Keri Nola, LMHC
(on The Bradens)

"[LOVERS AT HEART] Foster's tale of stubborn yet persistent love takes us on a heartbreaking and soul-searing journey."
—Reader's Favorite

"Smart, uplifting, and beautifully layered. I couldn't put it down!"
—National bestselling author Jane Porter
(on SISTERS IN LOVE*)*

"Steamy love scenes, emotionally charged drama, and a family-driven story make this the perfect story for any romance reader."
—Midwest Book Review (on SISTERS IN BLOOM*)*

"HAVE NO SHAME is a powerful testimony to love and the progressive, logical evolution of social consciousness, with an outcome that readers will find engrossing, unexpected, and ultimately eye-opening."
—Midwest Book Review

"TRACES OF KARA is psychological suspense at its best, weaving a tight-knit plot, unrelenting action, and tense moments that don't let up and ending in a fiery, unpredictable revelation."
—*Midwest Book Review*

"[MEGAN'S WAY] A wonderful, warm, and thought-provoking story...a deep and moving book that speaks to men as well as women, and I urge you all to put it on your reading list."
—*Mensa Bulletin*

"[CHASING AMANDA] Secrets make this tale outstanding."
—*Hagerstown* magazine

"COME BACK TO ME is a hauntingly beautiful love story set against the backdrop of betrayal in a broken world."
—*Bestselling author Sue Harrison*

Chapter One

JESSICA AYERS COULD hold a note on her cello for thirty-eight seconds without ever breaking a sweat, but staring at the eBay auction on her iPhone as the last forty seconds ticked away had her hands sweating and her heart racing. She never knew seconds could pass so slowly. She'd been pacing the deck of her rented apartment in the Seaside cottage community in Wellfleet, Massachusetts, for forty-five minutes. This was her first time—and she was certain her last time—using the online auction site. She was the high bidder on a baseball that she was fairly certain was her father's from when he was a boy.

"Come on. Come on. Come on." *Fifteen seconds.* She clenched her eyes shut and squeezed the phone, as if she could will the win. It was only seven thirty in the morning, and already the sun had blazed a path through the trees. She was hot and frustrated, and after fighting with her orchestra manager for two weeks about taking a hiatus, and her mother for even longer about everything under the sun, she was ready to blow. She'd come to the Cape for a respite from playing in the Boston Symphony Orchestra, hoping to figure out if she was living her life to the fullest, or missing out on it altogether. Finding her father's baseball autographed by Mickey Mantle was her self-imposed distraction to keep her mind off picking up the cello. She'd never imagined she'd find it a week into her vacation.

She opened her eyes and stared at the phone.

Five seconds. Four. Three.

A message flashed on the screen. *You have been outbid by another bidder.*

"What? No. No, no, no." She pressed the bid icon, and nothing happened. She pressed it again, and again, her muscles tightening with each attempt. Another message flashed on the screen. *Bidding for this item has ended.*

No!

She stared at the phone, unable to believe she'd been seconds away from winning what she was sure was her father's baseball and had lost it. She hated phones. She hated eBay. She hated bidding against nonexistent people in tiny little stupid phones. She hated the whole thing so much she turned and hurled the phone over the deck.

Wow.

That felt really, really good.

"Ouch! What the..." A deep male voice rose up to her.

Jessica crouched and peered between the balusters. Standing on the gravel road just a few feet from her building, in a pair of black running shorts and no shirt, was the nicest butt she'd ever seen, attached to a tanned back that was glistening with sweat and rippled with muscles. Holy moly, they didn't make orchestra musicians with bodies like that. Not that she'd know, considering that they were always properly covered in black suits and white shirts, but could a body like that even *be* hidden?

He turned, one hand rubbing his unruly black hair as he looked up at the pitch pine trees.

Yeah, you won't find the culprit there.

His eyes passed by her deck, and she cringed. At least he hadn't seen her phone, which she spotted a few feet away, where it must have fallen after conking him on the head. His eyes dropped to the ground...and traveled directly to it.

Jessica ducked lower, watching his brows knit together, giving him a brooding, sexy look.

Please don't see me. Please don't see me.

He looked at the cottages to his left, then to the pool off to his right, and just as Jessica sighed with relief, he crossed the road toward the steps to her apartment. His eyes locked on her. He shaded them with his hand and looked down at the phone, then back up at her, and lifted the phone in the air.

"Is this yours?"

She debated staying there, crouched and peering between the railings like a child playing hide-and-seek, hoping he really couldn't see her.

I've been seeked.

Darn it! She rose slowly to her feet. "My what?" She had no idea what she was going to say or do as the words flew from her mouth.

He laughed. God, he had a sexy laugh. "Your phone?"

He stood there looking amused and so damn sexy that Jessica couldn't take her eyes off of him. "Why would that be mine? I don't even have a phone." *Great. Now I'm a phone assaulter and a liar.* She had no idea that being incredibly attracted to a man could couple with embarrassment and make her spew lies, as if she lied every day.

He looked back down at the phone and scratched his head. She wondered what he was thinking. That it fell from the sky? No one was that stupid, but she couldn't own up to it now. She was in too deep. As he mounted the stairs, she got a good look at his chest, covered with a light dusting of hair, over muscles that bunched and rippled down his stomach, forming a V between his hips.

He stepped onto the deck and raked his hazel eyes down her body with the kind of smile that should have made her feel at ease and instead made her feel very naked. And hot. Definitely hot. Oh wait, he was hot. She was just bothered. Hot and bothered. Jesus, up close he was even more handsome than she imagined, with at least three days' scruff peppering his strong chin and eyes that played hues of green and brown like a melody.

"Hi. I'm Jamie Reed."

"Hi. Jessica...Ayers."

"How long are you renting?" He used his forearm to wipe his brow. She never knew sweating could look so sexy.

"For the summer." She shifted her eyes to her phone. "What will you do with that phone?"

He looked down at it. "I guess that depends, doesn't it?" The side of his mouth quirked up, making his handsome, rugged face look playful and sending her stomach into a tailspin.

Jessica needed and wanted playful in her too prim and proper life, but she needed her phone even more, in case her orchestra manager called.

"Let's say it was my phone. Let's say it slipped from my hand and fell over the deck, purely by accident."

He stepped closer, and suddenly playful turned serious. His eyes went dark and seductive, in a way that bored right through her, both turning her on and calling her on her shit. He placed one big hand on the railing beside her and peered over the side. His brows lifted, and he stepped closer again. She inched backward until her back met the wooden rail. He smelled of power and sweat and something musky that made her insides quiver.

"That's a hell of an accident." His voice whispered over her skin.

Jessica could barely breathe, barely think with his eyes looking through her, and his crazy, sexy body so close made her sweat even more. The truth poured out like water from a faucet.

"Okay. I'm sorry. I did throw it, but it's not my fault. Not really. It's that stupid eBay site." Her voice rose, and her frustration bubbled forth. "I don't know how I could lose an auction in the last ten seconds. My bid held strong for forty-five minutes, and then out of the blue I lost it for five lousy dollars? And it was all because the stupid bid button was broken." She sank down to a chair. "I'm sorry. I'm just upset."

"So, let me get this straight. You lost a bid on eBay, so you threw your phone?" He lowered himself to the chair beside her, brow wrinkled in confusion, or maybe amusement. She couldn't tell which.

"Yeah, I know. I know. I threw my phone. But it must be broken. I hate technology."

"Technology is awesome. It's not the phone's fault you lost your bid. It's called sniping, and lots of people do it."

"Sniping?" She sighed. "I'm sorry. I know I sound whiny and bitchy, but I'm really not like this normally."

He arched a brow and smiled, which made her smile, because of course he didn't believe her. Who would? He didn't know she was usually Miss Prim and

Proper. He couldn't know she never used words like *stupid* or even visited the eBay website until today.

"I swear I'm not. I'm just frustrated. I've been trying to find the baseball my father had as a kid. It was signed by Mickey Mantle, and somewhere along the line, his parents lost it. His sister had colored in the autograph with red ink, and I think I finally found it...and then lost it."

"That's a bummer. I can see why you're upset. I'm sorry."

"How can you be so nice after I beaned you with my phone?"

He shrugged. "I've been hit by worse. Here, let me show you some eBay tricks." He scrolled through her apps, of which she had none other than what came with the phone. He drew his brows together. "Do you want me to download the eBay app?"

"The eBay app? I guess."

He fiddled with her phone, then moved his chair closer to hers. "When you're bidding on eBay and other people are bidding at the same time, you need to refresh your screen because bids don't refresh quickly on all phones." He continued explaining and showing her how to refresh her screen.

She only half listened. She simply didn't get technology, and she was used to sitting next to men in suits and tuxedos, not half-naked men with Adonis-like bodies wearing nothing but a pair of shorts with all their masculinity on display. She could barely concentrate.

JAMIE COULD TELL by the look in Jessica's eyes that she wasn't paying attention. As the developer of OneClick, the world's second-largest search engine, rivaling Google, he'd been in his fair share of meetings with foggy-eyed people who zoned out when he started with technical talk. But refreshing a screen was hardly technical, which meant that either beautiful Jessica was really a novice and had lived in a cave for the past ten years or she was playing him like a cheap guitar. She sure as hell didn't look like she'd been living in a cave. She was about the hottest chick he'd seen in forever, sitting beside him in a canary-yellow bikini like it was the most comfortable thing in the world. Maybe she was a fashion model with handlers that did these kinds of things for her.

Her light brown hair brushed her thighs when she leaned forward, and her bright blue eyes, although looking a little lost at the moment, were strikingly sexy. She had a hot bod, with perfect, perky breasts, a trim waist, curvaceous hips, and legs that went on forever, but that didn't change the fact that she'd tried to avoid admitting that the phone was hers. The last thing Jamie needed this summer was to be played, even by a beautiful woman like Jessica. This was his first summer off in eight years, and he intended to relax and spend time with his grandmother, Vera, who was in her mid-eighties and wasn't getting any younger. If the right woman came along, and he had the time and interest, he'd enjoy her company, but he had no patience for games.

"Either your phone is new, or you don't use many apps."

"No. To be honest, I don't even text very often. I've been kind of out of the swing of things in that arena for a while. And after this I'm not sure that I really want to dive in."

He handed her the phone. "You can do this on your computer. Some people find that easier."

She closed her eyes for a beat and cringed. "I get along with my computer even worse than I get along with my phone."

He still couldn't decide if she was playing him or not. She sounded sincere, and the look in her beautiful baby blues was as honest as he'd ever seen. Oh hell, he might as well offer to help.

"Then you've met just the right guy. I can give you a crash course in computers and phones."

"I've taken up so much of your time already. I would feel guilty taking up any more on a beautiful day like today. But I really appreciate your offer."

Are you blowing me off?

Jamie rose to his feet. "Okay, well, if you need any help, I'm in the cottage on the end with the deck out front and back. Stop by anytime." He hesitated, knowing he should leave but wanting to stay and get to know her a little better. If she was playing him, she would've taken him up on his offer for sure.

Jessica rose to her feet, grabbed a towel from the back of her chair, and picked up a tote bag from beneath the table. "I'm heading to the pool, so I'll walk down with you."

They walked down to the pool together in silence, giving Jamie a chance to notice how nice she smelled. It took all of his focus not to run his eyes down her backside—he was dying to see her ass, but why rush things and make her uncomfortable? She'd walk into the pool and he'd have his chance.

Jessica dug through her tote bag. She placed a slender hand on her hip and sighed. "I forgot my key. Why do they keep the pool locked, anyway?"

He had no idea why, but she looked so curious that he made up a reason. "To keep the derelicts out."

"Derelicts? Really? My friend suggested that I rent here. He said there was almost no crime on the Cape."

Jamie wondered who her *friend* was. "We had some trouble with teenagers two summers ago, but other than that, your friend was right. There are no derelicts lurking about."

"Oh, thank goodness. I didn't think my coworker would lead me astray. I guess I'll go get my key."

She turned to leave and—*holy hell*—her bikini bottom was a thong. A thin piece of floss between two perfect ass cheeks. How had he missed that?

It was all he could do not to drool. "Nice suit," he mumbled.

She looked over her shoulder. "Thanks! I saw the Thong Thursday flyer and thought, why not? I bought this suit when we were overseas and wore it there once. I brought it with me, but I never would have had the guts to wear it here, until I saw that you guys had an actual *day* for one." She waved and disappeared up the steps to her apartment.

Jamie spun around and scanned the bulletin board where the pool rules were posted. A blue flyer had been tacked front and center: JOIN US FOR THONG THURSDAY!

Thank you, Bella.

Jamie jogged up to Bella's cottage. The screen door was open.

"Bella?" Bella Abbascia owned the cottage across from the apartment Jessica was renting. Bella was the resident prankster. Her favorite person to play tricks on was Theresa Ottoline, the Seaside property manager. Theresa oversaw the homeowner association guidelines for the community—including the pool rules, which included a rule that clearly stated, *No thongs on women or Speedos on men*.

Her fiancé, Caden Grant, walked out of the bedroom in his police officer uniform. "Hey, Jamie. Come on in."

Jamie stepped inside. "Hi. I wanted to thank your fiancée for Thong Thursday."

Caden shook his head. "She did it, huh?"

"Hell, yes, she did it, and..." Jamie looked out the window at the *big house* where Jessica was renting. The house was owned by Theresa. The apartment Jessica rented had a separate entrance on the second floor.

"Did you see the new tenant? Jessica Ayers?" He whistled. "Hotter than hell."

"I saw her sitting on her deck the other night when I pulled in, but I haven't met her. Bella's over at Amy's with the girls."

Evan, Caden's mini-me teenage son, walked out of his bedroom. Evan was almost seventeen, and this year he'd cropped his chestnut hair short, like his father's. Over the year he'd grown to six two. His square jaw and cleft chin, also like Caden's, had lost all but the faintest trace of the boy he'd been two years earlier.

"Dude. You went running without me?" Evan, Caden, and their other buddy, Kurt Remington, whose fiancée, Leanna Bray, owned the cottage behind Bella and Caden, sometimes ran with Jamie in the mornings.

"Sorry, Ev. Vera wanted to get a jump on the day, so I went early."

"That's okay." Evan glanced out the window in the kitchen and looked down by the pool, where Jessica was spreading a towel out on a lounge chair. "I was gonna go for a run, but if it's Thong Thursday, I think I'll go for a swim instead, then head over to TGG for the afternoon." Evan had worked with Jamie for one summer, learning how to program computers, and he'd been working part-time at TGG, The Geeky Guys, ever since.

Jamie set a narrow-eyed stare on Evan.

"What?" Evan laughed.

"Behave," Jamie said, before walking out the door. *Christ, now I'm jealous of a kid?* He glanced at the pool, tempted to put on his own suit and head down for a gawk and a swim. Instead, he headed across the gravel road to Amy Maples's cottage.

"Hi, Jamie. Just in time for coffee." Amy handed him a mug over the railing of her deck.

"Thanks."

Jenna Ward, a big-busted brunette, and Bella, a tall, mouthy blonde, followed Amy out of her cottage. They wore sundresses over their bathing suits, their typical Cape attire. The Seaside cottages had been in their families for years, and Jamie had grown up spending summers with the girls and Leanna Bray, who owned the cottage beside Vera's, and Tony Black, who owned the cottage on the other side of Leanna's.

"Come on up here, big boy." Bella waved him onto the deck and pulled out a chair.

"I owe you big-time, Bella." He sat beside her and set his coffee on the glass table.

"Most people do," she teased.

"I know I do." Jenna had recently gotten engaged to Pete Lacroux, a local boat craftsman, who also handled maintenance for Seaside—and had been the object of Jenna's secret crush for years. Bella and Amy had secretly broken things in Jenna's cottage for several summers without Jenna knowing, to ensure that she and Pete would have reasons to be thrown together.

"Thong Thursday?" Jamie shook his head. "You are a goddess, Bella."

She patted her thick blond hair. "Thank you for noticing."

"Leanna is going to be so mad at you for doing that," Jenna said. "She doesn't think our men need to see butt floss on any of us." Leanna ran a jam-making business out of Kurt's bay-side property.

Bella swatted the air. "She's staying at their bay

house for a few days. She'll miss it completely." The lower Cape was a narrow peninsula that sprawled between Cape Cod Bay and the Atlantic Ocean. The cottages were located between the two bodies of water, and both Kurt and Pete owned property on the bay. Caden and Bella had a house on a street around the corner from the bay, and all three couples spent most of their summers at Seaside and the rest of the year at their other homes.

Luscious Leanna's Sweet Treats had really taken off in the last two years, and since her business was run from a cottage on their bay property, she was spending more and more time there.

"I'm sure Tony won't complain," Amy said with an eye roll that could have rocked the deck. Tony Black was a professional surfer and a motivational speaker, and Amy had been hot for him for about as long as Jenna had been lusting after Pete, but Tony had never made a move toward taking their relationship to the next level. Jamie didn't get it. He'd seen Tony eyeing Amy, and Tony took care of her like she was his girlfriend. Amy was hot, smart, and obviously interested—Tony was a big, burly guy with a good head on his shoulders. They'd make a great pair.

"Speaking of Tony, I saw him leave early this morning. He's spending the day at the ocean." Jamie sipped his coffee.

"Good, then maybe he'll miss the thong show, too." Amy leaned over the table and lowered her voice. "Did you guys see the chick renting Theresa's condo?"

"All I know is that she's smokin' hot and she doesn't talk much." Jenna was busy resituating the top of her sundress, pulled tightly across her enormous breasts.

"I don't know what her deal is," Bella said. "But she was yelling at her phone the other day."

"You mean yelling on her phone," Jenna corrected her.

"No, I mean at. She was staring at it, smacking it, and yelling at it." Bella made a cuckoo motion with her finger beside her head.

Nothing new here from the girls. A little jealousy over the new hot chick. Jamie picked up his coffee mug. "Mind if I bring this back later? I have to get going. I'm running into Hyannis to pick up a few things. You guys need anything?"

The girls shook their heads.

"You're willingly going to miss Thong Thursday?" Bella put her hand to his forehead. "You must be ill."

No shit. "One look at my ass in a thong and she'll be chasing me around the complex. I wouldn't want to subject you three ladies to that. It could get ugly." He smiled with the tease.

"Ha! Yeah, right. Like you'd ever wear a thong." Jenna threw her head back with a loud laugh. "You're just worried about sporting a woody down by the pool."

She had him there.

"You've got woodies on the brain," Jamie said. "Are you guys coming to Vera's concert tonight?" Vera had played the violin professionally when she was younger, and this summer a group of older Wellfleet residents had put together a string quartet and invited Vera to play. They never saw much of a crowd, but it got her out of the house and playing for an audience again, which she enjoyed.

"I wouldn't miss Vera's concert," Amy said.

"Bella and I are going over together because Caden's taking someone's shift and Pete's hanging with his father tonight, working on a boat. I'll ask Sky if she wants to come, too." Sky was Pete's sister. She'd come to the Cape last summer to run their father's hardware store while he was in rehab, and she'd never gone back to New York other than to pack up her things. Now sober for almost a year, their father helped Pete with his boat-refinishing business.

"Vera will be glad to hear it, and she loves Pete's sister." He glanced down at the pool, then headed for his cottage.

"Wanna bet who's gonna bang the new chick? Tony or Jamie?" Jenna's voice trailed behind him.

Jamie slowed to hear the answer.

A crack of hand on skin told him that Amy had shut Jenna up with a friendly swat.

Chapter Two

JESSICA OPENED HER eyes at the sound of her cell phone ringing. She was lying poolside, having a nice little fantasy about sinfully sexy and ever-so-helpful Jamie Reed. Her phone rang again, and she reluctantly shoved the thoughts of him away and dug through the bag for her phone.

Her father's picture flashed on the screen, and she smiled.

"Hi, Dad."

"Hi, honey. How is the Cape?" Ralph Ayers was in his mid-fifties. Jessica was blessed with his dimples, blue eyes, and light brown hair—though his was now graying at the temples. Unfortunately, she was also blessed with her father's passive personality, which she was working this summer to change so she didn't end up railroaded by her mother her whole life.

She remembered how she'd thrown her phone over the deck. *Maybe I'm working a little too hard on that.*

"It's beautiful. I've been lying out by the pool all day." When Jessica was young, their family vacations were more like cultural lessons overseas with only a day or two spent on a beach, and always with her cello in tow. Her mother insisted she keep up her practicing. Jessica could still remember begging to stay on the beach rather than tour museums and countrysides. But her mother insisted that the more well rounded she was, the better she'd be accepted as a cellist.

Unfortunately, life as a cellist, with no social life to speak of, left her feeling like a culturally adept square.

"Not the beach? I'm surprised," her father said. "I was sure you'd be camped out on the sand all summer long."

"I will be." *But today I followed Jamie off my deck.* "Tomorrow maybe. How are you, Dad?"

"I'm well. Just worried about you. Your mother's been on the phone night and day with her symphony friends. She's concerned that you're jeopardizing your seat with the orchestra and any chance you have with the Chamber Players. I'm not so sure she's wrong. Are you sure this is what you want to do? After all that hard work at Juilliard?"

The Boston Symphony Chamber Players was one of the world's most distinguished chamber music ensembles sponsored by a major orchestra. It was made up of principal players of the Boston Symphony Orchestra, including first-chair string and wind players. It would be a miracle for Jessica to be invited to join such a prestigious group. Everyone in the industry knew how unique it was for a twenty-seven-year-old to hold a seat in the BSO in the first place. Although her manager had agreed to the hiatus after weeks of discussion and they'd found a suitable replacement, she knew just how cutthroat the industry could be. There was a chance she'd lose her place—and any chance she might ever have at the Chamber Players—and that realization made her feel sick and free at the same time.

"Yes, I'm sure." *I think*. "We've talked about this. Dad, I feel twenty years older than I am most of the time. I live in orchestra land, and that doesn't really lend itself well to experiencing life outside of the orchestra. And I've never done anything else. I just want to be normal for a little while. Live a regular life. Daddy, I'm twenty-seven. I love Mom, but I don't want to live my life like she does." Her mother played the cello in several smaller orchestras but had never made the cut for the larger ones. Eventually she gave up trying and put all of her energies into Jessica's success.

"I want to *experience* life a little, and besides, I have a summer project I'm working on. Something fun."

"Okay, sweetie. As long as you're happy. I trust your instincts, and you know we're here if you need anything."

"Thanks, Dad."

"Want to say hello to your mom? She's just upstairs."

Jessica shifted the phone away from her mouth and sighed. The last thing she wanted to do was talk to her mother, but, like her father, she tended to avoid confrontation. At least until that morning, when she'd forgotten and barreled headfirst into creating it with Jamie.

"Sure." She listened as he took the phone upstairs and said something to her mother.

"Hi, Jessica. How are you?"

"Fine, Mom. And you?" She forced a smile, but even she could hear the tension that had taken residence in her voice.

"How's your vacation? Are you practicing? You don't want to let that slip, not after all your hard work." Cecilia Ayers had always micromanaged her daughter's life, and Jessica was working on taking control of that, too. She didn't give Jessica a chance to respond. "I spoke to your—"

"Mom, please. I'm on vacation, remember? Aside from stressing out over my career, how are things with you?" She closed her eyes, envisioning her mother's thin lips pursed together, her eyes shifting upward as she blinked away her irritation in that proper, pull-herself-together-without-embarrassment way she had.

"I'm well, thank you," her mother finally managed.

"Good. I'm glad to hear it." Being the people pleaser that she was, she added, "Don't worry. I'll practice. I just need a few days away from it. You know I'll miss it and have to play."

"Okay. Well, good."

Jessica knew her mother only pushed her to help her be the best damn cellist she could possibly be, and as thankful as she was for that, Jessica always felt a pang of longing for all of the normal mother-daughter things she'd missed out on over the years.

She sat up on the lounge chair as an older woman wearing a big floppy hat came through the pool gate. "Mom, I've got to go, but it was good talking to you."

"Okay, honey. Enjoy yourself. Not too much, of course."

She ended the call and stuffed her phone back into her bag, unsure what enjoying herself too much even meant. Her life in Boston consisted of practicing, playing concerts, and an occasional evening out with her musician friends—whose idea of a wild night was spontaneously playing "Rum and Tequila" by the Tom Fun Orchestra.

The pool looked too inviting to pass up, and as she passed the older woman, she said hello.

"Good afternoon." The woman's gray hair was cut

in a pixie style similar to Judi Dench's hairdo. She had a kind, familiar smile, although Jessica couldn't place where she'd seen her before.

She felt the woman's eyes on her as she walked into the pool and sank beneath the water. When she broke the surface, she saw three more women, wearing sundresses, coming through the gate, carrying colorful plastic wineglasses and towels. They were holding on to one another and laughing like best friends. They looked like they knew how to have a good time.

A skinny blonde looked over and waved.

"Hi," Jessica said as the blonde walked past.

The brunette couldn't have been five feet tall. She flashed a friendly smile as she peered around the skinny blonde's back.

"Hi. I'm Jenna."

"Hi. I'm Jessica. I'm renting up there." She pointed to the apartment she was renting in the second floor of the only large house in the community.

"We know," the skinny blonde said. "I'm Amy, and this is Bella." She pointed to the tall blonde who was laying a towel out on a lounge chair by Jessica's.

Bella waved over her head without turning around.

Jessica got out of the pool, feeling the eyes of all three girls on her.

"Darn it. I forgot my thong," Bella said.

"Bella," Amy hissed. "Well, I remembered mine." She pulled her sundress over her head, and sure enough, she was wearing a pink thong bikini. She turned and wiggled her butt at Bella.

"I cannot believe you wore that. Who are you, and what have you done with my Amy?" Bella waved to the older woman. "Hi, Vera. Did you wear your thong?"

"Bella Abbascia, why, you know I *always* wear my

thong." Vera winked at Jessica, then returned her attention to the novel she was reading.

Jenna took off her sundress. She could have stopped traffic in her red bikini. She had the largest breasts Jessica had ever seen on such a petite woman, trapped beneath the tiniest bathing suit top. Jessica was sure the wrong move would send the top flying across the pool as if launched by a slingshot.

"I wore my thong. Looks like you're the odd one out," Jenna said to Bella.

"Has anyone seen Theresa?" Amy whispered.

Jessica spread her towel on the lounge chair and stretched out on her stomach. "Do you mean Theresa Ottoline? The woman I rent from?"

"Yeah," Jenna answered.

Jessica pointed at the woman walking through the pool gate. She felt something on her butt and was surprised to see Vera covering it with a towel.

"Stay as you are," Vera said with a serious tone.

What the heck?

Jessica waved to Theresa. Theresa lifted her chin in response. She'd been curt since Jessica arrived, but at least she usually smiled. Now she walked at a fast pace with her jaw clenched and her shoulders riding just below her ears. Her high-waisted khaki shorts hung nearly to her knees, and her polo shirt was primly buttoned. She had short layered hair, which, in combination with her outfit, looked a bit mannish.

Theresa crossed her arms and stared at Bella, tapping her foot on the concrete deck.

"Hi, Theresa. Here for a swim?" Bella set a pair of big round sunglasses on her nose and leaned back in her chair.

"I think I might." Theresa wiggled out of her shorts, exposing far too much of her bare, white, cellulite-covered ass, the tiny triangle of a thong peeking out at the top of her butt crack.

Jessica had no idea what was going on, but she covered her mouth to keep from laughing at the look on Bella's face.

Jenna and Amy clung to each other's arms with one hand and stifled their laughter with the other. Bella pressed her lips together, barely suppressing a laugh.

"How about it, Vera?" Theresa yelled across the pool deck. "You up for a Thong Thursday swim?"

Jessica looked up at Vera with wide eyes.

"Oh, I think I'll spare you the imagery. Thank you, though," Vera said.

Jessica chanced a peek at Theresa, whose eyes were still pinned on Bella.

"Actually, I think I'll go run a few errands. You girls enjoy the afternoon." Theresa pulled up her shorts and stomped out of the gate.

Amy and Jenna ran to Bella's side, whispering and laughing. Jessica looked at Vera, who motioned her over to the table where she was sitting. She handed Vera the towel she'd covered her butt with and sat across from her.

"Hi, I'm Jessica. Thank you for covering my butt. I think." She drew her brows together, still confused by what had just happened.

"Bella's a prankster, and Theresa is the property manager. As you probably guessed, thongs aren't allowed at the pool."

"Oh." Jessica chewed on her lower lip. "Gosh, I hope I'm not going to get in trouble. I had no idea, and the sign..."

"Bella made the sign. Every year, Bella plays tricks on Theresa. She's been doing it since she was a kid, and every year Theresa ignores her. But this year, it looks like Bella's getting a little payback."

Jessica scrutinized the three girls, still laughing and carrying on about Theresa's thong. She was a little envious of their fun.

Vera reached across the table and patted Jessica's hand. "Don't take it personally, hon. This wasn't about you. You should be proud of that body of yours."

Jessica felt herself blush. "Thank you. They look like they're a fun group."

"They are fun. Some of the nicest women you could ever meet. How long are you here for?"

"For the summer." She turned back toward Vera. "I'm here through the beginning of August, I think."

"You think? Where are you from, dear?"

"I'm from Boston. I've rented the apartment in the big house for the summer, so I'll probably stay if nothing comes up at work. Where are you from?"

"I'm from Boston as well, and I'm also here for the summer. I come every summer." Vera smiled.

Jessica glanced at the girls again.

"Why don't you go join them?" Vera nodded toward the others.

"Oh goodness, no. I couldn't do that. It's been a long time since I've had friends like that. I really have to be going anyway."

"Do you have a date?" Vera lifted her thin, gray brows.

"A date?" Jessica laughed. "It's been even longer since I've had a date than since I've had friends like that. No, no date."

"Well, then, why don't you come by Wellfleet Harbor tonight and listen to our little concert. Do you know where that is?"

"Yes, I think so. That's where the WHAT Theater is?" The Wellfleet Harbor Actors Theater was a small theater located beside the harbor.

"That's right. Just down the road, across from the

beach are tennis courts, and beside that there will be a tent set up where I'll be playing in a string quartet. I'd love it if you would stop by and listen. There won't be many people there. There never are."

A string quartet? She debated making up plans to escape going, for fear of the music spurring her on to pick up her cello, but in a split second the excitement of seeing Vera play stole any chance she had at conjuring up an excuse. "I would love to go. Thank you. What instrument do you play?"

"The violin. I used to play with symphonies all over the world."

Jessica's pulse quickened. She could hardly believe that she'd found someone she had something in common with in the little community. She wanted to tell Vera that she played the cello, but she didn't want to talk about her career, or worse, be asked to play something. The minute she picked up her cello, she'd remember the beauty of it against her, the vibration of the music, and her much-needed hiatus would be kaput. She was purposely not picking up her cello for a few days to separate herself from her love for it. She needed that space in order to make clearheaded decisions about whether this hiatus was temporary, or the beginning of a new direction altogether.

Chapter Three

JESSICA SAT WITH her feet buried in the sand and a dozen red roses in her lap, which she'd bought to give to Vera. She looked out at the harbor while she waited for the quartet to begin playing, having arrived early with the hopes of enjoying the view of the bay and pulling her thoughts together before the concert. The air was crisp, and it carried the salty, fishy scent of the bay. She wrapped her cardigan around herself and drew her knees up to her chest. She'd come to the Cape once as a teenager with a friend. It had been the one and only time she'd lied to her father about where she was going, and she'd felt so guilty that she'd come clean a few days later. He'd grounded her for a week, but his vibrant blue eyes had betrayed his words. *I'm disappointed in you,* he'd said, but it felt like his eyes conveyed that he was proud of her for breaking the rules. She was used to disappointing her mother. It seemed every missed note was a disappointment. But her father had never been critical of her playing, or of her. And when he'd said he was disappointed, it had crushed her. The combination of his stern words and that look had confused her for years, until her first year at Juilliard, when her mother had been disappointed in one of her performances, and her father, standing beside her mother, had said, *Next time you'll do better,* but his eyes clearly relayed the message, *I'm so damn proud of you.* At that moment she'd understood how very alike she and her father were—both willing to kowtow to her mother—and how very different they were from her mother.

She inhaled the sea air and blew it out slowly, sending her negative memories into the night. She'd been thinking about Jamie, the girls from the pool, and Vera, all afternoon and evening. For the first time in her life, she was free from the strings of performing that had bound her for so many years. She had time for friends, like the girls at the pool, or Vera, whom she was sure she could talk to for hours.

She also had time to date.

Date. She'd gone on a few dates in recent years, but without fail, her dates would go on and on about something and her mind would fall back to her need to practice. Or, maybe most embarrassingly, she'd simply rather spend time playing her cello than with any of the men she'd dated. But now, as the breeze brought the music from the string quartet to the beach across the street and the notes threaded their way around her like an old friend, images of Jamie and the idea of dating danced closely together.

She couldn't shake the look in his eyes as they rolled down her body, drinking her in as if he were dying of thirst. He probably thought she hadn't noticed, but that quick look had sent an unfamiliar, and surprisingly welcome, shudder through her. He had an easy smile, and when she'd lost her mind and snapped at him, he hadn't gotten angry or taken it as a personal affront. He'd simply offered to help her understand how to use eBay.

She'd put off thinking about how she'd lost that bid, too. She'd wanted so badly to win that auction that even now, thinking about it, made her throat swell. The music stopped, and she inhaled deeply, rose to her feet, and gazed across the street to where the string quartet was playing. The white tent rippled in the breeze as she made her way across the cool sand to the parking lot.

The music started up again, and she crossed the parking lot, her eyes on Vera, sitting proudly, playing her violin. She looked regal in a long black cotton skirt and blouse. Jessica had no hope of stifling the smile on her lips as she lowered herself to one of the metal chairs in the front row. Vera was right; there were only a handful of people in the audience.

A breeze picked up the hem of her dress, and she settled the bouquet she'd brought for Vera over it. She probably should have worn something longer to ward off the chill, but she loved the summery feel of the dress, and she felt more her age in it. She was so used to dressing conservatively for the symphony and social events surrounding her career that when she'd gone shopping for her vacation, she'd had to ask the salesgirl what women her age were wearing these days. She hadn't realized how out of sync she was with other twenty-seven-year-olds.

"Hey there."

She turned at the sound of Jamie's deep voice. She was so caught up in the music that she didn't realize he'd slid into the seat beside her, and now she couldn't take her eyes off of him in his slate-blue long-sleeved shirt, which looked so soft and worn that she wanted to cuddle up to him, and a pair of jeans that had the faded marks of an old favorite where his muscular thighs tested the strength of the denim.

"Hi," she whispered. "I didn't expect to see you here."

"My grandmother is playing." He nodded at Vera. "Vera Reed, on the violin."

"She's the one who invited me here. I met her at the pool." She glanced at Vera, who was watching them with a smile. "She plays beautifully."

"She does. I love to listen to her."

"Shh."

They turned, and a white-haired man sitting behind them pointed to the stage.

"Sorry," they said in unison.

Jessica knew better than to speak during performances, but she could barely restrain herself from talking with Jamie. Jamie lifted one shoulder in an easy shrug.

They listened in silence to the rest of the concert. Jessica felt the heat of his gaze as he stole glances at her, and it took all of her efforts not to shift her eyes to him. She held on to the bouquet to keep herself grounded. When the music ended, she finally allowed herself a good look at Jamie. His dark hair was rustling from the breeze, and his warm, contagious smile reached his eyes as he applauded and lifted his chin in Vera's direction. He glanced down at Jessica, and she didn't know if it was her newfound sense of freedom, the lingering loveliness of the music, or the way his lips turned up at the end and slipped into something more flirtatious, but butterflies took flight in her stomach.

She felt herself grinning like a sixth grader crushing on a boy when she spotted Bella, Amy, Jenna, and a beautiful, tall brunette coming toward them. She dropped her eyes, hoping they wouldn't notice the way she was swooning over him.

"Hey, handsome." The tall brunette embraced him.

She, like the others, had on jeans and a hoodie.

"Sky, this is Jessica." Jamie touched Jessica's arm. "She's renting at Seaside. Jessica, this is Sky."

She wished she could pretend that Jamie touching her arm had meant something, but his other hand was on Sky's lower back, and she realized they must be dating.

"Nice to meet you." Jessica shifted her eyes away from Jamie's hand connecting him with Sky and hoped the disappointment in her voice wasn't as evident to them as it was to her.

"Sky's my fiancé, Pete's, sister. She hangs out with us a lot," Jenna explained. "I'm sorry about the whole thong thing," she added.

"Yeah, that was meant for Theresa, but we didn't expect that you'd be there when she came down," Amy added.

"I did," Bella said. "That was the whole point, for all of us to do what we're not supposed to."

Amy elbowed Bella.

Jessica didn't know how to read Bella. If everyone was supposed to wear a thong, how come she was the only one who didn't?

"What?" Bella's brows knitted together at Amy. She sighed, and her voice softened. "Okay, so here's the deal. Theresa's a stickler for rules, and I like to break them. So...yeah, I knew you might go down to the pool, and if you did, I, like Jamie, hoped you'd wear a thong—"

"Don't bring me into this." Jamie held his hands up in surrender, which made Jessica laugh. "I wasn't even at the pool."

Maybe he wasn't dating Sky after all.

"Anyway, it was way more fun with you wearing one, but I never expected Theresa to bare her ass." Bella laughed. "What was up with that?"

"Oh my God, I know." Amy's eyes were wide.

"What's wrong with wearing a thong?" Sky asked.

Jenna explained Bella's prank to Sky, and Jamie leaned down close and whispered, "Sorry you got caught in the crossfire."

"Your grandmother saved me. She covered my butt with a towel before Theresa saw me."

Jamie glanced at Vera. "Did she? Good old Gram."

"Hey, are you guys up for a few drinks?" Sky asked. "We could go to the Beachcomber."

"I'm up for a few drinks, but I'm not sure I can handle the Beachcomber tonight. Why don't we light a bonfire in the quad?" Amy suggested.

"The quad?" Jessica asked.

"That's what we call the grassy area between the cottages. I have no idea why, but Bella said it one night when she had too many glasses of Middle Sister wine, and the name stuck." Jamie touched Jessica's arm again. "It'll be fun. Join us?"

"Sure." She tried to ignore the heat his hand was causing to sear through her veins.

"Okay, but there aren't any single guys at the quad, so you blew my chance at a hot date night." Sky set her hands on her hips. "Are you single, Jessica? Maybe you and I should hit the Beachcomber."

I guess Jamie's not your boyfriend after all.

"I am single, but I'm not really up for a bar tonight. Thank you anyway." No Jamie, no bar. *Quad, here I come.*

"Excuse me a sec." Jamie went to help Vera with her violin, and when he returned with Vera on his arm, Vera ran her eyes over the group and sighed.

"Do you know how much it pleases me to see all of you here?" Vera met Jessica's gaze. "Together."

Jessica handed her the bouquet. "These are for you. The consonance was lovely, and the capriccio at the end…" She covered her heart with her hand. "Took my breath away."

"Why, thank you." Vera exchanged a look with Jamie that Jessica couldn't read. "Do you play?"

"A little," Jessica answered. It was hard for her not to talk about her career, but she knew it would lead to all sorts of questions about how someone so young played with the Boston Symphony Orchestra, and then Vera would want to know why she'd taken an extended break. She wasn't ashamed of her reasons, but she also wasn't ready to give up being a regular person yet. Being a regular person, it turned out, was really fun.

"What's a capriccio?" Amy asked.

"A quick improv. The spirited piece they played at the end," Jamie answered.

Holy cow. You just got a million times hotter.

JAMIE HELPED VERA out of the car and into the small cottage. "Are you going to join us for the bonfire, Gram?"

"I think I'm going to turn in. We had a nice turnout tonight, didn't we?" She sat on the couch, and Jamie spread a throw blanket across her lap.

Jamie had enough money to buy one of the million-dollar estates overlooking the water, but he loved the three-bedroom cottage and the memories it held. Before his parents were killed in a freak accident while on safari, they summered at Seaside as a family. In addition to the few memories of his parents he'd retained over the years, the friendships he shared kept him in the community.

"Yes, and I got shushed." He laughed, remembering the look in Jessica's eyes when the man behind them had shushed them. Her cheeks had pinked up, and she looked so damn cute he'd nearly pulled her against him.

"That little Jessica is a sweet gal, isn't she?" Vera picked up her book and set it in her lap.

"She's not so little, Gram. She's probably in her mid-twenties, but yeah, she is sweet." He hoped to find out more about her tonight. "Do you want me to make you some tea?"

"No, thank you, dear. You go ahead and have some fun. I'll be just fine." She opened her book and leafed through the pages.

Jamie gazed down at the woman who had raised him. He loved her so much, and he knew how lucky he was that she was still in good health. She was the only family he had left, and he feared the day he would lose her, too. He wanted to spend as much time with her as possible, which was why he'd arranged to spend the entire summer here at the Cape, and now he felt a little guilty for hurrying out to the quad to see Jessica.

"Gram, I loved listening to you play tonight."

"Thank you, Jamie." She smiled up at him, then turned back to her book. She'd always been a big reader, and of course a music lover, and she'd traveled the world playing with some of the most prestigious orchestras. That was before Jamie's parents had been killed, when Vera said goodbye to the best parts of her life to raise him.

"I probably don't tell you enough, Gram, but thank you for everything you've done for me. I couldn't have become the person I am without you and Grandpa there to guide me." He wrapped his arms around her. "I love you."

She patted his back in the comforting way she always had. "I love you, too, dear. Now go see that pretty little thing before Tony arrives and steals her out from under your nose."

"I'm not looking for a girlfriend, Gram."

"Whatever you say, dear." She kept her eyes trained on the book.

"Besides, what's a six-two surfer got over a six-two computer nerd?" He rose to his feet and spread his arms out.

Vera shooed him away with her hand. "He's got nothing on you, but why give him a head start—even if you're not looking for a girlfriend?"

Behind the cottages, the fire blazed in the large hibachi that Pete Lacroux's brother had made as a gift for the community earlier in the summer. Hunter Lacroux worked with steel, and his hibachis and sculptures were favorites all over the Cape.

Bella and Caden sat together on a wooden bench, his arm slung casually over her shoulder. Jenna and Pete sat on the other side of the fire in deck chairs pushed so close together they could be sitting on the same one, with their female golden retriever, Joey, at their feet.

Jamie shifted his eyes to Tony, sitting between Amy and Jessica on the longer bench, leaving two empty chairs. Sky sat beside Blue Ryder on Jessica's other side. Blue was one of the best carpenters on the Cape. In addition to being the contractor of choice for the Kennedys, where he handled everything from new construction to renovations on their multi-home estate in Hyannis, he'd built an art studio on Pete and Jenna's bay-side property for Jenna, and he'd quickly become friends with the group.

"There's the man." Tony got up, pulled a beer from a cooler by the bench, and handed it to Jamie. "We had extras from this afternoon, so you gotta help me finish them off." With a quick shake of his chin, his dirty-blond hair flopped out of his eyes and then fell right back to center. Tony had on a tank top and board shorts, despite the chilly night. Every goddamn muscle was on display. Tony put an arm around Jessica and one around Amy with a *Hey man, it's all cool over here* grin on his face.

Hard to get his back up over a friend, but that didn't mean the streak of jealousy that tore through Jamie didn't make him stand up taller and pull his own broad shoulders back.

"Thanks, man." Jamie took a long pull on the beer and sat in a chair across the fire from Jessica. *Too damn far away*.

"Thanks for showing up to watch Vera tonight, you guys. It meant a lot to her." Jamie stole a glance at Jessica. She was still wearing the dress and sweater she'd had on earlier. Her exquisite long legs were crossed at the knee, and her foot kicked up and down nervously. He'd give his left leg to be Tony, with his arm around Jessica right then.

Jessica caught him looking at her and pressed her lips together in a sweet, embarrassed smile that brought out her adorably sexy dimples. Damn, what was it about her that had his interest so piqued?

"I really enjoyed hearing Vera play. She's very talented. Does she play every night?" Jessica lifted a wineglass to her lips.

Jamie was too busy watching her lick her lips to respond.

"Weekly," Amy said. "And sometimes she plays out on the deck here, which I personally love."

Tony squeezed Amy's shoulder. "Is there anything you don't love about Seaside?"

Jessica ran her finger around the rim of her glass and glanced at Jamie. If he didn't distract himself from her, he'd be the joke of the night. Bella would call him googly-eyed and other ridiculous names.

He shifted his eyes to Blue, who was sitting in the other seat he'd like to be in at the moment. "Good to see you, Blue. What's new and exciting?"

"Not much. I just wrapped up another renovation for the Kennedys in Hyannis, and I'm toying with the idea of finding a property to flip to give me something to focus on this winter." Blue ran his hand through his hair and nodded at Sky. "Unless I can convince Sky to renovate her father's place."

"You're dreaming." Sky tossed her dark hair over her shoulder. "Maybe I'll get a place of my own soon and you can knock down walls or whatever it is that you love to do so much." Sky and Blue had become close over the last year while he was working on Pete's property. Sky was as beautiful as Blue was handsome, and Jamie was surprised that they'd never taken their friendship to the next level, but Blue seemed more like an older brother to Sky than a potential love interest.

"Oh, Sky, you should let him," Jenna said. "I love my studio, and Blue's going to put in even more cabinets so that I can organize it." She spread her fingers, palms out, and her eyes widened. "I'll organize my paints, brushes, tarps…I can't wait."

Pete pulled her closer and kissed her cheek. "She's already organized everything in our house and my father's house. I'm ready to set her loose with Blue at the Kennedys."

"Shit." Blue laughed. "Their staff wouldn't know what to do with her. They have their own way of doing things, and I've seen the inside of their cabinets. They're neat and organized, but not *Jenna* organized."

Jamie and Jessica's eyes connected again, awakening the sleeping giant in his pants. He shifted in his seat. Jamie lived in Boston, and although he had a hectic work schedule and cared for his grandmother, he still found time to date. He had a handful of women he enjoyed spending time with. Women he was sure weren't after his money, of which he had millions. He lived like an average Joe, because if there's one thing Jamie learned from a very young age, it was that life was short and what really mattered wasn't what he had, but how he chose to spend his time. Hobnobbing with the wealthy would never bring him happiness, but hanging with the friends who knew and loved him always did. And he hadn't realized until just now that what was missing was a woman whom he could actually share his life with—and his friends.

"Hey, we have fresh strawberries. Anyone want strawberry margaritas?" Jenna jumped to her feet and reached for Bella's hand. "Come on."

"I have a beer." Bella held up her bottle.

"So what! This is Jessica's first bonfire with us. We need to initiate her." Jenna reached for Sky's hand next. Joey lifted her head, then used Jenna's escape to stand between Pete's legs and beg for more attention.

"I'm in!" Amy jumped up, too, as if they'd both swallowed Mexican jumping beans. "Come on, Jessica." She pulled Jessica to her feet.

"Sounds good to me, but I'm a lightweight. I never really drink," Jessica admitted.

Jamie and Tony exchanged grins. Not that either of them would take advantage of a woman when she was drunk. They never competed for women, either. Of course, neither had ever dated the women who rented here. Even so, Jamie sensed a hint of friendly competition...*Game on.*

He watched Jessica walk inside trapped between Jenna and Amy and knew that before the summer's end, she'd be considered one of them. The question was, would he be on the outside looking in, or the one sitting beside her by the fire?

JENNA'S ONE-BEDROOM cottage was nowhere near

big enough for the five of them. The kitchen was about five feet long and wide enough only to open the refrigerator. The counter barely had enough room for the five shot glasses Jenna was filling with tequila. When Bella reached above Jenna and pulled down the blender from a high cabinet, she squished Jenna against the counter.

"Hey," Jenna protested.

"Oh, hush. You wanted margaritas." Bella set the blender on the coffee table in the living room, where there was a little more room as long as Sky, Amy, and Jessica remained sitting on the couch.

"Come on, girlies." Jenna waved them over and they huddled next to the kitchen while Jessica stood a few feet away, watching them. Jenna handed a shot glass to each of them, then poured salt onto a cutting board while Amy squeezed past her and sliced lemons. Each of them sucked on the webbing between their finger and thumb; then they put salt on their wet skin and grabbed a lemon from Amy.

Having never done shots before, Jessica's stomach was all kinds of nervous. Sky took her hand and pulled her over to the counter.

"Just do what we do." Sky licked the webbing of her own hand, eyes wide, and nodded at Jessica, encouraging her to do the same.

"Um…" Jessica's pulse quickened.

"I think we have a virgin with us." Bella draped an arm over Jessica's shoulder.

"I'm not…" *Oh my God. You're talking about my virginity?*

Bella smiled down at her. "Good to know, but I meant the tequila."

Jessica let out a relieved sigh. *Oh, thank goodness.*

"To Jessica. The first victim of Thong Thursday." Jenna sucked back the drink and drew in air between clenched teeth. "Woo! Go on, girls."

Jessica watched as each tossed back her head and sucked down the tequila like they did this every night. Maybe they did, but Jessica never had. Not once. She rarely even drank wine. With her orchestra friends, drinking was never a part of their evenings out, and when she was by herself, she never had the desire to drink. Watching the girls, she realized again that she had been moving in a very small and sheltered circle. She stuck her fingertip in the tequila and sucked the alcohol off of it. It had a strange taste, not at all pleasant. She wondered what the excitement was all about.

Amy touched her shoulder. "Jessica, don't worry. I'm a lightweight, too. We'll take care of you."

"Like Tony takes care of you?" Jenna raised her brows in quick succession.

"So, you and Tony are a couple?" Jessica had seen the way Amy looked at him, and she imagined it was the same way she couldn't stop looking at Jamie. He looked so casual and sexy, and every time their eyes met, her body got hot and flustered.

"Don't I wish." Amy rolled her eyes. "We're just friends."

"Okay. Okay." Jenna bounced on her toes. "Come on, come on. We gotta do this before Petey comes in here and..."

Bella set a hand on her hip. "And what? Wants to get down and dirty? Trust me. He'll love it even more when you're three sheets to the wind."

Jessica had spent the last few years with people who were reserved, focused on excelling in a highly competitive, highly skilled field that was also cutthroat and unforgiving. This fun banter, this girl talk, was all new and exciting to her—and she didn't want it to end.

"Okay, here goes, but please don't let me

embarrass myself. And if I throw up, don't let Jamie see. And if—"

"Ha! Five bucks." Jenna slapped a hand out toward Bella and wiggled her butt from side to side in a celebratory dance. "Pay up."

Jessica's heart crashed to her feet. *Am I a joke to them?* Like Thong Thursday? Her face must have reflected her horror because Amy took hold of her shoulders and looked compassionately into her eyes.

"Honey. Jessica, honey. We do this to each other all the time. Don't take it personally." Amy put her arm around her. "You guys, she's as sensitive as me."

"Have a shot, Jessica. It'll take the edge off of our backward humor." Bella pushed her shot glass up toward Jessica's mouth.

"So, you aren't making fun of me? Because I'm kind of slow on the uptake, I think. I'm not used to this sort of joking around." Why was her throat thickening? Damn it. Why couldn't she be stronger, like her mother? At times like this it might help.

Sky pulled herself up and sat on the counter, while filling everyone's glasses again. "They do this to everyone. They just noticed that Jamie had his eye on you, and..." She motioned for Jessica to drink.

Jessica clenched her eyes closed and licked the awful salt from her hand, then tossed back the tequila—*Gross!*—and sucked the lemon. She drew in air between gritted teeth just like each of them had.

"Well?" Jenna brushed Jessica's hair from her shoulders. "You still with us?"

Jessica nodded, reeling from the taste. "It tasted like burning water. Is that what it tastes like to you?"

Bella licked her hand and began dabbing salt on it. "It tastes like *I'm about to get shitfaced* to me."

Jessica pressed her lips together, suppressing a smile. The four of them were so different from one another, but they got along like sisters. *Thong Thursdays and tequila shots?* What else had she missed out on while she was spending hour after hour with music instructors and, later, playing with the orchestra? Heck, what else had she missed out on since she first picked up the cello at *six*?

Two shots later, Jessica felt a little numb as they went back outside. The guys were standing by the fire, beers in hand. Jamie looked over and his mouth lifted in a crooked smile. Jessica returned the smile, or at least she thought she did. Her entire body felt relaxed, and all the proper rigidity in her back, shoulders, and even her neck had somehow disappeared.

And she liked it. She liked it a lot.

Jessica swayed a little and reached for the bench as the men came toward them. Jamie's jeans hung low on his hips, and there was no mistaking his flirtatious smile or the heat in his eyes as he raked them down her body. She held tightly to the bench for support.

"So the strawberries were a ruse?" Pete laughed and wrapped an arm around Jenna. Joey lay down beside his feet and rested her head on her paws with a loud huff of breath. Pete whispered something that made Jenna blush.

"Crap. We left the margaritas inside." Bella glanced at Jenna, then waved a hand in the air. "Oh heck. We're good." Bella plastered herself to Caden's side, and he looked up at Tony and shook his head.

Blue and Tony exchanged a laugh.

"It's a good thing I drove tonight." Blue pulled Sky down to a seat.

"Hey, don't even think about making a move on my sister," Pete warned.

"*Pfft*. Just getting her home safely. We're friends," Blue said.

"So were we," Pete and Jenna said in unison, then

shared a kiss.

"Come here, sweet one." Tony guided Amy to a chair and sat beside her, leaving Jamie and Jessica to look at each other like two kids at a middle school dance.

She couldn't look away, even though she was sure his gaze was burning a hole right through her and at any minute someone was going to yell, *Fire!* and douse her with cold water.

Jamie leaned in close and touched her hip. "I guess they initiated you?"

Good Lord, his hand was flaming hot.

"Care to share a bench with me?" Jamie asked.

His voice sent a shiver down her back. Her body was doing all sorts of things it had never done before, including walking with an extra little sway of her hips and getting warm between her legs. She liked that, too. *A lot.* She settled into the bench and pulled her feet up next to her. Jamie sank down beside her and draped an arm over the back of the bench. Somehow, even in her tipsy state she was aware enough to stifle the urge to see just how soft his shirt was and cuddle up beside him, because she knew she'd also want to see just how hard his body was.

She felt like she was drifting on a cloud, listening as everyone talked and laughed. Sometime over the course of the hour Jessica began sharing Jamie's beer, and sometime after that his arm warmed her shoulders. Pete and Jenna and Bella and Caden turned in for the night with promises of coffee in the morning. Or at least that's what Jessica thought they'd said. Her mind was still a little fuzzy.

"We'd better take off, too. I've got to be on a job site early tomorrow." Blue rose to his feet and pulled Sky along with him. "And you have that tattoo shop gig in P-town tomorrow, right?"

"Yup. Tattoo shop. I'm spending the day tatting up hot guys and girls." Sky leaned down and hugged Jessica. "See you soon, I hope."

"Me too. It was fun hanging out with you." After she hugged Sky, Jessica's hand fell on Jamie's leg, and she let it stay there.

"I'd better get our little lightweight to bed." Tony lifted Amy easily into his arms, and she settled in against his chest with a sigh. Her hand reached for his neck, then fell to her belly. "I have a way with women, don't I? Good night, kids."

"G'night, Tony. It was nice to meet you." Jessica watched him disappear into the darkness, and she wondered how Amy would feel in the morning. Or if they were friends with benefits, although it sure didn't seem that way when Amy was talking about him inside the cottage.

"Guess it's just you and me."

Jamie's rich voice slid over her, bringing goose bumps to her arms and heating up her girly parts even more. How the heck did he manage to pull off laid-back and sensual at the same time? And why was it such a turn-on? She looked down at her hand, still on his thigh, and felt his muscles flex. The fire was nearly out, just a few embers glowing in the darkness. She should probably go home. It was already far later than she was used to staying up, and she had a big day tomorrow. Didn't she? Didn't she always? She had to practice and...No. That wasn't right. She wasn't practicing. She was vacationing. She had all the time in the world.

She realized that she hadn't responded to Jamie's remark. Instead of answering him, she tilted her head and looked at him. *Really* looked at him. He was too beautiful, and she was pretty sure it wasn't just the tequila that made her think so. His hazel eyes were seductively dark and narrow. His tanned skin blended handsomely with the sexy scruff on his jaw, and his full lips were barely parted. She wanted to run her finger along his lips and feel their softness.

"What?" he asked quietly.

"I'm just..." *Thinking about touching your scruff. And maybe your lips. And that crease by your mouth when you smile. There it is. Oh, I love that crease. Oh, and your hands. I'm dying to know what your hands feel like.* "Thinking..." It was the only word she could manage without making a fool of herself.

"Thinking about throwing your phone at me again?"

She'd almost forgotten she'd done that. She trapped her lower lip between her teeth and shook her head, then reached up and stroked his cheek. Good Lord, what were her eyes doing? They were closing, and she was sinking into the feel of him. Oh my, his skin was soft, the stubble rough and prickly. She let her fingers trail down his jaw and dance lightly over his lips. They parted at her touch. His breath was hot against them, and it drew a sigh from somewhere deep inside her. A long, dreamy sigh, which she only realized she'd let out too late and brought her back to reality. She opened her eyes, her hand frozen on his lips.

His eyes darkened even more. Jessica held his gaze and lowered her hand to his chest. Why not? She'd already played her hand. He knew she was out of her mind. Why not take it further? She might neve have another chance. Oh Lord, his chest was hard, hard. She pressed her palm flat over his heart and it beating fast, which made hers beat even faster slid her hand over his pecs; all the while he looking at her like he was there solely for her pl His heart told her what she really wanted to k liked her touch as much as she liked touching him.

In the quiet of the night there was only the two of them and the sound of their quick, heady breaths. Her fingers traveled beneath his open collar, through his light spray of chest hair to the hot skin beneath. She'd never done this, taken her time touching a man like this, while he watched her every move. She'd never even made the first move. She wasn't a virgin. There had been one guy between her legs. In high school, when she was rebelling against being her mother's perfect cello-playing daughter. She'd dated a few men since then, but had never opened herself up to sleeping with them. She'd never wanted to do this to anyone. And just touching clearly wasn't enough, because she was already damp between her legs. Oh Lordy, it had been forever since *that* happened spontaneously. She withdrew her hand from his shirt, and he covered it with his, trapping it against his chest.

"Don't stop," he said quietly. "That felt nice."

You have no idea how nice. He held her gaze, and she wanted to sink into the sensual well of emotion in his eyes and bathe in it.

"I'm sorry. I'm not usually like this." Why was she
whispering? They were alone in the dark. The other
tages were dark. Surely no one could hear them.
he wanted quiet with Jamie. She wanted quiet
and—
fted his weight and brought his right arm
back, then gathered her hair and drew it
ulder.
sorry. I'm not usually like this either. I
ing at you, and it's taking all of my
o what I really want to do."
en know me." *Shut. Up. Shut. Up*.
ead. "But I'd like to."

Her pulse quickened. Her hand was still pressed to his chest, and she had no plans on moving it anytime soon.

"Wh-what do you really want to do?" She pressed her lips together, unable to believe she'd asked and so thankful that she had. Bella must be wearing off on her.

He drew his brows together. "Stay here all night and talk to you. Kiss those amazing lips of yours and see if you taste as sweet as you seem. Bury my hand in that gorgeous hair of yours—" He slid his hand beneath her hair and fisted his hand in it, angling her head back just a little. "And set my lips on your neck." He pulled her in close and pressed a kiss to the base of her neck, which zapped her brain cells.

He opened his mouth, his soft lips sending shocks of desire through her body. His tongue—*Oh God*—slid along her skin as he kissed his way to the tender spot below her ear. She didn't even know she was sensitive there, but she was trembling against him. "And taste you until you're squirming so badly you have to kiss me back."

His whisper stole her breath. She could barely think past the desires coursing through her. He took her earlobe between his teeth, then sucked it into his mouth, and she worried she might die on the spot, it was such a rush. She fisted her hand in his shirt and a heated whisper tumbled out.

"Kiss me."

Their eyes met for a split second before he lowered his glorious lips to hers and she got her first taste of him. She felt the first stroke of his tongue all the way to her toes, soft and unyielding at the same time. His mouth was hot, every stroke of his tongue, eager and hungry. He deepened the kiss, and it sparked an urgency for more that she didn't understand but didn't have any desire to fight. She threaded her hands in his hair, earning her a deep, masculine groan from deep in his lungs, which vibrated in his chest as he pulled her closer. She'd never been kissed like this before. Had no idea a kiss could consume her like this. How could anybody kiss like this and ever move on to anything else? Their kiss eased to a slow passion that burned through every inch of her shiver-ridden body. He kissed her more softly, drawing his lips away, and she pressed on the back of his head, unwilling to relent just yet. This was too delicious, too mesmerizing, too freeing. He met her need and deepened the kiss again. Their tongues crashed, air passed from his lungs to hers, then back again. She felt something inside her whir like a bird's wings, and as they finally, reluctantly, drew apart, she felt his tongue drag along her lower lip, and a needful sound escaped her lips.

"Christ Almighty, I've wanted to do that since I first saw you." His whisper was low and gravelly.

She opened her mouth to say something. What, she had no clue. She couldn't think. She couldn't speak. She could only want. She pulled his mouth to hers again and melted against him when their lips met again, and she went a little crazy—fisting her hands in his shirt, clawing for more of his sinfully delicious mouth. Oh God, what was she doing? She had to stop. She knew she should. She wasn't this type of girl. She didn't attack men with her mouth and cling to them like they were hers for the taking. But...he smelled so good, and he was so strong, holding her against him, returning her desire with an intensity she'd only dreamed of. She kissed him harder. She could kiss him all night. They didn't have to do anything more. Just to have this connection, this inferno blazing between them. It was more than she'd ever felt for anything.

Except the cello. She loved playing as much as she loved kissing him. *No, no, no!* This was so much better, hotter, more satisfying, all-consuming. She needed oxygen, but she couldn't pull away. Wouldn't. She'd rather drown in this kiss. Tomorrow the girls would come out and find her body seared from the inside out, lying lifeless on the bench with a smile on her lips, and someone would win five dollars. Just when she was about to draw away with the need to breathe, he breathed air into her lungs. Oh, she was head over heels for him, for his kisses. She was hopeless. She slowly became aware of his heart beating against her hand again. Of his erratic breathing mirroring her own. Of the feel of his hand pressed against the back of her skull, the other hand firmly holding her hip. Her clutch on his shirt softened, and everything in her mind settled and came together in one final, breathtaking press of their lips.

She had to move. She was dangerously close to going further, to pulling his lips to her breasts, her ribs...*Stop. Stop. Stop*.

She didn't even *know* him. She blinked several times to try to get past the heat that blurred her vision, and she forced herself to push away from his chest.

There. Space between us. Good.

Not good. Bad. Very bad. She didn't want that space. It didn't feel good at all.

His lips parted in a sexy, easy smile that nearly had her falling into him again.

"I should..." She pointed toward her apartment.

He cupped her cheek. "Jessica, what are you doing tomorrow?"

"Hopefully kissing you." Her hand flew to her mouth, and she slammed her eyes shut. She hadn't meant to say that aloud. When he laughed, a deep, devastatingly masculine laugh, it drew her eyes open. "I'm sorry. I blame the tequila."

"I'm buying a bottle tomorrow."

The flirtatious glimmer in his eyes nearly did her in.

"What are you doing tomorrow?" he repeated.

"Tomorrow. Um…I don't know." Her mind was a little clearer now, but her heart was still racing. She tried to remember what she was doing tomorrow. "I want to see if I can find out who won that auction."

"I'm taking Vera to the flea market in the morning. Want to come with us? We can get to know each other better."

Get to know each other better. *Oh God*. That drove reality home. They'd known each other only a day, and she'd hit him with her phone and mauled him like a ten-dollar hooker.

She suddenly felt very exposed. She realized she was practically sitting on top of him; her torso was stretched across his lap. She glanced at her legs—her dress was bunched up just below her private parts. She tugged at the hem and felt her cheeks flush.

He reached down and helped her right her dress. "I didn't look. Don't worry."

She smiled. Everything about him was easy. He was easy to kiss—way too easy to kiss—easy to like, easy to touch, easy to be with.

She scooted off the bench and wobbled when she rose to her feet. He was beside her in a flash, with one strong arm wrapped securely around her waist, the other holding her hand.

"You okay?"

"Yeah. I'm sorry. I'm not a drinker. Or a…" *Slut. Temptress. Oh my God, could you really think that about me?* "A girl who kisses a guy she's known less than a day."

He smiled again. Damn that smile. It pulled one from her, too. She couldn't even really be mad at herself for kissing him. Any woman in their right mind would have done the same. He was sweet, and hot, and hard bodied. *Really* hard bodied.

"It's not your fault. I'm hard to resist." His eyes brightened with the tease.

"That you are, Mr. Reed." She took a step toward her place to keep from going up on her tiptoes and kissing him again.

"So, you claim you're not a phone thrower or a kisser. What kind of girl are you?" His arm remained around her waist as they walked down the gravel road toward her apartment.

She shrugged. "I'm not really sure. That's kind of why I took the summer off. To find out."

"Well, even if we hadn't kissed, I'd have still asked you out for tomorrow, just so you know. So whatever type of girl you are, I like her." He moved behind her as they ascended the stairs toward her apartment. "What are you taking time off from?"

On the deck, she turned to face him, and for some reason her hands found his. This was so nice. She didn't want it to get weird, and her world was a weird one, full of proper manners, proper attire, and odd hours, which were all reasons she wanted to experience being *out* of it. He was looking down at her expectantly. He must know at least something about the life she led, given his grandmother's profession. She drew in a deep breath and blew it out slowly.

"I'm a musician." There. Simple, no big discussion.

His brows drew together, like he didn't quite believe her. Who was she kidding? She'd never believe the generic term *musician*. It wasn't like she could pull off being a rock star or even a singer. She was far too reserved for either.

"I'm a cellist." She couldn't help but smile at the word. She loved it. Everything about it—from the way it sailed off her tongue and felt feminine and exotic to the beautiful music it represented—everything except the life it made her lead.

"A cellist."

"Yes."

Jamie shook his head. "Vera is going to love you, and I have a feeling I'm going to be left in the dust tomorrow. Maybe I need to rethink my position on this date."

Her mouth went dry, and she dropped her eyes.

With their hands still entwined, he used his finger to lift her chin and gazed into her eyes. He leaned down and kissed away all the worry that had coiled in her belly. When they parted, he stepped closer, so they were thigh to thigh. Her body went hot with desire again.

"Jess, I reconsidered my position, and I like this one even better. Will you spend tomorrow with me?"

Jess. Four simple letters that her mother had fought her entire youth. Her given name was Millicent Jessica Bail-Ayers, after her paternal grandmother. Thankfully, her parents had been kind enough to allow her to use the name Jessica instead of Millicent, but professionally she was known as Millicent J. Bail. Her parents had been smart enough to guide her in that direction as well, allowing her anonymity when away from the orchestra. Along with the middle name concession of her youth, her mother didn't think shortened names were appropriate or appealing, and Jessica had gotten so used to hearing her mother correct people—*Jessica, not Jess, please. It's unbecoming of a lady*—that she nearly corrected Jamie. She'd corrected everyone before him, but she liked hearing it from him.

Her mother was wrong. *Jess* was soft and feminine, at least coming from Jamie.

She went up on her tiptoes and kissed him, because if she didn't, she'd think about how she'd wanted to all night long.

"Yes. I'd love to join you tomorrow."

She'd have to relearn how to behave between now and then. Step number one…no tequila.

Chapter Four

FRIDAY MORNING JAMIE was up with the sun, after staying up most of the night working his way through emails and thinking about Jessica. He'd been so taken with her that when he'd tried to review the trouble reports his staff had sent him by email, he'd been too distracted and had given up after a page or two. He'd half expected Jessica to push him away when he'd first pressed his lips to hers last night, even though she'd asked him to kiss her. She'd taken him by surprise when she'd kissed him back as ravenously as a starving woman might eat her first meal. And later, he'd seen a shadow of worry pass over her eyes and just as quickly disappear. He wasn't sure what to make of her, but after a kiss that reached inside his body and awakened senses he hadn't ever felt before, he wanted to explore the possibilities.

When he went out for his run, Caden had been on his deck ready to go. Now they were closing in on the end of their four-mile run. It was only seven thirty and already the sun was blazing.

"So you're going to the flea market with her?"

Caden asked. "You know it'll take the girls about ten seconds to get wind of this, right?"

"What makes you think they don't already know?" Jamie asked.

"Good point, but Bella said you don't date renters."

"It's not like it's one of Theresa's rules, or even one of mine. I just...haven't. Besides, there's a first time for everything." They jogged up a back road toward the Seaside entrance. Jamie focused on the cadence of their footfalls on the pavement, a nice, even rhythm.

"And a last," Caden said. "I'm convinced that something happens here on the Cape that makes couples come together."

"Yeah? I've been coming up to Wellfleet for thirty years and I can count the number of women I've gone out with here on one hand." Jamie waved his hand as they turned into Seaside. "If you haven't noticed, I'm still single."

"Did you OneClick her yet? Make sure she's not a freak?"

Even after eight years, it was still strange to hear his company name in place of Google. "No, actually. I made a conscious decision not to check her out online. There's so much crap on the Internet, and I don't want to stare down some old boyfriend on a Facebook page, or worry about some bullshit blog that snapped a picture of her at the wrong moment to make her look like a ho."

"Man, you think that's smart?" Caden asked. "There are a lot of money-hungry people out there, and you're not exactly middle class."

Jamie shrugged. "I can tell if a woman's after my money."

"Must be hard to be worth a couple million."

A couple? Try several hundred million. Jamie had

assumed Bella had told Caden by now. Friendships ran deep at Seaside, and now he understood exactly how deep.

Money was something Jamie had because he worked hard. He didn't think of it as who he was, and he didn't think it made him any different from anyone else. It gave him a sense of security, but he did what he did for a living because he loved it. Figuring out technical puzzles and coming up with solutions was about the biggest thrill there was to Jamie, outside of the usual male sexual fantasies, of course.

The gravel road forked at the entrance. It ran in a circle through the development with Bella and Jenna's cottages, the laundry building, and the house where Theresa lived and Jessica was renting down the fork to the left. The *big house*, as they called it, had been the only house on the property until the land was subdivided and the cottages were built. The road circled by the pool at the far end, and Jamie's, Leanna's, Tony's, and Amy's cottages were on the right side of the community. Jamie and Caden ran down the fork to the left.

"Glutton for punishment? You know they'll all be together at our place," Caden said.

Jamie knew there was a good chance that Bella and the girls were on Bella's deck with comments at the ready, but their harassment would be well worth the glimpse of Jessica if she was out on her deck.

Caden elbowed him. Jamie followed his gaze to Jenna's deck, where Jessica and the other girls were gathered around the table drinking coffee. Pepper, Leanna's fluffy white Labradoodle, barked and ran around their feet. Jamie slowed and crouched to pet Pepper. Caden took a knee beside him.

"You think they scared her off yet?" Caden cracked a crooked smile and lifted his brows.

"I guess we'll find out." Jamie looked down at Pepper. "Come on, Pep." Pepper ran ahead of them and leaped onto Jenna's deck.

"Morning, ladies." Jamie felt all of their eyes on him as he rested his hand on the back of Jessica's chair. It took all of his restraint not to lean down and kiss her cheek, and she surprised him when she reached up and touched his hand. He lifted his index finger and trapped hers beneath.

"Well, well, well. If it isn't the hottest running duo in Wellfleet." Bella reached for Caden's hand and leveled a stare at Jamie. "We hear you're going on a date to the flea market today."

Jessica looked up and smiled, flashing those dimples that shot something warm and nice through his chest. "I told them that we were going with Vera this morning."

He moved his hand from her chair to her shoulder and smiled down at her. She was wearing a white sundress and a pair of sandals. The tie of a pink bathing suit circled her neck. He glanced around the table at the others, and they were all dressed similarly, other than Leanna. Her brown hair was pinned up in a high ponytail, and she wore a blue tank top and cutoffs, both streaked with red jam. Jessica already fit in like one of the Seaside girls, and she looked about as comfortable as could be.

"Stop by and see me at the flea market, you guys. I'll give you each a jar of Strawberry Spice, my newest jam flavor." Leanna sold jam at the Wellfleet Flea Market on the weekends. "I make it with strawberry wine and habanero peppers. You get all the sweet and just enough heat."

She could have been describing Jessica. He couldn't help but squeeze Jessica's shoulder. She was all the sweet heat he needed.

"We will. Thanks, Leanna."

"Pepper and I have to go set up." Leanna hugged everyone. "It was good to see you guys. I miss being here, but I have huge orders this weekend, so we're going to stay at Kurt's house for a few days. I'll come by as much as I can, though."

"We love you, Lea, no matter where you stay." Amy picked up Pepper and carried him to Leanna's car. "And thanks for bringing my boy to see me. I've missed him, too." Pepper lavished her face with kisses.

"Where's Tony?" Caden asked.

"He went for a run on the beach," Amy said. "He's surfing at the Outer Beach in Orleans today. He said the swells there have been great lately."

"Did he behave last night?" Jamie asked. "I thought about chaperoning."

"I heard you were a little busy chaperoning your own party." Jenna laughed.

Jessica's cheeks pinked up.

"Sorry, Jessica. I couldn't help myself." Jenna handed her a muffin. "Here. This will help ease the embarrassment."

Jessica shot a quick glance at Jamie as she took the muffin, then lowered her eyes.

He was surprised she'd share what they'd done with the others, but then again, she could have just said they stayed up talking. If he and Jessica decided to pursue their relationship, he wondered if she'd share the intimate details with them. He pushed away the notion of Bella and the girls knowing about his bedroom escapades.

"On that note, I think I'll grab a shower. I'll swing by and get you when Gram's ready—about ten?"

"Sounds good." She smiled at him again, bringing back memories of her body pressed against his, which sent a surge of heat rushing to his groin.

Make that a cold shower.

SEEING JAMIE ALL sexy and nearly naked again sent dirty ideas whirling around in Jessica's head. She went back to her apartment before the girls saw right through her. She'd never had those kinds of thoughts before. *I mean, really...who thinks about running their tongue down the center of a man's abs? Apparently, I do.* She had to get a grip before they went to the flea market.

Had she been so entrenched in her career that she'd somehow missed these desires in herself for all these years? Or had she just never met the right man to bring them out? Had these naughty desires always been a part of her? She wasn't going to find the answer in the next fifteen minutes, so she tried to push the lust away and eyed her cello case leaning against the wall to distract herself.

She had promised herself that she'd go at least a week without playing, but after hearing Vera's quartet, she craved the vibration of the music as it resonated through the floorboards and vibrated through her body. She gave in to the draw of her cello and removed it from the case. She stroked the neck and scroll as if they were parts of a familiar lover. Oh, how she'd missed them. She'd brought a cello pillow with her, knowing she wouldn't have access to a cello chair, and now, as she settled it on the wooden chair in the center of the room and positioned herself in the chair, she breathed a little easier. If she were home, she'd play the Amati one of the benefactors of the orchestra had loaned her, but she didn't dare bring such an expensive cello on vacation.

As she positioned herself in her chair, years of coaching whispered in her ears. *Pelvis and lower back forward, chin parallel to the floor, knees out.* She grounded her feet flat on the floor and settled the body of the cello against her chest. The familiar lightness of it brought a smile. With her bow in hand, she closed her eyes and breathed deeply. It felt strange knowing she could play anything she wanted without the pressure of preparing for a concert. The choice was easy. Her fingers moved without direction. The familiar tension of the strings drew her eyes closed as the long glide of the bow brought the sarabande from the Bach's 6th suite for cello to life. The piece reminded her of angels singing. When she was alone, without the pressures of the symphony or the whispers of her mother's scrutiny, there was no place she'd rather be than behind her cello. Her mind drifted to someplace far away, as if carried by the music itself. Her body felt lighter, and all the stresses of the world fell away.

Kind of like kissing Jamie.

When the piece ended, she sat with the cello between her legs for a long time, relishing the feel of it, until she remembered the complexities it brought into her life, and her joy was stolen piece by piece.

Part of her wondered if it was the intense hours or the pressure and scrutiny that bothered her most. She knew it was the scrutiny and pressure to be the best that drove her to practice as hard as she did, and that scrutiny was what kept her nerves strung so tightly twenty-four seven. All she wanted was a normal life. To let go of the need to be perfect and to please her mother. She even wondered if it was her position with the orchestra that was causing the stress, or if it was the underlying pressure from her mother. She hoped to figure that out during her hiatus.

She gently packed the cello away again.

A normal life. Time to get back into it.

She forced herself to focus on tracking down the seller of the baseball. That was the distraction she'd chosen for herself—*although Jamie was proving to be an even better distraction*. As if she'd flicked a switch in her brain, she put the focus she'd once put into practicing her cello back into finding the baseball.

Only a laptop wasn't a beautiful cello. It was a stupid, technical hunk of metal that she didn't get along with. She opened the laptop and took a deep breath. If she could master the cello and graduate top of her class at Juilliard, then she could do this.

Maybe.

After twenty frustrating minutes of trying to figure out how to get back to the page on eBay where she'd bid on the baseball, she was ready to heave the darn thing over the deck. She'd used the Internet so little over the years that it was just one more thing she had to get used to. She narrowed her eyes at the evil thing, wondering how it could possibly be more difficult than anything else she'd ever tried. With a loud breath she tried one more time to figure it out. Finally, she found the Contact Seller link and sent a note to the seller of the baseball.

She pushed her chair back from the table. At least she was making a little headway in the normalcy department. She'd made new friends. In reality, that was anything but *a little* headway. It was huge, and wonderful, and uplifting. She'd been a little nervous when Jenna, Amy, Leanna, and Bella had invited her to join them for coffee earlier, but they were easy to be with, and after the first blatant question from Bella—*So, did Jamie make a move?*—to which she'd responded, *No, actually, I did,* she'd had fun and conversation had come easily. She didn't know where her answer had come from, and she still wasn't sure if it was true or not. Technically, she'd fondled his magnificent chest before he'd kissed her neck, so maybe it was true.

"Hi, beautiful."

She startled at the sound of Jamie's voice. Her legs once again turned to jelly, as they had earlier that morning when he was wearing nothing but a pair of running shorts. Jamie opened the screen door and, thankfully, he bent down to kiss her cheek. She needed a moment to get her legs to work.

"You startled me. I'm so used to being alone, and I forgot the door was open." She closed her laptop. He was wearing a pair of shorts and a black tank top that did nothing for her jelly legs.

"Sorry. What are you working on?" He reached for her hand and pulled her to her feet.

"I'm trying to track down the person who won that baseball." Her hands were drawn to his chest like magnet to metal. She didn't bother trying to fight the urge to touch him. She knew she'd lose. She'd lain in bed half the night thinking about all those muscles she'd been lucky enough to touch last night. And the kiss. Oh God, she couldn't think about it without wanting to kiss him again.

"I'll help you do that when we get back, if you'd like."

Before she could say anything, he pressed his clean-shaven jaw to her cheek and hugged her. Butterflies fluttered in her stomach again, and her lips were jealous of her cheek.

"I really want to kiss you hello," he said. "But if you have second thoughts about last night, just—"

She clung to the straps on his tank top and pulled him down close enough to press her lips to his. He wrapped an arm around her waist and deepened the kiss with slow, sensual strokes of his tongue until she had no brain cells left.

"I guess you don't have second thoughts," he said against her lips.

"Mm-mm." She circled his neck with her arms and pressed her lips to his again. This was bad, bad, bad. She really shouldn't be so aggressive, and she wasn't even sure how to channel her urges. It had to be *him*, something about him, or something he was doing...

Jamie Reed, kisser extraordinaire.

She forced herself to flatten her palms against his chest and push away from him. Her breath rushed from her lungs.

"I'm sorry." She covered her heart with her hand, as if she could stop it from racing. "I'm pawing at you and attaching myself to your incredible lips, and..." She looked up. He had the sweetest look in his eyes. She nearly kissed him again.

"My *incredible* lips?" The side of his mouth quirked up.

"Oh..." She felt her cheeks flush again. She hadn't blushed so much since she first began playing the cello—when she was six. But the words gushed from her still-numb lips. "You're irresistible. How did you make it this long without some woman snatching you up?"

He pressed his hand to the back of her neck and kissed her forehead. "I could ask the same of you."

He glanced at her cello case. "I heard you playing earlier. It was magnificent."

"You heard me? I hope I didn't bother anyone." She hadn't even considered the noise. She hoped Theresa didn't mind. She'd have to be more aware the next time.

"I'd love to watch you play sometime."

"You would? Maybe sometime." She tried to sound casual even though her mind was raging a silent battle. *Normal. I want normal. My life has never been normal.*

When they arrived at his cottage, Vera was waiting on the front deck with her purse on her lap and an open paperback in her hands. Her hair was nicely done, and she wore a pair of cotton pants and a white, button-down, short-sleeved blouse. Her shoes were stable and efficient, and she wore a wide-brimmed straw hat. She set the book on the table and smiled at them.

"Good morning, dear."

"Good morning," Jessica said. "Thank you for allowing me to tag along with you today. I haven't been to the flea market yet."

Vera glanced at Jamie. "I had nothing to do with it, but I'm pleased you're joining us. Was that you I heard playing the 'Sarabande'?"

"Yes. I didn't realize the sound would carry so far. I hope I didn't disturb you."

"Goodness, no. It was beautiful, one of my favorites. We should play together sometime."

"I would like that very much." This was the problem with trying to be a regular person. Such a big part of her craved playing the cello that she'd jump at the chance to have her hands on it. Jessica could already hear the beauty of the music in her head, feel it in her body—and every time it hit her, it came at the expense of everything else in her life.

"The most beautiful duo around. Ready, Gram?" Jamie took Vera's arm and walked with her to the car, then opened the back door for Jessica. He ran his hand down her forearm and smiled as she got in. It was a gentle touch, an I'm-glad-you're-here moment that brought a sense of comfort for Jessica and eased her nerves.

Jamie paid the entrance fee at a kiosk as they drove into the parking lot of the Wellfleet Drive-in Theater, where the flea market took place. It was only a little after ten in the morning, and there must have been a hundred cars in the lot already. Just beyond the parking lot was a snack bar and a playground, already full of children laughing and playing, and row after row of colorful awnings shaded vendor booths for as far as she could see.

Jamie took Vera's arm as they entered the first row of vendors. He smiled at Jessica and lowered his hand to her hip.

"If we go too slow, feel free to look around without us. We'll catch up eventually."

She was touched by his thoughtfulness. "Don't worry about me. I'm a meanderer. I could spend all day at a place like this, and I so rarely get to do anything like that, that it's probably me who will be moving too slowly."

"Never." With a casual smile, he turned his attention to the table of beaded necklaces and earrings before them.

Vera was picking up necklaces and running them through her fingers. "Come here, dear."

Jessica went to her side, and Vera held a pretty jade necklace up to her shoulder. She lifted her chin and assessed her selection.

"That's your color." Vera looked up at Jamie.

"It brings out your eyes, Jess."

"Thank you." Jessica wasn't used to people fawning over her in that way. As uncomfortable as it made her, it also made her feel welcome and closer to them.

Vera looked at a few more items and then they moved to the next booth. Colorful beach bags and purses hung from hooks around the perimeter of the awning. They spent the morning going from one vendor to the next. Each booth offered something different, from clothing and jewelry to hair products, knives, and leather goods.

When they came to Leanna's booth, she came

around and hugged all three of them. "I'm so glad you made it."

Jars of jam with bright green and red labels covered the tabletop. There were homemade breads and muffins, and in the center of the table was a tasting area with several open jars of jam.

Leanna handed Jessica a plastic knife and a hunk of homemade bread.

"You have to taste Strawberry Spice." She pointed to an open jar, then handed a piece of bread each to Jamie and Vera, too. "I'm swamped today, but help yourselves."

Jessica handed the knife to Vera to use first. "I can't believe she makes these. Look at all these wonderful flavors. Apricot and Lime, Frangelico Peach, Watermelon. I could eat them every morning I love jam so much."

"When I was your age I ate pound cake for breakfast, made with real butter." Vera smiled and touched Jamie's arm. "And even when Jamie was a little boy, I still ate about half a loaf each morning, didn't I, Jamie?"

"Yes, and if I tried to sneak a piece she'd say, *One slice, and then you need to eat your eggs.*" Jamie laughed. "I think she just wanted the loaf all to herself. I don't even remember my grandfather eating any."

Vera rolled her eyes. "Your grandfather abhorred sweets. Do you remember that time he came home early from work and found us eating ice cream right before dinner? I was sure he was going to have a conniption fit." She waved her hand in the air. "I'm sure you don't remember. You were barely seven at the time." Her smile faded, and Jamie shifted his eyes away.

The air around them thickened with a heaviness Jessica couldn't read. Jessica tried to lighten the mood.

"My mother never would have allowed ice cream before dinner."

Jamie smiled, but it was a slightly tethered smile. They ate their bread and jam, and by the time Leanna came back, the tension had eased.

Leanna handed Jamie a tote bag full of jam. "There's jam for all of you in here. Sorry I can't really chat, but..." She glanced at the group of people hovering behind them, waiting for their turn to taste the jam.

"Thank you, Leanna. That was delicious." Jessica stepped to the side to allow others near the table.

A few rows over they came to a booth that had a plethora of miscellaneous items, from old McDonald's Happy Meal toys to books, antiques, and much to Jessica's surprise, baseball cards, bobbleheads, and other sports paraphernalia. She knew her father's baseball wouldn't be there. Not after she was sure it had been sold just the day before, but her heartbeat quickened at the sight.

She felt a hand on her hip.

"Hoping to find your father's baseball?" Jamie asked.

She loved the way he moved closer to her and spoke softly, as if every word were meant only for her ears, no matter how generic the topic.

"Not really. The person just won it yesterday, but seeing sports memorabilia makes me think of my dad, and that always makes me happy."

"So you're a daddy's girl?" He moved to her side, keeping his hand on her hip.

She blinked up at him. She was a daddy's girl. Was it okay to be a daddy's girl, or would that make her seem immature? Did she care if it did? Hadn't she come on this vacation to figure out who *she* was—aside from a cellist? Aside from her mother's expectations? She was done pretending to be someone else. For any reason.

"I guess I am," she admitted, and it felt darn good.

He draped his arm over her shoulder. "Then we have something in common, because I'm sure you've noticed that I'm a bit of a grandma's guy."

Unless guys had totally changed in the last few years while she was busy playing her heart out, Jamie was as unique in his honesty as with his emotions. He kept surprising her, and the more he did, the more she liked him.

The morning went by too fast. Vera bought a scarf, Jamie picked up a few war novels, and they ate lunch beneath an umbrella at a picnic table in the courtyard beside the snack bar. Even though she was having a wonderful time and could walk around for another few hours without an ounce of boredom, it was nice to get a break from the hot sun. She and Jamie sat shoulder to shoulder across from Vera. Turkey sandwiches and iced tea had never tasted so good.

Vera set her napkin on the table. "Do you play the cello professionally?"

"Yes. I'm taking a bit of a hiatus at the moment." She sipped her iced tea, trying to ignore the way her nerves started to quiver. She wasn't quite ready to reveal that she worked for the Boston Symphony Orchestra.

Vera raised her brows. "A hiatus. Oh yes, how I used to dream of those. That's not something that is typically acceptable in the larger orchestras, unless there's illness, of course, or something as unavoidable. But dreaming I did, for a break from the long hours of practice and working most evenings. Of course, I was married and my husband might not have liked sweets, but he loved my music. He was very supportive. But a young, single girl like you? How do you fit in a social life?"

She did understand. Jessica breathed a little easier. She felt Jamie's eyes on her and glanced at him. *Yup, still devastatingly handsome.* And he was waiting to hear about her nonexistent social life. Why did she find it embarrassing that she didn't have one?

"I'm working on the social part of my life."

"Well, then, maybe this summer will prove to be good for both of you." Vera rose to her feet and Jamie went to her side. Vera patted his arm. "Relax, dear. I'm just going to the ladies' room. Sit and visit with Jessica."

"I'll walk you over." Jamie kept hold of her arm.

"I'm fine, sweetheart." Vera peered around him at Jessica. "He's worse than a mother sometimes. Thoughtful to a fault." She touched Jamie's cheek. "I raised you right."

Jamie watched her walk away. "I worry about her falling," he said as he straddled the bench beside Jessica. She loved how he fussed over his grandmother.

Why did everything he did make him sexier?

"She's wonderful. You're lucky. I barely knew my grandparents."

"Yeah." He touched the ends of Jessica's hair. "I am lucky."

"Did you and your parents live with your grandparents when you were younger?"

His eyes grew serious again. Jamie ran his fingers through the ends of her hair. Her hair was so long that people often asked if they could touch it. Jamie's touch was different, more intimate. As if they'd been dating for a long time and he was comfortable enough to do it without asking. Jessica wasn't used to this type of intimacy. She'd never played with girlfriends' hair or even worn her hair down often. Her *performance hair,* as she'd come to call it, was a tight bun secured with a million pins to ensure not a strand came loose.

He scooted closer, one strong leg behind her, the other touching her knee.

"My parents died when I was six. Vera and my grandfather raised me." Jamie blinked several times, and when he lifted his eyes to Jessica's, his heartache became hers. Her chest tightened, and her hand was drawn to his knee.

"I'm sorry. I can't imagine..."

"It was a freak accident while they were on safari in Africa. A lion attack." He breathed deeply.

"Oh, Jamie." Her heart ached for him.

"Thank God for Vera; that's all I can say. She was the best surrogate mother I could have had."

"Do you still live near her?" she asked. "She said she lives in Boston."

"When we're not at the Cape, she lives in an assisted living facility. I'm only five minutes away. I stop by and see her every day on my way home from work and on weekends. Take her out, that sort of thing." His eyes softened. "I usually come to the Cape on weekends to spend time with her during the summer, but time is going by quickly. That's why I'm here for the summer this year. I want to spend as much time with her as possible."

Vera returned with a pleasant smile that reached her eyes. "It's quite warm today. Why don't you bring me back to the cottage and the two of you can go enjoy the beach."

Having just heard that Jamie wanted as much time with Vera as possible, Jessica didn't want to monopolize him.

"Oh, goodness, thank you," Jessica said. "But you must want to go to the pool and cool off. I can fend for myself this afternoon."

Jamie took Vera's arm as they made their way through the parking lot toward the car.

"I've had enough heat for one day. You two kids should go enjoy the sunshine."

"You sure, Gram?" Jamie helped her into the car.

"Quite sure, dear."

Jamie opened the car door for Jessica. "What do you say? Want to hit the beach for a while?"

You in a bathing suit? How on earth will I keep my lips off of you?

"Sure. I'd love to."

Chapter Five

JAMIE HAD BEEN to the beach in the rain, fog, sweltering heat, and on gorgeous days such as today, and regardless of the weather, there was always a crowd. Cell phones didn't work on the ocean beaches of the lower Cape, which made days spent there even more relaxing. This was his first time at the beach with Jessica, and he was especially glad that cell phones didn't work there. The last thing he wanted was to be interrupted when he was with her. Besides, he worked hard, and he deserved a little private relaxation time without being tethered to emails and texts.

Jessica lay on her back in her light pink bikini, looking like she'd slipped off the page of a glossy magazine right onto the blanket. The bottoms tied on the sides and, thankfully, she wasn't wearing a thong, given that Jamie's body reacted to her every time they were close.

He lay on his side, perched on one elbow with a book beside him, although he hadn't made it through a single page. He was too drawn to Jessica.

"What are you reading?" Her eyes were closed, the

edges of her lips were curved in that sweet smile she sometimes tried to suppress, and she was so damn beautiful that it was hard for him not to stare.

"I'm not getting much reading done, but it's one of Kurt Remington's thrillers, *When Evil Comes*. Kurt is Leanna's fiancé."

She turned toward his voice and opened her eyes, shading them with her hand. "He's an author?"

He nodded. "Bestselling author. He's really good."

She rolled onto her side, and her bikini top shifted, exposing the milky white fullness of her breast. He tried not to stare, but his eyes kept revisiting the view.

"That's so cool."

"That's why he's not around much this summer. He's on a tight deadline, but I'm sure you'll meet him at some point. He's a great guy." He wanted to touch her, to lay his hand on her hip, to kiss her lips, but he didn't want to take a chance of embarrassing her on the beach. Instead, he set his book aside and moved closer, leaving only inches between them.

"I hope you didn't mind that Vera was with us this morning. I'm glad you came along."

"I really like your grandmother. She's so nice, and you're so sweet with her. I think I had more fun watching the two of you than looking around." She was leaning on her elbow, just as he was.

Jamie moved his fingertips on top of hers on the sand and smiled. "Do you want to go in the water?"

"Maybe in a minute. Right now I want to just lie here with you." Her eyes darkened, narrowed a little. "I like spending time with you."

As if his other hand had a mind of its own, it landed on the hot, sun-kissed skin of her hip. She narrowed her eyes in an inviting, seductive way, and he inched closer, bringing them thigh to thigh.

"I like spending time with you, too. When we get

back to Seaside we'll see if you heard back from the seller of that baseball." He loved that family was important enough to her that she wanted to track the baseball down for her father.

"I'd like that."

"Do you mind if I ask where you're taking a hiatus from? Where do you play your cello?"

A group of teenagers ran by and kicked sand on her legs and back before she could answer. She leaned forward, against his chest. Holy Christ, she felt good. Instinctively, he began brushing the sand from her legs, butt, and back. She leaned back, her hand still on his chest, her lips slightly parted. He flattened his hand on her back and pressed her to him as he lowered his lips to hers. She pressed her fingers into his chest and he deepened the kiss. Their tongues met in long, passionate strokes. He slid his hand up her back and buried it beneath her hair, cupping her head. She had the most sensuous lips he'd ever kissed, and as he angled her head, she opened them further and rolled onto her back. He was hard as stone against her thigh, and slid his leg over hers. Jesus, if he didn't stop he'd never be able to, but she smelled like warm coconut and tasted hot and sweet. He couldn't help but rock his hips against her thigh so she could feel what she was doing to him. The last thing he wanted to do was tear his lips from hers, but it's what he needed to do, because in his effort to keep from embarrassing her, he was practically making love to her right there on the crowded beach, just feet from the lifeguard chair.

Her eyes fluttered open and her lips curved up. There wasn't a hint of regret in her eyes. God, he loved kissing her, loved the way she looked at him. He touched her cheek, then pressed a soft kiss to her lips.

"I'm not even going to try to pretend that I don't want to keep kissing you."

She blushed. "I'd like that."

She opened the door and he walked right in. Their lips met in another heated kiss. His resolve to back off liquefied, and his hand slid down her ribs to her hip and over the soft swell of her thigh. He eased back, softly kissing her lips a few times before forcing himself away again.

"Now I'm going to pretend I don't want to kiss you, or we're going to get kicked off the beach for indecent activities."

That earned him a soft laugh. He moved his leg off of hers, allowing her the freedom to move. She remained on her back, the pulse at the base of her neck beating wildly, two taut peaks pressing against her bikini top, and a satisfied smile on her lips.

"Want to go in the water to cool off?" she asked.

"I think I need a minute." *Or ten, to get rid of my hard-on.*

They spent the rest of the afternoon swimming, kissing, and lying in the sun. As the afternoon sun disappeared and evening rolled in, they gathered their things and headed back to the parking lot. Jamie couldn't remember the last time he'd felt so relaxed and happy. They threw their things in the back of his car and he reached for her hand and drew her in close.

"I'm not ready for our day to end. How about if we go back to Seaside, see if you've heard back about the baseball, shower, then head into town for dinner and a walk?" He gazed into her eyes, and she flashed her dimples with a sweet smile.

"I'm not sure I know you well enough to shower together." She lifted her brows and he had to kiss her again.

"Damn. I had my hopes pinned on the shower." He opened the car door for her and helped her in.

"What about Vera? Maybe we should invite her to

dinner."

"I love that you're thinking of her, but I don't think she'll mind if we go alone." He slid into the driver's seat. "In fact, I'm pretty sure she's at home hoping we stay out all night. I smelled matchmaking going on with her this afternoon."

Back at Seaside, they checked her email and she still hadn't heard back from the seller, so they sent another message.

"You know, we can probably find the seller's actual store and then send a message there, too. Have you searched for it yet?" Jamie stood behind Jessica's chair, looking over her shoulder at her laptop.

"Searched on eBay?" She looked up at him with eyes so wide and innocent he had to lean down and kiss her forehead.

"No, on OneClick."

She drew her brows together. "Isn't that a thing like Google? I always get lost when I'm searching. I end up spending an hour going from website to website and never find what I'm looking for."

"Here, let me show you." He sat beside her and typed in OneClick.com and the OneClick search window came up. "Type in My Mom Threw Out My Baseball Cards."

"What's that?"

"The name of his store. Didn't you see it on eBay?"

She shook her head. "I only saw Seller."

He put an arm around her and kissed her cheek. "I'll give you a quick lesson on eBay after we do this."

"No, that's okay. After I find this baseball, I'm done. This stuff is hard for me. Give me sheet music or even just play a few notes, and I'll pick it up fast, but this?" She pointed to the computer. "It's like one big headache waiting to happen."

"What would make it easier?" He searched for the

store and found that it was no longer around. He turned his attention back to Jessica and made a mental note to do his own search later that evening.

"It would be easier if you did it for me." She leaned forward and kissed him. "I can pay you in kisses."

He drew her onto his lap. "Now, that's a deal I'll take."

He sealed his lips over hers, and she wrapped her arms around his neck and kissed him as she had the other night, only this time, he knew her mind was clear of alcohol. He liked kissing her even more without the distraction of wondering whether she'd remember it in the morning and if she'd regret it. She was still wearing her bikini beneath her sundress, and she felt so damn good that his hands began to wander, to her hips, her outer thighs, then beneath her dress to the curve of her ass. She tightened her arms around his neck and arched her chest into his. She was open to taking this further, but Jamie had never been a wham-bam-thank-you-ma'am kind of guy, and he really liked Jessica. Maybe more than he should after two days.

Tearing his lips from hers drew a groan from deep within him.

"You groaned." A playful smile curved her lips.

"Yeah, I know." He blew out a breath. "It was either that or...You've got to get off my lap before we head someplace you may regret."

She narrowed her eyes. "Why would I regret it?"

"I don't know. Because you're a woman, and..." He lifted her easily from his lap and set her on the other chair, then ran both hands through the sides of his hair to try to clear the lustful thoughts from his mind.

"And? Do women often regret being with you?" Her voice was serious, but her eyes were teasing.

He took her hands in his. "Not that I know of, but...It's easy to jump into sleeping together. Three moves and we're there." He lowered his voice. "Not that I don't want to be buried deep inside you—shit. I can't even think about it without getting all hot and bothered."

She pinked up again—hell, he liked her reactions.

He kissed the back of her hand. "I want to know you, Jess. I want to know about your life, your family, why you're on a hiatus. If we start with a sexual relationship, I don't know. It's just that I like you too much to do that. It would feel like we were working backward."

She let out a long breath. "Really? You don't mind waiting?"

"Don't mind? No. Jess. Do you mind? Maybe it's just me, but this feels different from just another date. Being with you feels different."

She dropped her eyes to their hands and bit her lower lip. He lifted her chin so he could see her eyes.

"What is it?"

"I...Okay, this is really hard to say aloud, but..." She closed her eyes for a beat, drew in a breath, then opened her eyes with a nervous smile. "I'm a little relieved."

"Was I pressuring you?"

"No, no. Nothing like that. My body was pressuring me. I keep wanting to touch you, to go further, but I'm not used to all of this. Well, any of this, really. I almost never date, Jamie. I don't spend the day at the beach or walk around flea markets with hot guys and a woman I could spend all day talking to. My life is hours of practicing my cello and evening concerts. I'm almost always in symphony mode. You know, prim, proper, demure. It's been ingrained in my very soul since the time I was a little girl."

"Jess, I like who you are. All of you." Jamie loved how open and honest she was being, and he could tell that it wasn't easy for her to reveal her innermost feelings to him. He wanted to reassure her, to let her know he wouldn't push her.

"We'll take it slow."

She nodded, swallowing hard and blinking away the dampness in her eyes. "I don't even know if I want to go slow. I've never felt like this before. I've never wanted to touch anyone the way I want to touch you. You're like...chocolate-covered potato chips. Sweet and salty. A guilty pleasure. Oh God, I'm making no sense." She covered her face and he folded her into his arms.

Every single thing she did endeared her to him. She was completely different from any woman he'd ever dated, and he liked her more for it.

"You're making total sense."

She pressed both hands to his cheeks and gazed into his eyes. "Make no mistake about me wanting you. Ever since I beaned you with my phone and you smiled at me, I've wanted you, and then we kissed, and...I was a goner. As relieved as I am that we'll take it slow, let's not take it too slow, okay?"

He laughed, then touched his forehead to hers. "What does that mean?"

"I'm not sure. Maybe we should have parameters, like a three-date rule or something." She lifted one shoulder and blushed.

"Babe, tell me what you want and I'll do the best I can, even if it means three cold showers a day. What is a three-date rule?"

"You know, like we won't be intimate for three dates, then..." She lifted her shoulders. "Then I guess we go with whatever we feel."

"Three dates? We went to the flea market, then the beach. Is that two?"

She laughed again. "I don't think that's how it

works."

"Okay, so no touching for three dates." He nodded. "I can handle that."

Her smile faded.

"What?"

"I thought we were talking about being *really* intimate, not touching."

He groaned again. "I have a feeling I'm going to get detention for misbehaving. There are too many gray lines I might cross."

"Okay, okay. How about this? Nothing below the waist for three dates." She drew a line across her waist with her hand. "For either of us."

"Thanks for the clarification. I thought I might get lucky." He pulled her into his arms. *Nothing below the waist.* He felt a little like he was a kid again, wanting more from a girl than he probably should. He wanted below the waist—he wanted above the waist. He wanted all of her. But for Jessica to feel comfortable and safe, he didn't mind holding back. "I'd wait a month if you wanted to."

"This means you can still kiss me, you know." She pursed her lips.

"If I have to." He took her in a greedy kiss that left them both breathless.

JAMIE PULLED THE car into a parking lot and parked in front of Zia Pizzeria.

"Are we having pizza?" Jessica loved pizza, though she rarely ate it. She didn't allow herself to indulge in much of anything outside of the cello. Now she wanted nothing more than to do just that.

"If you'd like." He cut the engine and stepped from the car.

When he opened her door, wearing a white tee that pulled tight across his chest and wrapped itself around his biceps like a second skin, the breeze carried the scent of his cologne, something masculine and spicy that sent a little thrill through her.

How on earth will I make it through three dates with you smelling like that?

Jessica wore jeans and a black lacy tank top. She was so used to wearing fancy clothing when she went out that she was taking full advantage of being on a break from her *real* life and wearing all the things she'd never had a chance to. Still on tap were her cutoffs, a tight minidress she probably had no business wearing, and she even hoped to find an appropriate place to wear a pair of overall shorts she'd loved on the mannequin when she was shopping for summer clothes.

She turned in the direction of the pizza parlor, her mouth already watering. Jamie draped an arm over her shoulder and turned her around, heading for an ice cream parlor.

"Everyone should experience ice cream for dinner."

She gasped. "You are a very bad influence, and I really, really like it." She rested her head against his shoulder, feeling like the luckiest girl on the planet. Not because of the ice cream, but for the thought behind it. Jamie had listened to what she'd said when she was talking to his grandmother, and that meant a lot to her. The few men she'd dated were very self-important, and she'd always felt like an afterthought.

After getting waffle cones bursting with enough ice cream to feed three people, they drove down to Nauset Beach and walked along the shore while they ate. Jamie held her cone while she put on the sweatshirt she'd brought and rolled up her jeans; then she held his cone while he rolled up his jeans.

"Aren't you cold?" she asked as she handed him

back his cone.

"You keep my engine running pretty hot." He reached for her hand, and even after all they'd said to each other earlier in the day, she felt herself blush.

In the distance, a red light blinked up high in a lighthouse. It was nice walking hand in hand with the sounds of the waves lapping at the shore beside them.

"You have to taste this." She held up her cone for him to taste.

"I don't think I like chocolate. Let me try it this way." He pulled her close and kissed her. "Yup. I like Jessie chocolate better."

"You're a goof."

He laughed. "Tell me about yourself, Jess. I know you like chocolate ice cream, you play the cello, you dislike technology—which I'll change if I have my way—and you love your father. What don't I know?"

"That's a tough question, because I'm so used to focusing on my work that I'm sort of at a loss about the rest of myself. The only thing I know for sure that I don't like—other than technology—is being twenty-seven and feeling like I'm living the life of a much older person. But here's what I have discovered that I do like. I really like your friends, which made me realize how much I've missed all these years by not having close friends. And one day I might like to do something to help kids, although I have no idea what that might be. I love to read, and right now I have a love-hate relationship with my cello. Mostly love, really. I always wished I had siblings, and I live in Boston." She finished her ice cream and then added, "And my favorite thing in the world as of this very moment is chocolate ice cream eaten while holding your hand." She smiled up at him. "Your turn."

"Well, let's see. I'm kind of loving holding your hand and finishing my cone, too, but I think it has more to do with you than the ice cream." He pulled her against his side as the tide rose and water crept toward them. "I never wished for siblings, because that would have meant sharing my grandmother, and I really treasured her. Still do. I live a pretty simple life, also in Boston, as you know."

"What do you do for a living?"

"I'm a computer geek."

"Oh God. Really? I'm sorry. I shouldn't have said anything about not liking technology."

A wave crashed against the shore and raced toward them. Jamie wrapped an arm around her waist and lifted her up and over the rushing water. She squealed and laughed as he ran up the beach toward the dunes with her in his arms. They tumbled onto the sand in a fit of laughter.

"You're fast!" She was out of breath from laughing, and it felt so good that her cheeks hurt from smiling. She couldn't remember the last time she'd laughed so hard. Her hair was whipping in the wind. She gathered it and twisted it into a knot at the base of her neck.

"Wow." His eyes danced over her face. "You're always beautiful, but now I can see your face better, and your neck, and..." He leaned closer and kissed her; then he pulled his knees up and casually rested his arms over them.

The air around them heated, and she knew he pulled back to cool the passion brewing between them in an effort to respect their new rules.

"Tell me..." She swallowed past the urge to kiss him again. "Tell me about your computer geekiness."

He leaned his shoulder against hers and laughed. "My computer geekiness? Well, you know that search engine you hate so much, OneClick?"

"If you mean the *evil* search engine, yes, I know it too well for my liking," she teased.

"I developed it." He stared out at the ocean as if he'd just told her that his name was Jamie or his hair was black.

"Developed it? Like, created it?" She couldn't fathom the amount of technical knowledge it would take to create such a thing.

He nodded. "Don't hold my geekiness against me."

"I won't if you won't hold my inability to master it against me." She scooted closer so their sides were pressed against each other. "I'm stealing your warmth."

He put his arm around her and kissed her temple. "I'll happily share my warmth."

"So what's it like to do what you do?" She envisioned him sitting in front of a computer all day, but she had no idea what he'd actually do beyond that.

"It's kind of like juggling about fifty balls at once. My company has twelve hundred employees in Boston and another fifteen hundred overseas. I just launched a new project last summer that integrates several arms of our search engines and brings results to users quicker and with more options using various algorithms—" He tightened his grip on her shoulder. "I'm rambling about something you have no idea about. Talk about boring. Sorry. Basically I do geeky stuff all day and go to a lot of meetings." He dug his toes into the sand.

"Your eyes light up when you talk about it, so you must enjoy it." She loved the smile that came with those happy eyes and the creases by his mouth that made her want to kiss him again.

"I wake up excited to get started, and when I finally go to bed at night, which is sometimes at two or three in the morning, because I do my best work at night, I hit the pillow feeling satisfied."

"Sounds like you're talking about a lover." She

wrapped her arm around his leg and cuddled in closer, soaking in the ocean breeze as it washed over them.

"Yeah, I guess. But a different type of satisfaction." He stroked her back, warming her all over. "How about you? Tell me about prim and proper symphony mode."

She turned and looked at him, expecting to see a taunt in his eyes, but they were dark and serious. "Do you really want to know?"

"I want to know everything you're willing to share with me."

Everything? That gave her pause. She'd never felt like her life was very interesting. "Okay, well, in a nutshell, I've been playing since I was a little girl. My mom says I always wanted to play, and I don't remember a time I didn't want to, so I have to believe her. But I think I also wanted to please her. She's an incredible cellist, but she never made the cut for the more prestigious symphonies, and I wanted to do that for her. I think I did, anyway. I'm no longer sure about the whys of it all, but I can't go backward. I can only keep moving toward the brass ring. This summer is my brass ring." She rested her head on his shoulder. "When I see how your grandmother treats you, it drives home how much I missed with my mom. I long to have a mother who treats me like I'm special for reasons other than my musical abilities. Vera looks at you like she adores the person you are. My father does that, and it makes up for what my mother never did, but still."

"Babe." He stroked her back.

"It's okay, really. I can't feel bad for myself, because while my mother wasn't warm when I was growing up, she taught me all the proper things I needed to know to succeed in my field, and I inherited her musical talents, so I should really thank her."

He gathered her in his arms and held her tight. She closed her eyes and soaked him in. She'd never shared those worries aloud, and she hadn't realized how deep they cut until that very second when she felt her throat swell and tears dampen her eyes.

"Wouldn't it be great if we could choose our parents?" Jamie's voice was solemn.

Jessica remembered that his parents had died. She lifted her head and saw compassion in his eyes. "Jamie. I'm so sorry. I wasn't thinking. Here I am complaining about my mother, and yours is..."

"Gone."

"Yes." More tears welled in her eyes. "I'm so sorry."

He nodded. "You know, I used to carry a lot of anger. I've never told anyone this before, but I'm sure my grandmother knows how angry I was. My parents had a lot of money. My father worked on Wall Street. He'd come home late at night, and I'd hear them talking after I was in bed. He'd come into my room, rub my back a little to wake me up, and talk to me about my day. I don't remember much, just bits and pieces of things. I remember my mom always smiling. She was a nature lover, and I think that's why she was so excited to go on the safari. She could finally see all the beautiful creatures she had dreamed about and watched on television. And my dad? He would do anything to see her smile. The thing that stood out most about him was the way he looked at my mom, like she was the most incredible person he knew, almost like he fell in love with her over and over again every time he saw her. We used to spend weekends as a family, and I have this feeling, more than a memory, of how much they loved me. But when they were planning their trip, I remember begging them not to go. That I remember clearly."

"Oh, Jamie." She caressed his cheek.

He shook his head and looked off in the distance. "I don't know why I was so against them going. They showed me brochures, and they were so happy about going on this safari that for some reason scared the shit out of me."

"Do you think you knew they were going to run into trouble? I've heard of that, young kids having premonitions. They say kids are more open to those types of things." She could never have this New Agey type of conversation with her parents, and yet, with Jamie, she felt as though she could talk about anything.

He shrugged. "Maybe. Or maybe I was just a scared little boy who didn't want to go to the African bush for a month, or maybe I just didn't want my parents to go. I don't know."

"Were you with them when...?"

"Vera wouldn't let them take me. She told them that it wasn't good for me to miss a month of school, and she came to New York to stay with me. I've always felt a little guilty about that." His eyes became hooded, and he looked away.

"I'm so sorry, and I hate that nothing I say can take that pain away." She climbed into his lap, wrapped her arms around his neck, and pressed her cheek to his. "I wish I was there when you were little. I'd have hugged you and told you how loved you were. I'd have listened when you were angry and cried when you were sad."

His strong arms wrapped around her body and he sighed. "I believe you would have. It was a long time ago."

They sat like that for a long while, their silence buffered by the sound of the ocean and the smell of the sea. Eventually—Jessica didn't know how much time had passed—his grip on her eased. Their eyes connected, and when their mouths came together, the rest of the world fell away. All that was left was the sound of their breathing, the feel of their hearts beating fast and hard against their chests, and the passion that had them kissing with desperation, grasping at each other's bodies. She ran her hands through his hair, over his neck, and all over every inch of his muscular back she could reach, while his hands traveled up her sides, brushing the sides of her breasts, making her crave more of him. The sadness of their confessions swirled around them and morphed into something thinner and smaller with every breath, then changed shape completely, spiraling into a common thread that wound around them and bound them together.

"Jess," he said in a heated breath.

Three dates. Three dates. Three dates. Oh God! Three whole dates?

She couldn't answer. She could only kiss him more. His hands slid beneath her shirt and—*Oh God, yes*—he caressed her breasts, sending a shudder of need right through her. Her nipples hardened with the first brush of his fingers. Shivers of heat chased that shudder deeper, and when he used his other hand to hold the back of her head as he kissed her neck, then licked it with his tongue, it was all she could do to fist her hands in his shirt to keep from begging for more. But, Lord, did she want more. He used his teeth to unzip her sweatshirt, and it just about killed her to have his mouth that close to her skin. He drew back for an instant.

"Waist up?"

"Waist up." *Ohgodohgodohgod*.

He lifted her shirt and palmed her breasts through her lacy black bra, then ran his tongue along her cleavage. Her body felt electrified. She could hardly believe she was making out *on the beach*. She didn't do things like this! But every pass of his tongue took her higher, until she couldn't think and couldn't take it anymore. She reached down and unhooked the center clasp of her bra. He moaned, a guttural, masculine sound of appreciation, as his mouth found her nipple and he taunted her with his talented tongue while squeezing the other between his finger and thumb. She was going to hyperventilate. She was sure of it. She couldn't catch her breath, except to beg.

"More. Oh God, Jamie."

He sucked and licked until her mind went numb and her body turned into a bundle of oversensitive nerves. Every kiss, every touch, took her closer to the edge.

They tumbled to the sand, groping and kissing, their hips gyrating against each other. He was hard and she was wet, so wet. With her shirt pushed above her breasts, her bra open, the cold air hit the wet skin of her nipples. Goose bumps raced across her flesh as his big hands gripped her ribs and he kissed a path down the center of her stomach and lingered around her belly button. He circled it with his tongue, then thrust into it. His thumbs stroked the sensitive skin beside her hips, and she felt as though she might come apart right then. She buried her hands in his hair and he grazed his teeth along her waist, his hard length pressing into her thigh. He moved up her body, positioning his hips over hers, and pressed his erection against her center. He felt so good, so hard, so...*Oh Lord.* He was sucking on her neck while putting pressure on her damp center with the heat of his arousal. Tingling began in her arms and legs. Something unfamiliar, wicked, and wild coiled deep in her belly, tugging, reaching, teasing, making her swell and ache between her legs. She'd read about these sensations, but she'd never actually felt them. *Oh God.* Her heartbeat quickened. She was so close. She had to be. This had to be what all the fuss over sex was about. She sensed the titillation of an impending orgasm. Her mouth went dry, numb, and she slammed her eyes shut, wanting it so badly. Wanting this with Jamie. It was just out of reach, making her chest feel icy and hot at the same time. Oh God, she wanted this.

Above the waist. Above the waist. Oh good Lord, they were totally clothed below the waist, and she was embarrassingly close to having her first orgasm. His hand slid down her body and grabbed her ass. *Ohgodohgodohgod*. She sucked in a breath, and he trapped her earlobe in his teeth, as he'd done the other night.

"How close are you?" he whispered.

She mewed. *Mewed!* He knew? She was mortified and even more turned on.

"Close…I think."

He squeezed her ass tighter and gyrated his hips so every inch of him was rubbing against her. Then he sealed his mouth over hers and kissed her hard, demanding, plunging his tongue deep into her mouth, in sync to his pelvic thrusts. It was erotic and sensual and so damn hot that she lost all control, and fireworks exploded behind her closed lids. Her muscles clenched and pulsed between her legs, sending heat and lightning through her entire body. Whatever had coiled in her stomach erupted, soaring through her body and out her lungs. He captured her cries in his mouth, holding her tight even as her hips bucked up off the sand. Then he did the most miraculous thing—he breathed for her. In and out, one long breath after another, until she'd eked out every last pulse of the mind-numbing orgasm, and he drew back with the need for air.

She was panting, embarrassed, and totally and completely taken with this patient and compassionate man who also happened to be sexier than hell and able to turn her world upside down while almost fully clothed. Jessica covered her eyes with her arm. He gently moved her arm aside and kissed her eyelids.

"Hey," he whispered. "Don't hide. You're stunning, Jess."

She clenched her eyes shut. She wished she could disappear, slip beneath the sand and tunnel to the sea. But even from behind closed lids, she sensed his smile and felt the heat of his gaze. She opened her eyes, and he was indeed smiling down at her.

"Oh God," she whispered.

"Stop." His whisper washed over her, soothing her worry. "You're beautiful."

"But I..." She glanced down at her body. Her breasts were exposed, her shirt tucked up beneath her arms, and he was fully dressed and hard as a rock. "You..."

"I'm fine." He clasped her bra, then kissed the skin between her breasts and pulled her shirt down before rolling onto his side beside her, one arm draped over her belly.

"But I...and you didn't."

"Above the waist, remember?" He kissed her softly.

"Well, that whole show was below the waist on me." She turned onto her side, still reeling from how her body reacted to him. "And you nearly turned me inside out." She grasped for the right thing to say and do. "I can...use my hand."

He brought her hand to his lips and kissed it. "No, babe. I didn't do that because I wanted payback. I wanted you. Badly. I did what I felt."

"Wow, you're a real giver." She laughed and

buried her face in his shirt. "I'm terribly embarrassed. I've never done that, and I didn't even know I could."

"Why are you embarrassed? We dig each other. That's a good thing."

"Yeah, but I don't...you know. And to do it without...you know." *Oh God, shut up!* Her cheeks felt like they were on fire.

"You don't *you know*? Well, we'll have to fix that, now, won't we?"

He gathered her in his arms again and kissed her tenderly. "You're incredible. Don't ever be embarrassed around me. I think you're lovely." He kissed her again. "And sexy as hell." He kissed her neck. "The sweetest person I know." He gazed deeply into her eyes. "And I want to spend more time with you, and I want to make you...you know."

Oh yes, now she knew.

And she wanted to...*you know*...even more.

Chapter Six

JAMIE STAYED UP half the night answering emails, working through issues that had come up at OneClick, and thinking about Jessica. The best thing about being a computer professional was that he could work from just about anywhere, but he was a hands-on guy when it came to his business, and he'd learned the hard way that giving too much authority away could bite him in the ass. Luckily, Mark Wiley, his attorney, had been with him since the inception of OneClick, and he was in the office daily, keeping an eye on the goings-on at the company from a legal standpoint. Jamie no longer sealed deals with a handshake, and although Mark was a bit overprotective of Jamie and his interests, warning him off of money-grubbing, ladder-climbing employees and women, they made a good team.

He read a brief email from Mark alerting him to a situation. *We have a potential bug with the search engine. Checking into it. Don't worry. Enjoy sun and fun. Will call if any further issues arise.* Mark could handle just about anything. He shot off a quick note of thanks, then began his hunt for the owner of the baseball card store. It was a piece of cake tracking him down through public website records and forums, and Jamie could hardly believe that the owner, Steve Lacasse, lived in Plymouth, Massachusetts. According to the information he'd dug up, Steve sold his goods on eBay, and like many other local collectors, he worked the Wellfleet Flea Market over the summers.

Jamie arrived at the flea market Saturday morning while vendors were still setting up their booths. He traipsed up and down every aisle, stopping at every booth that had a single sports item, but had no luck finding Steve.

He climbed back in his car and drove over to Kurt Remington's house on the bay to see Leanna.

Kurt's house, and the separate cottage from where Leanna ran her business, were built on a dune overlooking the water. Jamie parked behind Leanna's old Volkswagen Bus that her father had refinished and painted with colorful seaside scenes when she'd graduated from college. He didn't bother going to the front door. Kurt was a creature of habit, and he was as methodical as Leanna was disorganized. He went for his morning run, then had coffee while he scanned the news. By nine o'clock he had his fingers on the keyboard pounding out his next bestseller. Leanna was his polar opposite. She would surely be scrambling to get to Seaside to see the girls before heading over to the flea market to set up her booth—late, as usual. At least that's what Jamie was counting on.

He heard their voices before he reached the steps to the rear deck. Pepper bounded toward him, tongue lolling from his mouth as he tried to climb Jamie's legs, barking for a little love. Jamie scooped him into his arms and petted his tangled white fur.

"How's it going, Pep?"

"Jamie?" Leanna peered over the deck as he ascended the stairs. Her hair hung loose over her shoulders, and her white tee was streaked with jam. Her eyes were wide with the smile on her lips. "Want a scone? They're fresh."

"No, thanks. I just wanted to pimp you for a little info." He set Pepper on the deck and hugged Leanna, then gave Kurt a brotherly pat on the back.

Kurt looked up from the news site he was reading. "Hey, man. How's it going? I hear you've got a line on the new Seaside babe."

"Hey!" Leanna leaned over his shoulder and ran her hands down his chest. "Don't call her that. Her name's Jessica, although she is a total babe."

Jamie flopped into a chair. "Everyone? That didn't take long."

"Jenna called me this morning. I'm running too late to stop by there." Leanna went inside and came out with a mug of coffee for Jamie.

"Thanks, Leanna." One of the things Jamie loved most about his summer friends was that their doors were always open. They didn't rely on cell phones and email to communicate. Even though he loved his work and he loved Boston, being at the Cape with his friends rejuvenated him in ways no place else, and no other friends, ever could.

"Leanna, do you know a guy named Steve Lacasse at the flea market?"

Leanna furrowed her brow and shook her head. "I don't know the last names of people there, but I know a few Steves. What does he sell?"

"I assume baseball memorabilia, but I'm not really sure. He used to own a store called My Mom Threw Out My Baseball Cards in Orleans, and he closed it down a little over a year ago. I did some checking, and he works the flea markets, here and in Dennis, and sells his stuff on eBay too. I just want to have a conversation with him."

"There are about three sports guys at the flea market, but I can't remember a Steve. I'll check it out when I'm there today."

Kurt ran his hand through his thick dark hair. "There is the Steve with that yellow truck. He sells all sorts of stuff—records, books, fishing rods—but I've seen sports memorabilia at his booth too. He might be the guy to ask." Kurt opened a document and perused it.

"You know, you're right." Leanna picked up a big, colorful bag and hoisted it over her shoulder. "He might at least know who the guy is. If you want, I can talk to him today and let you know what he says. What's this for anyway?"

Just thinking of Jessica brought a smile to his lips. She'd been so beautiful when she'd come apart beneath him last night, and she'd been so open and honest with him afterward, that as hard as it was to wait to get even more intimate, he was glad they were. He already felt like this was the beginning of a much more meaningful relationship than those that he'd had in the past.

"It's for Jessica. He sold a baseball on eBay that she thinks was her father's when he was a boy, and she wants to track down the new owner."

"Fate." Kurt's eyes never left the laptop. He continued typing. He was a man of few words, but this one had Jamie stumped.

"What do you mean?"

"Steve. My Mom Threw Out My Baseball Cards? I assume her father's parents lost the ball somewhere along the way and this guy got it, maybe after it passed hands a few dozen times?" Kurt shifted his eyes to Jamie. "Think like a writer. Connect the dots."

Until then it hadn't struck him how ironic the name of the store was, given Jessica's situation. "So it's fate that he works here?"

Leanna kissed Kurt's cheek and patted his shoulder. "I'll see you later. I've got to run. I'll talk to the Steves I know and specifically the Steve that Kurt mentioned, and I'll text you after I do."

"See ya, Leanna. Thanks." Jamie turned his attention back to Kurt. He wasn't a big believer in fate, given his parents' untimely deaths, but he was curious about what Kurt meant.

Kurt leaned back and clasped his hands behind his head. "Fate. You know, something that's destined to happen. The development of events beyond a person's control. Jamie, look at me and Leanna, or Bella and Caden. Would you ever have put us together as couples? Fate, man. Jessica's here, you're here, Steve *might* be here. It's all fate."

Kurt went back to typing, and Jamie knew it must be nine o'clock.

Jamie thought about fate on the short drive back to Seaside. How could that be? Would fate have caused his parents' safari vehicle to break down in the bush? Would fate have driven them into the bush without their guide that morning? Or placed the hungry lions there when his mother left the vehicle, he assumed to go to the bathroom? Would fate have put the video camera in his father's hands as he filmed in the opposite direction and caught her screams as a backdrop to the beautiful scenery—or when the camera crashed to the ground and his father's frantic footfalls and guttural, terrifying screams could be heard sprinting toward his dying wife? Against Vera's pleas, Jamie had insisted on watching the video when he was in his late twenties. That video had taken the story of his parents' deaths and made it real. He'd watched it over and over ten, twenty, maybe thirty times in a row—and then he'd buried the sights and sounds so deep he hoped they never resurfaced. But sometimes, when his mind was unoccupied, they did.

As Jamie pulled into Seaside, a painfully familiar thought pressed in on him. Had his father died saving his wife, or had he given himself over to the lions because he loved her too much to live without her?

Jamie wasn't buying fate, no matter how well it fit his and Jessica's lives at the moment. Fate was an invisible enemy with, in his eyes, an evil history that he didn't care to have touch his future.

JESSICA BALANCED HER laptop on her hip and crouched at the bottom of the stairs to her apartment to pick a few wildflowers. She carried them across the quad toward Jamie's cottage, intending to give the flowers to Vera and to ask Jamie for help finding the eBay seller again, since they got a little sidetracked last night. *Deliciously sidetracked.*

"Jessie, Jessie, Bo-Bessie!" Jenna waved from Amy's deck. "Come on over and join us."

Jessica loved that they included her. She stepped onto the deck and noticed that Bella and Amy were still in their pajamas. Bella's nightshirt barely covered her ass, while Amy had on pink plaid pajama pants and a tank pajama top with a picture of a sexy cat with an hourglass figure, wearing a black bikini and holding a bottle of wine, and MAKE ME PURR embroidered above it. Jenna grabbed Jessica's arm and guided her into a chair. She put her hands on her hips and looked pointedly up and down Jessica's outfit.

Jessica swallowed hard. She and Jenna were both wearing cutoffs and white tanks, each with bikinis beneath. Of course Jenna was as voluptuous as Megan Fox while Jessica was less curvy, like Jennifer Aniston, but they looked like they'd coordinated their outfits, and from the look on Jenna's face, Jessica guessed this wasn't a good thing.

"Well, well, look at us." Jenna narrowed her eyes and raked them down Jessica again as Amy disappeared inside the cottage.

Gulp.

"Now we're total Seaside sisters!" Jenna leaned down and hugged Jessica. "Don't worry. I can help you match your sandals a little better. Something blue to go with your suit would be nice." She lifted her foot and wiggled her toes. "See? Green. Matches my suit."

"It's way too early for one of your OCD matchy-matchy lectures." Bella rolled her eyes as Amy came out with a cup of coffee and set it in front of Jessica. "Sit down, Jen. Jessica, don't let her anywhere near your apartment, or everything you own will be color-coordinated, alphabetized, and God only knows what else."

Jenna flopped into a chair and stuck out her lower lip.

Amy patted Jenna's shoulder. "We love your organizational skills. Don't worry. Bella just didn't get any last night, so she's cranky."

Bella slid her a *shut up* look.

"Did you get any?" Jenna asked Jessica with wide eyes.

"Me?" Jessica froze.

"Oh, come on. We know you spent the entire day with Jamie, and he's such a doll. I mean, really. Easy on the eyes and sweet as pie."

"Cliché," Bella said. "Sweet as jam."

"That's a good one," Amy said.

"Kurt gave me a thesaurus because I kept calling Caden *hot* and he got sick of hearing it." Bella smiled and tucked her thick blond hair behind her ear. "So now I use other words, like *sexy, smoldering, scorching*..."

"Okay, okay, back to Jessica and Jamie." Jenna touched Jessica's arm.

"Jenna! She doesn't have to kiss and tell," Amy chided. "She's nosy, Jessica. Sorry." She sipped her coffee, then added, "But we are all curious. We love Jamie, and we only want him to be happy."

"Yeah, so if you plan on using him and then tossing him aside, just forget it, because it'll bring my claws out." Bella blew on her fingernails with a serious, dark stare.

I wouldn't know how to use a guy and toss him aside.

A smile spread across Bella's lips. "We take care of our own."

She didn't know what to say, but her heart was galloping in her chest.

"They terrified me when I was younger," Amy whispered to her.

Jenna playfully pushed Amy's arm. "We did not. Bella's all talk, Jessica. So, how was your date?"

Now she was afraid to answer, and she was pretty sure the word flying through her mind wasn't appropriate. *Orgasmic.* She opened her mouth, intending to say something benign, like, *It was nice*, or, *We had a lovely time*, but her voice had a mind of its own, and out came a long, dreamy sigh, followed by, "A-ma-zing."

The girls squealed. She felt her cheeks pink up, but she had no hope of keeping to her prim and proper upbringing. The girls were just as excited as she was. She sensed she could trust them as much as she feared Bella's threat. She had a feeling that the threatening banter, the inquisition, and the smiles they were sending her way were all part of the sisterhood they shared, and she wanted in.

"He's so...I need that thesaurus." She laughed.

"Oh my." Amy raised her brows.

"We didn't do *that*." Here came the prim. "He's warm and kind, a great listener. Interesting and generous."

Jenna and Bella rolled their eyes.

"And?" Jenna pushed.

Forget prim; she wanted girlfriend talk. She leaned in close and lowered her voice. "And the best kisser on the planet."

Bella and Jenna high-fived.

"You guys, she'll never talk to you again if you do that," Amy warned. "Jamie never dates girls up here, and he never talks about the women he dates back home. He's like our sweet, very private brother. We're happy for you."

"Thanks. Honestly, I'm happy for me." Just thinking about Jamie made her smile.

"So were you going over to pretend that you needed computer help?" Jenna pointed to her laptop.

"Pretend? My computer hates me. I'm like the anti-geek. Give me a cello and I'm right at home. Give me a phone or computer? It might as well have dropped into my lap from Mars. But Jamie's helping me. I'm trying to track down a baseball my dad had as a kid."

"I knew you were some kind of musician. You were watching Vera with stars in your eyes the other night," Amy said.

"She was looking at Jamie, goofus," Bella added.

"Both, probably," Jessica admitted.

"Speaking of Mr. Amazing Kisser." Bella nodded toward Jamie's car as it came up the gravel road and pulled into his driveway.

Jessica's pulse ratcheted up a notch. "Please don't

say anything to him about what I said."

All three of them pretended to lock their mouths and toss away the keys.

Jamie crossed the road, a lustful look in his eyes as they connected with Jessica's.

"Hi, handsome," Bella said.

"Want some coffee?" Amy asked.

He walked right past them, making a beeline for Jessica. "No, thanks." He leaned down and pressed a tender kiss to her lips. "Hi, beautiful. Did you sleep okay?"

I can't breathe. Heat swirled between them so thick she was sure it would sear the deck around their feet.

"Yeah," she finally managed.

He placed a hand on her shoulder and eyed the girls' wide-eyed gazes, the smirks on their pretty faces. His lips curled up.

"Did you get the scoop? Am I *all that*?"

Oh God!

"You've been all that since you were a kid." Amy smiled at Jessica. "Now you're all that with an awesome girlfriend who refuses to kiss and tell."

She wanted to run over and hug Amy. *Thank you! Thank you! Thank you!*

"But we love her anyway." Bella winked at Jessica.

She looked up at Jamie, standing behind her, his hands on her shoulders, that easy smile she adored on his lips. "I brought Vera flowers, and I was hoping you might help me with tracking down the baseball guy."

He leaned down and whispered, "Already done. Come on. I'll explain."

When he kissed her cheek, all the girls *aww*ed in unison. She must be getting used to them, because she didn't feel her cheeks pink up this time. Thank goodness. It was embarrassing to be a blushing twenty-seven-year old.

Jessica thanked Amy for the coffee and followed Jamie across the gravel road to his cottage.

"His store was in Orleans, but he closed it a while ago. He lives in Plymouth, and you won't believe this, but he works the bigger flea markets around the Cape in the summers, and of course sells his stuff on eBay."

"How do you know all of this?"

"Bread crumbs. Geeks know how to follow them. Anyway, I went to the flea market, and he wasn't there, so I went to see Leanna. She's going to talk to the Steves that are at the flea market today and figure out if one of them is the right guy. Kurt seemed to think one of them was. Anyway, she'll text his info if he's the right guy so we can call him."

They were standing on his deck. Jessica hooked her finger into the front pocket of his shorts. "You did all of that for me?"

He smiled with a casual shrug.

"Thank you so much." She went up on her tiptoes and kissed him just as the glass door slid open. Jessica stumbled back on her heels, and he caught her by the hip as Vera stepped outside carrying a beach tote.

"I'm sorry to have startled you. Please, continue." She waved her hands with a conspiratorial grin and sat in one of the deck chairs.

As Jamie ran his hand down Jessica's arm, his gaze lingered on her, warming her all over.

"Good morning, Gram. Want some coffee?"

"No, thank you, dear. I had some already. Did you two have fun last night?" Vera took a paperback out of her tote.

"We did," Jamie answered.

The way the corner of his mouth kicked up combined with the heat Jessica saw in his eyes brought back the memory of being beneath him.

Feeling his weight on her thighs and hips, the power behind each pelvic thrust, the passion in every heated kiss. *Oh, good Lord, I am breathing hard again.*

He squeezed her arm. She saw the recognition of her heady state in his eyes and had to look away. She handed Vera the wildflowers to distract herself from thinking of Jamie.

"I picked these for you."

"Aren't they lovely. Thank you, Jessica."

"I'll get a vase." Jamie went inside the cottage and Jessica sat across from Vera.

"It's going to be a beautiful day. Do you and Jamie have plans?" Vera asked.

"No, we don't." She just realized this was true, and yet it felt like a given that they'd do something together.

Jamie brought out a vase full of water and arranged the flowers in it. "There you go. What do you want to do today, Gram?"

"I'm still a little tired, so I'm going to sit and read for a while. Why don't the two of you go do something fun?" She smiled up at Jessica.

Jessica recognized the matchmaking Jamie had mentioned, and when she glanced at Jamie she knew he felt it, too.

He touched her shoulder. "Do you like to bike?"

"Bike? Gosh, I haven't been on a bicycle since I was little." She honestly couldn't remember how long it had been, but she had a vague memory of riding a bike before the cello took up all her free time.

"Oh, Jamie. Good idea. Jessica can use one of ours." Vera patted Jessica's leg. "It's like reading music. It'll come right back to you."

"Sounds perfect."

Jamie loaded the bikes on the rack on the back of his car, and they drove down to Salt Pond Visitor

Center in Eastham. The glass and brick building was built just off of Route 6, with a large amphitheater off to the side.

"Have you been here before?" Jamie took her hand as she stepped from the car.

"No. Other than one weekend trip as a teenager, this is the only time I've been to the Cape." The air smelled like wet earth and sulfur. "What's that smell?"

"Nauset Marsh. It's behind the building. Let's go inside before we ride. This is something you shouldn't miss. I come every year, even though I've seen everything a million times."

His hands were big and slightly calloused, manly and strong, like him. She loved how her hand felt in his. He had on a pair of army-green cargo shorts and a white tee, and he looked like every one of the words Bella had used to describe Caden. Only better.

"Did the girls grill you this morning?" he asked.

"A little, but it was obvious that they were just looking out for you. Especially Bella."

He held open the door to the visitor center. "Bella's protective of everyone, but her bark is worse than her bite."

The atrium of the visitor center was spacious and busy with people milling about, talking to the forest rangers behind the information desk and hovering over a diorama of the Gulf of Maine ecosystem in the center of the room. The glass back wall offered a spectacular view of Nauset Marsh. Jamie led Jessica through the atrium and down a hallway.

"There's a bookstore we can check out afterward." He nodded to a small bookstore as they passed, but continued walking through a set of heavy wooden double doors. "This is my favorite exhibit."

They walked into a small museum, with stuffed birds and other animals perched around the room.

There were articles and artifacts detailing the changes in boating, industry, and other aspects of the Cape's seafaring heritage. It was fascinating, and Jamie didn't rush her through, even though he'd seen it many times. He stood patiently beside her while she looked at each exhibit, and when they finally made it to the bookstore, which also served as a gift shop, he bought his and hers key rings engraved with their names on one side and an outline of the lower Cape on the other. He gave Jessica the one that said Jamie.

"Now you're branded." He kissed her softly.

She loved that he'd given her something so simple and so meaningful.

"Don't worry," he said. "I am, too." He put the one with her name on his key ring and then ran his finger down her cheek. "I figured that since you grew up under an iron thumb, you probably never had much time for these types of boyfriend/girlfriend things."

"I never even had a real boyfriend in high school." She'd been too busy practicing.

"Well, I know it's silly, but every girl should experience things that let them know how special they are. Even if it's about ten years later than what's typical."

She reached into her purse and handed him her keys, and he slipped the silver ring that said Jamie onto her key ring. He was right. She did feel special.

They walked around for a while longer, and then they unloaded the bikes and hid her purse in the trunk.

"Why don't you ride around the parking lot first to make sure you're comfortable?" He took care of everything, just as he had earlier that morning with tracking down the eBay seller.

"I feel so silly needing to practice," she admitted.

"Well, you look hot as hell, so if that's what silly

looks like, I'm all for it." He patted the bike seat. "Come on. I want to make sure you're comfortable."

She climbed on the bike, and after a minute of wobbling and finding her balance, the muscle memory returned, and she sailed across the parking lot feeling free and light and incredibly happy.

They followed the paved bike trail as it wound through woods and behind several businesses all the way to the Orleans Rotary, where they passed several bikers coming in the opposite direction. For the first time in as long as she could recall, Jessica felt normal. How she'd longed to experience life the way others did, without every hour spoken for, without always being properly attired, aware of giving appropriate answers. Here, she was meeting friends, laughing, and enjoying herself more than she ever had, and she never realized how wonderful a relationship could be until she met Jamie. No matter what they were doing, it felt natural to be with him. He looked out for her, and he treated her well, not to mention those heart-stopping kisses he doled out like candy.

The trail was cool beneath the umbrella of tall trees. They rode side by side where the path was wide enough, and when Jamie was forced to pull ahead, he looked back often to check on Jessica. They were surrounded by woods, with the smell of the sea in the air; it was like they'd entered their own private paradise. The path widened and the trees became sparse as they entered reality again and came into town. They followed the bike path behind a bike rental shop, and a few feet ahead, the path crossed Main Street. Jamie looked handsome with his windblown hair and glistening skin as he came to a stop beside her and grabbed hold of Jessica's handlebars, then leaned in for a kiss.

"I want to show you something." He nodded up

Main Street toward the traffic light.

"The Chocolate Sparrow?" she asked hopefully. The Chocolate Sparrow was a chocolate specialty store across the street. She'd seen it in the tourist magazines, and now, as the scent of chocolate hung in the air, she could practically taste it.

"Sure, but I had something else in mind."

She followed him to a stoplight, where they crossed the street and turned down the main road. They came to what looked like an abandoned office complex and parked their bikes by the empty parking lot.

"What is this place?" She took in the cedar-sided offices. The windows were filmy, the offices void of all signs of life.

"I'll show you." He took her hand and led her up a set of stairs between two buildings, to the entrance of an office. Above the door was a sign painted to look like a baseball and the words MY MOM THREW OUT MY BASEBALL CARDS written in black.

"Oh." Her breath left her in a rush of hot air. "Jamie, how did you find this?" She ran her hand along the flat metal door.

"Bread crumbs." He pulled his phone from the pocket of his shorts and checked his text messages. "Leanna said the owner, Steve, isn't at the flea market, but she got his phone number from the flea market admin staff." He smiled at her and handed her his phone. "You can call him."

"Jamie, you did this. I can't believe you did all of this for me."

They sat on the top step. "I like puzzles."

The way his eyes darkened and his voice softened told her that wasn't the only reason he'd done it.

"Thanks for helping me try to solve mine." *In so many more ways than one.*

"Are you going to call?"

"Yeah, in a second." She reached for his hand. "I don't have a lot of friends outside of work, and I want you to know that I really appreciate what you've done. It means a lot to me. I'm a little nervous about calling, though. When I came to the Cape it was with the intention of figuring out how to be normal, and finding my dad's ball was supposed to be something for me to focus on so I didn't think about playing the cello day and night."

"What are you worried about? That if you find the baseball you'll suddenly begin practicing for hours on end?" He gathered her hair in his hands and laid it over her shoulder, then kissed her cheek. "What's so bad about that?"

"What's so bad? I'd lose this. You. The ability to be normal." Her stomach twisted.

"Babe, there are twenty-four hours in a day. Two, three, four, or even five hours of practice? That's nothing." He touched his forehead to hers. "Besides, I've just found you. There's no chance in hell that I'm going to let you get away that easy."

"You don't get it. Practicing is just a piece of my life. I work crazy hours. Maintaining friendships outside of other musicians is nearly impossible, and musicians can be cliquey, like any other industry, I guess, but they can be whiny and bitchy. *Ugh*. It's a whole different world."

"That doesn't sound very different from any other industry. Maybe you just think your life is really different because it's the only one you know. I work at night all the time, and every office has cliques and complainers. You just rise above it, work around it, ignore it as best you can and move on." He pressed his leg against hers. "What else?"

"Maybe you're right. I don't know. As you said,

playing with an orchestra is really all I know. All I've ever known. I could go on and on, but it's not that I hate what I do. I *love* it. There are times when I crave it like addicts crave a fix. But there are aspects that make it difficult. There's a lot of travel, some international. It can be exhausting, and…lonely." She hadn't realized that until just now, but after spending time with Jamie, she knew what she was missing out on. "Listen to me. I have a job millions would give their eyeteeth to have, and I'm complaining like a child. I just want a little break from it, and the baseball was supposed to distract me from playing, because I really am drawn to it like it's my drug of choice."

"Okay, so what I'm hearing is that you love playing, you get lonely, and you want this vacation to be about something other than playing. So if you find your dad's baseball, you need another distraction until you figure out what you really want to do with your career, right?" He had a serious look in his eyes.

She rolled her eyes. "Ridiculous, right?"

He folded her into his arms and touched his lips to hers. "Not at all. I'd say it's my lucky summer, because I'm really good at being distracting and even better at keeping you company." He took her in a deep, passionate kiss that made her tingle all over.

"You are incredibly good at that," she said against his lips.

"Here, let me distract you again."

She melted against his lips, her whole body warm and wanting. He was so much more than a distraction. He was becoming the air she needed to breathe.

She made the phone call, hardly able to believe she was getting that much closer to finding her father's baseball. Her father didn't even know she was looking for it. She'd struck it lucky when she found what she was sure was his baseball on eBay, and she'd only found eBay because a fellow musician said she was selling her violin on eBay and they got to talking about the website. She'd shown her how to find the site on her phone and how to bid. Luck had been on her side—even if she hadn't won the baseball, she'd met Jamie, and that made it all worthwhile.

Steve didn't answer. She left a message with her name and phone number and gave Jamie back his phone.

"Now we wait, I guess." She told herself not to be too hopeful, but she couldn't help it. Hope swelled within her.

"Hardly. Now we go enjoy life a little." He drew her up to her feet and took her in another delectable kiss. "You'll be sick of me by the end of the day."

"Not a chance in the world."

"This is our second date, you know." He dragged his eyes down her body lasciviously as they descended the stairs.

She felt naked under his heated gaze, and she could hardly believe how much she wished she was.

They ate lunch on the lawn of the Orleans Windmill, overlooking the water, and soaked in the sun before heading across the street to the Bird Watcher's General Store. By the time they got back to the car at the Salt Pond Visitor Center, it was nearly six o'clock.

"Do you mind if I call Vera and make sure she's okay?"

"Not at all. I'm going to use the ladies' room." Inside the ladies' room, the fluorescent lights were bright and unforgiving, and as she patted her face dry, she assessed herself in the mirror. Even in the harsh lighting, she noticed a difference in her looks. Her eyes were brighter, and despite being up half the night thinking about Jamie, the fine lines she'd seen around her eyes for the past few months were gone. Not only did she feel happier and more at ease, she was pleased to see that she looked less stressed as well. Before coming to the Cape she'd begun to feel twice her age, and she wondered how much of what she was seeing was caused by Jamie and how much was a result of taking a break from the orchestra.

When she came out of the restroom, Jamie was waiting for her.

"How's Vera?" she asked, feeling a little guilty for monopolizing his day.

"She's fine. She spent a few hours at the pool, and she's already eaten dinner." He wrapped his arms around her waist. "How do you feel about wine tasting?"

She glanced down at her clothes. "I should probably shower and change first, but it sounds fun."

"You're such a tease. You really need to stop talking about showering together." His eyes darkened.

Her mouth went dry at the idea of being naked beside him. *Beneath him. Oh God.* "I...I never used the word *together*."

"Maybe I made that part up in my fantasies."

His lips met hers in a succulent kiss that turned her mind to mush. His hands slid to her lower back as their hips came together, and her entire body flushed at the feel of his arousal. He was so hot. Everything he said and did was hot, sensual, sexy. No wonder her brain melted every time she was near him. If this kept up, he'd have to pour her into bed by the end of their third date.

Chapter Seven

THE TRURO WINERY wasn't normally open in the evenings, but this was the week of the annual wine festival, and tonight they had tastings and tours until midnight. The event was sold out, but Jamie knew the owner of the winery, Cliff Warner, and after calling Vera, he'd put a call into Cliff, who was thrilled to hear from him and more than willing to open their doors for them. Like every other event on the lower Cape, it was a casual affair. They could have come directly from their bike ride, but Jessica had insisted on showering—*alone*, unfortunately. She was a sight for sore eyes in a midthigh-length, forest-green tank dress that gathered at the waist. Her simple gold bracelet and matching necklace were dainty and feminine, and perfectly accented with a pair of dangling earrings.

They moved with the crowd from one room to the next in the old captain's house. The interior boasted cathedral ceilings with views of thick wooden trusses and roughly finished hardwood floors and cabinetry. In each room they were given a different type of wine to taste while the staff explained the origin.

Jessica held Jamie's arm as they shared a glass of strawberry wine. She licked her lips after taking a sip, leaving them glossy and inviting.

"That's so sweet. Taste it," she urged, flashing her baby blues at him.

He ignored the glass and went straight for her lips. As Cliff and his wife led the tour out of the room, Jamie ducked into an alcove with Jessica. She had a tentative look in her eyes as he backed her up against the wall in the dark area.

"We're going to get in trouble," she whispered.

"No, we won't."

He lowered his mouth to hers and kissed her like he'd been aching to do all evening, as he'd been forced to watch every man in the place steal glances at her. He couldn't blame them. She was so gorgeous he wanted to devour her right that second. He had to at least taste her, and as he deepened the kiss, she rocked her hips into his and slid her hands into the back pockets of his jeans. He was so hard, and her body was so soft. He wanted to disappear into their kiss and let their bodies take over. It was all he could do to tear his lips from hers.

"Definite trouble," she said in one hot breath against his lips. "We'll get caught making out like teenagers."

He ran his hands up her sides and brushed her breasts with his thumbs.

"Jamie."

Holy hell. He heard the plea in her voice for him not to stop—he loved her voice and loved the way she looked at him like she could barely think when they were close—but he saw a shadow of worry flash in her eyes, and he knew she was worried about getting caught.

"Okay, we'll stop." He slid his hands back down

her sides and clutched her hips.

"No. I meant, *kiss me*, Jamie."

She pressed her lips to his and held on to him like she was never going to let him go. Their mouths crashed together in a tangle of tongues and clashing of teeth, and he couldn't help it. He had to have more of her. He slid his hand beneath her dress and felt the sweet curve of her bare ass. He drew back and stared into her eyes, suppressing a groan at the tease of her bare flesh.

"Thong." She hungrily pulled his lips to hers again.

He fondled and grabbed, and dear Jesus, his fingers swept between her thighs and she was hot, damp.

"Above..." She kissed him again. "The waist."

Goddamn it. With a groan, he let her dress drop and gripped her ribs over the top of the thin material.

"Weren't rules made to be broken?" he mumbled against her lips.

Voices neared in the room they'd just escaped. Jessica sucked in air and stilled. He pressed his body to hers and covered her lips with one finger, then used his mouth to silence the question in her eyes. His tongue swept hers until all of the tension rolled from her body and she warmed to his touch once again. The voices became louder, closer, and they both opened their eyes, mouths still pressed together. Jessica began to giggle, and he kissed her harder. Her eyes closed and a moan of pleasure escaped her lungs. Then her eyes flew open and she squeaked. Squeaked! Which made him laugh as she covered her mouth with her hand. He smoothed her dress, save for the points of her nipples giving them both away.

With her hand in his, he led her past the elderly couple talking beside the alcove. "Excuse us."

They laughed as they hurried into the next room.

As soon as they cleared the doorway, he swept her into his arms again.

"Too close for comfort?"

She nibbled on her lower lip. "Kind of exciting."

"Holy...Come here, you little vixen." He took her in another greedy kiss, then peeled his lips from hers. "Another whole day?"

"Another whole *date*," she corrected.

"By the time we come together, I'll be so hot for you I'll barely last."

She raised her brows with a blush on her cheeks. "Maybe I need to rethink this whole relationship."

"Maybe you have to..." The hell with that. "You're such a sweet and naughty girl. Everything you do turns me on." He ran his knuckle down her cheek. "Trust me, baby. I can last so long you'll be begging me to stop. But that first time we come together? It's not going to be sweet or careful." Jesus, the way his heart swelled with emotions every time he was near her and the desires that raged through him, he couldn't even begin to imagine how good it would feel to finally sink into her. He settled his cheek against hers and held her so close he felt every breath. "But the next time, and the next, and every time thereafter? Sweet, hot, sensual, rough, playful. We'll do everything you've ever dreamed of. Only better."

She sucked in a jagged breath. "Promise?"

Christ Almighty, he'd died and gone to heaven.

Chapter Eight

JAMIE REED WAS patient to a fault. He was kind, generous, and just about the best friend a person could have. He was as loyal as a puppy and as trustworthy as the law. Or at least he always had been, until that very second. He'd spent half the night working through company issues again, and the other half of the night convincing himself not to beat off. His patience shattered about five thirty Sunday morning, when the crows started cawing and images of Jessica lying in her bed played in his mind like a pornographic rerun. Of course, in his fantasies she wore nothing but a silky little negligee and every word out of her mouth had to do with fucking her or sucking him. By the time it hit six o'clock, he was ready to burst. Even a cold shower didn't help.

He tossed a few bagels into a paper bag, threw in a jar of instant coffee, and headed for the door.

"Where are you rushing off to?" Vera asked from behind him.

"Going for a run." He had never been a very good liar.

"With a paper bag, and dressed like that?"

Jamie closed his eyes, his back to his grandmother. "I have a breakfast date with Jessica."

"Well, don't you want to bring something a little nicer? Muffins, maybe?" He heard the smile in her voice. "I could make some for you."

He heard her shuffling toward the kitchen in her slippers. Jamie turned, knowing she'd see right through him, the same way she'd known the first time he snuck out of the house to meet a girl when he was sixteen.

"Thanks, Gram, but I think she likes bagels."

She crossed the cozy cottage in her pink housecoat, a smile on her thin lips and love in her eyes. Vera reached up and brushed his hair from above his eyes.

"You worked until very early this morning."

"I kept you up? I'm sorry. I'll try to be quieter." He was trying his best not to sound anxious, but he wanted to see Jessica more than he wanted anything else in the world.

She took his hand and led him to the couch. "Sit with me a second before you rush out. I'll only take a moment."

He'd do anything for her, but at that moment, every second felt interminable. He sat beside her and tried not to seem too anxious. The paper bag crinkled in his grip.

Vera patted his hand. "I like her, Jamie. She's just like your mother was."

That sucked the wind from his sails. They rarely talked about his parents. There wasn't a reason, that he could remember, or a time when they suddenly stopped talking about them, but they'd somehow faded into the background of their lives. It was strange how that happened. One day he was consumed with grief, and a year later, he had shaped and molded that grief into something he could shift to the side in order to continue living.

"She is? I don't remember Mom very well. The images in my mind feel like they're pieces of pictures you've shown me rather than real memories."

"Your mother was in love with love, Jamie. She was so in love with your father that it seeped from her pores, and you? You were her very heart and soul."

His throat thickened at her words.

"She used to watch you when you were sleeping, and she'd brush your hair from your forehead in that way that mothers do."

"You do that to me." His voice was barely above a whisper.

"Yes." She nodded. "I do. And I did it to her when she was just a girl, too. It's love, Jamie. There's nothing more powerful than the draw of the heart."

He dropped his eyes to keep her from seeing the emotion in them.

"There's a glimmer in someone's eyes when they're in love. Your grandfather had it the first time he met me. I wanted to savor that look and put it in my pocket. You know that feeling when you want to remember something until the day you die?"

Vera had a way with words that cut to the chase. "I think I do now."

"He looked at me like that every morning for the rest of his life. Oh, he had his moments. The ice-cream-before-dinner moments." She laughed. "But when something is as right as rain, no umbrella in the world can keep you from getting drenched. Don't expect it to be all flowers and prettiness. Real love isn't like that. Love is painful and beautiful at the same time. Sometimes it grips your lungs so tight you're sure you'll die for lack of air, and then it drags you down and beats you until you wish you would die. And just as quickly, it fills your lungs with helium and you think you might float away. And eventually, when you've paid your dues and knocked down the walls that kept the sweet, soft middle of your heart safe for all these years, that's when you settle into togetherness."

"Why are you telling me this now, Gram?"

"Because you're a careful man. You see women a few times, and then you bury your feelings in the computer. It's time to break that cycle and let yourself love and be loved. This is your summer, sweetheart. I can feel it in my bones. I see that glimmer in your eyes, and that little honeybee up there with the beautiful smile and eyes that look at you like you're a gift of the sweetest nectar she's ever encountered? I have a feeling it's her summer, too. Go. Be happy."

Jamie hadn't thought he needed his grandmother's approval to allow himself to let his feelings come forth, but as he ascended the stairs to Jessica's apartment, he realized that there was a piece of him that hadn't wanted to spread himself too thin, for fear of not being there for Vera. How could she have known that when he hadn't had a clue?

It wasn't yet six thirty when he knocked on Jessica's door, paper bag in hand, as transparent a ruse as Saran Wrap.

The door opened just a crack, and Jessica peered up at him. A smile spread across her lips and filled her eyes.

"Hi."

Her voice had that sleepy, sexy, just waking up sound, and it made him want to gather her in his arms and become one with her while her body was still warm from the sheets. He couldn't even begin to pretend otherwise.

"I..."

She opened the door and leaned her shoulder against it, her legs crossed at the ankle, her back slightly arched. Her hair was tousled, cascading over the silky, spaghetti-strap camisole that stopped just short of her belly button, exposing a path of skin that Jamie knew intimately. His mouth watered at the memory of how sweet and hot her skin was against his lips, how responsive her body was to him. His eyes slid lower, to the lace panties she had on, and he was a goner.

"I brought our third date. I mean, breakfast."

Her dimples came with her smile as she pushed open the screen door and he closed the distance between them. She smelled like a springtime afternoon—only warmer. With the bag in one hand, he leaned down and kissed her. She circled his neck with her arms and he kicked the door shut behind him. Good Lord, he lost all control around her. He should take her out for a three-course champagne breakfast. God knew she deserved it, but as the bag slid from his hand and he caught the edge of it and set it on the floor, it was all he could do to remember to breathe. With one strong arm around her waist, he lifted her to him, and her legs naturally circled his waist as he deepened the kiss and backed her up against the closed door. She tangled her fingers in his hair and held on tight—Jesus, that amped up the heat—and she slicked her tongue along his lower lip, pulling a hungry moan from his lungs.

"Is this our third date?" Her eyes darkened, narrowed seductively.

"Hell, yes. Hungry?"

"Only for you." She pressed her lips together and smiled that Cupid-like smile that shot straight to his heart and nearly killed him every time.

He settled his mouth over the pulse point on her

neck, feeling the quickening beneath his tongue. She fisted her hand in his hair and held him to her. He kissed and sucked a path along her collarbone, up along her jaw, to her mouth once again. The urgent kiss was rough and greedy. He needed her more than he'd needed her five seconds earlier. With her pressed against the door, one hand on her ass, he drew her camisole over her head and tossed it away.

"Jesus, you're beautiful." He took her breast in his mouth, loving first one nipple, then the other, bringing them both to taut peaks as she pressed his mouth harder to her breast.

"More, Jamie. Oh God, you feel so good."

He grazed his teeth over her nipple, licking, tasting, sucking hard as she rocked her hips against him.

"Bedroom," she said in a heated breath.

He carried her into the bedroom, but before lying her on the bed, he cupped the back of her neck and gazed into her eyes.

"I want more than this with you, Jess. So much more. More than a day, more than a night. More than just sex."

He sealed his lips over hers and brought her back down to the mattress. The sheets were still warm. He reached behind him and ripped his tee over his head, then reached for the button on his jeans. She came up on her knees and put her fingers on his.

"Let me." She licked her lips and it did him in.

She kept an eye on him as she unbuttoned his jeans, unzipped them so slowly he nearly tore them off for her. He forced himself to be patient. She hooked her fingers in the hips of his jeans and in one forceful tug they were down to his thighs, his eager arousal an inch from her lips. With her eyes trained on his, she licked him base to tip, sending a bolt of heat right through him. He watched, barely breathing as she wrapped her slender hand around his thick length. The sight, and feel, of her stroking him, licking the tip, then burying him in her mouth, had him on the verge of coming. She clutched his hips and drew them forward and back as she took almost all of him in, and he felt the back of her throat again and again.

It was the most titillating and beautiful sight he'd ever seen, and his carnal desires took over. He pulled out from between her beautiful, sensuous lips. She stuck her lower lip out in a pout and drew her eyebrows together.

"Hey." She wrapped her hand around him again and swallowed him deep.

He clenched his teeth against the need to come and fisted his hands in her hair, drawing her forward and back once, twice, then pulling out completely and stepping from his jeans.

"I've got to have you, Jess."

He lifted her to her feet beside the bed and took one breast in his mouth, sucking hard, testing the waters. She held his head against her again, moaning for more. He used his teeth, teasing her as he slid his hand beneath her panties, down between her legs, to her hot, wet center.

"Yes, more, Jamie."

He slid his fingers inside her velvety heat at the same time he squeezed her nipple between his finger and thumb and took her other breast in his mouth. She cried out and he released her nipple.

"Sorry, babe."

She pulled him back to her breast. "More. Harder. I'm so close."

Oh, hell yes. She liked it rough, which suited him just fine. He kissed her hard as he thrust his fingers deep and pinched her nipple. She grabbed his ass and pressed his erection against her belly.

"Look at me, Jess," he said against her lips. "I want to see you when you come."

Jessica opened her eyes, their tongues still stroking each other, his fingers moving deep and fast inside her. Her eyes narrowed, fluttered closed, then sprang open again as she cried out into his mouth and dug her nails into his ass. Her body shivered and shook, pulsated around his fingers. When she drew back, panting, still holding a handful of his ass, Jamie took a step back. He had to drink her in. Bare from the waist up, her pert nipples pink from his touch, she was reaching for him, heaving with every needy breath, and his fingers were still buried inside her.

"You're too fucking beautiful." He tore her panties off.

She reached for him, and he was ready, aching to be inside her, but he needed more of her. He wanted to make her come again, to let her feel all of the desire that had built over the last few days, so when she finally took him in, she wasn't rushed or anxious, but ready. So ready he could take his fill. He slid one hand beneath her hair and tugged her neck back; her lips opened to him with a rush of air. His other hand circled her body, and he slid his fingers between her cheeks from behind, then buried his tongue in her mouth, tempting her until she was trembling with need again. Her breathing hitched. He spread her legs with his thighs, feeling her body quake beneath his touch, and then he slid down her body, licking her from sternum to belly button. He dragged his tongue along the sweet skin above her pubic bone, smelling her luscious scent, needing to taste her. With one hand still teasing her from behind, he ran his tongue along her sensitive, wet skin.

"Yes," she commanded.

He stroked her again with his tongue, and she gripped his shoulders, her body quivering against him.

"You're so sweet, so deliciously responsive to my touch."

He used his hand to tease the swollen bundle of nerves he knew would send her over the edge again as he loved her with his mouth. She fisted his hair again and tugged—heightening his arousal even more with the mix of pleasure and pain—and held him firmly against her. There was no place he'd rather be than pleasuring her with his mouth and hands, priming her for his full, heated desire. He felt the orgasm rolling in. Her thighs tensed and her nails dug into his skin. She stopped breathing for a second; then her head fell back and her hips bucked as her inner muscles pulsated time and time again, and his name sailed from her lips in a cry of pleasure so vibrant and wonderful it filled his chest.

"Don't...stop."

He licked and sucked. "You're so beautiful when you come. I'll never stop."

He felt the tension ease in her thighs and he carried her to the bed, then set his mouth on her again. In seconds she was coming again, her head tossed from side to side as she gasped time and time again. He reached for his jeans to retrieve a condom and she grabbed his arm.

"Make love to me," she pleaded.

"Protection," was all he could manage.

"On the pill. I need you, Jamie. Now, please."

He settled his hips over hers, feeling her heat and wetness on the tip of his arousal.

"You're sure?" He always used condoms, but he wanted to feel her so badly he wasn't about to turn her down.

"More than anything I've ever been sure of in my

life. Please, Jamie. Don't make me wait."

He sealed his lips over hers, slid his hand beneath her thigh and lifted her knee up beside his hip as he slid into her. She was so incredibly tight that it took effort to enter her. Too much effort. He forced his mind to focus, stilled his movements, and searched her eyes.

"Jess. Have you done this before?"

She nodded. "Once."

Oh, dear Lord. "Once?" Guilt coiled deep in his belly. She must have seen it in his eyes, because she reached up with both hands and touched his cheeks.

"I'm not a virgin. You didn't do anything wrong." She was smiling, and the depth of emotion in her eyes brought his forehead to hers.

"I was aggressive. I shouldn't have been so rough. Jesus, Jess, you deserve sweet tenderness." He was panting. She felt so damn good, he was nearly ready to come, but now he worried. She deserved slow loving, and he figured they'd get to that, but if he'd known, he wouldn't have rushed it, and he definitely would have led with more care.

"I wanted it just like this. With you. I didn't want sweet tenderness. I mean, I do, but this is exactly what I dreamed it would be like making love with you. I'm happy, Jamie." She leaned up and kissed him, arching her hips, taking in more of him.

"You said you were on the pill. You touched me like you'd done it a million times. I just assumed..." *I'm an asshole. I know better than to assume.*

"I'm on the pill to regulate my cycle. I touched you like my heart told me to, not out of practiced precision. It's embarrassing to admit I haven't done those things."

He kissed her softly, brought his hands under her and cradled her head. "Baby, you have to tell me these things so I don't hurt you, or ask you to do something you aren't comfortable with."

She nibbled her lower lip and nodded. "Okay."

"There's no need to be embarrassed with me. I adore you. I want to bring you pleasure in every way, sexually, in our daily life, but I have to trust that you'll clue me in on things." He touched his forehead to hers again.

"I promise. I didn't mean to deceive you."

"You didn't—that's a harsh word. I just—I like you so damn much, Jess. I want to do all the right things."

"Then make love to me how you want to. Hard, slow, fast, whatever your heart tells you to. Jamie, I wish you *were* my first."

Making love to her how he wanted to was easy, because after she alleviated his guilt, at least enough that he could push past it, what he wanted most was the physical and mental connection with Jess. And knowing that she believed he was as special to her as she had become to him, his urgency subsided, and deeper emotions grew.

Each time he entered her, he went a little deeper, soaking in the intensity of her tightness and drawing out the pleasure for them both. Their kisses heated up, and they moved in sync, faster, deeper, kissing and groping until the guilt subsided completely. He gripped her ass and tilted her hips, just enough to hit the spot that would bring her to the edge, where he held her, panting, grasping at his shoulders, begging for more. Until he was ready, too, and he took them both over the edge in a frenzy of pleasure-filled cries, groans, and loving strokes that awoke parts of him he never knew were sleeping.

He'd thought about making love to Jessica since the first time their eyes met, and now, afterward, there was a peace that overtook him, a desire to be closer than he'd ever felt with another woman. He usually rolled off and his mind moved on to other things. With Jessica, he didn't want to move away, but he worried he was too heavy for her. He shifted his weight, and she pressed her hand to his hips, keeping him inside her.

"Please don't move. I've dreamed of being in your arms, beneath you, feeling you inside me, for days. Please don't go."

Jesus, they were so in sync. "I'm not going anywhere, but I have to know, Jess. You've only been with one man. Why me? Why so fast? We could have waited."

Her fingers moved lightly along his skin, up and down his back, and when she spoke, her eyes filled with seriousness, laced with emotion so deep he could fall into them.

"I always thought I'd know when the right man came into my life. The man I'd want to give myself over to completely. The first time I...did that was when I was very young. I was trying to fit in during my sophomore year in high school. We never even dated. It was like I dared myself to do it. I met him after school and we did it in his bedroom while his parents were at work." A shadow of sadness washed over her eyes and just as quickly disappeared. "I was rebelling in the stupidest way imaginable."

"Oh, babe. I'm sorry. High school boys can be such jerks." He kissed her softly and shifted his weight so his thigh was over hers, his arm draped over her chest. He imagined some jerky kid sweet-talking her into giving up her virginity, and it pissed him off. He felt protective of her and wanted her to feel safe. He drew the sheets up to her waist and tightened his grip around her.

"It's okay. It was a good lesson, actually, and it was

my choice. I wasn't forced or anything. I *wanted* to be normal badly enough that I believed that might do it. It didn't, but it wasn't horrible. It was kind of like when you try a food you don't love, but maybe if someone else had cooked it you would try it again, because you know it's supposed to be *really* good. Anyway, after that night I decided that rebelling would have to happen in safer ways, and it made me realize that sex was in no way tied to not feeling lonely. I still felt lonely. But that, I realized, came from within. I learned how to deal with the loneliness, and I rebelled by playing the music I wanted instead of what my mother chose. I'm lame, a nerd, whatever. I know, but it served the purpose."

"But, Jess, all these years? Didn't you miss being touched?" He was a sensual man, and Jamie loved being touched as much as he enjoyed touching. He couldn't imagine going all those years without being intimate with a woman.

"I don't think you understand how focused I've been all these years. Dating wasn't ever part of my daily life. In Juilliard I practiced nonstop, graduated top of my class, and after..." She shrugged. "It's not like I'm a saint, Jamie. I went out with a few guys, but I never *felt* anything for them, so they never got past second base." Her cheeks pinked up. "And now here I am."

"So was this...was I...some sort of rebellion?"

She ran her finger over his lips. "No. I'm past rebellion. I've moved on to self-discovery. When I arrived here the week before I met you, I was hit on by guys. Several over the course of that week, actually. If this were rebellion, any of them would have done. I told you, I don't rebel with my body any longer. I'm twenty-seven, Jamie, and in all those years, I've never felt drawn to a man like I was, like I am, with you." She inhaled deeply and blew it out slowly. "Besides, I never knew what I was missing. I imagined what it might be like to make love with someone I cared about, and I hoped it would be like this, but before the…what we did on the beach, I hadn't, you know."

He blinked several times, wondering if she was saying what he thought she was. "You never had an orgasm?"

She shook her head.

"You've never pleasured yourself?"

She bit her lip and shook her head. "Never even considered it."

If I had your body, I'd never stop touching it. "But you were so open with me. You knew just what to do, how to act." He'd never met anyone like her, so pure and honest. So openly loving.

She shifted so they were nose to nose. "That's because it wasn't an act. I finally allowed myself to let go of what I'd been taught about how to act and of right and wrong. You know, they didn't cover *proper orgasm etiquette* at Juilliard." She laughed, a sweet, sensuous laugh that he wanted to always remember. "I just let myself feel, accepted what you had to give, and I gave what I wanted to share."

He drew her body against him, wanting to take care of her and show her all the ways she deserved to be loved and cherished.

"Was it okay for you?" she asked just above a whisper.

He leaned back and met her gaze. "Being with you before we made love was never just okay. You make me think and feel and want in ways I never have before. I've never felt closer to anyone in my life."

And I doubt I ever will.

Chapter Nine

AFTER MAKING LOVE again and finally eating those bagels, they spent the day with Vera and the others down by the pool. Jamie, Caden, Kurt, and Tony sat at one of the round tables, playing poker beneath an umbrella. Bella brought a radio, tuned to a top forties station. Jessica, Bella, Jenna, and Amy were lying in the sun on lounge chairs. Leanna was still at the flea market, and Vera was reading beneath an umbrella close to the girls.

Jamie's head was still spinning from making love to Jessica earlier in the day. He couldn't get over how trusting she was. Not that he couldn't be trusted. He was a trustworthy guy, but with Jessica he had nearly zero control. She barely knew him. He could have been an asshole. Maybe he was one. How would he know? Would an asshole have continued making love to her when he realized he was only the second man she'd ever been with? He couldn't have stopped if his life had depended on it. She had a crazy hold over his emotions, and it became stronger with every second they were together. He'd been a second away from asking her to shower with him, and he'd forced himself to back off, because he knew if he saw all those naked, luscious curves glistening wet beneath the shower spray, the memory of how good she felt beneath him would be too fresh. He'd go back for more without thinking. Instead, he'd rinsed off alone, smelling her scent all around him in the small bathroom.

"Dude, you going to stare at her all day, or are you going to make a move?" Tony arched a brow.

Double entendre noted, Jamie gave him one right back. "Can't beat an ace in the hole."

"Unless you're wielding a longer sword," Kurt added with a smirk. "Come on, boys, put away your dicks and play your cards."

Jamie set down four aces. "I was talking about my cards." *And thinking about Jess.* He'd never had sex with a virgin, but if he had, he imagined it wouldn't have felt much different from making love to Jess after only one kid had been there before him, at least ten years earlier. Heat streaked through him. He shifted in his seat and tried to distract himself as best he could.

"Son of a bitch." Tony tossed down his cards. "I thought you were day dreaming."

Caden laid his cards facedown. "You guys are too hot for me today. I've got to pick up Evan at TGG. Anyone need anything in town?"

"Condoms, Jamie?" Tony asked. "They sell 'em small."

"Yeah, that's why I can't buy them at the same places as you." Jamie clasped his hands behind his head and relaxed back in his chair. "They don't carry triple XL."

Kurt shook his head. He threw his cards on the table and leaned closer to the others. "I think Tony's jealous."

"*Pfft.* I've got women coming out my ass." Tony ran his hand along his muscular pecs.

"That's the problem." Caden rose to his feet. "You're supposed to come in them. They're not supposed to be coming out of anywhere, especially your ass. I'll see you guys later."

Kurt pushed out from the table. "Hold up. I'll walk with you. I have to get some writing done."

Jamie's phone rang. He watched Jessica walk over to the pool steps and stick her toe in the water. She held on to the metal railing and stepped down onto the first stair, looking sexy as hell in her pink bathing suit. His phone rang again.

"Get your phone, bud." Tony pushed the ringing phone closer to Jamie.

He answered the call from Mark, but his attention was focused on Tony as he joined Jessica on the steps of the pool. Tony's dirty-blond hair had sun-kissed streaks of lighter blond. His muscles glistened in the sun, and Jamie knew the way he was leaning against the concrete edge of the pool, his palms flat, elbows behind him, was a purposeful pose to pump up his enormous biceps. *Bastard*.

"Sorry, Mark. What were you saying?" He'd been too busy watching Tony to catch what Mark had said.

"Jesus, Jamie. Focus. This is important. There's something going on with the search engine, and it's worse than we thought. A bug. Every time kids search for..." Jamie lost focus on Mark's voice as Jessica walked into the water and Tony reached for her hand, drawing her deeper. *What the fuck is he doing?*

"What do you think?" Mark asked.

"What?" Jamie snapped, angry about Tony fucking around when he knew Jamie was with Jessica. Tony never did shit like this. Jamie didn't know what was up with him today, but he was acting like he was looking for a fight.

"Damn it, Jamie. What are you doing? This vacation was a mistake. I told you it was. You should be here dealing with this shit," Mark seethed.

"It's my first vacation in eight years, Mark."

Tony grabbed a raft and lifted Jessica onto it. His goddamn hands wrapped around her waist, and when she shifted, her ass was about an inch from his face. *Asshole*. Jamie shot a look at Amy, who was scowling, unlike Bella and Jenna, who were rolling their eyes.

"I've got to go, Mark. You can handle it however you see fit." He ended the call, stalked to the deep end of the pool, and dove in. He broke the surface on the other side of Jessica's raft and shot Tony a dark stare.

Jessica reached for his hand. "Hi."

"Hey, babe. Enjoying the sun?" He shifted his eyes to Jessica. Good Lord, it was a good thing he was in the water, because he was getting turned on just looking at her, despite his annoyance at Tony, who swam away.

"Yeah. It's nice. Want to climb up with me?" She patted the raft.

"I don't think that's a good idea."

She wrinkled her brow; then her eyes bloomed wide as understanding dawned on her and she dropped her gaze to the pool with a sexy smile. "Oh."

Bella, Amy, and Jenna jumped into the water, splashing both of them. Jamie pulled himself up halfway on the raft to shield Jessica from the splashes.

"Mr. Chivalrous, look at you," Jenna yelled as she doggie paddled around the deep water.

"Lame excuse to get closer," Tony hollered.

"What's up with him today?" Jamie asked Bella.

"Ames had a date last night." Bella swatted Jenna as she tried to cling to her. "He's been grumpy ever since."

"Poor bastard. He had his chance. How'd it go, Amy?" Jamie climbed off of Jessica but kept his hand on hers.

Amy had a foam noodle beneath her arms as she floated around the pool in her baby-blue bikini. "It was nice. We're going out again tonight."

"We're all going so we can check him out." Jenna grabbed a noodle and floated over to Jessica's raft. "You two should come. We're going to listen to a band play at Marconi Beach. I'm going to make Petey dance with me."

"I've never even seen a band on a beach." Jessica squeezed Jamie's hand. "Do you think Vera would want to go?"

"You have no idea how much I love that you want to include her, but she's been going to bed early these days. I'll ask her, but it'll probably be just us. Do you mind if I go spend a few minutes with her?"

"Of course not. Go."

After a quick kiss, he swam the length of the pool, grabbed a towel, and joined Vera, the call with Mark all but forgotten.

"YOU CAN BURN a hole through a man if you stare too much," Bella teased.

"Do they sell full-body heat protectors, then? Because there's no chance that I'll be done staring at him anytime soon." Jessica couldn't believe she'd admitted that out loud, but she was practically salivating over Jamie's muscles as they bunched and flexed while he dried his delicious body—the taste of which was too fresh in her mind to forget.

"Said by the woman who suspiciously didn't answer the door this morning at seven thirty." Bella raised her brows.

"Bella!" Amy yelled. "We said we wouldn't

embarrass her."

Jessica pulled Amy's noodle closer and asked quietly, "Did you guys really come by?"

Amy nodded. "Don't worry. We didn't stick around and listen or anything. But we heard enough to know that we shouldn't bother you."

"Oh my God. Oh my God." She covered her mouth and shot a look at Jamie. He was laughing with Vera. She loved how attentive he was to his grandmother. "Oh no. Did Vera hear us, too?"

"No, Vera was playing her violin," Amy assured her. "Tony was too angry about me going on a date to be aware of anything, Kurt had his nose in his computer, and Caden was out running, so it was only us girls."

"Oh, thank God. I'm sorry I didn't answer the door." No, she really wasn't. She'd had the best morning of her life, and every time she revisited the feel of Jamie lying on top of her, or remembered the feel of his tongue stroking her most private spots, or... She had to stop thinking of him. Her nipples were already erect.

"Don't be. At least you're not like Leanna." Amy laughed. "She leaves her windows open and all of Wellfleet can hear her. That's probably the real reason they stay at their house on the bay instead of the cottage."

"Oh, that's awful. If we ever do that, please, please tell us, because I'd be mortified." She realized she'd used the term *us*. It felt natural. It felt good.

"You guys are such a cute couple. I wish my favorite surfer dude would ask me out. I've been in love with him forever." Amy's eyes went soft when she looked at Tony lying on a lounge chair.

"If he's that mad over you dating, it means he likes you. I know he was only helping me onto the raft to make you jealous." Jessica lowered her voice to a whisper. "He looked right past me and stared at you."

"Well, he sure doesn't act like it, but I do like the guy I'm going out with," Amy explained. "Jake Ryder, he's Blue's younger brother."

"Much younger brother. She's a cradle robber," Jenna said.

Did that make Jamie a cradle robber, too?

"He's only twenty-eight, but he's some kind of hot, mountain rescue guy, so..." Jenna wiggled her eyebrows in quick succession.

Amy swatted Jenna's arm.

Jamie and Vera walked by, and Jamie crouched beside the pool. "I'm going to help Vera get situated. She doesn't want to come this evening, so it will be just us. Okay?"

"Sounds good." Jessica waved to Vera. "We'll miss you tonight."

"Thank you, dear. Have a nice time."

She watched Jamie escort Vera out of the pool gates and sighed, feeling like the luckiest girl in the world. She got out of the pool to lie in the sun, and her phone rang with an unfamiliar number.

"Hello?"

"Hi. Is this Jessica Ayers?"

"Yes." She watched the girls fight over the raft she'd used.

"This is Steve Lacasse. You left me a message the other day." His voice was energetic and friendly.

"Oh! Steve, yes, thank you for calling back. You had a baseball for sale, the one with Mickey Mantle's signature all colored in with red ink."

"Yes, but that's been sold. Shipped it off the other day."

"Yes. I know it was sold. I'm ninety-nine percent sure that was my father's ball from when he was a child, and I'd like to contact the new owner to see if I can buy it from him. I was wondering if you could share his contact information with me." *Please, please, please.*

"I'm sorry, Jessica, but I can't give out any personal information. You can probably track him down on eBay."

"Yes, I've tried that. Could you please pass along my information to him?"

"I suppose I could do that. What's your email address?"

"It's Jessica at BSO dot com, but could you please give him my phone number instead?"

"Darlin', I'm not sure that's a wise thing to do. Email is much safer."

She smiled at his concern for her, but she hardly ever used email, and the less she had to rely on the computer, the better. "Thank you, yes, I understand that, but if you wouldn't mind?"

He agreed, and Jessica hung up the phone feeling hopeful about finding her father's baseball.

She lay down on the towel as Amy dried off a few feet away.

"Do you think I'm crazy to go out with someone a few years younger than me?" Amy laid her towel on her chair and tucked her wet hair behind her ears.

"I'm not the best person to give dating advice, but I'm younger than Jamie. I think you should follow your heart."

Amy sighed. "I tried that." She glared at Tony, who was nose deep in a novel. "I want to run down to the crazy store. Want to come with me?"

"What's the crazy store?"

"Oh, right. Sorry. You know the two souvenir shops that are across the street from each other in South Wellfleet? Right on Route 6?"

Jessica shook her head.

"The ones with all the inner tubes and blow up stuff all over?"

"Oh, those. Yes."

"We had a renter here once whose little girl called them the crazy stores, and it kind of stuck. Anyway, they have tie-dyed dresses, and I want to see if I can pick one up for tonight."

An hour later Jessica, Amy, Bella, and Jenna came out of the crazy store with bags in hand. Jessica had a fun new dress to wear, which went perfectly with her new life. She'd bought Jamie a mood ring, and she'd picked up a cute beach bag for Vera.

When they got back to Seaside, Jessica heard Vera playing her violin. She walked around to the back deck of Jamie and Vera's cottage to listen and found Jamie sitting with his back to Jessica, working on his laptop. Vera was playing "Czárdás" by Vittorio Monti, a piece that Jessica had always loved. She closed her eyes for a minute and let the music wash over her. Her fingers moved out of habit. She ached to play again. She opened her eyes as Jamie looked up from where he was working on his laptop and smiled.

"Hey, Jess."

"Hi. I got Vera a little something. I've always loved that piece she's playing."

"It's one of my favorites, too." He reached for her hand as she stepped onto the deck and kissed her cheek.

"I saw this bag at the crazy store and thought Vera might like it for the pool."

"The crazy store. You must have gone with the girls." He held up the bag and showed it to Vera. "Look what Jess brought you."

Vera stopped playing and joined them at the table. "That was very sweet of you. Thank you. This is lovely."

"I'm glad you like it. I love listening to you play." Jessica decided to wait and give Jamie his gift when they were alone. A mood ring wasn't just silly. It implied intimacy, and she was still a little shy after what Amy had said.

"Thank you. Until my fingers won't allow it, I'm going to play to my heart's content."

Jessica knew that feeling. She'd been working hard at ignoring the urge to pick up her cello. She focused on her father's baseball to stifle the urge to join Vera. "Jamie, I heard back from Steve, and he's going to give the buyer my number."

"That's awesome." Jamie folded her into his arms and hugged her tight. "You might get that baseball after all."

"I hope so. I'm going to run this stuff home. I want to call my father and catch up on a few things."

"I still haven't given you a lesson on eBay or the computer. I'm sorry that fell through the cracks. Want to do that now?"

She couldn't tell if the desire in his eyes was her imagination or if he was making up an excuse so they could be alone and intimate again. She already missed the feel of him, and ever since he made the innuendo in the pool about being aroused, she'd been fighting memories of lying in his arms and being spoiled by his hands, his mouth, his body. *Oh Lord.* She had to go home before Vera saw right through her.

"That's okay. You're working and spending time with Vera. Hopefully, the buyer will call me, so there's no rush."

"Jessica, why don't you bring your cello down and accompany me in a piece? I would love to hear you play." Vera patted Jamie on the shoulder. "Go on, Jamie. Help her bring her cello down."

"I don't want to interfere." Jessica couldn't ignore the goose bumps racing up her arms at the idea of playing with Vera. Playing for Jamie was one thing, but Vera was an accomplished musician. She'd appreciate the musicality of Jessica's style, which would be thrilling, but she would also notice her weaknesses.

"What do you say, Jess?" Jamie rose to his feet.

How could she say no to Vera? "Okay. Sure. Thank you, Vera." They walked across the quad toward her apartment.

"Where are y'all going?" Bella hollered from her deck, where she was grilling. The smell of seasoned steaks rose around her cottage.

"Jess is going to play with Vera," Jamie answered. "Come on over." He turned to Jessica and lowered his voice. "You don't mind, do you?"

"No, it's fine." She wasn't sure if she was so nervous about playing in front of everyone, or because once she did, she might not be able to keep herself from playing again and again.

"I'll bring steaks." Bella hung over the edge of her deck and hollered, "Jenna! Pete! Jessica's playing with Vera. Grab some salad!"

Jenna ran outside in her new tie-dyed sundress with Joey on her heels. "Really? Oh, yay! I'll get Ames. Can you tell Kurt and Leanna? Oh, and Tony?"

"Amy left to meet Jake." Bella stepped off her deck.

"And Tony's right here." Tony waved from his side yard. "I'll be over in a few minutes."

"Go get ready!" Bella shooed Jamie and Jessica away.

Jessica looked nervously at Jamie, who was smiling with pride in his eyes, while her stomach twisted and turned.

"See? Everyone wants to hear you play." He draped an arm over her shoulder as they headed up the stairs to her apartment.

Jessica realized the real cause of her stress. She'd played in front of thousands of people, the media, even the president, and she wasn't as nervous as she was to play in front of her new friends. She wanted to be plain old Jessica Ayers to them, and she knew the minute Vera heard her play, she'd know how accomplished she really was, and even though the others may not realize the level of expertise she possessed, surely they'd recognize that her cello playing was above average. She hoped Jamie was right and that she was misjudging how she could fit her cello into the real world, and more specifically, into their relationship.

In her apartment, she fisted her hands in Jamie's shirt and kissed him. She needed to get her mind off her nerves and she'd been thinking about his lips all day.

"I've waited all day for that." He sealed his mouth over hers again, and within seconds her legs turned to jelly and her nerves eased.

She was blissfully under his spell. When he pulled back, she was breathless.

"Are you nervous?"

"You can tell?"

He covered her hand with his on his chest. "You've got a handful of chest hair in there. Some skin, too."

She opened her fists. "I'm sorry."

"Why are you nervous? Didn't you say that you play in an orchestra?" He drew those sexy brows together.

"Yes." She went to get her cello before either of them could make another move and they ended up between the sheets instead of down on his deck where everyone would be waiting to watch her play.

Oh God.

Chapter Ten

JESSICA'S EYES WERE closed as her fingers danced along the fingerboard of the cello against the backdrop of the setting sun. The bow moved gracefully, then forcefully, then full of grace once again, across the strings. In the few days Jamie had known her, he'd never seen such a peaceful expression on her beautiful face. It was as if the music had seeped into her body and filled it with serenity. Surrounded by the people he loved most, she opened her eyes for a split second and immediately sought his, and in that second, she leveled him flat.

Her lips curved up and her dimples appeared, making his entire world spin on its axis. In the next moment her eyes closed, and the combination of the music and Jessica made his chest feel full.

"Dude, she's amazing," Tony whispered.

"Yeah," was all he could manage. Jamie had listened to his grandmother play in enough orchestras to know expert cello playing when he heard it.

After they played, Vera lowered her violin and gazed at Jessica. Jamie had never seen his grandmother in awe of anyone. There was no mistaking the look in her eyes as she watched Jessica humbly look down at her cello with something akin to love in her eyes. Jamie looked over the others, as they clapped and smiled and told both Vera and Jessica how marvelously they'd played, and on their faces he saw the same admiration for the duo that swelled inside him. Jessica's eyes found Vera's and held. Jamie couldn't read the silent message that passed between them, but he felt the power of a secret world, a secret love. A kinship. If there was one thing he understood, it was that his grandmother had recognized something in Jessica that none of them could see, and he wanted to be in the know.

While the others gathered around the table filling their plates with the potluck dinner everyone had pitched in to make and Jessica settled her cello in the case, Jamie went to Vera's side.

"That was beautiful, Gram."

"Yes. Magnificent," she said as she tucked her violin into its case. Vera pulled her thick sweater around her shoulders and crossed her frail arms over her chest with a slow exhalation. "Magnificent," she whispered, as she shifted her eyes to Jessica again. "Be a dear, would you, please? I'd love a plate of food. I'm famished."

Jamie knew when he was being dismissed. He could see that she wanted to speak with Jessica alone, and again he wished he could swim in Vera's brain long enough to understand what she'd seen.

He grabbed a plate and filled it with salad, steak, and a slice of Leanna's homemade bread and layered it with her delicious Strawberry Spice jam.

"Didn't Jessica say she played *a little* the other night?" Bella asked.

"Yeah, she sure did." Jamie respected his

grandmother's privacy and purposely didn't try to eavesdrop on her conversation with Jessica, but he couldn't help glancing at the woman who continually proved to be so much more than he ever expected. In every way, from her kindness and generosity, to her sweet demeanor and sensual instincts. She was standing with her hands laced together, swaying just the slightest bit, like a blade of grass in the breeze. Her lips were pressed together in that I'm-embarrassed-but-happy way that he'd fallen head over heels for, but her beautiful blue eyes were serious as she spoke to Vera. She nodded, said something that caused Vera's mouth to open wide and then ease into her own pleasant smile.

"Well, I think she more than plays a little." Bella handed a plate to Caden, then turned to ask Evan if he wanted her to fill one for him.

"Damn, Jamie. Gorgeous and talented." Tony had a plate loaded with steak, potatoes, salad, and bread. "Lucky dude."

Vera reached out and embraced Jessica, and they both headed his way.

"That I am. What's up with you and Amy? Did you blow it altogether?" Jamie asked.

Tony clenched his jaw. "Nothing to blow."

"Really? Could have fooled me, but what do I know?" Jamie patted him on the back. "You going to the beach party tonight?"

"Of course." Tony tossed his chin to the side and his hair fell over his brows as he draped an arm around Jamie's shoulder and lowered his voice. "Surfing only satisfies one type of desire in this hard bod."

The ache of jealousy in his friend's voice wasn't lost on Jamie, and as Tony joined Kurt, Caden, and the others and Jessica came to his side, he couldn't help but feel empathy for him. He knew that hookups would only lessen a fleeting desire. And now that he'd experienced what being with someone he cared about felt like, he knew that making love could be a deeper, more fulfilling experience, and he hoped his friend would find that one day, too.

"Thank you, dear." Vera took the plate from Jamie, pulling his attention back to the group.

"Sure." He turned his attention to Jessica and wrapped his arms around her waist. "You didn't tell me that you played even better than Jacqueline du Pré." He kissed her softly and noticed her eyes flash to Vera, who was settling in at the table.

"Please. I'm not that good, but thank you." She dropped her eyes.

"Hey, are you okay?" he asked quietly. "You should be beaming with pride, and you look a little worried."

"I need to tell you something, and I've kind of been holding it back because I didn't want it to make things weird between us, but I've told Vera, and now I feel bad for not telling you first." She hooked her finger in the waist of his jeans. "Jamie, I'm on hiatus from the Boston Symphony Orchestra."

The Boston Symphony Orchestra was one of the country's five major symphony orchestras, and it was more than a big deal. It was a major deal, and taking a hiatus from such a prominent orchestra was not something the orchestra or, he imagined, Jessica would take lightly.

"That's amazing, to play with such a prominent orchestra. Why would you keep that from anyone, especially me?"

She shrugged. "I just wanted to try to live a normal life and see what I was missing. People get weird when they hear you play for one of the Big Five, not to mention that I'm being considered for a seat with the

Chamber Players, which is just another thing that would set me apart from other people my age." The Big Five orchestras were designated based on musical excellence and caliber of musicianship, as well as a few other determining factors. In addition to the BSO, the Big Five included the New York Philharmonic, Chicago Symphony Orchestra, Philadelphia Orchestra, and the Cleveland Orchestra.

"The Chamber Players? That's huge, isn't it? Very prestigious." Jamie knew how prestigious it was, and he wondered how Jessica wasn't jumping with joy to tell everyone she knew.

"Yes, it is." She sighed, and when she shifted her eyes away, he sensed her discomfort with the discussion.

Jamie had seen firsthand how people reacted differently to Vera once they knew of her pre-Jamie career, and he knew all about people acting differently when they learned he held a coveted status, which was why he chose to live a low-key lifestyle rather than that of the rich and famous. But he wasn't sure their friends at Seaside would be clued in to the symphony industry, or that they'd care, given that they'd always treated him like he wasn't a billionaire. He wished she'd give them the chance to show her how they would react, but he was beginning to realize just how central the orchestra had been to Jessica's life, and how she really must have lived a life very far removed from anything outside of the orchestra and the music world. It was all beginning to make sense—her inexperience with men, her fear that she might not fit in. She was so beautiful that if she were out in bars at night, she'd have been swooped into the arms of any number of men quicker than she could have said the word *cello*.

He wondered if there was more to her hiatus than

just wanting to live a normal life, especially knowing that, as Vera had mentioned, taking a break from one of the biggest symphonies around was frowned upon. Whatever the reason, he didn't want to make her any more uncomfortable than she already was.

He kissed her and whispered, "Your secret is safe with me."

Chapter Eleven

MARCONI BEACH WAS just a few minutes south of Seaside. Known for being a family-friendly beach during the day, with ample restroom facilities and lifeguards, Marconi Beach transformed at night into an oceanfront dance club. Colorful spotlights illuminated a makeshift stage that was brought in for the band and disassembled and removed before the next morning. Tonight there were crowds of people milling about the wide beach at the bottom of the high dunes. Some people danced barefoot in the sand, while others gathered in groups, talking and laughing. Beach chairs were set up in circles around bonfires and down by the shore. Jessica had never been to an event like this, and although she felt dressed for the occasion in her new tie-dye dress with a hoodie hanging open over it and flip-flops that she left dune side, her heart was racing.

Tony opened the cooler and handed them each a beer. “Party on, my friends.”

“Thanks, Tony.” Jamie opened one bottle and handed it to Jessica, then opened his own.

"Come on." Leanna pulled Jessica's hand, leading her toward the band. "Even Kurt is going to dance. Come on, Jamie! Everyone's over here." She guided them through the crowd, with Tony on their heels, and there in the thick of scantily clad dancing twentysomethings were all of their friends, including Pete's sister, Sky, and Blue—and Amy and Jake.

Jessica shot a look at Tony. His eyes were narrow and his jaw was clenched. She went up on her tiptoes and whispered to Jamie, "Can Tony dance with us?"

"Three's a crowd," he said with serious eyes. "But as long as I don't have to share you later, it's fine with me."

He settled a hand on her hip, but before Jessica could say anything to Tony, a cute brunette began dancing with him.

"Sorry. I just felt bad for him."

He touched his forehead to hers. "You're too sweet for your own good." Jamie began swaying to the music, and Jessica fell into the rhythm effortlessly. It was easy to be in sync with him. He moved fluidly, without tension or worry about what other people thought. While their friends danced and laughed around them, making funny comments and drinking their beers, Jamie's eyes were locked on Jessica's. His hips pressed to hers, and the seductive smile on his lips sent a shiver right through her.

He pressed his unshaven cheek to hers. "I've been thinking of your sweetness all day, and I can't wait to taste you again tonight."

His heated whisper on her skin, the prickles of his five-o'clock shadow on her cheek, and the enticing innuendo had her entire body hot. Jessica circled his neck with her arms, and their hips took on their own slow, sensual rhythm, while the band played a fast beat. Jessica had never worried too much about safety, as she'd always traveled with the group of musicians she worked with, but here, on the beach amid all those people, she felt safe in Jamie's arms. She'd seen him come right over in the pool when Tony closed in on her, and later, instead of peppering her with questions about the symphony and her hiatus—or her future—he kept her secret close to his chest. And now, as she pressed her cheek to his chest and breathed in his scent, feeling the steady beating of his heart, she knew she was falling for him, and at some point, all those important questions would have to be answered. But not tonight. Tonight she wanted to enjoy her new friends and disappear into Jamie's touch.

"I bought you something today." She slid the mood ring off her thumb and held it out to Jamie.

"A ring? What exactly are you proposing?" He arched a brow.

"That we see what you're feeling. See how it's purply right now? It's a mood ring. This color means *I'm amorous, sensual. Mischievous.* Put it on. Let's see what you are." She watched him slide it on as they danced. "We only have to worry if it turns black."

"What's black?"

"Intense nothingness. A black hole. Angst so deep you can't push your way out of it."

"I can tell you what I'm feeling without a ring." He pressed his hips to hers, and the feel of his arousal sent another thrill through her. The ring turned dark blue.

"Ooh, you're love-struck. Deeply relaxed," she whispered.

He pulled her close. "I am *not* deeply relaxed. Intensely turned on, hard as a rock, but not relaxed." His voice was low and deep, and it pulled her under his spell again as he lowered his lips to hers and took her in another brain-numbing kiss.

The song ended, and Jenna waved everyone over to one of the bonfires, where Pete handed out sticks and marshmallows. Jamie leaned down and kissed Jessica passionately, pressing her body to his, stroking her tongue as if he were making love to her mouth. She came away breathless, momentarily unable to think, much less walk.

"Damn, I love how your body reacts to me," Jamie whispered in her ear.

"My legs are jelly," she admitted.

"Too bad I can't lay you down right here and make your whole body feel that way."

Oh Lord. Every nerve in her body was on fire. She was already damp between her legs, and they'd only just arrived at the beach. How was she supposed to make it through the evening without falling to pieces? Everything he said, every brush of his cheek, every glimpse of his sexy smile, made her insides quiver. With her body aching for him, now that she knew what it felt like to be naked in his arms, to be as close as two people could possibly be, she could barely clear her mind enough to think of anything else. The ocean breeze, the music, Jamie…it was all so romantic. The perfect night to hang out with friends and relax, and there she was, wanting to tear off his clothes and play him like an electric guitar, wild and uninhibited, then slowly, memorizing the feel of every inch of him.

She shook her head to clear the dirty thoughts and realized Jamie had been watching her the whole time. He pressed his cheek to hers again and whispered, "I love that look in your eyes. It makes me want to take you right here."

Oh God, yes. She clutched his waist.

"Want me to cook you a marshmallow to take your mind off of what we really want to be doing?" he asked.

Marshmallow, yes, that's good. Marshmallows have nothing to do with sex. That should help get her mind out of the gutter. She'd never had a dirty mind before, and as surprising and new as it all was, she didn't fight it. She reveled in it, wondering what was happening to her.

She looked up at Jamie. *You're happening to me.* "Sure. A marshmallow sounds great." They joined the others by the fire.

"Petey's making mine golden brown," Jenna explained. "Not golden, not brown, golden brown. Which reminds me..." She ran her fingers through her dark hair, then reached into her pocket, pulled out a plastic tiara, and settled it on her head.

"And your marshmallow has arrived, princess." Pete held the marshmallow up for Jenna to inspect.

Jenna lifted her chin as she assessed the marshmallow with a scrutinizing gaze. She slid it from the stick with a wide smile.

"Perfect! Thank you!"

Pete leaned down and kissed her lips, then smiled at Jamie. "Gotta treat her as she deserves."

Jenna stared adoringly up at Pete.

"Oh my God. That's too cute. How long have you been together?" Jessica asked.

"In my mind? Six years, but in real life? A year," Jenna explained.

Bella, Caden, Leanna, and Kurt joined them as Jenna was talking.

Pete wrapped his arms around Jenna from behind. "Guys can be thick-headed, or so I'm told." He slid his eyes to Tony, still dancing with the brunette.

"Not all guys. Caden and Kurt knew what they wanted and went for it." Bella leaned against Caden's side.

"Hey! Are you dissing my man?" Jenna put up her

fists and pretended to box with Bella.

"Put those puppies away, Jen, or I'll unorganize your closet," Bella teased.

Jenna dropped her hands and looked up at Pete. "I tried to defend you."

"That's my girl." He kissed her again.

Bella draped an arm over Jessica's shoulder and looked at Jamie as he crouched by the fire. "At least Jamie's not thick," Bella said with a smile.

Jessica bit the insides of her cheeks to keep from saying, *Yes, he is. Thick and long, and oh so good.* "No. He seems to know exactly what I'm thinking all the time."

"You kicked ass on your cello tonight," Bella said. "You should play professionally."

"That's what I'm trying to decide this summer. If I should continue to play with my orchestra, or if I want to back off for a while. Maybe teach music to children or something similar." She hadn't really considered anything beyond making a decision about the orchestra yet, but the idea of teaching kids was appealing. She hoped one day to have a family, and she loved children. She imagined it would be fulfilling to bring children and music together in a fun way, rather than the high-pressure tutoring sessions she'd endured.

"Come on, babe. Let's dance so I have an excuse to have your body against me." Caden pulled Bella to his side.

"You never need an excuse." Bella laughed and waved as they walked down the beach arm in arm toward the band.

"Wait for us!" Leanna grabbed Kurt's hand and they followed Caden and Bella.

Jessica tucked the idea of teaching away for later consideration. There was so much love in this group of friends. She felt as though she'd left Boston and been plunked down on a whole new planet. She sat beside Jamie by the fire.

"Hey there." He pulled the marshmallow he was roasting off the stick and fed it to her.

She bit part of it off, then guided the rest into his mouth and tried not to laugh when the sticky marshmallow stuck to his fingers. He shook his fingers up and down.

"I think it's stuck for life," he joked.

She swallowed the piece she was eating and captured his hand in hers. Their eyes met. He knew what she was about to do. She saw it in the darkening of his eyes, felt it in the tension in his hand. She had no idea that following her heart would take her down such a dirty trail, but follow she did as she drew his finger into her mouth and rolled her tongue over the sugary sweetness, sucking until all that was left was the taste of him. She held his gaze as he drew his finger slowly out of her mouth. Jamie was breathing hard. His hand came around the back of her neck, hard and hot against her skin, and their lips came together in a hungry kiss that had her mind sprinting down the dirty trail again. She was one stroke of the tongue away from climbing onto his lap, wondering if they could unzip his pants and make love beneath her dress with no one knowing. She pawed at his shoulders, his chest, and—*Oh God*—a moan slipped from her lungs into his. Surely everyone around them was thinking they were going to rip each other's clothes off any second—because man, oh man, did she want to.

She forced herself to tear her lips from his. A quick scan of the beach told her that nobody cared that she was wet and he was probably hard as a freaking rock, or that she'd been ready to make a spectacle of both of them.

"Let's get out of here." It wasn't a question. Jamie pulled her to her feet and crossed the sand like he was on a mission. "We're taking off!" he yelled over the music in their friends' general direction. Then with one arm around Jessica's back, her take-charge boyfriend led her toward the dunes.

Chapter Twelve

JAMIE WAS HOT, hard, and hornier than a bunny on Viagra. The image of Jessica sucking his finger with that seductive look in her eyes that did him in every time played over and over in his mind. They were halfway to the dunes—the parking lot was three minutes away. Four, tops. And there was no way he was going to make it. He had to feel her against him. They were shrouded in darkness, far away from the band and the lights. He swept Jessica into his arms and cupped her perfect ass. Her eyes were at half-mast, full of desire and the same well of emotion he'd seen earlier. Jesus, he was so far gone, he couldn't ignore his feelings for her if his life depended on it. He forced himself to slow down. After how aggressively he'd taken her the first time, he wanted to cherish every inch of her, show her how good she could feel with tenderness instead of heady need. He ran his thumb over her lower lip and heard the breath leave her lungs.

"Jess." He breathed deeply, reminding himself to be sweet and tender, and forcing his greediness away.

He lowered his mouth, a whisper away from hers, so they were breathing the same air. He had to taste her, to feel the woman who had seared herself into his heart so fast. He dragged his tongue along the swell of her lower lip, and she inhaled a jagged breath. A seductive, intoxicating sound that nearly brought him to his knees. He grazed her lips with his, kissed her softly, resisting the urge to deepen the kiss. His hands slid lower on her ass, and he felt her heat through the silky fabric of her panties. His tongue slid over hers, to the smooth enamel and jagged ridges of her teeth. Her jaw dropped open and she melted against him, giving herself over to him as she'd done from their very first kiss. Allowing him to lick the insides of her lips, the creases and corners, as he memorized every dip and curve of her sweet mouth.

He could barely think for the need to be inside her. He drew back, putting distance between their lips, if not their bodies. There was no way in hell he was letting go of her.

Her eyes opened and her lips curved into a contented smile. "Hi."

Her whisper brought his forehead to hers. "Hi."

"Kiss me more," she pleaded.

"I'm going to kiss you all night long." He forced his hands from her butt and circled her waist, lifting her into his arms. Her legs wrapped seamlessly around his waist as their lips met again in another interminable kiss. At some point, maybe a minute later, maybe ten, he became aware of his hands on her ass again, beneath her panties and inching closer to the promised land. *What the hell am I doing?*

He parted from her delicious lips, and his powerful legs carried them up the sandy path to the top of the dunes. Jessica rested her head on his shoulder, her hot breath on his neck, and ran her fingers through the ends of his hair.

"Hurry," she whispered, as he picked up her flip-flops from where she'd left them.

The word shot through him like a bullet. The temperature had dropped, and a chilly breeze swept over them. Her body was so damn soft as she gripped him tighter and cuddled closer.

"Dune or bed?"

"Whatever's fastest," she answered.

He tangled his hand in her hair and tugged softly, so he could see her eyes.

"Baby, I want to love every inch of your body the way you deserve to be loved. I want you to feel how good your body is capable of feeling, learn each of your most sensitive spots. Hurrying is the last thing on my mind."

Her eyes went dark. "Bed."

He carried her to the car and settled her into the passenger seat. God, he loved taking care of her. Jamie climbed into the driver's seat and leaned over for another kiss. *Bed. Bed. Bed.* He started the car and set one hand on her thigh as he drove. He was surely going to hell, because he slid that hand up until he could feel her heat. When she spread her legs and rested her head back, eyes closed, he slid his fingers beneath her panties and stroked her already slick, sensitive folds. He tried to pay attention to the road, but his eyes darted toward Jessica. He loved the way her body responded to him. She was practically panting for more. She licked her lips and shifted in her seat so he could slide his fingers into her.

"Mm." She fisted one hand in her dress and clenched the edge of her seat with the other. "Oh God."

Someone behind him honked, and Jamie realized he'd eased off the gas. He wasn't about to leave her hanging, and they were still a few blocks from Seaside.

He turned down a dark, deserted road and cut the engine. Without the rumble of the engine or the road noise, the car was silent, save for Jessica's heavy breathing. He leaned over the console and drew her panties down to her thighs. She tried to spread her legs, but they were restrained by the thin material. He slid his fingers in deeper, and then he lifted her dress and leaned across the center console, bringing his mouth to her clit, swirling his tongue, taking it between his teeth and sucking, licking, teasing. Sexy little noises filled the car as she squirmed against his touch, pleading for more and holding his head so he had no choice but to continue. A thrill rumbled through him. He loved when she took a little control, and he couldn't wait to explore more of what she liked. He stroked her wetness with his tongue and felt her thighs tense.

"Look at me," she whispered.

The mimicking of his words brought his arousal to a whole new level as he met her gaze, and she cupped her breast, then squeezed her nipple as he'd done the night before.

"Holy Christ, you're sexy." He quickened every stroke of his tongue, feeling the orgasm grip her, her body pulse and swell. He watched as her eyes slammed shut and her jaw dropped open.

"Jamie. Jamie. Jamie."

A rush of whispers that made him want to drive his hard length into her.

A few blessedly hot minutes later, she opened her eyes and he brought his mouth to hers. It was a desperate kiss, each clawing for more as she licked her sweetness from his tongue.

"Home," she whispered.

Less than five minutes later they were unlocking the door to her apartment. Jessica fumbled with the keys as Jamie kissed the back of her neck, his hands exploring her taut stomach and the undersides of her breasts, beneath her dress.

She turned in his arms and held her hands up by her head, surrendering herself to him again. "I can't unlock..."

He settled his mouth on the curve of her neck.

"Unlock the door," she whispered.

He pressed his hips to hers and held her wrists against the door.

"I think it'll be a little embarrassing if everyone comes home and finds me buried deep inside you right here on your deck." Just the thought had his body twitching.

She strained against his hold, craned her neck, trying to kiss him. He lowered his mouth, leaving a sliver of air between them.

"Or they might find me on my knees between your legs."

"Jamie..." she said with pleading eyes.

"Or you on your knees."

She narrowed her eyes seductively and licked her lips. "Open. The. Door."

He slid her wrists closer together against the smooth wood and held them both in one hand, then pulled down the strap of her dress and lowered his mouth to the silken crest of her breast.

"Now you're just getting demanding." He smiled up at her as he kissed a path between her breasts.

"Please open the door? You're killing me."

His heart sank, and he released her wrists. "Did I hurt you? I'm sorry, babe." He cupped her cheek, and she leaned forward and kissed him.

"No, silly. You're killing me in a good way." She handed him the keys, then wrapped her arms around his middle and pressed her cheek to his chest.

He blew out a relieved sigh.

"We need a safe word." He fumbled with the keys.

"Safe word? Like to make you stop?"

Jamie closed the door behind them and tossed the keys on the table. He wrapped his arms around her waist and touched his forehead to hers.

"Yeah. You know, so I know I won't hurt you."

She furrowed her brow, obviously thinking it over. "What if I hurt you?"

He laughed. "I somehow doubt that's going to happen."

"What if I tie you up and it's too tight? Or I do something you don't like?" She pressed both hands against his chest and smiled playfully up at him.

"Tie me up? I thought you'd only been with one other guy."

"Two. *You*, remember?" She slipped off her flip-flops and tossed her long hair over her shoulder.

"And you want to tie me up?" Jamie arched a brow.

"No. Not now." Her cheeks pinked up and she turned away.

He turned her by the shoulders and drew her closer to him. "You can tie me up, tie me down, or ride me to heaven and back, Jess. You don't need to be embarrassed."

She placed her hands softly on his chest again in what he'd come to think of as her spot. "I don't know what I'll want to do, but if I need a safe word, then I want you to have one, too."

"So this is all about being fair?" The side of his mouth quirked up. "Okay, how about the word *red*?"

"Red?"

"Red."

She slid her hands beneath his shirt and pushed it up to his armpits. She pressed her lips to his abs and trailed kisses up to his pecs as her fingers danced over his nipples, making every nerve stand on end.

"Then if I say green, does that mean *go*?" she asked.

He pulled her dress over her head and the air rushed from his lungs.

"Green. Green. Green," she whispered.

MUCH LATER, SATED and a little sore, Jessica lay on her side, spooned against Jamie's chest, listening to the even cadence of his breathing. As promised, he'd made love to her slowly and sensuously, and after a brief reprieve, he'd made love to her hard, fast, and every way in between. She looked at the chair by the bedroom door, where Jamie's jeans were hanging over the armrest, his shirt spread across the back. She could get used to falling asleep in his arms, but she knew that until she made a final decision about her career, that was a dangerous thought. He had a business to run and a grandmother to care for. She'd have to travel, and there was no way she'd ask him to give up his time with Vera. It was easy to play house on vacation. She wasn't so sure it would be as easy back home when she was bunned, busy, and working crazy hours.

She thought about how good it had felt to play her cello with Vera and the accolades Vera had rained on her afterward. She'd even asked her to play with her quartet Thursday night. *And I forgot to mention it to Jamie*. She'd even forgotten about checking her cell phone for the call from the new owner of the baseball. She wrapped her hand over Jamie's, and in his sleep he hugged her closer to him. Before she'd come to the Cape, her life was regimented, her schedule dictated by playing the cello, and now she knew exactly what she'd been missing. Now she knew Jamie.

I love playing the cello.

She eyed the case propped against the wall just outside the bedroom and felt her heart squeeze. Was she wrong? Could she maintain a relationship and find a healthy balance between the man she was falling for and the instrument she adored playing? Her eyes drifted upward to the clock on the wall. It was three fifteen in the morning. Should she wake Jamie? Didn't he need to go home so his grandmother didn't get upset? Would she? He was a grown man. Maybe she didn't care. But that generation? Maybe she did.

Oh God. What was she doing? She needed to wake him and let him decide, but he felt so good, so warm. So safe. She tried to hold back the last thought, but it pressed in close until it nearly suffocated her and she had to get it out.

So loving.

She shifted her hips a little and pulled the blanket up over her thighs. She'd never imagined herself being comfortable naked in front of anyone, much less a man she'd known for only a short while, but with Jamie, everything felt natural.

"Careful moving like that. You'll wake certain parts of me you might rather leave sleeping." Jamie's voice was low and rough against her neck.

She turned in his arms so they were nose to nose and touched his stubbly cheek with her hand. "Don't you have to go back home?"

He opened his eyes and pulled her against him. "Are you kicking me out?"

"I don't know. Have you spent the night out before when you were here with Vera?" She lowered her voice to a seductive whisper. "Or will you staying over make me a bad girl?" She felt him get hard as he tightened his grip on her.

"I think you have the whole bad girl thing down

pat, but we'll keep that our little secret." He kissed her softly and smiled. "I haven't left Vera overnight while I was at the Cape before, but I'm fairly certain that she knows we're sleeping together."

"Well, yeah, but why throw it in her face?"

He pulled back. "You *are* kicking me out."

"Not because I want to," she protested. "Just because I don't want her looking at me sideways tomorrow. Like I soiled her perfect grandson." She stroked his cheek.

He rolled onto his back with a dramatic sigh and arced his arm over his eyes. "You don't want people seeing me take the walk of shame—that's what this is about."

She draped an arm over his chest and pushed herself up so she was peering down at him. Her hair curtained their faces.

"Walk of shame? I don't care who else sees you leaving. I just don't want to disrespect Vera."

"Yeah, yeah, yeah." He said it with a serious tone, and although she couldn't see his eyes beneath his forearm, she had a clear view of his sexy little smile.

She pressed her lips to his.

He pulled her on top of him, chest to chest, thigh to thigh, only his hard length between them. Her engine revved up again, and she wondered how she'd gone twenty-seven years without Jamie Reed's arms around her.

"Okay, I'll leave in a minute." He gathered her hair and draped it over one shoulder, then traced her cheekbone down and around her jaw with his finger. "I'm falling hard for you, Jess."

Ohgodohgodohgod. He felt it too. "So you aren't this loving and sensual with every woman you date?"

"Not even close." He searched her eyes and drew his brows together. "Uh-oh. I played my hand too soon, didn't I?"

She smiled at that. How could he think that she wasn't falling head over heels for him? She felt like everything she did screamed it. "Not even close to too soon."

In the next breath, he rolled her beneath him and kissed her. His hazel eyes were filled with emotion mirroring her own intense feelings.

"I'm not falling for you." She tried to keep a straight face, but when the smile in his eyes faded, she couldn't play out the ruse. "You've swept me away, Jamie, like Vivaldi's *Four Seasons*. You start out soft and magical, and then there's this intensity that takes my breath away and makes my body ignite into flames, and then there's the softness again. And just when I think we're as close as we could get, you surprise me with something as simple as a kiss on my temple—which I love by the way. And..." She realized she was going on and on, and he was smiling down at her like she was all he ever needed.

"I don't mean to ramble, but I'm so comfortable with you, like we've been together forever, and there's still so much we don't know about each other. And that should scare me silly, but it doesn't." She breathed deeply.

"Because you have nothing to fear when you're with me, Jess."

She sensed he was right, but suddenly it wasn't enough to say she was comfortable with him, because what she felt was so much bigger than comfortable.

"Did you know that without rosin, the bow slides across the cello strings and makes a faint whispery sound, or no sound at all? It's the rosin that provides the friction in order to produce sound when it's pulled across the strings. Before you, Jamie, I was whispering through life. With you, I'm whole. I'm melodious and tuneful. Pure musicality." She smiled up at him. "You're my rosin, Jamie."

"Jessie," he whispered, and touched his forehead to hers.

He didn't need to say anything more. She felt his feelings seep through his skin to her very soul, coming together with hers and filling all the lonely, empty spaces she'd always known were there.

Chapter Thirteen

JAMIE AND JESSICA spent the next few days enjoying each other, the sun, and their friends. Jamie took his normal morning runs with Caden, Evan, and Kurt, if he was around. Yesterday Pete joined them while Jessica had breakfast with the girls. After worrying about just how much of their relationship Jessica had shared with them, Jamie finally got up the courage to ask her if she was sharing the intimate details of their lovemaking. Jessica had pinked up when she'd said, *I didn't, but not because I'm embarrassed about it. I didn't tell them because I don't want them thinking about you in that way.* He'd loved the little possessive comment, especially since she didn't act possessive in any other way. He'd never dated a woman who didn't watch him when other women were near, but Jessica had a quiet confidence about her. It was like his straying never crossed her mind—which was a good thing, because he was as loyal as a junkyard dog, and he would never hurt her in any way.

Vera joined them for afternoon outings to the bay and visits to nearby towns, like Chatham and

Brewster. Jessica and Vera got along well, and both were excited about Jessica's joining the quartet tonight. Come evening, Jessica and the girls from Seaside threw together salads and grilled, and they all ate dinners together in the quad. When the stars came out, they fell into Jessica's bed or the dunes by the ocean, and made love until they were too exhausted to move. Jamie went back to his own cottage in the wee hours of the mornings and tried to catch up on his emails, but after one or two emails, he was just too wiped to focus, and caught a few hours' sleep instead. All the while, he craved the day he could wake up with Jessica in his arms. For now, they chose not to take advantage of their close living situations to the fullest extent. Vera was kind enough not to make mention of Jamie's early-morning returns, and although he doubted she'd care if he stayed with Jessica until morning, that didn't lessen the guilt that he knew he'd feel for doing so. Self-inflicted guilt, of course, but it was what it was.

Thursday morning he was heading out for a run with Kurt and Caden when his phone rang. He blew out a breath, debated ignoring it, but gave in to responsibility when he saw Mark's name on the screen. *Shit.* He'd blown off a few emails from Mark and a number of other employees the last two nights out of sheer exhaustion, and he hadn't checked them yet this morning.

"Hey, Mark. How's it going?" He twisted the mood ring on his finger. Every time he looked at it he thought of Jessica.

"How's it going? Really? You knew we had shit going down over here and you've completely ignored my emails and my texts."

"What? Hold on." Jamie scrolled through his phone. He didn't have a single text from Mark. "Mark. I don't have any texts from you." He paced the cottage, anxious to get on with his run and hoping Mark was overreacting.

"My ass, you don't. I texted you about seven times between ten in the morning and two in the afternoon yesterday. I called, but it went straight to voicemail, *and* I sent you emails."

Fuck. He and Jessica had gone to the beach yesterday. There was no cell phone reception on any of the lower Cape ocean beaches. It was like a time warp. Once someone descended the dune, they were off radar until they headed back up to the parking lot.

"What the hell's going on?" Mark demanded. "Are you dodging me for a reason?"

"Mark, chill a minute. You must have texted while I was on the beach. Texts don't come through at the ocean here. You know that." Jamie went outside on the deck. Vera looked up from the book she was reading and smiled at him. He squeezed her shoulder as he passed.

"Don't you check your messages?"

"They don't come through. It's all fu—" He glanced at Vera. "Messed up. They don't even register. What's going on that's got you wound so tight?"

"What's got me wound so tight? I'll tell you what's got me wound. Remember that issue you told me to handle?"

Jamie ran his hand through his hair, racking his brain. He vaguely remembered something he'd told Mark to handle while he was at the pool, but he'd been distracted by Tony and Jessica. "Remind me."

Mark blew out another frustrated breath. Jamie pictured him stalking across his fifteenth-floor office, bushy brows drawn together, dark eyes seething. "I'll remind you, all right. Search engine bug. Young kids searching for toys, video games, and movies with dragons are getting ads for military equipment and ammo. If the media gets wind of this, we're screwed. Mothers are already bitching a blue streak."

Shit. "All right, so our team tracked it down, right? Get PR on it. Do some damage control, and we're back in business."

"Are you fucking kidding me? Did you hear what I said? Kids and guns don't mix. What are you smoking at the Cape, Jamie? Do you hear yourself?" He mocked Jamie. "*So, our team tracked it down, right?*" He blew out a breath again, a habit he had when he was too mad to form a response.

"It's all fucked up. If our team had tracked it down, would I have called you? We've got our cyber investigation team on it to see if we were hacked," Mark explained. "You need to be here. You've got to come back and take charge of this situation."

"Mark, you've got our teams on it and the cyber investigators. Let them do their jobs." Before meeting Jessica, Jamie would have packed up and driven back to Boston. But that was then. Now he didn't want to miss a minute of time with her, and he trusted his team of professionals to handle the issues without him micromanaging.

"Jamie, if this hits the news, you're going to have a media shit storm to deal with."

Mark was right. If it got that far, they'd have a bigger issue on their hands, but he'd hired the best programmers in the country. His being there wasn't going to change a damn thing. Or at least that's how, for the first time in his life, he was rationalizing putting his business second to his personal life.

Jessica came out of Amy's cottage wearing a nightshirt without a bra and a pair of cutoffs. She waved to Jamie, her perky nipples poking against the sheer material, and the evening before came rushing back. They'd washed her bedsheets at midnight, after spilling body oil on them, and when they went into the dark laundry room to get them from the dryer, the room was hot, and so were they. They'd ended up making love on top of the warm dryer.

"Are you even listening to me?" Mark snapped.

Shit. He'd zoned out. He waved to Jessica as she walked toward her cottage. Jesus, she had a sweet ass.

"Jamie!" Mark yelled.

"Yeah, sorry. Listen, I'm not leaving the Cape. Whatever I need to do, I can do from here. Just set up a videoconference. Give me a time."

"Bad move, Jamie. You need to be here to light a fire under their asses. I'm telling you, nipping this in the bud is critical."

Jamie was sure his being there in person wouldn't do any more good than a videoconference. He trusted his cyber investigators, and he trusted Mark, but he also knew Mark didn't like his advice to be ignored. He had to level with Mark or Mark would never let up. He also knew how protective Mark was of him. He practically had the FBI check out every woman he dated, and while it pissed Jamie off at times, he was equally as thankful that Mark had his back.

"Mark, I met someone. I'm not leaving."

Vera raised her eyes and smiled. Jamie knew that Vera understood how serious he was about Jessica, because he rarely shared his personal life with anyone. Especially Mark. But Mark had his ways of finding things out, so one way or another, his attorney and buddy since college would have figured this out without him.

"You're blowing off business for a chick? Eight years of a stellar rep that you could lose over some dipshit hacker…for a chick?"

"She's not just a chick." Anger simmered in Jamie's

gut.

Mark laughed. "She better have a golden pussy for this risk, my boy."

"Mark! Cut the shit." He wanted to tell him not to ever refer to Jessica that way again, but Mark was already hot under the collar and he needed him to focus on the issues, not on his relationship.

"Fine. I'll come there. I can be there this afternoon. We'll structure a game plan and I'll take care of it. You're at Vera's?"

Jamie let out a frustrated breath. Mark was a good friend to come all the way there instead of relying on a videoconference, and Jamie appreciated his efforts. He'd gone over and above the call of duty for Jamie many times, and in turn, Jamie paid him well. Not to mention that their friendship ran even deeper than their business relationship. Tonight was Jessica's performance with Vera's quartet, and he wanted to be there. His parents' deaths had taught him how precarious life really was, and he wasn't about to miss Jessica's performance, even for Mark.

"Fine. I have plans at seven thirty, so make it early."

"I SAY WE go chunky-dunking tonight," Bella said as she looked out over the water. The girls were having a late lunch at Mac's Seafood on the harbor. Pete, Kurt, and Caden were working, and Jamie had a meeting to prepare for with his attorney.

"What's chunky-dunking?" Jessica was only half paying attention. She was thinking about Jamie. He'd been so sidetracked that morning when they had coffee with Vera after his run. He'd mentioned how many calls and texts he'd missed from his attorney, and Jessica worried that she was interfering with his work.

"Skinny-dipping," Jenna explained. "For normal-sized women." She glared at Amy. "Pin-thin girl over there can still go *skinny-dipping*."

"Oh, please." Amy waved a dismissive hand. "You think you're normal sized? Miss Young Dolly Parton?"

Jenna cupped her breasts and pushed them up. "Mine are so much better than Dolly's, and I'm a brunette, much sexi—"

"Don't even go there." Bella pointed a finger at Jenna. "We are *not* having the brunettes have more fun argument."

"I'm not sure I can go skinny-dipping," Jessica admitted.

"What? Why?" Bella asked.

"Because I'm playing with Vera's quartet tonight." Thank God, because she'd never gone skinny-dipping, and she didn't like the idea of running around naked in front of anyone other than Jamie. "Besides, aren't there sharks feeding at night?"

Leanna reached across the table and patted her hand. "We don't chunky-dunk in the ocean. We go in the pool."

"In the pool?" She couldn't keep her eyes from popping open wide. "What about everyone else? Don't you care if their boyfriends see you naked?"

They all laughed. "That's why we do it after midnight when everyone's asleep. And whatever you do, don't tell Theresa. It's against the rules."

"Oh." Now she really wasn't sure about this. Jessica wasn't a rule breaker, even if she and Jamie had fooled around on the beach. It was nighttime, after all, and they were fully dressed. When she was younger, she'd felt so guilty after sneaking out of her parents' house to go to the Cape she'd told her father and then *thanked him* for grounding her. *I have lived a sheltered life.*

"You're playing tonight, so after you and Jamie…you know." Jenna raised her brows in quick succession. "When he goes back to Vera's and falls asleep, then we'll go."

She dropped her eyes so they wouldn't see her shock that they knew about him leaving in the middle of the night.

"She thought we didn't know," Amy said gently. "Jessica, we're all friends. And we're all women. We get it, and Jamie's not a player, so we know he's really into you."

She breathed a little easier. A little. This summer of self-discovery was becoming way more than that. If they knew the sexy stuff she and Jamie did, would they still understand? Or would they think she was a tramp?

"Yeah, as long as we don't have to see the pink fuzzy handcuffs attached to the bedpost…Bella." Jenna pushed Bella's shoulder.

"What?" Bella laughed.

"What if Evan had seen them?" Jenna asked.

"He's a teenage boy," Bella said. "The last thing he wants to do is walk into his father's bedroom."

"True," Jenna agreed.

"We don't. I don't…" No, not handcuffs, but his hands worked damn well.

"Really?" Bella asked. "You should try them. But on a more serious note, we don't judge each other. That's not what girlfriends are for. Girlfriends are for calling each other on their bullshit, supporting each other when we're down or frustrated, and…" She shrugged. "Maybe most important, we always, unconditionally and without judgment, have your back."

She couldn't stop envy from tumbling from her lips like pebbles. "You guys are so lucky to have each other."

They all exchanged a glance she couldn't read, and in the next second they were gathering around her for a group hug.

"You're lucky, silly," Amy said.

"Yeah. You're a Seaside sister now." Jenna kissed her cheek with a loud *mmmwwwwaaahhh!*

"Welcome to our little circle," Leanna added.

As they settled back into their seats, leaving Jessica reeling with appreciation, Leanna asked, "So, Jamie's meeting with his attorney today?"

"Yeah. There's some issue at his office." Jamie had assured her this morning that she hadn't been keeping him from taking care of the work he needed to do, but even with his reassurance, she still worried.

"The guy's a prick," Bella said. "He came up a few years ago to meet with Jamie about something and he was like…I don't know. He's slimy. I don't like him."

"He's an attorney. What do you expect?" Leanna sipped her drink. "They have to be cutthroat."

"I met him," Jenna said. "When he was down that time. Remember, Bella? He's not cutthroat. He's like a snake in the grass. He stared at my boobs the whole time, then sidled up to me and propositioned me with a no-strings-attached offer of the best sex I ever had." She said the last part with air quotes.

"Jamie said he's a close friend. It sounded like they'd been friends forever. Did you tell him about it?" she asked Jenna.

"Of course I did." Jenna pointed to a little girl in a pink bathing suit running in and out of the water's edge beside the pier. "Oh my God she's cute. Anyway, Jamie kind of blew it off. Made a joke or something. I got the feeling Mark did that stuff all the time, and really, what could Jamie have done about it? I mean, if he had touched me, Jamie would have torn him apart, but a proposition?" She shrugged.

"Really," Bella said. "They've been buddies forever. I think Jamie ignores how slimy he is because he keeps Jamie's business in line. It's probably a good tradeoff. You don't want a wussy attorney. You want a snake in the grass."

"I can't even imagine Jamie around a guy like that." Jessica's cell phone rang while she was still processing the information about Mark.

"Five bucks says it's Jamie," Jenna said. "Oh, Jessie. I miss you so much. Please, please come back!" She burst into a fit of laughter.

"Actually, I don't recognize this number." Jessica put the phone to her ear. "Hello?"

"Hello. Is this Jessica Ayers?" Each word was pronounced with careful precision, with a shaky, elderly sounding voice.

"Yes, this is she." She met the girls' curious gazes and shrugged.

"This is Mr. Elliott. Steve Lacasse sent me a message and indicated that you were interested in the baseball that I won from him."

Without thinking, she reached for Amy's hand.

Amy exchanged a worried glance with the others.

"Yes, sir," she answered. "I think...that's my father's baseball from when he was a little boy, and I was wondering if I could buy it from you. I'll pay double whatever you paid."

"Oh." The man was quiet.

"It would mean the world to me. My father is a wonderful man. He's done so much for me, and I want to do this little thing for him." She realized she was rambling and cut herself short. "I'll pay triple. Whatever you want. Please."

"I'm sorry, Jessica," he said.

Jessica's heart plunged as he explained.

"I bought that ball for my grandson, and it's already in his hands. I can't very well take it away from him. He's six and an avid baseball fan already. Why, it would squash his excitement."

"No, I suppose you can't very well do that. Thank you for calling, and I hope your grandson enjoys the ball." She ended the call and sat in disappointed silence.

"Asshole," Bella said.

"Jerk." Amy patted Jessica's back.

Leanna's eyes went soft. "I'm sorry, Jessica. I know you were hoping to get the ball for your father, but maybe there's something else he'd want instead?"

"Yes! I'm sure we can find something," Jenna said with far too much enthusiasm. "Tell us what he does. We'll figure out the best present ever!" She sat back down and leaned across the table. "I could paint a portrait of you. What parent wouldn't like that?"

Jessica managed a smile. "Thanks, you guys, but it's okay. He doesn't *want* anything. He's never asked for a darn thing. He puts up with my mother's stoic personality, works his butt off to pay for everything she could ever want, and he's never asked for one single thing."

"He sounds like a good man." Amy stroked Jessica's back. "I'm sure he'll understand."

"Yes, he will." Jessica rolled her eyes as if she weren't heartbroken. "He always understands." She hadn't realized how much she wanted this for him. It was supposed to be a silly little diversion, and it had worked as just that. In fact, being with Jamie had distracted her even from her own diversion. But now, as that door shut, she realized that the only reason she'd seen it as a silly little diversion in the first place was because her mother's voice echoed in her head. *Remember, Jessica, nothing compares to what you are working toward. Sports, dances, and the like? Silliness. Sheer silliness. Where will that get those kids in ten years? But you...you're going to be a star. The best cellist ever.*

Her mother had said it forever. When she was just a little girl, practicing her cello by the window of the observatory in her parents' home, listening to the laughter of the children outside. Every time her mother drove by the park where her friends were playing on the way to practice, and as a teenager, when the other girls were going to homecoming football games and dances and she longed to be included.

The best cellist ever.

She looked around the table at her new friends' worried faces. The women who, without even having all the details, had heard bits and pieces of her conversation, read her body language, and instantly came to her defense. She considered Jamie and how her world was brighter with just the thought of him, and she wanted all of it. She wanted these friends, she wanted Jamie, and she wanted to be around Vera, to play their music together, drink coffee, talk, and sit by the pool.

She pulled on the reserves she'd relied on through Juilliard, when getting down on herself wasn't an option, and when she was in the middle of playing for a huge audience. She drew her shoulders back. Coming to Wellfleet and finding her father's baseball might have started as a diversion, but now it seemed like it was part of a path to a door to her new life, waiting to be opened.

"So, if Theresa doesn't see us," Jessica asked. "Can we drink wine when we go chunky-dunking?"

Chapter Fourteen

JAMIE SCRUBBED HIS hand down his face, trying not to show the depth of his worry. No wonder Mark had been so upset. He'd arrived at Seaside two hours earlier, armed with files and data that painted a much darker picture of the issues than Jamie had assumed they were dealing with.

They were sitting on the back deck of the cottage with four laptops set up on the table, open files and initial investigation reports laid out on the extra chairs.

"Mark, I had no idea it was this widespread."

Mark sat back and exhaled loudly. He'd dressed casually for their meeting in a pair of khakis and a white polo shirt. His thick dark hair and brows gave him a brooding look. Jamie had seen him at his best and his worst. Mark was a workaholic. Jamie's weekends at the Cape had always seemed like a luxury compared to Mark's stringent work schedule. When Jamie first brought up that he'd be working remotely and spending the summer at the Cape with Vera, Mark had nearly had a heart attack. He'd spent three weeks trying to convince Jamie it was a bad idea, and not for selfish reasons. He had valid points about employees easing up on their work if the boss was gone and giving division directors more leeway to make decisions than they already had. Jamie, however, couldn't be swayed. Vera wasn't getting any younger, and if his employees worked a little less diligently, that wasn't the end of the world. They worked their asses off every day of the year, just as he did. And now, having met Jessica, he realized that coming to the Cape had been the best decision he'd ever made.

"I figured you didn't realize it, and I forgot about the goddamn cell phone reception out here. Can't you do what normal billionaires do and go to the Hamptons?"

Jamie silenced him with a no-fucking-way stare.

Mark held his hands up in the air. "Fine, whatever. I get it. Your grandma's place, family ties and all that, but, Jamie, you've taken sidetracked to a whole new level."

"Yeah. I get it. I'll be more on point. I got a little lax."

"A little lax?" Mark laughed. "Dude, a year ago you would have driven back to Boston the second I said the word *issue*. You built OneClick with nothing more than your brain and those talented programming fingers. Don't fuck it up."

He'd never allow anyone else to talk to him that way, but Mark had stuck with him when he first opened the doors to OneClick and could barely pay him a tenth of what he should have. Days when Jamie wasn't sure the hard work was worth it, Mark had talked him off the ledge. He owed Mark the respect of answering his emails in a timely fashion.

"I'm not fucking it up. It looks like our team has a handle on it."

"Yeah, yeah. I've taken care of it all as best I could, but you're the best programmer there is, Jamie. Interpreting code is in your DNA. But these reports?" He slid a stack of papers across the table to Jamie. "You used to go over these with a fine-tooth comb. If you'd looked at them you might have caught this before it blew up."

He hadn't reviewed the trouble reports in a week. Mark was right. He'd fucked up.

Jamie turned at the sound of Amy's car pulling into the driveway across the road. He peered over Mark's shoulder as the girls got out of the car. The first thing Jessica did was look over at his cottage. He watched her beautiful eyes skim over his car, to the front deck, then around back. Their eyes caught, and he felt her gaze all the way to his gut.

He smiled and waved.

Mark turned and looked at Jessica. "This is the girl?"

"Yes. Jessica."

Mark leaned toward Jamie and lowered his voice. "She's pretty, Jamie, but pretty women are a dime a dozen for a guy like you. What is it? Does she give the best blow jobs on the East Coast?"

Jamie gritted his teeth against his rising annoyance and reminded himself that this was how Mark had always joked. He ignored Mark's comment altogether and went to greet Jessica as she came into the yard.

"Hey, babe." He stepped off the deck and kissed her.

"Hi. I don't want to interrupt." She smiled at Mark, who lifted his chin in response.

Douche. He could be a douche. Jamie knew it and had always overlooked it, but when that jerkiness was turned toward Jessica, it struck a whole different chord in him.

Jamie shot Mark the narrow-eyed stare that Mark had seen a million times in business meetings when Mark wanted to play the tough negotiator and Jamie was sure it wouldn't suit the situation.

Mark stood and held out a hand. "Mark Wiley, Jamie's attorney."

Jessica shook his hand. "Jessica. Nice to meet you."

"Jessica...?" Mark waited for her to answer.

Jamie knew exactly what he was doing—fishing for information.

"Jessica Ayers." She drew her brows together in question.

"Sorry. I'll remember your name if I have the full name in my head. There are a million Jessicas out there."

A million Jessicas? Jamie's patience was wearing thin.

"So you're the pretty little filly that's been keeping Jamie from concentrating on work. I can see why," Mark said.

"Watch it, Mark," Jamie warned.

Mark lifted his chin in acknowledgment. "What do you do, Jessica?" He slid his hands into his pockets. Jamie knew the casual stance all too well. Mark was trying to put Jessica at ease while he slithered in to gain information, and even though this was what Mark did with most of the women Jamie dated, when it came to Jessica, it made every nerve stand on end.

"She plays for the Boston Symphony Orchestra." Jamie put a protective arm around Jessica's shoulder and walked toward her apartment. "I'll be right back, Mark. Go ahead and do your thing."

When they were on her deck, safely away from Mark, Jamie took her hand in his and kissed the back of it. "I'm sorry about Mark. He can be an ass around women, and he's very protective of me. But I'll set him straight. You won't have to worry about that kind of stuff anymore."

She circled his waist with her arms. "He didn't bother me. Well, except for the million Jessicas comment. That kind of felt like he was trying to make me jealous."

"Don't worry. You're the only woman I want in my life." He tilted her chin up and took her in a sensuous kiss. "I missed you, and I'm sorry this is taking so long. The issue goes much deeper than I thought."

"That's okay. Will you be there tonight to hear me play? It's okay if you can't. I don't want to stand in the way of your work."

"Are you kidding? I wouldn't miss it for the world, and you're never in the way. Work is work." He shrugged, but he knew Jessica would see right through his shrugging it off so easily.

"Well, I'm sorry that you have a much bigger issue to deal with."

"It's nothing I can't handle." He glanced over the quad and caught Mark watching them. "I'd better get back if we're going to be done in time. We're going to work straight through dinner. I'm really sorry, babe. I hate to leave you hanging."

"That's okay. Oh, and I almost forgot to tell you that the guy with the baseball called. He gave it to his grandson and doesn't want to sell."

He read the sadness in her eyes. "We'll just have to up the ante."

"No, I tried. I told him I'd pay him three times whatever he paid, but he said it was important to his grandson, who apparently is a baseball fanatic. It's okay. It's not like my father asked for it or anything. It was just something I was doing to distract—" No, she wasn't going to minimize her feelings any longer. "It was something I was doing *for* him. But we did the best we could, and thanks to you, it was much more than I ever could have done on my own."

"Don't thank me yet. This isn't over. We'll think of something." He kissed her and saw Mark walking across the quad. *Jesus Christ.* "Vera invited Mark to come listen to you guys play tonight, but he's leaving tomorrow morning. I'm sorry about today. I hope you know I'd rather be with you."

She pressed her hands to his chest and went up on her tiptoes to kiss him.

"I do know, and after he leaves we can sneak some time in."

"Yeah, about that. I'm about ready to just tell Vera I won't be home until morning. She won't care, and she knows we respect her."

"Jamie," she whispered.

"About ready, Jamie?" Mark called from the bottom of the stairs. "We've got hours of work ahead of us."

"Be right there." *Christ.* "Sorry, babe."

"Wait, are you sure about Vera?"

"Of course I'm sure." He pulled her close and shifted his eyes to Mark, who was standing at the bottom of the stairs with his back to them. "I'm sure of you, too."

Chapter Fifteen

"NOT QUITE THE Boston Symphony Orchestra, is it?" Vera smoothed her long black skirt and patted her hair. She and Jessica had driven to the harbor together. It was almost eight o'clock and they, along with the other musicians in Vera's quartet, were preparing for their show.

There were only a handful of people seated in the metal chairs waiting for them to begin. Jessica had been watching the parking lot, waiting for Jamie to arrive. She knew that the girls were having drinks down the street at the Bookstore Restaurant with their significant others, and they'd be there any minute.

"It's better than the symphony in many ways," she answered Vera.

"How so?" Vera asked.

"Well, for one thing, Jamie will be here, so that makes it a million times better." She inhaled deeply. "And this is so comfortable, Vera. Don't you think so? With the breeze coming off the sea and children playing behind us. It's casual and much less stressful.

Although I have to admit that my heart is going crazy. I'm not sure why I'm so nervous."

Vera touched her arm. "It's because you care. You're an accomplished musician, and when you play, every note carries a piece of you with it."

Vera truly understood, and it made her realize that she would miss the camaraderie of her musician friends if she didn't return to the orchestra, and she did sort of miss having people around who understood the pressures of a musician's lifestyle.

A little boy darted past the tent and Vera laughed. "I miss little ones."

"I'm sorry about your daughter, Jamie's mother. That must have been very difficult for your whole family."

Vera dropped her eyes for a beat. Her eyes were warm when she met Jessica's gaze again. "Yes, it was beyond difficult when we lost our daughter, but I had Jamie to focus on. I think there is only one thing that could be worse than losing my child." Vera watched the children play for a moment, then brought serious eyes back toward Jessica. "If I had never had her in the first place. I would have missed out on all those wonderful years that we had together. Nothing can replace time spent with family."

Vera paused, looking into the distance with a sorrowful gaze. "Do you hope to have a family some day?"

"Before this summer, I didn't have time to think about what I wanted. I've spent a lot of time thinking lately. I do want a family one day, but I have a lot of decisions to make before that can happen."

"Oh, I have faith in you." Vera squeezed her arm. "You'll figure everything out."

They settled into their chairs.

"Try not to be too nervous tonight. We're like

family now. And as far as making your decisions goes, you'll know the right thing to do. Sometimes the heart tells us things in whispers, and we miss them. When we're ready, we hear them loud and clear."

Jessica loved the words Vera chose. *Sometimes the heart tells us things in whispers, and we miss them.* She wondered how many whispers she'd missed in her life—or if she'd missed any at all. Thinking about what Vera had said, she assumed that one day she'd know that answer—she'd hear it loud and clear.

She looked into the sparse audience. Her Seaside friends were all there, except Jamie. Jessica closed her eyes as they began to play, trying not to focus on missing him. The music carried her worries away. After they were done playing the first piece, Jessica opened her eyes and was immediately drawn to the dark-haired man in the second row, wearing a dark blue tee and gazing right through her. *Jamie. My Jamie.* She was so happy to see him, and he looked so proud of her. He was sitting beside Mark, whom she suddenly realized looked a lot like the actor Peter Gallagher.

Jamie blew her a kiss as they began playing the next piece, and Mark shook his head. She closed her eyes again, choosing to ignore Mark's head shake and soaking up the comfort of having Jamie nearby. She allowed herself to get swept into the vibrations of the cello, the higher notes of the violin, and the energy of the musical piece.

By the time they finished playing for the evening, the children were gone from the playground and the metal chairs were nearly full. The audience clapped and lingered, talking to the musicians, asking questions, and telling them how lovely they played. Jessica's friends from Seaside hugged her and Vera and doled out accolades that made her head spin. As the crowd thinned and Jessica began putting her cello in its case, Jamie and Mark finally joined her.

Jamie handed her a bouquet of white and pink roses and kissed her cheek. "You were incredible. You're so beautiful when you play. It's as if the music is a part of you."

"Thank you. These are so pretty."

"Pink, for your graceful elegance when you play, and white, for our new beginning."

The roses were gorgeous, but it was the thoughtfulness of the color roses he'd chosen and the meaning behind them that made her swoon like a schoolgirl.

Jamie drew her into his arms and kissed her.

"Jesus. I am right here, you know." Mark turned away, crossing his arms over his chest.

Jessica stepped back, feeling her cheeks pink up. "I'm sorry." She turned to finish putting her instrument away as Jamie and Mark joked around about their kiss.

"Babe, I'm going to help Vera with her violin. I'll be right back." He turned to Mark. "Behave yourself."

"Me? I'm not the one playing tonsil hockey." Mark laughed as Jamie walked away.

Hearing them joke with each other made Jessica feel a little better. Maybe Mark wasn't as crass as the girls thought.

"You were good," Mark said in a hushed tone as his eyes darted around the tent. Their friends were gathered just a few feet away.

"Thank you."

"Working for the BSO is an important job," he said in a voice that sent an icy chill down Jessica's spine. Gone was the joking smile he'd flashed so easily when Jamie was with them, replaced with a manipulative look in his eyes, even as they jumped from person to person, to the beach across the street, and to the tennis courts to their right—everywhere but where she stood.

"Yes. It is."

"You know who Jamie is, right? Of course you do." He moved closer to her, pressed his shoulder to hers as she closed her cello case. "You also probably know that he needs to focus on his billion-dollar business and all this playing around is just that. *Playing around*."

Stunned into silence, Jessica held her breath.

"Jamie's not a knight in shining armor. He's not going to swoop you off your feet and make everything in your world flowers and bunnies."

She froze, unable to think. Her limbs trembled, and it was all she could do to grab the edge of the table to remain erect.

"Jamie Reed can have any woman he wants," he said in a low growl. "You're no different from any of the others he's been with, no matter how pretty you are. He needs to focus, and unless you want to be the cause of his empire's demise, I suggest you back off."

Ohgodohgodohgod. She couldn't even begin to process the things he'd said. *You're no different from any of the others...Back off.*

"Smile pretty. Here comes Mr. Reed."

Jessica couldn't face Jamie. She couldn't move at all. She felt his hand on her hip. His cheek brushed hers and she closed her eyes.

"Hey, babe. The gang's going out for drinks. Want to go?"

She opened her mouth, but no words came. The world was spinning out of control, draining her of her strength. She felt dizzy and reached for Jamie's hand.

"Babe?" Jamie whispered.

"She's probably tired. Come on. Let's go grab a few

hours of fun before I go back to the Sheraton." Mark grabbed Jamie's arm.

"Hold up." Jamie shrugged him off and moved around Jessica so he was facing her.

She kept her eyes trained on the ground. *Breathe. Breathe. Breathe.* If she looked at him, she'd cry.

"Babe, are you okay?"

She nodded. "Just...not feeling too well."

"Then we'll stay in. We don't have to go," Jamie assured her.

"I'm here for one night and you're going to blow me off?" Mark's voice was light and carefree, as if he hadn't just shattered Jessica's world.

"You're a big boy, Mark. I think you can handle a night alone," Jamie said.

"Go," she whispered.

"What, babe?" Jamie leaned closer.

"Go with him. I'll be fine. I'm just tired." *And I need to think about what Mark said.*

"I'll stay with you. We can relax, go to bed early." Jamie's voice was laden with concern, and love, and all the things that had made her fall for him in the first place.

Even if Mark was just trying to scare her off, there had to be a reason. *You're no different from any of the others he's been with, no matter how pretty you are. He needs to focus, and unless you want to be the cause of his empire's demise, I suggest you back off.* As much as she didn't care about the other women he'd dated, Mark's words still stung, and she did worry about taking Jamie away from his work. Hadn't she done enough of that? Wasn't that why Mark was there and why Jamie's company was in the situation it was in?

She managed a glance at Mark, who shook his head the slightest bit, which she read clearly as, *Back off. Stop monopolizing his time.* Just enough of a sign for her to feel it like a knife to her heart.

"No, go with Mark. I'm fine." *I need to think.* She'd been putting off making her own decisions, too. Maybe this was fate. Maybe this was the whisper Vera was talking about, and she should open her ears and listen.

"Are you sure, Jess? I don't mind." Jamie lifted her chin and searched her eyes.

She tried to smile, reached out and touched his stomach. She loved him so much it hurt. She nodded.

"I hate to leave you," Jamie said quietly.

Mark turned a way-too-comfortable smile in her direction. She swallowed the bile that rose in her throat.

"Jessica, do you need Jamie to stay with you tonight? If you do, hey, I'll back off. Who am I to come between two lovebirds?" He held his arms up in surrender.

"I'm fine. Go. I'll take Vera home."

Jamie folded her in his arms and kissed the top of her head. "You sure you're okay to drive?"

"Yes."

"Okay. I'll come by afterward if you're not asleep."

It was all she could do to nod her head.

Chapter Sixteen

THERE WAS A time when hanging out at the Beachcomber would be a five-hour, enjoyable affair, but Jamie had been there for two hours with Mark and his other friends, and it felt like two hours too long. He'd tried texting and calling Jessica, but her phone went to voicemail.

"Why don't you go see how she's doing?" Bella asked. "And tell her I'm totally bummed that she's sick, and that we'll table our chunky-dunking for another night."

"Hey, hey, hey." Mark tapped the table. "Let the man enjoy life a little. He needs to blow off some steam."

Blow off steam? That was the last thing he needed to do. How had he ever overlooked all the things about Mark that were rubbing him the wrong way? What he needed was to know that Jessica was okay. He never should have left her in the first place.

He glanced around the table at his friends. Caden and Bella were forehead to forehead, whispering. Leanna was sitting on Kurt's lap, as she almost always was, and Jenna was dragging Pete onto the dance floor. Pete rolled his eyes in Jamie's direction, but the light in Pete's eyes gave away the truth. He was so in love with Jenna that he'd do anything for her. Amy was texting someone, probably her new beau, Jake, and Tony hadn't even come out tonight. *Self-preservation*, he'd told Jamie. Jamie hadn't bothered to ask what he'd meant by that. And then there was Mark, eyeing every woman in the place.

What the hell was he doing here? He should be with Jessica. He didn't want a drink, and he certainly didn't want to dance without her. Hell, he needed to be with her, and he could tell by the look in her eyes earlier that she'd needed him just as badly as he needed her. But, as usual, he'd allowed himself to be swayed by Mark.

Enough was enough.

Jamie pushed away from the table. "I'm taking off. Mark, thanks for driving out tonight. Are you okay to drive back to your hotel?"

Mark waved a dismissive hand, avoiding Jamie's gaze. "Yeah, fine, fine."

Amy eyed Jamie. "Can you give me a ride back?"

"Sure." He draped an arm around Amy and said goodbye to the others.

"You okay, Ames?" he asked on the way to the car.

"Yeah. This is just a weird summer." Amy was like a sister to Jamie. As much as he didn't want to get involved with whatever was or wasn't going on between her and Tony, he could tell by the drag of her voice that she needed an ear to bend.

"Tony?" Of course it was about him.

Amy shrugged.

He opened the car door for her, then settled into the driver's seat. "What's happening with Jake?"

"Jake." She smiled and rested her head back. "He's

amazing. Did I tell you he's a mountain rescue guy? Really rugged and sexy. He's so nice, and always a gentleman." She turned and looked at Jamie with a sigh. "He's also twenty-eight and probably way too wild for me in the long run."

Jamie took the back roads up toward Seaside. "Too wild?" He glanced at Amy. Her head was still back, and her hair hung straight, past her shoulders. She wore a pair of white shorts and a pretty blue crinkled cotton top. Her skin was tanned and flawless. She was smart and generous to a fault. He had no idea why she was still single. Then again, he had no idea why Jessica was still single either.

"I'm wild, don't get me wrong. I'm a fun-loving girl, even if I'm not as loud about it as everyone else," Amy assured him.

"Oh, I know you are," he said with an arched brow. She was about as wild as a lily.

She swatted his arm. "I am! I may not be able to hold my liquor, or be as dirty mouthed as Bella, but I am wild in my own way."

"Amy, is that what you think guys want? Wild women?" He couldn't believe he was having this conversation with Amy, but she was so damned sweet, she'd get eaten alive if she told men she was wild—even if she had a secret wild side like Jessica did.

"Well, don't they?" She furrowed her brow and spoke softly. "Jamie, I know I'm the good girl of the group. I can't help it. I just am. But, you know, all women have other sides to them."

"Amy, you are sweet, and yes, you're a good girl, and smart, funny, beautiful. You're everything the right guy will look for. Guys talk about wanting wild women, but those aren't the women they marry. Those are like, I don't know, something to say you've had."

She covered her face with her hands and groaned

as they pulled into Seaside. "So then it's just hopeless. I don't know what I'm supposed to be, but obviously being me isn't working out so well in the guy department."

Jamie parked the car and turned to Amy. "Amy, I've got to be honest with you. If Jessica was a wild woman in public, I'd never have dated her, and I highly doubt Caden, or Kurt, or Pete would have gotten serious with Bella, Leanna, or Jenna if they had been either. Bella's not wild; she's brazen. There's a difference. At the end of the day, she's stable, loving, and head over heels for Caden and Evan. Younger guys like wild. Guys our age like to keep our wild moments with our women private, and I think wild's the totally wrong word. I can't speak for all men, but I think most guys want a woman who's not afraid of taking control in the bedroom or to be seductively sexy when you're on a date. You know what I mean—privately passionate, but even keeled the rest of the time. Flirty with us, maybe, but just us. No guy wants to worry about what his woman's doing when he's not around."

"Really? You're not just saying that because it's me?"

Her eyes were so serious and her words were so full of worry that he reached out and hugged her. "*You* are amazing just as you are. The right guy is going to come along, and you'll realize that all this worry was for nothing. Amy, is this all about Tony, or did Jake make you feel this way?"

She sighed. "No. It's about me. I'm always the friend, never the girlfriend. Do you know that I can count the men I've been intimate with on one hand? Lame, right?"

He thought of Jessica and how good it had felt when they'd finally come together—and the conflicting emotions of her having been with only one other man. She'd given herself over to him so completely, and continued to on a daily basis. The fact that she'd waited until it felt right to be with a man made everything about her that much more special. Some women used sex for power, others to make up for whatever daddy love they never received. Jessica had waited because in her heart it had felt like the right thing to do, and Jamie respected that because he'd done the same thing with his feelings. He'd kept them trapped inside him until the right woman came along. And he had no doubt that Jessica was that woman.

"Honestly, Amy, I think it speaks volumes about your self-worth. That's a good thing. Don't ever let anyone convince you otherwise." He came around the car and opened her door.

Amy wrapped her arms around him and hugged him tight. "You're such a good friend, Jamie. Thank you for not telling me I'm a loser."

He laughed. "You're not a loser, and don't worry. The right man will love you just as you are."

"I keep hoping the right man will realize that I'm the right woman." She shifted her eyes to Tony's cottage.

After making sure Amy got inside okay and then checking on Vera, who was fast asleep, Jamie grabbed clean clothes, penned a note for Vera telling her he'd be back in the morning, and headed over to Jessica's apartment.

Jessica's apartment was dark, but Jamie heard the faintest music playing inside. He knocked lightly on the door, and a few minutes later the door opened a crack. Jessica was looking down, and he couldn't see her face.

"Hey, sorry I'm so late."

She opened the door, eyes trained on the floor.

Jamie followed her in and wrapped his arms around her from behind.

"How are you feeling?"

She shrugged.

"Babe, why aren't you talking to me? Are you that sick?" He turned her in his arms, and his stomach plunged. Her eyes were swollen and red, her nose was bright pink, and her lower lip was trembling.

"Jess? What happened?" He pulled her against his chest.

She fisted her hands in his shirt, and her body trembled. He realized she was still crying. He gathered her in his arms and carried her to the couch, and held her, safely enveloped against him, as tears streamed down her cheeks.

"Jessie, what can I do? What happened?"

She shook her head, and he stroked her back, hoping to soothe whatever ache she had.

"Did something happen to your father? A friend?"

Again she shook her head.

Jessica sucked in a jagged lungful of air and lifted her head from his tear-soaked shirt. The minute their eyes met, she burst into tears again.

"Shh. Whatever it is, it's okay. I'll take care of it. We'll get through it together." He stroked her back, while his own chest tightened with worry. He surveyed the apartment for clues about what was going on. Her cello was propped against the wall in the corner; her laptop and phone were on the table. The small kitchen was tidy, and he had a clear view into the bedroom, and other than the bed being rumpled, everything was in its place. The sounds of her sniffling and the feel of her trembling against him made his gut clench tight.

"Jess, please tell me why you're upset."

She pushed away from his chest again.

Jamie wiped her tears with his thumbs.

"It's okay. Whatever it is, I'll take care of it."

"I'm…sorry." A lone tear accompanied her whisper.

"Jessie, don't be sorry. It's okay to cry. I just want to help fix whatever's wrong."

She nodded and wiped her eyes. "I'm afraid to tell you, but I want to."

"Tell me what? You can tell me anything." He searched her eyes and saw so much worry and sadness that he couldn't imagine what was causing her so much pain.

"I'll tell you, but you have to promise me to be one hundred percent honest, even if it'll hurt me."

He cupped her beautiful cheek, his chest tight and his heart in his throat. He wished he knew what the hell was going on. He had nothing to hide from her, and to think she was this upset over something about him knocked the wind out of him.

"I promise. I'll always be honest with you. Always."

She shifted her body so she could sit up straighter and inhaled deeply. She pressed her lips together and nodded, as if she were nodding to herself, telling herself she was okay. Her eyes fell to his chest again.

He was ready to crawl out of his skin with worry.

"Baby, please," he whispered.

"Tonight, after the concert was over and you were helping Vera…" She drew in another uneven breath. He felt her fingers grip his shirt. "Mark said…"

His body flashed hot. His muscles constricted. *Mark? Motherfucking Mark caused this?* He clenched his jaw to keep from raising his voice.

"What did Mark say to you?"

She swallowed hard but held his stare. "He said that…" Her breath hitched and she swallowed again, then gripped his shirt—and chest—tighter. Her jaw began to tremble again.

"He said that you're just playing around with me and that you can have any woman you want. That I'm no different from any other woman you've been with and if I don't want to be responsible for the demise of your career, I should back off."

She spoke so fast it took him a minute to process what she'd said. Breathing harder as understanding dawned on him, he was powerless against the rage that filled his veins. His hands fisted and his biceps flexed. Without a word, he lifted Jessica off of him and set her on the couch.

"Jamie?" Tears streaked her cheeks as she huddled on the couch, looking small and fragile and so damned broken it killed him.

Every muscle tensed. Fire seared his veins, but beneath that rage was his love for Jessica, and it battled the anger. He was afraid to touch her, afraid to get too close for fear that his anger toward Mark might move him to act too roughly.

"I'll be back." Blinded by anger, he moved for the door. He had to fix this shit, had to get to Mark and beat the living shit out of him for hurting Jessica—for putting any doubt in her beautiful mind.

"Jamie, wait!" She scrambled off the couch and followed him out to the deck. "Wait. Is it true? Was this all a game to you?"

"A game? Is that what you think? Do I act like it's a game?" *A fucking game? This is anything but a game.*

"No, but—"

He stilled, his gut burning. "But?"

"I *am* a distraction. I know I am, so the most important part is true," she whispered with a trembling voice. "I could cause you trouble in your business. I could make you fail."

He closed his eyes to try to gain control of the storm brewing inside him. When he turned to face her, she looked impossibly small and scared, like a wounded bird. And goddamn Mark was the one who'd wounded her—and it was Jamie's fault. He'd left her alone with a shark. What the hell had he been thinking?

"You're not a distraction." He hated that his teeth were clenched and his face was probably red, but the words were true, even if the emotions putting them forth were misconstrued. He wanted to hold her until she knew, without a shadow of a doubt, that he loved her—but he was incapable of being gentle at the moment. This was the best he could do. "You're the woman I love. The only failure was mine, for letting him near you."

Chapter Seventeen

JAMIE SPED DOWN Route 6 and was at the Sheraton in less than five minutes. He cut the engine and gripped the steering wheel so tight his knuckles turned white, wondering what the fuck he'd been thinking to let Mark anywhere near Jessica. He had too much fucking faith in Mark; that much was clear. His muscles corded tight, frustration brought his fist down on the dashboard, once, twice, three times—and after he'd cracked the damn thing—a fourth.

"Motherfucker," he seethed.

More than ten years of friendship, and this was how Mark paid him back?

His eyes dropped to the stone on the ring on his right hand. *Black. Nothingness. Angst so deep you can't push your way out of it.* He breathed heavily, his chest aching with anger and love and all the out-of-control emotions in between. He stormed from the car and into the hotel, nearly blasting through the glass doors that opened so damn slowly he wanted to shatter them. He blew past the reception desk, oblivious to the greeting of the woman behind it, and stalked down the hall, head bowed, blinded with rage.

Room 189 was in the back of the building, which was good. No one would hear him killing Mark. He pounded on the door, rattling it on the hinges.

"Open the fucking door, Mark." He didn't care that it was midnight, or that there might be families sleeping in the nearby rooms. He couldn't have registered such a coherent thought if his life depended on it. He felt the weight of his anger like a two-hundred-pound gorilla, digging its claws into every muscle, snaking into his body and electrifying his nerves until they burned so hot, he could barely see straight.

He banged on the door again. "You have three seconds before I break it down," Jamie seethed.

He heard the slide of the lock, the chain rattle, the doorknob slowly twist. He thrust the door open and grabbed Mark by his white T-shirt, lifted him off the floor, and slammed him against the wall, barely registering the door clicking closed behind him or the woman screaming in the center of the bed as she scrambled to pull sheets over her naked body.

"What the fuck?" Mark hollered.

"What. Did. You. Do?"

"Nothing. Jamie, what the hell?" Mark's body shook; his eyes shot to the bed.

Jamie turned and looked at the bed, his knuckles digging into Mark's chest. "Leave. Now," he said to the frightened woman, then turned back to Mark, ignoring her as she whimpered and cried, gathered her clothes, and tore out the door.

"Jamie. Put me down. We'll talk." Mark's eyes were wide and fearful.

"Pleading is ugly on you, motherfucker, and talking is the last thing on my mind."

Mark touched his shoulder and lowered his voice.

"Jamie. It's me, Jamie. We're friends, remember? Put me down. We'll talk, and then if you still want to rip me to shreds, you can." He dropped his eyes to his bare, limp dick between them.

Fuck. How the hell had he missed that? Jamie shoved him toward the bed. "Put some fucking pants on." He paced the hotel room. Mark's clothes were thrown over a chair, a woman's high heel was beside the dresser, and a half-empty bottle of wine was beside the bed. Goddamn it. He spun around as Mark pulled on his khakis, fear in his eyes, but beneath that, Jamie saw the calculating eyes of the manipulator that he'd always known was there but had chosen to ignore. Jamie never imagined Mark would use that sleazy, manipulative side against him.

"What the fuck did you say to Jess?" They stood a foot apart, Jamie's hands fisted, ready.

"What? That's what this is about?"

Jamie landed one punch to the side of Mark's jaw, then grabbed his tee as he reeled sideways and yanked him up, so they were nose to nose. "Don't fucking play with me."

Blood dripped from Mark's nose. His eyes went dark as he lifted his hands in surrender. "Okay, okay."

"Say it. I want to hear it from your fucking mouth." Jamie's arms shook from the storm blazing through his body.

"Let go. I'm not saying a fucking word until you do." Mark held his stare.

Jamie threw him backward. He stumbled into the large, low dresser. He touched the blood streaking over his lips and chin, grabbed something that was bunched up on the dresser—a shirt, pants, who the fuck knew or cared—and he wiped his face.

"Assaulting an attorney isn't smart."

Jamie closed the distance between them and

pinned him to the floor with another dark stare.

"Fine, fine." Mark went to the chair by the small wooden table beside the bed and sat down.

Jamie paced, his anger leashed by a fraying thread. He planted his legs like pilings in the earth and crossed his arms over his chest, locking another dark stare on Mark.

"I told her the truth, that you need to focus on your business. Jamie, you don't even know her."

Jamie reached for Mark's shirt and Mark held his hands up. "I don't give a rat's ass what you *think* I know. What the fuck else did you say to her?"

"Okay, okay, okay." He wiped the blood from his nose with his forearm. "Fuck that hurts. I told her that she was no different from the other women you dated, and you're not some fucking knight in shining armor who's here to save her. You're a businessman who needs to focus before you lose everything you've worked for."

Jamie put one hand on each arm of the chair and loomed over him. His voice was cold as ice. "And what makes you the expert on what I feel?"

Mark blinked up at him, rearing back as far as he could from his seated position. "Jamie, I'm your best friend. I've known you for years. You trust me with everything. I protect you. Jesus fucking Christ, without me you'd have lost half your business years ago."

There was an ounce of truth in what he said. *Fuck*, Jamie hated that. Mark had saved Jamie too many times to count.

"She's the woman I love, and I don't need your protection from her." Jamie pushed away from the chair and paced again, hands fisted by his sides.

"The woman you love? Jamie, Jamie, Jamie. Get a grip here. How long have you known her? A few days? A week?"

He spun around, venom in his voice. "I don't give a fuck how long I've known her. What makes you think you have the right to say any of that shit to her?"

"Because I've never seen you turn your back on your business, and someone had to think with their head instead of their dick."

Jamie stepped closer, and Mark held his hands up again.

"Jamie, you didn't run a check on her. What do you really know? What she told you? You've been down that path before. She could be playing you like a two-dollar fiddle, for all you know. How many women have told you they were models when they were working at some rancid topless bar, looking for a sugar daddy?"

"You fucking heard her play. She's not lying about what she does for a living." He had no proof, but he didn't feel like he needed it with Jessica. Sure, she'd been a little cagey giving up that particular information, but he understood her reasons, just as he kept his own career from most people.

"Okay, so she plays the cello. BSO? OneClick will tell you if that's true in five seconds or less. What else do you really know about her? Where does she live? What do her parents do? Has she ever been arrested? Holy hell, Jamie. Do you even know how many men she's slept with?"

Jamie stopped pacing and stared at Mark. He didn't know any of that shit, except how many men she'd been with. But he knew he loved her. Damn did he ever love her.

"Jamie, your look tells me that you have no fucking idea about any of this. Well, maybe the sex part. If she's inexperienced, she'd be a novice in the bedroom, but..."

A novice in the bedroom. He remembered the way she'd watched him as she took him into her mouth and took him higher than any woman ever had. The way she climbed on top of him and rode him, brushing her breasts against his face until he was ready to explode, and how she'd enjoyed being restrained by his strength. She'd told him it was all new to her, and her eyes had been full of truth and such depths of emotion that he hadn't questioned it.

No, he refused to believe she'd lied about that. He'd felt her—been inside her, felt her tightness, saw the heady excitement of newness in her eyes. No way had he misread those things.

"Let me do one quick search. Right now. Just one. It'll tell you what you need to know in under five seconds. I can run a full background check later, but let's just see if she's with the orchestra." Mark moved toward his laptop.

"No." He grabbed Mark's arm. "Don't fucking search her name. This is my life, not yours. I appreciate your concern, but if you ever..." He pulled Mark closer and tightened his grip on his arm until he saw pain in Mark's eyes. "If you ever say one word to her again, I will kill you with my bare hands." He tossed him to the bed and stormed out.

Chapter Eighteen

JESSICA PUSHED HER coffee cup across the small table. She couldn't stomach looking at it, much less the smell of it. It smelled like the acid swirling in her stomach. She glanced into the bedroom at her unmade bed. Tears welled in her eyes as quickly as if someone had struck her with a hot poker. She turned away and shuffled across the floor in her sweatshirt and underwear. She was cold to the bone despite the warm seventy-five degrees of the second-story apartment and the sun-drenched air blowing in through the open window. She sat on the couch, then rose to her feet again. Nothing felt right anymore. Would it ever? Was this her window into reality? That life outside of the orchestra could be blissful and heavenly and then barf her up like a bad meal without ever looking back? She didn't want to believe it, but all night she'd waited for Jamie to return. She'd even turned on her stupid cell phone in case he texted or called.

She hadn't heard him go jogging this morning, and she'd sat with her ear to the goddamn window from dawn until ten minutes ago, when she dragged herself into the kitchen for the rancid cup of coffee that nearly made her curl into a ball and remain there.

With a loud sigh, she headed for the bathroom to shower. Even the girls hadn't come by this morning. Of course they wouldn't. They were his friends, not hers. They hadn't come by to go skinny-dipping the night before, either. Jamie probably filled them in last night when he got back.

Her cell phone rang, and her chest filled with hope as she ran to answer it. Her heart sank when the orchestra manager's name appeared on the screen.

"Good morning, Charlie." She tried to sound like she wasn't drowning in sadness.

"Millicent. How are you, dear? You sound deathly."

It took her a minute to recall her professional name. Had it been that long? Had she tossed aside all that she'd worked for that easily? She forced herself to answer.

"Just a little off this morning." *Deathly*. How perfect.

"Well, I hope you can shake it off, because your substitute has taken ill. She can't shake it off, and we need you back by tomorrow." Charlie said this like it was a given that she would agree. It had been part of their agreement. If there was an issue with her substitute, she'd return within twenty-four hours.

But she didn't know she'd be heartbroken.

How could her fingers even work when the ache of missing Jamie was pulsing through her body with the force of a tsunami? She couldn't push it away, could barely breathe through it.

"Millicent?"

She cleared her throat and held on to the table for support. "Yes. I'm here."

"Tomorrow morning. Rehearsal's at ten. You might want to come in early, as the others will want to welcome you back, and you know how pitiful reunions can be. You'll have to relive every detail of your little vacation fifteen times over."

He ended the call before she could say another word, and really, what would she have said? *I'm not sure my arms will work well enough to pack my bags?*

WHEN THE SUN rose over the horizon, Jamie was still sitting on the dunes at Nauset Beach, where he'd been since he'd left Mark at the Sheraton. He wanted to be as far from him as he could, and even the Wellfleet beaches seemed too close. *Fucking Mark*. Nauset was serene in the early dawn hours, which he needed to balance the fury within him. The sand was cool on his bare feet, and the dune grass swished in the morning breeze. He'd walked far across the dunes, past the homes overlooking the water, past the divots where teenagers slid down the dunes, leaving a butt-shaped path all the way down to the beach. He'd walked until he'd come to an island of untouched dune grass, where he'd been sitting ever since, thinking about all the things he'd learned with his own OneClick search. There was no Jessica Ayers listed with the Boston Symphony Orchestra—or in Juilliard, for that matter. He no longer knew what to believe about Jessica, but his heart felt as though it were coming apart inside him, leaving shards of glass etching her name, her touch, her image, into him.

When young families began arriving at the beach, Jamie still wasn't ready to move. Two hours later, he twisted the ring on his finger. The stone was orange and green. What the hell that meant, he had no idea. He stared at the damn thing. It was probably a three-dollar gift, and yet he knew that every time he saw it, it would carry the emotions and memories of being with Jessica. He leaned back on his palms and watched the beach become dotted with people. Laughter and voices carried in the air and faded around him. When he could take their happiness no more, Jamie finally rose to leave.

He pulled into Seaside and purposefully took the fork to the right to avoid driving by Jessica's apartment. He wasn't ready to talk. Not nearly ready to see her beautiful face. One look at her soulful eyes and he'd fall headfirst into her without having time to think. He'd never known how close two people could become, or how intense lovemaking could be, until he'd opened his heart to her. She hadn't even tried to win him over, or at least not that he could tell. She didn't play any of the games other women did. She'd never expected expensive restaurants or lavish dates. She hadn't asked for a damn thing. She'd even tried to talk him out of spending the night for fear of it upsetting Vera, when any other woman would have used the opportunity to stick their claws in deeper. She was happy just to be with him, to take whatever he wanted to give. And he'd wanted to give her the world, which now, as he stepped from his car, seemed a little crazy after a week. Why did it feel like he'd known her his whole life? Was Mark right? Had she played him like a two-dollar fiddle and he'd been too taken with her to notice?

"Hey!" Bella yelled as she stalked off of Amy's porch. "Hold it right there."

He closed his eyes for a second, closed the car door, and then turned to face her, hoping he had the strength not to snap.

"What the hell did you do to Jessica?"

If looks could kill, she'd have driven him six feet under.

"Bella, I—"

She held up her hand. "Don't even try to explain,

Jamie Reed. I always thought you were a good guy. I would protect you to the ends of the earth, but you brought her into our group and we all fell in love with her. Not just your sorry ass."

Amy stepped off the deck in a pretty yellow sundress and walked across the road with sad eyes cast downward.

"Hi, Jamie."

She sounded so distraught, he reached out to her. "Are you okay?"

Amy nodded. "Just bummed that Jessica left. I was sure you two were the real deal. Are you okay?"

"Left?" His eyes ran between Bella and Amy. "What do you mean *left*?"

"She got a call from her manager," Amy explained. "She had to go back to Boston. She came to talk to you, but you weren't home. I think she left a note and some of your clothes with Vera."

Bella rolled her eyes. "Like you didn't know about all this? Come on. Her eyes were so red from crying all night she looked like she had been Maced. She said the last thing you needed was to be distracted from your work, and we all know that had to come from you, because no woman would make that shit up."

"Mark." He turned on his heels and ran inside.

Vera lifted worried eyes from the book she was reading and held up an envelope. She didn't have to say a word. In an instant, he read her expression and knew she wanted to reach out and hug him, but he needed to be left alone to deal with whatever was going on with him and Jessica. Vera had the same look in her eyes she'd had his senior year of high school, when the girl he'd been dating had called the night before the senior prom and left a message telling him that she was going to the dance with someone else.

"Thanks." He tore it open and walked to the back

of the small cottage while he read the handwritten note.

Jamie,

Thank you for showing me what it was like to live and to love. Being with you was the best feeling I've ever experienced. Not just when we were intimate, but walking through the flea market, lying on the beach, just being near you. Vera's a lovely woman, and she's raised a wonderful man. I'll miss you both so much that it hurts. I never knew I was capable of being so happy, but then again, I never had the chance to know you. I'll cherish the memories of our time together forever, and I'll never love another man as I love you. Yes, I fell in love with you, Jamie, and I'm not sorry for that. I do wish I could have told you to your face, but this is probably best. It's amazing to me that two people can feel so close so fast, but I've lived a sheltered life, so maybe you've experienced this type of connection many times before and I'm alone in my wonder. In any case, I understand how much of a distraction I was, and I hope I didn't cause you too much trouble. Please don't be too angry with Mark. He obviously cares very deeply for you. Take care of Vera. She's everything I always wished I had with my own mother, and more. Warmest wishes for your success and happiness.

—Jess

He sank to one of the chairs on the deck. His throat swelled with emotion as he reread the note in fits and spurts a few more times. *I fell in love with you, Jamie... Don't be too angry with Mark...Take care of Vera.* He breathed deeply. *Warmest wishes...*She'd climbed back into the prim and proper cocoon she was so afraid of, and it broke his heart.

Don't be too angry with Mark. That was so *Jessica*, always thinking of others before herself. He was angry with Mark, and he was angry with himself, and now with Jessica for leaving a shitty-ass note to say goodbye.

He turned the paper over in his hands and read it again, his heart aching with every word. It wasn't a shitty-ass note. It was a very thoughtful, precisely written goodbye.

He jumped to his feet and flew past Vera.

"Where are you going?" Vera grabbed the arm of the couch and leaned forward.

Jamie heard hope in her voice. "Errand. I'll be back."

He sped down Route 6. Jessica couldn't have gotten far. He called her cell as he drove—the call went to voicemail, and he contemplated leaving a message. *Call me. Let's talk.* But he ended the call without leaving anything more than a few seconds of dead air.

"Let's talk? What the fuck am I going to say?" He shook his head. "Hey, I didn't see your name in the Boston Symphony Orchestra listing of musicians? There's no record of Jessica Ayers at Juilliard? What am I doing? I'm talking to my fucking self in my goddamn car."

He pulled into the next parking lot, knowing he'd never say any of those things to her, because he felt guilty as hell even thinking them. And if he saw her in person, he'd want to kiss her, to hold her, to hear her tell him she loved him and look at him like he was all she ever wanted or needed again. He wouldn't have the heart to say a damn thing other than how much he loved her. If he did that, if he allowed himself to soak her goodness up, even for only a few minutes, and he found out it *was* all a lie, a game, a play for a successful boyfriend, he'd never recover.

Ever.

Chapter Nineteen

"JAMIE, ARE YOU sure this is what you want to do?" Vera stood in the doorway of his bedroom in the cottage as he packed his things the next morning. "You can't just bury your feelings in work, no matter how easy that is."

He met her worried gaze, then zipped his suitcase closed. "I'm not burying my feelings. I'm going back to work to handle the issue that Mark uncovered. I should have been there days ago."

"Sounds to me like Mark came here to uncover issues."

His muscles constricted. He gritted his teeth while he tried to calm the anger that had been gnawing at his gut ever since yesterday, when he'd found out Jessica had left. He'd held out hope that maybe his doubts were wrong until he'd broken down and called her—only to be met with her voicemail. Fifteen hours later she still hadn't returned his call. His feelings were so tangled that he didn't know if he was coming or going. Was she avoiding his calls because she knew he'd discovered she'd lied to him, or was it something else altogether? Had he hurt her too badly by not being there for her and leaving her in limbo while he tried to drown his doubts in ocean views, pretending he could cast them away with each rolling wave?

He picked up his suitcase and set it on the floor beside Vera. "I don't know, Gram. I can't figure out if his coming here was a blessing or a terrible mistake. I usually know what's right and wrong, and this time..." He twisted the ring Jessica had given him, unable to convince himself to take it off.

Vera took his hand in hers. "That's because this time it isn't about right and wrong. This time it's not about code or computers or puzzle pieces that fit into nice little niches and make sense. This time, Jamie, it's about your heart. You're not supposed to understand it, but it's a good thing you're feeling something. You've got a big heart. God knows you do. You take care of me so well, Jamie. Now take care of you."

He nodded, not sure he knew what taking care of himself even meant anymore.

"I'll come back next weekend. I just need to get this work thing under control." *And hopefully get in control of myself again.*

"I'll be fine, sweetheart. If I need anything, Bella, Kurt, and the others will take care of me." She hugged him and stroked his back, as she'd done when he was a little boy.

He kissed her cheek. "Okay. I love you."

"I know you do. I love you, too, dear."

Jamie reached for the door.

"Jamie."

He turned around. "What is it, Gram?"

She shook her head, and her thin lips curved into a semi smile. "I just wanted to say that there are some things in life that are meant to be. Sometimes they're good, and sometimes they're the most hurtful, treacherous things you can imagine. Those things can't be stopped. They can't be thwarted by fighting or changing your course, because they're like air. Shapeless and fluid. Odorless and silent. They move through hearts and closed doors, and travel the globe until they find their prey."

Her tone sent a shiver down his spine. These were the words she'd used the day she told him that his parents had died. The very same words, being delivered in the very same fashion. A flash of memory he'd buried so deep he thought he'd never be able to revisit it burst forth in his tortured mind. Just before those words left her lips all those years ago, she'd stumbled at the kitchen counter where she'd been making his grilled cheese sandwich. He'd jumped from his chair—*Gram!* He was a little thing at six years old. He could still feel the cold linoleum on his bare feet as he ran toward her. He could still feel the weight of her, as if it were yesterday, as he'd put one lithe arm around her waist and guided her to the kitchen table. His hand was barely big enough to wrap around the wooden spindles of the chair as he tugged it from the table and guided her into it. What he didn't remember, had never been able to recall, was a phone call telling her of their demise. No matter how many nights he'd stayed up replaying the moment in his mind, he never could recall the shrill ring of the phone.

Now she patted his hand and nodded. "Go. You'll know what's right."

"I..."

"Jamie, just as you knew then, you'll know. We couldn't stop them. I warned them, begged them to stay, but your mother insisted, and your father, he'd have followed her into a volcano without a thought."

"You...You believed me."

"I believed you. You told me then that they

weren't coming home. As a boy, you were very in tune to your parents, but after...Jamie, I prayed you'd lose that connection over time, and you did. You got busy filling your mind with everything and anything you could. It was as if you never wanted to feel that connection again. Not that I blamed you. No. I knew you were right. You dove into puzzle after puzzle. Oh, the hours you spent doing every puzzle imaginable. Figures, crosswords, math calculations, and any other puzzle you could get your sad and angry little hands on. You put enough chaos in your head to fill those lonely spaces your parents left behind."

"Gram." He laughed at the notion. "Are you saying that it wasn't just a feeling, but that I had a premonition about Mom and Dad dying?"

She squeezed his hand. "I'm not one to give names to things. I don't believe like your generation does, that everything needs a label. All I know is that you knew that they were not coming back, and when I couldn't convince your parents to stay home, I moved into your house and insisted that you stay with me." She smiled and waved her hand in the air. "You probably don't remember, but they put up quite a fight about leaving you home. Your mother called me every name in the book." She paused, and her eyes filled with sadness.

He must have blacked that out, because he didn't remember any of it, but he remembered clear as day, standing on the front porch of his parents' house waving to them as they left for the very last time. His mother's face was streaked with tears, her thick dark hair loose and wild, tickling his cheek and nose as she clung to him. *I love you, Jamie. You're the best boy in this world. I'll take pictures of your favorite animals, and I'll write to you. I love you so much.* And his father, dressed in a pair of jeans and a black tee, looking virile and powerful. Jamie remembered feeling like his father was as big and solid as the oak tree in their front yard, and when he picked Jamie up and wrapped those powerful arms around his only son, the scent of Old Spice filled Jamie's senses. *Take care of Mama*, he'd said to his father. *I'd die before I'd let anything happen to her,* his father had answered with his deep voice, full of tethered emotion. He wasn't one to openly cry, and when he set Jamie back down on the ground and palmed Jamie's hand with his big hand, Jamie knew his father was a man of his word and meant what he'd said.

Vera squeezed his hand again, pulling him from the memories he'd thought he'd buried long ago.

"Go," Vera urged. "Before it gets late and you have to drive in the dark. Put the past behind you and concentrate on your future. That's where you'll find your answers."

Chapter Twenty

MONDAY MORNING JESSICA sat in front of her computer staring at the OneClick search screen with her cell phone pressed to her ear, listening to her father talk about the show he and her mother had seen. Other than Saturday's concert, which she'd attended in a zombie-like state, she'd spent the entire weekend home alone, wallowing in the ache of missing Jamie. How would she survive another day? She typed in Jamie's name for the millionth time, just so she could see his picture appear on the screen. The sight of him never failed to bring fresh tears to her eyes and an ache to her chest, and still she tortured herself.

"Sorry we weren't able to cancel the tickets to the show and go to your concert, honey," her father said. "How did it go?"

It took her a second to realize he'd asked her a question. "Uneventful."

"Oh, well, I guess that's better than if it went poorly. What did you do yesterday? I was really hoping you'd come by for dinner after we heard you were home, and when you didn't return my calls, I worried."

I spent Sunday in a fog. "I'm sorry. I've been pretty tired, that's all. I'll try to come by soon."

She'd received Jamie's phone message, but she couldn't bring herself to call him back. *It's me. I'd like to talk to you. Please.* He'd sounded as sad as she felt, but every time she thought about calling him, she heard Mark's voice. *He needs to focus, and unless you want to be the cause of his empire's demise, I suggest you back off.* And immediately after, she'd remember the determination on Jamie's face when he left her apartment that very last time, as he said, *You're not a distraction. You're the woman I love.*

"Jessica, I don't want to pry, but I've never heard you this down before. Did something happen while you were away?"

"Sort of. I met someone, but we aren't together now." She was so emotionally exhausted that she didn't trust herself to make a sound decision. If Jamie loved her, then why hadn't he come back that night—or the next morning? She hadn't left Seaside until the next afternoon, and from the surprise Vera expressed over Jamie not being with Jessica when Jessica went to say goodbye to him, it was obvious he'd stayed out all night. Vera had said that he left a note saying he'd see her in the morning. Where would he have gone if he wasn't with Jessica? And why would he wait so many hours before calling her?

"I'm sorry. Dating can be difficult."

She heard a strain in her father's voice. They'd never talked about dating, and come to think of it, they'd never talked about much besides the world of academics and the orchestra.

"Dad, how did you know you loved Mom?"

"Well...I guess I just knew. I'm not sure how I knew, but everything just fell into place in our lives. It was like once we met, we knew, I guess."

Jessica could tell by the way he laughed that he was uncomfortable with the question.

"I couldn't think of anything other than her, believe it or not," he explained. "I know you'll find that hard to believe, given how stoic your mother can be, but to me, she's everything. That doesn't help you much, but I guess I'm not very good at these things."

She sighed. "I don't find it hard to believe. I just...I think we were big distractions to each other's work. I'm not sure it would have worked out with my career anyway."

The truth was, she was a distraction. A big one. So was he, but he was the most welcome distraction she'd ever encountered. She closed her laptop, crossed her arms over it, and rested her head on them. With her eyes closed, she could recall his touch as he brushed her hair from her shoulders or pressed his cheek to hers, the way he'd filled her so completely that he'd stolen her breath the first time they'd made love, and the guilt in his eyes when he'd realized that he was only the second man ever to be there. Tears rolled down her cheeks. She'd found what she was sure was her father's baseball *and* she'd fallen in love. Two things she'd never imagined she had a hope in hell of accomplishing. Then she'd gone and somehow lost both.

"Sweetheart, if he didn't think you were worth the distraction, then he's not the man for you. Every love is a distraction. That's what makes it so special."

"Maybe not," she agreed. Then why did it feel so right to be with Jamie, and why did it hurt so badly to lose him? If he wasn't worth the energy, how could anything else be? Including the cello? There wasn't any lingering doubt about who Jamie was or why he loved her. How could that be so wrong?

Because he doesn't love me. How could he? He never came back.

Maybe her mother was right, and everything outside of being an excellent cellist was not worth the energy. Maybe she'd just needed a good dose of reality to slap her into realizing how lucky she was to hold her position with the orchestra. With every tear that fell, she weighed her thoughts, and not one of them took hold.

"I think I'd better go, Dad."

"Jessica, honey, if you're this torn up over him, maybe you should talk to him. Tell him how you feel." He lowered his voice, and it sounded as if he was walking as he spoke. "Honey, some things are more important than being the best cellist. But if you tell your mother I said so, I'll deny it until the cows come home."

She heard the smile in his voice.

"Okay." She wiped her tears.

"I'd do anything for your mother, and you know that, but, Jessica, you don't have to. You have choices in your life. I know you've put your all into your career, and you've done a damn good job of it. Whether or not you make the Chamber Players doesn't matter. Don't put that pressure on yourself, and I'm sorry if I did."

Don't put that pressure on myself? A spot with the Chamber Players is what everyone strives for. Her mother had ingrained that in her mind since she first started playing with the symphony. "You deserve to let yourself be happy. There are ways to have both, you know. Your career and a relationship. Your mother and I did it."

She couldn't stop a laugh from slipping out. "No, *you* did it. She does whatever she pleases and you conform."

"Okay, maybe to some degree, but that's what relationships are. Compromises. I love you, honey, and if you want to talk any more, just call me. But at least think about talking to this man if you think he's worth it."

"Okay. Thanks, Dad." Now more than ever she wished she'd found that baseball for him.

After they ended the call, she once again debated calling Jamie, and after a few minutes, she decided against it. There was only one way to distract herself from her heartache. She took out her cello and began to play.

She jumped when her phone rang twenty minutes later.

Amy.

She debated not answering, but the thought of losing the friends she'd made in addition to losing Jamie was too painful.

"Hello?"

"Hi, hon. It's Amy. I was just thinking about you and wondering how you were doing."

Jessica wasn't sure how much to confess to Amy. She was, after all, Jamie's friend first, and she knew how close he and the girls were. She decided to be a little vague.

"I'm okay, thanks, Amy. How's the Cape?" She missed having breakfast with the girls. She missed talking to them and listening to them share advice and give each other a hard time. She never even got to go chunky-dunking.

"It's quiet without you and Jamie here. But you know, it's the Cape, so it's still amazing."

"Jamie's not there? I thought he was there for the summer." He left? His business must be in trouble. *I must have been a worse distraction than I thought.*

"He went back to handle whatever was going on at

work."

"So he's here. In Boston?" Her pulse quickened, even though there was no reason for it. Boston was a big city, and it wasn't like he was there to see her, but still, somehow knowing he was in the same city set a slew of butterflies loose in her belly.

"Yeah. I guess. He left the day after you did. I wish you'd come back. Do you think you can make it up for a weekend? You said you rented the apartment for the whole summer, right?"

Jessica heard the hope in her voice and knew it was genuine. "I don't know. My schedule with the orchestra is really busy, but even if I could, I think it would hurt too much."

"Oh, hon. Have you talked to Jamie yet?"

"No. I can't. It'll just hurt more. I know it's over. I just...I can't believe it. And being there, where we fell in love..."

Amy gasped. "Jamie told you he loved you?"

She couldn't hold back the tears any longer. It felt good to have someone to talk to, to get it out of her system. "Yes. Right before he left to see Mark and never came back."

"Well, Mark's a big turd. I've known Jamie since he was a little boy, and as far as I know, he's never been in love before, so that has to mean something. Don't give up hope."

I already have. "Yeah, it means he either didn't mean it, or that he realized I really was too much of a distraction to be worth it."

"Want me and the girls to come visit you for a night? You're only two hours away."

She couldn't imagine trying to maintain a brave face in front of the girls, and they were Jamie's friends first. She was so confused. Even though Amy was reaching out, what if she came between the girls and

Jamie? She'd never forgive herself.

"No, thank you. I mean, I'd love to see you, but I don't want to put you guys out. Besides, with my schedule, I don't know when I could spend time with you."

"Well, if you change your mind, let me know. And, Jessica, even if you're not with Jamie, you're welcome here. We all miss you."

"Thanks, Amy. I miss you guys, too."

After they ended the call, she went to the den to practice. The roses Jamie had given her were in the window overlooking the park. She smelled the pink and white roses, noting the petals that had fallen to the windowsill, the brown edges of several others. Maybe it's a sign. *Nothing lasts forever.* Even the thought felt wrong.

She went back to the living room and picked up her cell phone.

Call him. Just call him.

She tried to imagine their conversation. She'd apologize for being a distraction, and he'd tell her she wasn't one. But she was, and she didn't have a solution to that. There was no solution. She loved him and she wanted to spend time with him, and having no solution to her being a distraction sucked. Or, she could call and say she missed him. Eventually they'd get back to the whole distraction thing. *Another sucky scenario*. She didn't understand why he didn't tell her the reasons he was ending things. He didn't seem like the kind of guy who would end things like this—and in her heart, she knew he wasn't.

She stared at her phone. *He called. He wants to talk*.

She pressed her voicemail icon and listened to his message again. His voice sent a shiver through her chest. She had to talk to him. She sat on the couch and leaned her elbows on her knees. Holding the phone between her hands, she brought her forehead to it and closed her eyes.

A few minutes later, she called him, and when his voicemail picked up, she froze. *Talk. Talk. Talk.* "Hi. I miss you, and I'm sorry. Oh God, Jamie. I miss you so darn much." She ended the call before she could say anything else and dropped the phone on the couch like a hot potato.

What am I doing? I sound desperate.

I am desperate.

For him.

THE AFTERNOON SUN shone through the window of Jamie's fifteenth-floor office. He'd been elbow deep in computer code since five in the morning, trying desperately to think through the bug that plagued the search engine. The issue had escalated with an article in *Tech News Today* that had already been picked up across too many newswires to count. His analysis was stopped cold every few minutes as thoughts of Jessica broke his concentration. He wondered if she was still on hiatus, and just as fast as that thought entered his mind, he wondered what she was really on hiatus from—sending his mind into a whirlwind of confusion. Why had she made up the story about playing for the Boston Symphony Orchestra? Was she as lonely for him at night as he was for her? A Tilt-A-Whirl ran in slower cycles than his brain lately.

There was a knock at the office door. He stared at it for a moment, debating his escape. He was in no mood to speak to anyone. The door cracked open and his assistant, Amelia Carr, poked her head into the office. Her dark hair fell over her shoulder, almost as long as Jessica's. She had a pensive look on her young face.

"I know you wanted privacy, but Mark Wiley has already come by twice, and he's here again."

The door crashed open, pulling Amelia into the room with it, her hand still glued to the doorknob. Mark pushed past her.

"He'll see me." He sat in the leather chair across from Jamie's desk with a large manila folder in his lap, casual as could be.

Amelia's eyes widened as she inspected her hand, then rubbed her arm.

Jamie glared at Mark on his way to Amelia. "Are you okay?"

She brushed her skirt and blouse, as if she could brush the embarrassment away. "Yes, thank you. I'm sorry. I didn't mean to let him in."

"It's fine. Thank you, Amelia, and I'm sorry for his rude behavior."

She closed the door behind her and Jamie turned on Mark. "You're an ass. She didn't deserve that."

"You're probably right, and if you had seen me the first two times I'd stopped by, I wouldn't have had to barge into the room." His nose was still a little swollen.

"You should have apologized, and when you leave, I expect you to do just that. She's not your issue. I am." The sight of Mark brought back the shattered look in Jessica's beautiful eyes, the tremulous shaking of her arms as she clung to him, her heart broken by what Mark had said to her. Why had it taken Mark hurting someone he loved for Jamie to see him so clearly?

"Even if you might have been right about Jessica, you had no business going after her in such a hurtful way. You had no business slamming past Amelia, and, come to think of it, you sure as hell had no business propositioning Jenna a few years back. You were way out of line, Mark. You have a problem, you come to me. Got it?"

Mark's expression was blank as a piece of paper. "I might have done you a favor. You weren't thinking straight."

With fisted hands, Jamie rose to his feet and leaned across the desk. "You're riding a very fine line right now. Friend or no friend." He gritted his teeth to keep from climbing over the desk and pounding the shit out of him. "Think before you speak, and tell me what the hell you want. If it has to do with Jessica, take your ass out of here, because I don't ever want to hear her name from you again."

Without a word, Mark tossed the manila folder on his desk and walked out of his office, closing the door too loudly behind him.

Jamie stared at the large black letters written across the front. JESSICA AYERS.

"Goddamn it."

Jamie picked up the envelope and sat in his leather chair. He knew what was inside without looking. Goddamn Mark had done a background check on her without Jamie's permission. Worse than that, he'd done it when Jamie had specifically told him not to.

Between a rock and a hard place didn't come close to describing Jamie's position. Mark had risked their friendship and gone against his direct order—and Jamie knew he was just looking out for him and for OneClick, the way he always had.

Fuck.

He ran his fingers over the envelope. One read would tell him everything he wanted to know, from her work history and previous addresses all the way down to traffic citations and, knowing Mark, a list of the men she'd dated in the past twelve months. He was nothing if not efficient.

And he was a complete ass to women.

To Jessica.

Jamie tossed the envelope on his desk and paced his large office, which was lined with windows overlooking a park and furnished with mahogany and leather. Jamie had chosen this office over the corner office that offered windows on two sides. The corner office overlooked the street, which offered nothing to Jamie other than noise and distraction. The green lawn of the park, people strolling rather than rushing from one destination to the next, offered him relaxation, inspiration, reminders that life was about more than what existed in the four walls of his office.

He breathed deeply, trying to clear his head, and gazed out the window. A young family with two small children bought food from a street vendor and then walked into the park. The mother wiped the little boy's face, then kissed his cheek. The father put his arm around her as the kids skipped a few feet ahead, and Jamie's mind went to Jessica. He'd never considered settling down before meeting her. He'd never met a woman who had made him feel so much, want so much—for both of them.

Did it really matter what she did for a living? She obviously played the cello, and he didn't care if she did it professionally or for shits and giggles. He saw the way she was carried away when she played, the blissful look that drew her eyes closed and her body to move through the motions of playing in an ethereal fashion. She was a beautiful woman, but when she played, she radiated happiness; her movements were fluid and even more graceful. He sighed with the memory, exhaling all of the tension that had buried itself in his muscles. He'd felt the same happiness coming from her when he was buried deep inside her, their bodies joined as close as two people could be, their hearts opening more to each other with every embrace, every kiss, every breath.

Jamie glanced at the envelope again and sank into his chair. She'd lied to him. Wasn't that enough? Shouldn't he forget her? Move on?

He thought about the issue he was working on and the long journey it had taken for him to reach the pinnacle of his career. The years spent meeting with executives, building capital, working eighty-hour weeks while everyone around him told him he was wasting his time. Spinning his wheels. Going up against an eight-hundred-pound gorilla that no one could compete with. Still he'd pushed forward, driving himself harder, working his fingers to the bone, because after all, Google had started somewhere, hadn't it? What made the founders of Google better than Jamie Reed?

The people who had been there from the beginning and encouraged him rather than try to dissuade him were Vera, Mark, and his Seaside friends. They believed in *him*. They'd never doubted that he'd do what he intended. And yet the only people he'd ever spoken to about his most intimate, hurtful time, when he'd lost his parents, were Vera and Jessica. He'd sidestepped the details around even his Seaside friends. But he'd opened up to Jessica in less than a week.

That had to mean something.

The phone on his desk beeped, and Amelia's voice came over the intercom. "Excuse me, Jamie?"

"Yes, Amelia?"

"The management team is ready to meet with you in conference room three."

He had to pull his head together and dig deep if he was going to find the root of this issue in miles and miles of code. "Thank you."

He scrubbed his hand down his face, still thinking

about Jessica. He couldn't reconcile the look in her eyes as being that of someone who was lying. No matter how hard he tried, no matter how much the pieces weren't fitting together in the real world, in his gut, and more than that, in his heart, he believed she'd been honest with him from day one, despite the fib about the cell phone not being hers. He smiled at the memory of her clocking him in the head with it.

Before going to the meeting, he made two phone calls. The first was to one of Blue's brothers, Gage Ryder. Gage was a sports director for No Limitz, a community center in Allure, Colorado, where he developed and ran sports programs for teens. He was well connected in the sports world, thanks to having played Division 1 baseball in college and being scouted by the major leagues. His father had played professional baseball, and Gage had seen firsthand how the rigorous travel and practice schedule affected their family. He'd chosen not to go that career route, in hopes of one day having a more stable and less stressful family life.

Jamie's call went to voicemail. He left a brief message. "Gage, it's Jamie Reed. I need a favor. Call me when you get a chance."

The second call he made was to Kurt Remington. Kurt's brother Sage was well connected in the arts community and could get him tickets for anything at the spur of the moment. He didn't want to rely on reports; some things he needed to see with his own eyes to believe. He hated to call in so many favors at once, but if ever there was a time he needed them, it was now.

After talking with Sage, he picked up his files, laptop, and the envelope, and headed into the meeting.

Chapter Twenty-One

"FIVE MINUTES." CHARLIE patted Jessica on the back and lowered his voice. "It's nice to have you back."

"It's nice to be back." It was Monday evening, and they were already playing the second concert of the week. Although Jessica was prepared, her stomach was queasy and her hands were shaky. Not sleeping and eating very little was not a good combination for such a rigorous schedule as the one she'd had to keep lately, but apparently this was what being heartbroken did to a person. She had no experience with this sort of thing, and she wasn't enjoying it one bit. Going from hopeful to hopeless, then finding an inkling of hope to cling to again—even if made up in her own head. *He'll call. He'll hear my voice on his voicemail and miss me just as much as I miss him*. She had no idea how women went through this roller coaster of emotions over and over, some starting as young as high school.

Charlie leaned in closer. "I was going to wait to tell you, but it's too exciting to keep to myself. You're going to be invited into the Chamber Players. The formal invitation is forthcoming." He squeezed her arm and smiled, then put a finger up to his lips.

Jessica couldn't have responded if she'd wanted to. She was stunned silent.

An invitation to play with the Boston Symphony Chamber Players would be the pinnacle of her career, what her mother had always hoped she'd achieve. The icing on her already perfect career cake, and still, her heart ached.

"I..." She couldn't figure out how to express what she was feeling. She knew she should feel overwhelming joy and pride, but she felt numb. Any happiness she was supposed to feel was buried deep inside her grief over losing Jamie.

"Exciting. I know. We'll talk." Charlie hurried off to talk with another musician.

The Chamber Players.

How was she supposed to concentrate now? This was the chance of a lifetime, and she was too heartbroken to enjoy it.

"Put your phone away," Greg, another musician, said sharply.

She hadn't realized she had it clenched in her fist. She checked for a return message from Jamie one last time and realized that for a woman who hated cell phones, she'd become awfully adept at texting and checking messages in the last two weeks. She had two text messages. One from Jenna and one from Bella, both telling her they missed her and she should come back to the Cape. Even with the happiness over their friendships, her stomach still took a nose dive when she realized that Jamie hadn't returned her way-too-desperate message.

It's really over.

She tried to swallow past the lump in her throat as she shut the phone off and tucked it into her purse.

Don't cry. Don't cry. Don't cry. She closed her eyes for a beat and conjured up her mother's stern voice. *No pouting. No whimpering. No frowns. Up, up, up with your chin.* Jessica lifted her chin, doing her best to swallow the ache seeping from her heart and filling her chest, tightening her throat, and making her heart race. With another deep inhalation, she recalled her mother's voice again. *Shoulders squared. Eyes forward, serious and happy, happy, happy. Remember, when you're on that stage, there's no place else you'd rather be.*

Shoulders back, chin up, she followed the group to the stage.

There's no place else I'd rather be. There's no place else I'd rather be.

Liar, liar, pants on fire.

AMELIA WALKED ACROSS the conference room where Jamie was meeting with the directors and managers of several divisions, strategizing new ways to track down the drone in their system. The large conference room looked like a war zone, with empty coffee cups scattered around the table, whiteboards filled with strategies for deciphering where the drone in the code might be, and documents and files spread across the large mahogany table. There were twenty-seven managers and directors around the table, each looking worn-out and frustrated, but because of their dedication to OneClick, and in turn, Jamie, they were still there, hours past closing time.

The group continued discussing the issue while Amelia handed Jamie an envelope and whispered, "Sage's contact had this delivered. It's for tonight at eight. It was the best he could do."

Jamie glanced at his watch. *Seven thirty*. "Thank you."

"I had Marcia bring your tux. It's in your office, and she said to tell you not to spill anything on it this time." Amelia smiled at that. Marcia was Jamie's housekeeper. In addition to cleaning, she ran various errands for him, and after six years as his employee, she knew him well.

"Please thank her for me. I'll never make it in time, but maybe I'll catch the tail end."

"I'll tell her."

Jamie turned his attention back to his division managers and programmers. They'd spent hour upon hour trying to track down the damn bug, and still, no one had any clue where to look. There were too many levels of code, too many paths to follow. Jamie was stymied as badly as his staff was, and it made the situation that much more untenable. Jamie was a master troubleshooter, and when it came to coding, whatever his highly effective, experienced staff couldn't handle—which was almost nil—he always could. But after days of going through enough code to scramble his brain, he was still at a loss.

Jamie listened to his top-level managers tossing ideas back and forth and realized that there was only one way to ensure nothing had been missed. It was late, and no one wanted to be there, least of all him, but he had to try to get to the bottom of this.

He addressed the group. "Obviously we're missing something, somewhere, and the only way I can see to do this is to start at the top again. We'll work our way through each level with a fine-tooth comb and find this goddamn drone."

A collective groan rose from the group.

"Jamie, we've gone over this, starting from scratch, for over a week. Do you really think starting from square one is going to help? Maybe we need to start someplace else." Rick Masters was the director of programming at OneClick. He had a wife and three young children waiting at home, including a newborn baby. He looked like he'd been up all night, and Jamie hated to keep him even later, but he had no choice.

"Do you have a specific suggestion of where to start?" Jamie asked. "I'm all ears, Rick, but if we don't find this, you know the consequences."

Computer glitches happened. Users knew that and to a large degree generally overlooked those things, but when an issue lingered, it tended to magnify in the eyes of the public, and the glitch had already hit the media. Not to mention that children and military hardware did not mix. It was only a matter of time until they began losing credibility *and* users at an insurmountable rate, not to mention sponsors.

"I don't know. I just can't imagine that we missed something at the top level," Rick said.

"I hear ya, Rick. And believe me, I have more faith in the people in this room than I have in the Oval Office, which is why I think we start at the very beginning." Jamie held his gaze. *Time to hit home*. "If your son were being bombarded by ads for guns and ammo, would you want us to start at square one, or would you want us to sit and knock our heads against the same wall for another few hours?"

Rick sighed loudly. "Point taken."

"Okay, let's start at the top. We've got kids searching for dragons, toys, games, movies, and videos, and they're resulting in ads for military hardware. What do they all have in common?"

Two hours later, they were still knocking heads. Selfishly, Jamie ended the meeting, and they agreed to regroup in the morning.

Traffic was thick for a Monday night, and as he watched the minutes tick by, his nerves started to get the better of him. He glanced at the sealed manila folder Mark had given him. Maybe he was being stupid, following his heart instead of his head. Mark had never led him astray before. Why would he now? What did he have to gain? Jamie was too nervous to think it through. He debated opening the envelope. It would be the most efficient way to know the truth, but Jessica wasn't a job. Jessica wasn't an employee. She was the woman he'd fallen hopelessly in love with. The woman he thought about night and day, and ached to see, to touch, to love.

He reached Symphony Hall at ten minutes after ten and punched the cracked dashboard as he drove into the lot. He'd missed the concert. *Damn it.* Was this what Vera had been trying to tell him? That he just needed to see for himself that he and Jessica were not meant to be together?

He floored it to the rear entrance where the musicians came and went, still refusing to believe she'd lied.

The devil on his shoulder whispered, *You're a fool. You saw the musicians' roster on the BSO website. She wasn't on it.*

He cut the engine, feeling as though he was living on deep breaths lately. The devil tried to be heard again, and this time Jamie made a deal with him. He was good at deals. *If she doesn't walk out that door, I'll walk away and never look back.*

With his heart hammering against his chest, he stepped from the car and into the dark night. He was parked over to the side, beyond the bubble of lights illuminating the lot. He didn't need strangers thinking he was some poor sap stalking one of the musicians.

The thought made him feel even more stupid. What was he doing standing in a dark parking lot waiting for a woman who probably didn't even exist? *She wasn't on the list.* Jessica Ayers could have been a made-up name, for all he knew. Christ, she could be anyone, anywhere.

And still, he had to see for himself.

He paced in the dark, every second sucking more air from his lungs. Finally, an interminable number of minutes later, the doors opened, and musicians carrying large black instrument cases walked out. Jamie's heart slammed against his chest as he watched them file out, say their goodbyes to one another, then turn and get into their cars. He waited as the parking lot emptied, his hopes deflating further with each passing car.

When the last car left, the remaining air left his lungs in a rush. He couldn't believe it. He'd *felt* her honesty. Felt it!

He was a fool.

An idiot.

Thank God for Mark. He'd never doubt him again.

He went back to the car and grabbed his phone to call him. The message light was blinking. He'd forgotten to turn the volume on after the meeting. Probably Mark wanting to know if he'd opened the fucking envelope. He pressed the voicemail icon and listened to the messages.

The first one was from Mark. *Listen. I know you're pissed, but after you read the docs, call me. I apologized to Amelia, and…sorry, man. The whole thing's a pisser.*

He lowered the phone for a beat. *Fuck.*

Then he lifted it to his ear again as the next message played.

Hi. His pulse quickened at the sound of Jessica's voice. *I miss you, and I'm sorry.* She sounded so sad, so sweet. He reached for the car as his throat thickened. *Oh God, Jamie. I miss you so darn much.*

He turned at the sound of the heavy metal door opening, and beneath the haze of the bulb above the door, he made out two dark forms. A large man and a lithe woman appeared. The man was carrying a large instrument case. The woman carried nothing other than a purse over her shoulder, her arms crossed, shoulders rounded forward as they walked toward the front of the building.

Numb with anticipation, he pressed Jessica's speed-dial number into the phone. He had to talk to her, regardless of his deal with the devil, or what the fucking papers said, or the Internet, or anything else in the entire universe. He had to speak directly to her and hear her tell him that she'd lied.

The phone rang once.

Twice. *Pick up. Pick up.*

He turned at the sound of a man's voice behind him as the phone rang a third time.

JESSICA DUG HER phone from her purse and stumbled at the sight of Jamie's name on her screen.

"Millicent, are you okay?" Charlie caught her by the arm. "Careful in those heels."

It took her a second to remember to respond to her given name. "Mm-hm. I um…I have to answer this. Thank you for carrying my cello." She took it from his hands.

"Are you sure you don't want me to wait? Call you a cab?"

They had planned on sharing a cab, but Jessica could barely think. It probably wasn't a good idea to be in a cab with her manager when she fell apart. She'd need time to recover from whatever Jamie had to say—good or bad.

"No, thank you. I'll get one. Thanks again." She waved as if everything was fine and turned back toward the rear of the building for privacy. The interaction took three seconds, but in those three seconds her legs had gone weak, and she felt like she was riding a roller coaster to an impossible height. Reaching for that shred of hope she allowed herself to dream of a hundred times over the last few days, she made it five steps before needing to lean against the railing next to the building as she answered the call.

"Jamie." She sounded as breathless as she felt.

"Jessie."

She heard the smile in his voice, the tenderness that she remembered, and it stole the rest of her strength. She crumpled to her knees, right there beside the building. The cello case banged against the pavement. She was riding that coaster down. Down, down, down from that impossibly high peak.

"Yes," she whispered as tears streaked her cheeks.

"Jessie. I'm sorry. Please, don't say a word and—"

"Jamie." She swiped at the salty tears sliding between her lips. "I'm sorry I—"

"No, please, Jess. Listen to me." His words tumbled urgently from his lips.

Jessica tried hard to concentrate through her anticipation.

"Jess, I don't care that you lied to me. I don't care who you work for or what you do. I just want to be with you. I don't care if you've slept with a hundred guys, or...Jessie. I love you, and I'm sorry. Please give me another chance."

Breathe. Breathe. Breathe.

"You...you think I lied to you?" Her entire body shook and shivered on the hard pavement. She covered her eyes with her hand. "Jamie?"

"I don't care. That's what I'm trying to tell you, Jess. I love you. I made a mistake. I...I..."

She heard his tethered emotions and knew he was holding back how much he wanted to see her. He sounded just as he had the night on the beach, when he'd wanted to make love to her, and the same way he sounded after they kissed that very first time in the quad, when the bonfire had burned down to embers and the fire between them had come to life.

"I need to see you. Please," he pleaded. "Tell me where you are and I'll come get you."

You think I lied to you? She couldn't bring herself to say it aloud again. She didn't want him to hang up. Couldn't fathom another night apart. "I'm…" Her voice hitched.

"Baby, I'm so sorry. I'll spend my life making this up to you. Please, tell me where you are, Jessie. I can't go another day, another hour without seeing you."

"I'm at the Hall. Next to." Her breath hitched. "The Hall."

"Hall?" He sounded confused.

"Symphony Hall, where we play." She didn't recognize her own voice, could barely hear it.

"Where? Where are you next to it?" His voice grew louder, and she could tell he was walking—or running.

She grabbed hold of the railing and pulled herself up to her feet, clinging to the metal bar for dear life and looking out at the main road. Thankfully, Charlie was gone. He hadn't seen her fall to pieces.

"Boston Symphony Hall. Are you in Boston?"

Silence.

Oh God. No!

"Jamie? Jamie?" Her lower lip trembled, followed by fresh tears as her voice escalated. "Jamie, oh God, Jamie, please be there. Ohgodohgodohgod."

"Jessie."

She spun around and her arm fell to her side. The phone landed on the pavement with a high-pitched crash. Goose bumps chased her rapid heartbeat as she drank him in. In that instant, she knew she must be dreaming. He was too close, and closing the gap between them fast. She was powerless to move a muscle. His strong arms circled her, his big hands pressed against her back, and his heart—his generous, loving, tender heart—beat at the same frantic pace as hers.

"Jessie. Forgive me, please."

"Okay," was all she could manage. She was too confused to think straight. He smelled so good, so familiar. Her throat swelled with emotion, threatening to silence her. She had to figure out what was going on. "What...What did I lie about?"

"I don't know. I don't care." He took her face in his hands, and she saw a flash of the mood ring, still on his finger.

"You kept it." She breathed heavily. "You...You're wearing it."

He smiled—*oh, how she'd missed that smile*—and she felt it all the way to her toes.

"You're here." She grabbed the lapels of his tuxedo and held on tight, with no plans of ever letting go. "And you're beautiful."

"No, Jessie. You're beautiful."

"Kiss me, Jamie. Please, don't make me wait another seco—"

He sealed his lips over hers. His mouth was warm as their tongues met and found their familiar rhythm, as if they'd never been apart. His low moan told her he'd missed her as much as she'd missed him, and when he deepened the kiss, to a hungrier, rougher kiss, she pulled herself tighter against his hard body. His hands moved over her hips, down her ass, up her back, one hand tangled in her hair, the other gripping the curve of her ass. She was his. So very his.

"I've missed you," he said against her lips and tugged her hair back a little, opening her mouth so he could take his fill.

She wrapped her arms around his neck as he slid his lips to her jaw and nipped, then dragged his tongue slowly over the tender spot, drawing a moan from deep inside her. His forehead touched her, and he looked deeply into her eyes. She nearly crashed to the ground again at the well of emotion that lay there. For her. For them.

"Come home with me, and I promise we'll talk, but I need you with me, Jessie. I don't want to let you go again."

She nodded, still shaken to be near him again. He picked up her cello and phone, and wrapped a powerful arm around her waist, pulling her against him so hard that he was practically walking for her.

In the car, she needed to get the rest out of the way before they fell into each other's arms again, because once they did, it might be a very long time before she remembered how to speak. But no words came.

He drove with one hand holding hers, the other on the steering wheel, bringing back memories of when they'd left Marconi Beach and pulled over on the dark side street. A rush of heat shot through her with the intimate memory.

"When you didn't call back, I thought I'd lost you for good." His voice was rough with desire, his eyes were dark and sensual, and as hopeful as she felt.

"I was a distraction and didn't want to make it worse." She glimpsed his reflection in the window. With the starched white collar against his tanned skin and his five-o'clock shadow, he was more handsome than any movie star, but it was his voice that shot to her heart. The love and desire, the hope and apology, all wrapped up in one, made her pulse quicken and her heart feel full.

"No. You were never a distraction. I love you,

Jessie. I was stupid not to come right back to your apartment that night."

She lowered her eyes, catching a glimpse of the stone on the mood ring. Pink and violet. She'd never seen one turn both of those colors at once. *Amorous. Heat. Sensual. Happy. Curious.* She'd memorized all of the meanings in the days they'd been apart.

Jamie pulled down a residential street. The houses sat far back from the road, each different from the next, and, she realized as they drove slowly past them, these were no houses. They were mansions. Sprawling homes with several wings and stories, set on several acres of perfectly manicured lawn. Vera's cottage at the Cape was modest, small even. She hadn't pictured Jamie in anything as lavish as a mansion. She glanced at him again, in his perfectly pressed tux, driving the expensive vehicle that she had somehow overlooked. *How did I miss this?* She must have been so taken with him that everything else fell away. Another trick of love, she assumed.

Jamie turned off the residential road onto a dark, tree-lined street. With the umbrella of trees blocking the moonlight, the road was pitch-dark, save for the beams of the headlights.

"Is this your street?"

"This is my driveway. It's a little long."

They'd been driving on the same dark road for at least three minutes already. No wonder Mark was ridiculously protective of Jamie. Probably every single woman within a hundred miles who knew anything about the Internet was after him.

They rounded a bend and in-ground lights spilled onto the pavement. Aboveground lights illuminated the night like magical fountains, and just beyond the circular drive was a beautiful and unique stone cottage. A round stone tower with a conical roof anchored the home on one side, with various-sized peaked roofs over nooks and bay windows in the recessed center of the home, and a three-car garage rooted on the far side. The ornate variations in size and shape of stone, evident even from the driveway, gave the home a warm, aged appearance.

Jamie parked in the driveway, and before getting out of the car, he took Jessica's hand and, for a minute, gazed into her eyes.

"Jess." His voice was soft as his eyes rolled over her face, neck, and shoulders like a caress. "The way I see it, we have two options. I can carry you up to my bedroom and make love to you until neither of us can remember anything about the last few days, or we can go inside, open a bottle of wine, and clear the air before going any further."

His voice was tender and patient, his words carefully chosen. He didn't move to get out of the car or try to rush her to make a decision. He was just as patient with her as he'd always been, which made the decision even more difficult.

"What if...?" She closed her mouth tight, debating if the question was worth asking. Maybe she should choose making love. She wanted that connection. To be that much closer and lose herself in him the way she had days earlier. But somewhere deep inside her, even though she didn't have experience with this type of thing, she knew that was a bad idea.

"What if we talk, and then something one of us says changes everything?" She didn't want to believe it could happen, but after the last few days, she realized that she didn't know squat about how quickly relationships could go awry.

He slid his hand beneath her hair and stroked the nape of her neck with his thumb. "Then maybe it's better if we do clear the air first, so you have no regrets later. Jess, I love you, and I'm ready to commit regardless of what happens when we talk. Nothing you could say, short of telling me you're a child-abusing heroin addict, will change that."

She laughed at the quirky smile on his beautiful lips as he spoke.

"I would rather know that you're just as committed to me—to our relationship—before making love to you, so maybe it's better if we talk and then decide where we go next."

A nod brought his arms around her in a warm embrace that her body took as an invitation to go soft against him. Talking was not going to be easy.

Jamie held her hand as he guided her through the wide hardwood foyer, over inlaid mosaic tiles in a spacious living room, past a fireplace and several sets of French doors.

"Your home is gorgeous." There were so many textures, she wanted to reach out and touch them all, from what looked like reclaimed wooden planks on the wall, which jutted out at different angles and depths, to the rough stone surrounding the fireplace.

"Thank you. Let's talk in here." He held her hand as she stepped down two deep wooden stairs into a cozy nook furnished with upholstered antique armchairs in rich fall colors, a deep chocolate sofa, and dark wood bookshelves against two-story stone walls. Sconces were placed on either side of two arched windows, making the room even more inviting. But when Jamie turned her in his arms and touched his forehead to hers, she no longer wanted to talk, no matter how inviting the deep sofa and intimate setting was.

"In case you decide that you no longer want to be with me after we talk, I want you to know that I adore you. I know it happened fast, and we only know about a tenth of what we should about each other, but I have never missed anyone as much as I've missed you these last few days, and if anyone knows about missing people, it's me." He pressed his lips to her forehead.

"Let's skip talking and just be close, Jamie. I missed you, too, and I want to be closer. As close as we can be."

His lips curved up, but he shook his head. "On the way inside I realized that I don't want to use our passion as a bandage to cover what happened these last few days. I want to make love to you with a clear conscience, and I want you to have the same peace of mind. You deserve to be cherished. I dropped the ball and doubted."

Doubted?

"Come on, baby." He led her to the luxurious sofa.

She watched him pour the wine at a bar in the corner of the room. He glanced up and smiled as he moved the bottle from one wineglass to the next, and when he came to her side, she couldn't imagine how she'd gone the last few days without him. Jamie handed her a glass and slid in beside her, one arm draped over her shoulder.

"I don't want any secrets between us, Jess. Our relationship can't work if we're constantly looking over our shoulders for skeletons to come out of the dark."

"I know. I've never lied to you, which is why what you said earlier rattled me."

Jamie dropped his eyes to his glass. "I know. I'm not proud of how I've acted. That night I went to meet Mark, I went a little crazy. I punched him and kind of lost my mind over what he'd said to you."

Her eyes widened. She'd never known a man to hit someone else. Especially over her. "You punched him?"

Jamie nodded. "That night, he had me so confused that I didn't know what to believe."

"So, he *made you* doubt me?" Her stomach sank again.

"God, this is so hard to admit. I'm such an idiot. Yes, he said things that made me doubt you a little. I didn't know what to believe, and then you were gone. Jessie, I'm sorry. I'm ashamed for all of it. I should have left his hotel room and gone straight back to you to talk it through, but I was confused, and..."

"And he's your attorney and friend, who has always given you solid advice and looked out for you for all these years regardless of how much of an ass he was to me, or Jenna, or probably half a dozen other women in your life." She lowered her eyes to his hand. The stone on the ring was green. *Worried.*

"Yes. And I know he's a total douche. Christ, I hated how he treated you. I gave him hell for that, and I'll fire him if it'll bring you back to me."

"Jamie, I'm confused. What did he make you doubt about me?"

"I promised to be honest with you, and I will." He exhaled and brought his hand to her shoulder. "I just have to sit with you for a minute in case you decide this is it. I just want this moment to remember."

She had no idea what could be that difficult to talk about. In her life, if there were issues with other musicians, she talked with them. With the few friends she had in the orchestra, she told them when things bothered her and they did the same, without hard feelings. They weren't close friends, but how could this be so difficult? What had she done that would warrant such a reaction? She began to imagine that it wasn't her he was worried about. Maybe he'd turned to another woman for comfort. Oh Lord, that made her a little queasy.

His brows drew together and his lips parted, and just as quickly they closed again.

"Jamie, you're scaring me a little."

"It wouldn't be too far off to say that he had me doubting just about everything about you."

"I don't understand. Why would I ever be untruthful to you?"

"I don't think you would be, but when he said all that he did to me, it made me wonder, and…I'm sure it was a website error," he said with an uneasy smile. "Jess, there's no Jessica Ayers on the musician list for the Boston Symphony Orchestra."

"You looked for me?" Her heartbeat sped up.

"Yes." His jaw clenched, and she could see he had something else to say.

"You think I lied about where I worked? Why? Why would I do that?"

"I never believed that you did. That's why I was going tonight, to see for myself."

"I don't know if I should be mad that you think I lied or happy that you looked for me." She traced condensation on the side of the wineglass with her finger.

"I'm sorry, Jess. I wish I could take it back, but we can't fix the past; we can only learn from it and create a better future, which is what I hope to do with you."

"Jamie, I..." *I want that, too.* But trust was everything in a relationship. Even with her lack of experience, she knew that much. "It wasn't an error. Jessica Ayers isn't on the symphony musician list. Jamie, I have never lied to you about a thing. I never even considered lying to you. When you like someone, you're honest with them. It just goes hand in hand, doesn't it?" She set her wineglass down on the end table beside the couch and rose to her feet.

Jamie watched her intently, his dark eyes narrow

and serious, his thighs tense against his slacks. "Yes, of course. I haven't lied to you either."

"Then why would you doubt me?" Her stomach twisted again and she felt flustered.

"Because Mark is manipulative and..." He stood and paced, then stopped before her, looking impossibly handsome and worried.

Totally unfair. Wasn't she confused enough?

"It's not Mark's fault. He didn't do anything different than he's always done. He pointed out the obvious. I'm not a fast-moving, carefree guy, Jess." He paced again and ran his hand through his hair, which only made him sexier because she happened to love that particular mannerism of his.

Jessica tried to keep up with what he was saying, but she was getting distracted by her feelings. She sat back down on the couch and lowered her eyes to her lap.

"I was never a carefree guy, Jess. Never. Not as a kid, not as a teen, and definitely not as an adult—until I met you. You made me forget that I'm supposed to be chained to my work, that I lost my parents, that there's more to life than working myself into the ground to forget the pain I've buried for so long but never really healed from." His back was to her when he stopped pacing. His broad shoulders rolled forward; he turned slowly, his eyes catching the light from the wall sconce. They were suspiciously damp, shadowed with pain.

"Jamie." It came out as a whisper. She went to him, circled his neck with her arms and ran her fingers through his thick hair. "My full name is Millicent Jessica Bail-Ayers. I use Millicent Bail professionally."

His lips curved up and he squeezed her hand. "I wish you had told me that."

"Didn't I ever?" She tried to recall every second

they'd been together, the things they'd talked about, but her recollections were tangled and fuzzy. Her body wanted to comfort him, hold him, kiss him, help him heal from the loss of his parents, which still plagued him. But her mind was spinning circles about what else he thought she'd lied about, confused about how these types of things could get so convoluted and hurt so badly.

He shook his head. "No. And that shouldn't have mattered. I should have asked you. I should have dealt with it instead of thinking the worst."

She took a step back to ground herself for whatever else was yet to come. "What else?"

She watched his Adam's apple slide up, then down his throat. His hesitation brought her back down to the couch.

"Jamie?"

He knelt before her and placed his hands on the outsides of her thighs. "Jessie. I promised honesty. It would be easier to tell you there was nothing else, but there was. I didn't know what to believe. Mark was throwing things at me, one after another, when I told him I loved you. Asking how long we had really known each other, where you lived, where you grew up. Christ, Jess, I didn't know even the basic things about you, and it didn't bother me at all. Then he reminded me about women I've dated who have pretended to be something that they weren't. He's an ass, there's no doubt, but he's also been my friend. A good friend aside from the asinine things he's said to women. He's had my back and saved me from a lot of shit." He ran his hands up the outsides of her thighs and fisted them in the fabric by her hips. The strain in his voice mirrored that in his face and arms. "Jess, I'm not making excuses, for him or for me. I'm just doing a lousy job of explaining."

"I'm still confused, Jamie. I'm sorry. What on earth did you think I lied about?"

"Jessie, I've been lied to by men and women."

"Jamie. Just tell me." She was breathing harder now.

He closed his eyes, and when he opened them he met her gaze and held it. "I didn't know what to believe about any of it. Where you lived, what you did for a living...how many men you'd slept with."

JAMIE FELT HER body go rigid. *Fuck. Fuck, fuck, fuck.* He had to make her understand before he lost her forever.

"Jess, I...there was so much going on in my head, and things were so messed up. You were crying, I kicked a naked woman out of Mark's room, clocked him and left him bleeding."

Jamie never knew so many things could happen in the space of two breaths. Jessica's eyes went from confused, to appalled, to angry, to distraught. Her face fell flat, her lips drawn south, and he felt her slipping away. She leaned back and turned her head, her eyes cold and distant.

"Jessie, please. I knew you didn't lie. In my heart I didn't think you were playing me, but—"

"But the doubt was there." Her voice was a thin thread. "You weren't sure if you could believe me after I opened my heart to you. Opened my soul and my body, Jamie." Her voice shook. "I know for other women it's easy to open themselves up to men, to let them touch their most intimate parts and to reciprocate." She turned toward him, looking battered and bruised from the inside out.

"Jessie, I'm sorry. I didn't—"

"Please," she whispered. Tears streamed down her cheeks, each one dragging his heart deeper into hell.

"What hurts the most is that it *was* easy to open up to you. To *you*, Jamie, because I trusted you."

Trusted.

"Jess, you can trust me. It was a momentary doubt. I called you that night and wanted to talk about it, but you never called back. I looked for your address online, but there was no Jessica Ayers listed anywhere. I didn't know what to do. You weren't listed with the BSO, so I didn't think I'd find you there. Mark gave me an envelope with what I'm sure is everything anyone could ever want to know about you, and I never opened it. I have no intention of opening it, but you need to know it exists." This time it was him drawing in a hampered breath. "And then...I couldn't take it anymore and I had to see for myself. I called Kurt's brother, and he arranged for me to get tickets for tonight's concert. But the nightmare at my office ran late, and by the time I got there it was over."

Her expression had gone blank.

"None of that matters. You trusted me, and I doubted your honesty." He touched her fisted hands. He loved her hands. They were delicate yet strong, and so very loving when she touched him. It struck him that he might never feel her hands on him again, and it was all he could do to pry himself from her and rise to his feet, feeling defeated by his own stupidity.

"I understand, Jess, but I didn't want to keep anything from you. I wanted you to know where my head was and why. I'll drive you home."

He extended his hand. When she placed her fingers in his, he felt his chest tighten again.

"Jamie?" she said softly.

"Yeah, babe?" He couldn't look at her. It hurt too much to see the disappointment written all over her unhappy face.

"Would you mind if I stayed with you tonight?"

He tried not to hold on to the thread of hope that trailed behind her question, but it was damn hard not to.

"Would I mind? Jess, you can stay with me for the rest of your nights."

"I just..." She looked away, touched her lips with her hand. "I'm not ready to walk away."

Thank God. "Tell me what you want, Jess." He forced his voice to remain even, not too hopeful or smothering, as he sank onto the couch beside her.

"I don't know, exactly." She touched his leg. "The only thing I know for sure is that you were as honest with me as a person can be, and even if you didn't trust me"—she sucked in another uneven breath—"I...My feelings for you are still here." She covered her heart with her hand. "And I don't know if I'm supposed to try to ignore them, which is really, really painful." Tears slid down her cheeks again.

Jamie couldn't help reaching over and wiping the tears he'd caused.

"I'm not sure what I'm *supposed* to do, because I've never been down this road before, but I'm not sure I really care what I'm supposed to do. I can't even think about walking out that door, Jamie. I walked away when I left the Cape, and I thought that was the most difficult thing I'd ever done in my life. But then, just when I was sure it was some big sign about us not being meant for each other, you showed up at the Hall." She tightened her grip on his leg.

"You showed up, Jamie. Part of you trusted me, despite what you read online, or what Mark—who you *do* know and trust—told you." She wiped the tears from her cheeks and breathed deeply.

She'd spoken softly, easily, without anger or venom. Didn't she always? Hadn't she always spoken to him from the heart, without weighing the calculated gain or risk of what her words might cost her, like so many other women before her had done? Not for the first time, or even the tenth, Jamie wondered how he'd gotten so lucky to have been in the right place at the right time to meet Jessica. And how he could have been stupid enough to doubt her.

"Something in your heart still believed in me, Jamie. In *us*. And even though it feels a little like you've sliced my fingers off, I just want to be with you. I'm not sure what it means, or how I'll feel tomorrow, or even in a few hours. But right now, I'm not ready to walk away from us."

Chapter Twenty-Two

THERE WERE THINGS that Jessica was very good at. Dedication to her craft was at the top of the list. Working with others and melding together in a musical environment was another. But lying ensconced in Jamie's arms and trying not to love him was not anywhere on the list. That particular part of her was gawking at the list like the list was a leper. Jamie had offered to make up the guest room for her, but that felt too far from him. She was glad Jamie hadn't tried to be intimate with her before he'd fallen asleep. She somehow knew he wouldn't. He seemed as content to hold her as she was to be wrapped in his arms as he drifted off to sleep, and this...His soft breath against her neck, his chest pressing against her back with each inhalation, the soft hairs on his legs tickling the backs of hers, this felt right.

Her eyes were used to the darkness after she lay awake for almost three hours. During that time she'd discovered things about Jamie that endeared him to her even more. He was a man of gentle, understated comfort and luxury. The king-sized bed was strikingly masculine and dark, with touches of ornate carvings along the ridges of the substantial headboard, which matched the long dresser and the taller one between the windows. His burgundy comforter and cream-colored sheets were soft as satin, though made of something altogether different and lovely. Probably Egyptian cotton with an impossibly high thread count. The comforter was as thick as two high-end comforters others might buy from expensive stores in New York or Paris, but the simplicity of the other elements in the room made them feel understated and modest. From the frosty sconces above the bed and the shaggy, deep throw rug at the foot of the bed to the photographs atop the dressers that told of his years before his parents died, his bedroom felt like a world in and of itself. Like his private hideaway, and in Jamie's arms, she felt like she belonged right there with him.

She turned to face him, and in his sleep he tightened his grip around her with a sated sigh. He'd looked so sorrowful when he'd explained all that he'd gone through, and the reality of his doubting had cut her to her core. But apparently her core wasn't as thin as other women's, because beneath the swollen, raw flesh of that cut, lay something too thick to damage with misunderstandings, the very foundation of what made her the determined cellist that she was. Beyond the pushing and micromanaging of her mother, beyond the desire to please her, lay her heart. And no matter how much prodding and encouragement she was given, it was her heart that she played with, just as it was her heart that had her reaching her hand up to stroke Jamie's cheek.

Lying there in the dark had allowed her to discover things about herself, and she hadn't even been looking. Apparently, she didn't have to look, because her heart led those discoveries as if it were weaving fine fabric, replenishing the frayed edges and thinly worn center of her being, repairing the pieces of flesh that had been cut through with Jamie's admission.

He was right. It would have been easier for him to say he'd only doubted where she worked, but Jamie was a moral, ethical man, good-natured and thoughtful through and through. Hadn't he proven that with the way he took care of Vera? The way he took care of her, up until that very last day? Jamie wasn't about the easy way, and she could see by the way his friends protected him—even if Mark was a mean bastard—that he'd earned that love and dedication moment by moment.

She ran the pad of her thumb over the prickly and soft edge between his scruff and his bare cheek. A low, sweet moan slipped from his lips, and again he pulled her closer. In his cotton tee and her panties, she couldn't feel the planes of his bare chest. Carefully, trying not to move too much and rattle him awake, she slipped the shirt over her head and placed it beside her. All it took was a graze of his chest with her breasts for her entire body to fill with desire and her nipples to remember his touch and rise against him. Her eyes welled with fresh tears again, but the pain from earlier was gone. She pressed her lips to his, selfishly drenching herself in his taste, his scent, his slumbering softness, and, moments later, his strength as his body awoke and his embrace tightened. His breathing became more urgent, and the muscles in his chest, legs, and all the delicious places in between hardened.

His hand slid up to the back of her neck, sending pinpricks from his touch to her toes as he deepened the kiss, and she fell into it. Opening to Jamie again was easy, because she'd never been closed, not any part of her. He breathed air into her lungs, stroking the hairs on the back of her neck, loving her mouth, deeper, more intensely, as salty tears slipped between their lips.

He drew back, inhaling as he touched his forehead to hers and exhaling her name. "Jessie."

Her name carried so much love, it brought certainty. With her heart in her throat, she managed, "I know why I couldn't leave."

His eyes opened, hooded, cautious, as he kissed tears from her cheeks.

"Because I'm yours, Jamie. I think my phone had Jamie radar when I threw it over the deck."

"Even after...?"

She touched his cheek again. "Even after. Maybe because of."

Their lips met again, sweet and loving, as their bodies and minds overcame the crinkle in time that had parted them, filled it in and smoothed it out with every caress, every kiss. Her hands traveled down the familiar planes of his back, hard and warm, to the curve at the base of his spine, where she pressed, bringing his hips to hers.

"Jessie," he whispered, as he trailed kisses over her dimples, down her chin, to the hollow of her neck.

They rolled together easily, as if their two bodies were one. Jessica's back touched the sheets as Jamie's mouth touched her shoulders. He kissed the sides of her breasts, down her ribs, sending shudders of desire between her legs. His mouth moved carefully, as if he were relearning the curves of her body, kissing, loving, sucking every bit of her flesh. Her fingers found his cheek, and he moved from her belly to her fingertips. He kissed each one, then drew them slowly into his mouth. His tongue swirled gently around each one before taking in the next and stealing her ability to think with each erotic stroke. He took her wet fingers and placed them between her legs, then lifted his eyes to hers, and she knew what he wanted. Without hesitation or embarrassment, she held his gaze as she slid her fingers over her slick center, and his eyes went impossibly darker. He gripped her hips and dragged his tongue down beneath her belly button, loving her with open-mouthed kisses along the creases of her legs. Her hand stilled, and she felt his eyes on her, but hers were closed. When he touched her hand and guided it over and back, caressing her wetness, she opened them, unsure if she'd survive the wait to be even closer to him. When he brought his mouth to her, expertly stroking over and around her fingers, a heady moan escaped her lungs. She felt an orgasm clawing at the periphery. Her fingers stopped, unable to function past the need to reach the edge. Jamie lifted her hand and drew her fingers into his mouth again, sucking them dry. He reached up and squeezed her taut nipple, his mouth working miracles down below, and she tumbled over the edge. The world exploded in lights behind her closed lids, fire moved through her veins, and her hips bucked and rocked against his restraint as he held her down with one strong hand.

"Need," she panted. "You."

Jamie moved swiftly up her body and buried the tip of his arousal as he gazed down at her. His biceps flexed, his broad chest slick with sweat, her scent on his lips. His expression was a mixture of desperation and desire.

"There's no going back for me. The moment I'm inside you, Jessie, I'm yours again."

Mine. The most beautiful word she'd ever thought.

"You've always been mine, as I've been yours. We

just took forever to find each other."

He moved into her, filling her so completely with not just the beauty between his legs, but the depths of emotion in his eyes, so raw and real it threatened to drown them both.

And as they fell over the edge together, in a tangle of limbs and lips, sighs and heady pleas, she knew there was no threat of drowning when she was with Jamie, only a sea of pleasure, a world of love, and a promise of truth.

Chapter Twenty-Three

EVERYTHING REALLY DID look better in the light of day, or maybe it was just the view of Jessica sitting on the back patio wearing Jamie's soft cotton tee, bare from the waist down save for her panties. Her long legs were tucked beneath her as she sipped coffee, her eyes on the manila envelope between them. The sight of it made Jamie's muscles cord tight, but Jessica was relaxed as could be as she lowered her cup from her lips and lifted her eyes to him.

"It's not going to open itself," she said with a mischievous smile.

She knew he didn't want to open the damn thing. They'd talked about it after they'd finally pried themselves from each other's arms, briefly, at least. They'd showered and made love again beneath the warm spray of the shower, and they'd discussed the envelope again as they'd dressed—Jessica in one of his fresh T-shirts and him in a pair of faded jeans. She said she didn't want to wear her skirt. *Not yet. I like the feeling of being back at the Cape, where we could just be ourselves. We can deal with the real world after eight o'clock.*

He liked that idea. He liked it very much.

While Jamie called his office, Jessica had retrieved the envelope from the car. He'd protested, not wanting it inside the house, but she'd carried it out back, barefoot and smiling.

"I have nothing to hide, Jamie. Let's see what he's found out about me."

She was teasing him again, egging him on. He had no doubt that she had nothing to hide—he only wished he'd followed his instincts days earlier. But maybe this was what was meant to be.

"The last few days are like a bad memory I'd rather forget. Besides, if I see what's in it, I'm going to get mad at him all over again and fire his ass." He reached for her hand, the memory of the night before coming back to him. Watching her touch herself, open herself to him again, even after everything they'd gone through, all that he'd admitted, she still trusted him without hesitation.

He kissed the back of her hand, knowing he'd never do anything to jeopardize her trust again.

"Jamie, Mark did this because he loves you. I know that now. I understand that, and I can look at it knowing that and not be bothered, the same way that I know that you doubted me because of what you knew of people other than me. We can't hold on to anger and frustration, or it eats away at us." She set her cup down and smiled, then furrowed her brow. "I think, anyway. I'm not one hundred percent certain about this, but that's how I've always dealt with my mother's overbearing personality. She lives vicariously through me, and I know that, so I put up with it. Well, at least I did, until this summer. I'm done putting up with it, but it doesn't mean that I'm going to hold a grudge or be angry when I see her. She loves me. She did what she thought I'd want, or what she thought would be best for me, and I can hardly blame her for doing what she felt was right. I get that now. It's the same with Mark." She pushed her hair from in front of her eyes. "I think I'm going to tell her how I feel. Clear the air, and let it all be water under the bridge so I can move forward. She's my mom. I love her. I think you can do the same thing with Mark, can't you?"

Jamie shook his head in disbelief, then cupped her cheeks and planted a kiss on her luscious lips. "You are remarkable. You're the one he treated so badly, and you're sticking up for him."

"No. I'm definitely not sticking up for him. I'm seeing things more clearly, that's all. When you love someone, you do things that feel right at the time. Sometimes that means hurting someone else—with words or fists." She looked down at his hands, her eyes serious and contemplative. "And other times, you hurt them in other ways, like leaving the Cape, hoping not to cause any more trouble for them."

Jessica moved into his lap and rested her forehead against his. "And if you're lucky, the person you hurt realizes why you did those things, and you work through them and come up with guidelines and understandings that create a safety net around the two of you."

"Like the three-date rule?" He kissed her again.

She rolled her eyes. "That was the one rule I'm glad we broke." She looked away, twisting the ends of her hair in her fingers, and sighed. "You know what?"

"I know lots of *whats*, but probably not the *what* you're asking about." He patted her butt, drawing her eyes back to his.

"That is very true. For a woman with almost no relationship experience, I think I'm getting the hang of it."

"Yeah, you are." He took her in a delicious, greedy kiss. How could he leave the envelope unopened after everything she'd said? Maybe it was time they cleared the air and put this all behind them. "Before we open this, I just want to be clear. You don't want me to fire Mark? After everything? After this?"

She shook her head. "Would you stop being friends with him if he'd been right about me?"

"No, but..."

"Jamie, you have to admit, I have a strange situation with my name, and we did move very fast, and that night, heck, even now, you don't know *where* I live." She handed him the envelope. "But I have a feeling you're about to find out."

His chest constricted as he tore the top of the envelope and withdrew the papers. He held them against his chest. "This is your last chance. I can burn them. There's a fire pit right across the patio. One match..."

She took the papers from him and read the cover letter clipped to the front. Her hand covered her mouth. "Oh, Jamie."

He closed his eyes. "There are matches in the kitchen."

"No, Jamie. You have to read this."

He opened his eyes. "Read it to me."

She shifted her eyes to him, and when she spoke, her voice was filled with compassion, and sorrow, and all the emotions Mark had written and been unable to say.

> *Jamie,*
>
> *If you ever repeat this to anyone, I will take you down slowly and painfully.*

Jamie shook his head. *Mark. Idiot.*

She continued reading.

You know I'm always right. Of course you do. I'm laughing, and know you are, too. It appears that in this instance, I jumped the gun. I know I went against your wishes by checking into Jessica's background, but you also probably knew I would. We've known each other too long for you to expect otherwise. It's why we make a great team. In these pages you'll see that Jessica is everything she's claimed to be, but I've found that she's far more than you led me to believe, or maybe more than you were aware of. All that stuff aside, I'm truly sorry for the pain I caused you both. I know this is big. Huge. You love her enough to hit me, man. I owe you one for that, by the way.

Jessica paused and reached for Jamie's hand. Their eyes connected, and he nodded, wanting to hear the rest of what his friend had to say. She cleared her throat before continuing, obviously as touched by Mark's confession as he was.

I know you might fire me, and I wouldn't blame you, but before you pull that card, remember this one. The dragon and the warrior, through thick and thin, and all things in between. Brothers until the end. Eyes to the sky, Dragon II.

Jessica set the papers on the table and sighed. "See? I guess he knows, or he's learned, more about relationships, too."

"Eyes to the sky." Jamie shook his head with the memory. "We made that up when we were in college. Every time one of us did something stupid, or we broke up with a girl, or blew off a class, we said, *Eyes to the sky. Eyes to the sky*. We never even really defined what it meant. The closest we could come to defining it was to say that whatever we did, whatever mistakes we made, we'd keep moving forward, push ourselves harder to reach whatever it is we were going for at the time. Grades, graduation, business deals." He laughed with the memory.

"What does *dragon and the warrior* mean?"

"Silly nicknames. You know, college stuff. I was the warrior, the one who braved cleaning up Mark's reputation and moving forward with my life despite losing my parents, that kind of stuff. And he..." He shook his head with the memory. "He was always a bit of a snake when it came to women. So we called him the dragon, but that didn't seem strong enough, so I dubbed him dragon II, like the biggest and ugliest of all—" Jamie's eyes widened. "Holy shit. Baby. Baby, you've got to get up." He patted her hips to hurry her from his lap.

Jessica stood. "What's wrong?"

"Nothing. Absolutely nothing. Everything is right." He took her hand and dragged her inside. "Come with me. Holy shit. I can't believe it. That idiot solved the bug in our search engine."

Jessica tried to keep up as he dragged her through the living room and the dining room, and into his office. "Sorry. I'll explain." He booted up his computer and handed her a throw blanket from a chair. "I keep it cool in here; you may need this. When I was in grad school, I put a little Easter egg in the code for the search engine."

She sat on the chair across from his desk and covered her legs with the blanket. "What does that mean? I'm picturing bunnies and chocolate."

"That's because you're the cutest person on

earth." His fingers flew across the keyboard as he cut through miles of cyber security to access the original code. "An Easter egg. A drone. A little piece of code that I created in grad school and totally forgot about until that damn letter." He glanced up at her with no hopes of suppressing his relieved smile or the rapid beating of his heart. "This is the thing we're looking for on OneClick that's pulling up military equipment when kids type in the words *dragon two*."

She gathered her hair over one shoulder and nodded, but her confusion was still evident in her eyes.

Jamie continued working. "We were kids, and to a computer geek, this type of stuff is fun." He glanced up again to catch her smile. "I put this piece of code in the program and totally forgot about it. It was a joke, you know, that one day, just by the law of large numbers, eventually it would rear its head again and we'd laugh."

"Law of large numbers?"

"Yeah, you know. A principal of probability and statistics. As the sample size grows—or in this case, the number of people searching for certain words—its mean will get closer and closer to the average of the whole population. The more people searching, the more the bug appears."

He looked back down at the monitor. "And it's been so long that when it happened, we didn't laugh, because I totally forgot about it. I have to call Mark and tell him. I can't believe this. Jesus, it might have remained there forever, and there's no way our coders would have known where to look."

"*Dragon Two*? Isn't that the name of a kids' movie?"

He was too excited to slow down. "Holy crap, you're right. That's exactly why it's coming up now. A million people are searching the terms *Dragon* or *Dragon Two* on a daily basis." He scanned the screen and typed faster. "I'm sorry, babe. I shouldn't be working when we only have an hour or so left before our real world time starts, but this is vital."

She came to his side and rubbed his shoulders while his fingers flew over the keyboard. "I love that you have a strong work ethic, and I love watching you work. I don't want to take you away from any of this, Jamie."

He slowed long enough to pat her hand, look up at her beautiful face, then went back to work. "You won't. I can't believe it took all of this for us to find this drone." His hands slowed. "It took all of this." He spun in his chair and wrapped his arms around her waist. "As much as I hate to think about it because of what happened to my parents, maybe things really do happen for a reason."

Chapter Twenty-Four

"SO THIS IS where the nonexistent Jessica Ayers lives." Jamie parked in front of Jessica's building. He'd been grinning ever since he'd fixed the coding issue that had mothers all over the world in a frenzy.

Having lived a life that relied so little on the Internet, it seemed odd to her that entire newspaper articles could be written about a search result error, but then again, to those who relied on the Internet, a broken cello would probably seem trivial.

"This is it. It's not very glamorous, but I like it." She'd changed back into her concert skirt, blouse, and heels, bringing her much closer to Jamie's height. He looked handsome from any angle, but she liked being that much closer to his lips, and as they rode the elevator to the top floor she took full advantage. She stood between his legs and kissed him until he was hard as a rock again, and when the elevator doors opened, she walked out with a satisfied grin on her lips.

"So unfair," he mumbled.

With the emotional roller coaster of last night, and

then again this morning, Jessica hadn't had time to process her feelings on the Chamber Players position. Now she felt a little dizzy, knowing she was about to take them from this amazing high to a place of serious discussion again, but she needed to at least share with him that the offer was on the table.

Her two-bedroom loft was a far cry from the spacious home Jamie lived in. She wondered what Jamie was thinking as he crossed the light-colored, wide-planked hardwood floors and passed the arched windows that overlooked the park. He picked up photographs of her family from her bookshelves as she went to her bedroom to change.

She was zipping her jeans when he came to the doorway and leaned casually against the edge of the doorframe, holding a photograph in his hand.

"You're beautiful, Jess. Maybe I should skip work today."

"Don't even tease me with that. You just solved the world's dragon dilemma. I'm sure your employees will want to cover you in roses or something." She loved the way he laughed, a masculine sound that came from deep in his lungs.

"More like throw them at me." He came to her side as she pulled on her top.

"Are these your parents?" He showed her the photograph he was holding of her with her parents, taken a few years ago after one of her concerts. She and her father were smiling wide; her mother's face was more serious, though still smiling. It was a strained smile, a familiar one to Jessica. Her mother's emotions were always tethered.

"Yeah, it was taken after a concert a while ago."

Jamie settled a hand on her hip. "You look a lot like your father."

"I know. He blessed me with his dimples. When I

was little, he used to tell me that we had them because an elf came into our bedrooms when we were babies and stole the divot of skin for good luck. He concocted a whole fairy tale about how the elves planted the divots and grew these glorious forests of good luck trees." She pictured the way her father's eyes lit up, and if she tried hard enough, she could hear the hushed tone he used to tell his tale. The memories were comforting.

"I love that idea."

"Me too. Jamie, you never finished reading the information Mark gave you about me."

He pulled her closer to him and kissed her softly. "I know. I'm not worried about that. I know everything I need to know."

"There is one more thing I need to tell you. It's a big thing, and I can't believe I didn't mention it yet, but we've been so sidetracked..."

"A big thing?" He sat on her bed and patted the bedspread beside him.

She sat beside him, and he draped an arm over her shoulder.

"Give it to me straight." He smiled at the joke.

"Okay." She felt a wave of excitement wash through her—an emotion that she now realized she'd been ignoring. Or maybe she'd been too upset to realize it was there. Whatever the reason, she couldn't ignore the pride she felt as she explained. "Well, last night, before the concert, my manager told me that I was going to be invited to play as one of the Chamber Players for the orchestra."

Jamie's eyes widened. "That's good news, right?"

"Well, it's big news." Her pulse accelerated. "At my age, it's really pretty phenomenal, but it comes with more commitments, and with our relationship, I'm not sure it's the best move for me. For us."

"What do you mean?"

"I mean, if I continue playing with the orchestra, there are times I'll have to travel. And I told you that I practice sometimes three or four hours a day *and then* go to work late into the evenings. It's not exactly conducive to a relationship, or a family."

"It's not?" Jamie's eyes grew serious. "I never realized that, because my grandmother played and she raised my mother somehow. And although she wasn't playing with an orchestra when I was growing up, there were times that she played with different groups, and my grandfather took me to see her play or spent the evenings with me. They worked it out."

"Yes, but you have Vera to take care of, and you have an entire empire, according to Mark. I can't be a distraction, or drag you away from what you've worked so hard to build, or from the woman who raised you."

"No, you really can't." He drew his brows together and his mouth formed a tight line.

Her stomach lurched. *No, you really can't.* Hadn't she known it might come to this? Hadn't she dreamed of other things while she was at the Cape? Maybe teaching cello instead of playing for an audience? She hadn't felt sad when she contemplated those things at the Cape. But after coming back and playing again and being accepted into the Chamber Players, she realized how much she enjoyed playing for the orchestra, even if the schedule was grueling. She reached for Jamie's hand. She loved him more than she loved playing. That much she knew, and she could still play, just for a different group. She could make this concession for them.

"I won't take the position. I've been thinking about doing something different anyway. Maybe teaching cello or something."

Jamie lifted her chin so they were eye to eye and pressed a kiss to her lips. "Jessie, you can't drag me away, because I'm too big for you to *drag* anywhere. I can make my own decisions. I want to support what you've worked your whole life for. I'm proud of you, for how beautifully you play, for your determination." He kissed her again. "For being willing to give it all up for us. But there's no need. I want you to live your dream, not push it aside. So we'll travel a little, and you'll work late at night, just like I program late at night. We're the perfect pair."

She couldn't believe he was saying all of this so easily, like he meant every word, which she was sure he did, but how could it work?

"But Vera?"

"Vera lives in the assisted living facility around the corner from my house when it's not summertime. She's well cared for. I see her after work because I can and because I haven't really had much of a reason not to. If you wouldn't mind, she might want to travel with us sometimes, if she's able, to see some of your concerts."

"Jamie—" She flung herself into his arms. "Really? You don't mind? She wouldn't hate me for taking you away?"

He took her face in his hands and gazed into her eyes. "Babe, Vera would be more upset if you gave up a chance to live your dream. Her only hope is that I'm happy. I love her, but I don't need to give up living my life to care for her, and she'd never want me to."

"But what if one day we decide to get married, and we want kids? I'm not saying we are, or we will, or trying to push you." He was searching her eyes, and she was talking so fast that she couldn't stop. "I'm just thinking long-term, because I don't think I could take it if we dated for a couple years and then broke up because you wanted kids and my career made it too hard. Not that I wouldn't give up my career for kids. But what if—"

He pressed his lips to hers, swallowing her words and all her worry along with them.

"Breathe," he said against her lips.

She did, and he kissed her again.

"You okay?" He held both her hands in his.

Jessica nodded, but she was anything but okay. Her heart felt like it was going to crash through her chest and leap the distance between them just to be closer to him. Her mind spun in circles, trying to figure out if he really understood what she was saying, but before she could ask, he was kissing the back of her hand again, sliding one hand to the nape of her neck in that way that made her insides go all warm and mushy and gazing lovingly into her eyes.

"I love kids. And if you're enjoying the orchestra when we decide to get married and have children, then we'll figure it out. I'll do as my grandfather did, and gladly take care of them. Neither of us has to give up what we love to have this relationship or a family. Odd hours? Long practices? More time for me to do my geeky man things, and I love to travel."

She exhaled a breath she felt as though she'd been holding for three days and wrapped her arms around his neck. "Just one more question."

"You've used up your allotment, but I might dole out an answer for another kiss."

"Are all men this easy?" She kissed him then, and in one quick move he rolled her onto her back and braced himself above her.

"I don't date men, so I can't answer that question."

As he lowered his lips to hers, she whispered, "I think Mark was wrong. You're not a warrior at all. You are my knight in comfy armor."

Chapter Twenty-Five

OVER THE NEXT two weeks their lives fell into sync, feeling less like a frantic gigue and more like a romantic rhapsody. Jamie worked around Jessica's schedule, and she around his. And for those times when they felt as though they'd gone too many hours without seeing each other, Jamie taught Jessica how to use FaceTime, and they connected that way. It was a strange feeling to know that the man she loved was only an icon away from her at all times. They'd FaceTimed twice this week. Once when she was scheduled to play in an evening concert and he'd had a late meeting, and once when he'd gone for a run and missed her in the forty minutes he was gone. He'd stopped running and FaceTimed her, sweaty and panting from an uphill sprint. Technology, it turned out, wasn't such a bad thing after all.

Finding time together wasn't as crazy as Jessica had imagined. Jamie really did enjoy working at night, and on the nights she wasn't playing with the orchestra, she often waited to practice until he was working. To a large degree, Jamie had been right.

Jessica had so little experience with relationships and life outside of the orchestra that creating a life for themselves wasn't nearly as difficult as she'd anticipated it would be. It took some coordinating, but they were even able to finagle two nights up at the Cape.

The flames of the bonfire danced in the center of their circle of benches and chairs on the quad at Seaside. Everyone had been so happy to see them together that they'd made a big show of preparing a barbecue, complete with margaritas—of which Jessica knew to have only one, so she could focus on her hunky man later in the evening. And focus on him she did. Before the girls came to get her to go chunky-dunking, Jamie lay beside her in the bed where they'd first made love. Their bodies glistened with sweat, each sated and spent.

"I never want to leave the bedroom again," he'd said sleepily.

"Unless they make beds with twenty-seven-inch monitors, I'm pretty sure your geeky side will need to be satisfied at some point," she'd said. It was a joke of theirs. His life was as ensconced with technology as hers was depleted of it.

She'd turned to kiss him and he'd already fallen asleep. She'd slipped out of the house when Amy, Bella, and Jenna had come to get her, after Caden and Peter had fallen asleep, too.

"We have to get Leanna," Amy whispered.

Dressed only in towels and flip-flops, they held on to each other as they headed for Leanna's house.

"Kurt…Right there."

Jessica grabbed Amy's arm and froze as Leanna's voice filtered out the open window of their cottage.

"Is that…?" she whispered.

"Yes. She forgets to close her window," Amy

explained.

Jessica wondered how much they'd heard of her and Jamie making love. She wasn't exactly quiet as a mouse.

Bella dragged Jenna toward the pool. "We'll go without her."

They hurried down the gravel road. Jessica's heart beat so fast with anticipation she couldn't stop smiling. "I've never broken rules like this before."

"Yes, you have," Amy reminded her. "Thong Thursday, remember?"

"Yeah, but I didn't *know* I was breaking the rule. It's different."

Bella slung an arm over her shoulder. "Well, get used to it. You're a Seaside sister now, and this is what we do."

A Seaside sister. She wondered if she'd ever get tired of hearing that, or if it would always carry the same thrill it did now. It was almost as good as hearing someone call her Jamie's *girlfriend*.

Jenna wrestled with the lock on the fence. The thick metal chain clanked and rattled.

"Shh!" Bella grabbed the chain, glaring at Jenna.

"I'm trying. It's stuck." Jenna tried shoving the key in again.

"You need to caress it, not jam it," Amy instructed.

"How would you know? The last time you caressed or jammed a long thing into a hole was a long time ago." Jenna laughed.

Amy swatted her arm. "You're a pig, and you have no idea how long it's been."

"Well, I know you and Jake didn't do the dirty because you never came back from a date smiling like a Cheshire cat." Jenna gritted her teeth and gave one more quick turn of the key. The lock sprang open and she bounced on her toes and beckoned them in.

"Hurry. Hurry!" She closed the gate quietly behind them.

"We usually put our towels by the stairs," Amy said as she guided Jessica toward the far end of the pool.

Jenna ran by them naked, her butt cheeks bouncing, arms crossed over her enormous breasts. "Brr."

"Why did she run from back there?" Jessica whispered.

"She always does. It's a Jenna thing." Amy slipped out of her towel and walked straight past Jenna, who was shivering on the first step, and into waist-deep water, then ducked down until she was covered up to her shoulders. "It is cold, so you have to get right in."

Jessica dropped her towel and followed Amy. Jenna grabbed Jessica's arm as she stepped into the water.

"Let's go in together," Jenna whispered.

They walked down the steps, holding hands, and submerged themselves up to their shoulders, as Amy had.

"Look, I'll never drown." Jenna looked down at her boobs bobbing at the surface and laughed.

Amy and Bella shushed her in unison.

"Sorry," she whispered. "Doesn't it feel good to be naked in the water?"

"Yeah. I never knew it would feel different." Jessica looked up at the apartment, thinking about how good it would feel to make love to Jamie in the water.

Bella dove under the water from the deep end and broke through the surface in the middle of the pool. Moonlight reflected off the water as they doggie paddled around the deep end, each taking hold of a noodle or a raft.

"Vera was so happy to see you and Jamie together again." Bella hung with her arms over the foam noodle.

"Yes, she was," Jessica said. "When Jamie asked her if she'd mind if we spent the night at the apartment, since I've paid through the end of the summer, she said we could sleep anywhere we wanted as long as we were together. Wasn't that sweet?"

"Really sweet," Amy said. "While you guys were gone, she kept talking about how you were meant to be together. I heard her tell Jamie that she was glad the air had carried him in the right direction. I'm not sure what that meant, but he hugged her really tight, so he must have understood."

"Air? I have no idea either, but I'm glad we're together. You guys don't know this about me, but I haven't had many relationships, and I swear to you, the sadness felt like it could drown me at any second. And getting through every minute was like wading through concrete."

"We've all been there way too many times," Bella said in a quiet voice. "You're lucky you haven't had to go through it much."

"Well, I don't know how you survived it more than once." Jessica shifted the noodle beneath her arms. "Hey, what do you do if Theresa shows up? I mean, we're naked."

"She's fast asleep. She caught us last summer, and Jenna told her we were cleaning up around the pool or something," Amy explained. "Then the dingdong asked her if she wanted to go skinny-dipping."

"Well, you left the cookie dough wrappers down here, remember?" Jenna swam over to the side of the pool. "Speaking of cookie dough…"

"I don't have any," Amy whispered.

"Me, either." Bella swam to Jenna's side. "Some person under five foot tall ate all of mine."

"I was having a meltdown." Jenna feigned a frown.

"Why?" Jessica asked.

"Petey reorganized my rocks on the deck. It totally threw me off."

Amy mouthed *OCD* to Jessica.

"I have cookie dough. Jamie and I bought some to make cookies for the barbecue but then forgot." She let go of the noodle and kicked her feet to stay afloat.

"Want me to go get it?"

"Yes!" the others whispered.

Jessica laughed and swam to the shallow end of the pool. Eating cookie dough after midnight, swimming in a pool naked...She never would have imagined herself doing these things. Ever. And now she couldn't imagine ever not doing them, with these friends. She climbed from the pool and Bella whistled.

"Hottie on deck," Bella said quietly.

"Yeah, right." Jessica wrapped her towel around herself, slipped on her flip-flops, and hurried toward the gate. "I'll be right back."

She passed Tony's cottage and ran across the gravel road, then took the steps to the apartment as quietly as she could. Inside, the apartment smelled like Jamie. She turned to close the door as quietly as she could.

"Hey, babe."

"Ack!" She spun around and found Jamie sitting on the couch in his boxer briefs. "Holy cow, you scared me."

He arched a brow and smiled. "Because robbers often address you as babe?"

She sat beside him in her towel. "No, because you're supposed to be asleep."

"So you can play naked without me? I like to play naked with you." He tugged teasingly at her towel.

She turned away with a soft laugh. "I need to get

the cookie dough."

He arched a brow.

"We're chunky-dunking."

"There's nothing chunky about your sweet little body, but uh…I've got a little something chubby in my drawers that would like to do a little dunking." He nuzzled against her neck.

"Oh my God, you feel good." Goose bumps raced up her arms. "That's not fair."

"Why?" he whispered against her ear.

"Because they're waiting for me, and…oh God, I love when you kiss my neck."

"Mm-hmm."

"Wait. Stop." She pressed her hands to his chest and pushed him away. "This is bad, bad, bad. What kind of a friend am I if I promise to bring them cookie dough and fall into bed with you instead? They need cookie dough."

Jamie sat back. "Blown off for cookie dough. That's a new low."

She pressed her lips to his. "I promise to make it up to you after we're done."

"Sounds like a plan." He drew her into an embrace. "That's not really why I was out here."

"Oh. Why were you?"

"Because I thought you were coming in for the night, and I wanted to surprise you with something."

"What is it?"

"Don't you have cookie dough to deliver?" His lips curved into a teasing smile, and he pulled her into his lap. "Are we still having dinner with your parents when we get back to Boston?"

"Yes, Monday night. Why?" Her father had been overwhelmingly happy for them, while her mother had said she was happy, with no change in the inflection of her voice. She'd followed that statement with a question about how their relationship would impact Jessica's career. Her mother's reaction had been a harder pill to swallow than she'd anticipated, but Jessica had drawn upon the advice she'd given Jamie about not blaming Mark for his wanting to protect him. She'd taken that advice and bitten her tongue.

"Remember the day we met?"

"Of course. How could I forget? You walked up to the deck and stole my heart with your smile."

He rolled his eyes. "Before that."

"When I pegged you with my phone?" She rubbed his head. "I'm so sorry about that…sort of. If I hadn't, we'd never have met."

He smiled. "Right. Totally worth it."

He reached behind him and handed her a clear glass box. She peered inside. It was hard to see in the dark apartment, but there was no mistaking the shape of the baseball, or Mickey Mantle's autograph colored in with red Magic Marker.

"Jamie," she whispered. She squinted, turned the glass in her hands so she could see each side. "How on earth…?"

"Let's just say that that little boy likes Mickey Mantle's clear signature a whole lot more than he liked the colored-in one."

She couldn't believe it. She'd given up so easily, and not only had he not given up, but he'd kept it a secret this whole time.

"I can't believe you did this. Do you know how happy my father will be?" Her eyes welled with tears.

"I knew how happy it would make you to give it to him." He brushed her wet hair from her shoulder.

"We'll both give it to him. Thank you, Jamie. This is the nicest thing anyone has ever done for me."

"Jessica? Are you in there?" Jenna's whisper came

through the front window.

Jessica covered her mouth with her hand, feeling guilty for taking so long and still reeling from Jamie's thoughtful gift.

"Of course she is," Bella said. "Where else would she be?"

"She probably went back to bed with Jamie," Amy added.

Jamie gathered her in his arms and whispered, "I'm about to do something even nicer for you and pretend I'm asleep so you can go eat cookie dough naked with the girls, when what I really want to do is put that cookie dough all over you and nibble it off."

He took her in his arms and crashed his mouth over hers, pressing her back to the couch. Her body went hot and soft all over, while his went hard above her.

"I think she's sleeping," Jenna whispered. "I see the edge of the couch. I see her feet. I think."

Jamie tore his lips from hers and pressed his finger over her lips. Jessica opened her mouth and twirled her tongue around his finger, earning her a heated stare and a press of his hips to hers.

"Let me see," Bella whispered. "Those aren't feet. Oh wait, yes, they are. Wait."

"Oh God! It's her and Jamie!" Jenna laughed. "Guess there's no cookie dough for us tonight. Go, go, go."

As their feet scampered down the steps, Jessica pushed out from beneath Jamie and grabbed the cookie dough, then flung open the front door and hurled it over the deck, pegging Bella in the back.

"Ow! What the...?" Bella said. She and Jenna bent over and searched the ground, finally spotting the cookie dough.

Jenna snagged it and waved it over her head at Jessica. "Thanks, babe!" she yelled. "Go, go, go." She shooed Jessica back inside.

Jessica shut the door feeling like she'd come home to the friends and the man she was meant to be with. Jamie closed the distance between them, sealing his lips over hers again.

"Sorry," he said against her lips. "I suck at pretending."

"Then don't pretend." She dropped her towel. "Think you can bring me more pleasure than that cookie dough would have?"

The End

Please enjoy a preview of the next
Love in Bloom novel

Seaside Secrets

Seaside Summers, Book Four

Love in Bloom Series

Melissa Foster

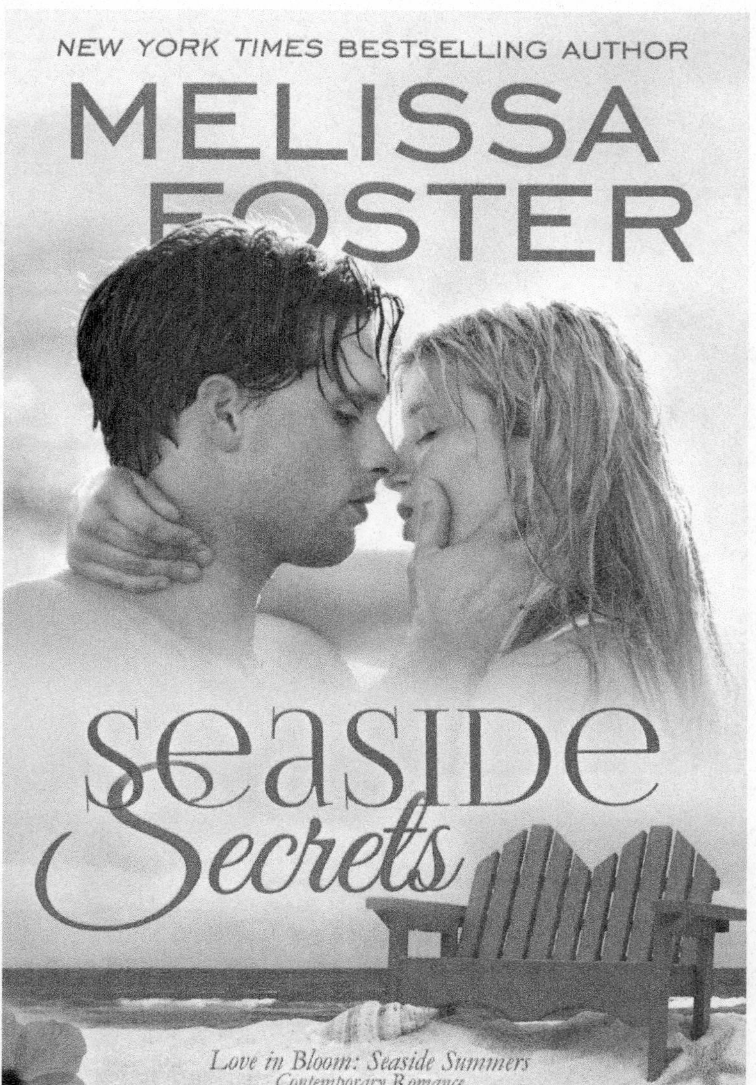
NEW YORK TIMES BESTSELLING AUTHOR
MELISSA
FOSTER
Seaside
Secrets
Love in Bloom: Seaside Summers
Contemporary Romance

Chapter One

"I JUST CAN'T believe that Jamie's the first one to get married. I mean, Jamie? He never even wanted to get married." Amy Maples was three sheets to the wind, sitting in a bar at the Ryder Resort in Boston. That was okay, she rationalized, because it was the night before her good friends Jessica Ayers and Jamie Reed's wedding, and she and her friends were celebrating. Besides, now that Jessica and Jamie were getting married and her other three besties had gotten engaged, Amy was the only single woman of the group. Drunk was the only way she was going to make it through the weekend.

"But that was before he met Jessica and she rocked his world." Jenna leaned across the table in the dimly lit bar and grabbed Amy's hand.

Amy saw Jenna's lips curve into a smile as she shifted her eyes to Tony Black, another friend they'd known forever, sitting with his arm around Amy, as per usual. Jenna raised her brows with a smile, implying something Amy knew wasn't true. She rolled her eyes in response. Tony always sat with his arm around her, and it didn't mean a damn thing, no matter how much she wished it did.

Amy and her besties, Jenna Ward, Bella Abbascia, and Leanna Bray, had grown up spending summers together at the Seaside community in Wellfleet, Massachusetts, and to this day they continued to spend their summers there, along with Jamie and Tony. The six of them had spent eight weeks together every summer for as long as Amy could remember. Their parents had owned the Seaside cottages, which they'd passed down to them. Summers were Amy's favorite time of year. Now that Amy's company, Maples Logistical & Conference Consulting, was so successful, she was able to take eight weeks off while her small staff handled the workload. Amy had spent seven years building and nurturing the business, and over the last three years she had turned it into a six-figure venture with clients varying from accounting to full-on logistical consulting. She could hardly believe how her life, and her summers, had changed. Just four years ago she was working part-time during the summers at one of the local restaurants to keep a modicum of income coming in. She loved summers even more now that she didn't have to work. Of course, her love of summers might also have something to do with being in love with the six-foot-two professional surfer and motivational speaker currently sitting beside her.

If only it were reciprocated. She tipped back her glass and took another swig of her get-over-Tony drink.

"Petey, can you please get me another drink?" Jenna batted her lashes at her fiancé, Pete Lacroux. She and Pete had gotten engaged last year. Pete was a boat craftsman and he also handled the pool maintenance at Seaside. Pete nuzzled against her neck, and Amy slid her eyes away. Maybe if Sky, Pete's sister, were there, she'd feel a little better. Sky wasn't currently dating anyone either, but Sky had to work, so Amy was on her own.

Bella and her fiancé, Caden Grant, were whispering nose to nose, Leanna was sitting on Kurt's lap with her forehead touching his, and Jamie and Jessica were looking at each other like they couldn't wait to tear each other's clothes off. Amy stole a glance at Tony, and her heart did a little dance. Delicious and painful memories from the summer before college tried to edge into her mind. As she'd done for the past fourteen years, she pushed them down deep as Tony leaned in close.

God, she loved how he smelled, like citrus and spice with an undertone of masculinity and sophistication. She knew he wore Dolce & Gabbana's The One. She kept a bottle of The One beside her bed at home in Boston, and every once in a while, in the dead of winter or on the cusp of spring, when months stretched like eons before she'd see Tony again, she'd spray the cologne on her pillow so she could smell him as she drifted off to sleep. It never smelled quite as good as Tony himself. Then again, Tony could be covered in sweat after a five-mile run, or laden with sea salt after a day of surfing, and he'd still smell like heaven on legs. Since they were just friends, and it looked like there was no chance of them becoming more, she relied on her fantasies to keep her warm. When she was alone in bed at night, she held on to the image of Tony wearing only his board shorts, his broad shoulders and muscular chest glistening wet, muscles primed from the surf, and those delicious abs blazing a path to his—

Tony pressed his hand to her shoulder and pulled her against him, bringing her mind back to the present.

"Time for ice water?" he asked just above a whisper.

So much for her fantasy. She was always the *good girl* who did the right thing, the only exception being occasionally having an extra drink or two when she was with her Seaside friends. At least that's what she led everyone to believe. Only she and Tony knew that wasn't the only exception—and she made sure that was a taboo subject between them. He wouldn't dare bring it up. She might not survive if he did. She sobered a little with the memory and shifted it back into the it-never-happened place she buried deep inside her. Her secret was lonely in that hollow place, being the only one kept under lock and key.

She met Tony's denim-blue eyes and felt a familiar rush of anticipation in her belly. Maybe tonight she wouldn't be the good girl.

"Um, actually, I think I want another drink."

Tony arched a brow in that sexy way that made his eyes look even more intense. He pressed his cheek to hers and whispered, "Ames, you can't show up for the wedding tomorrow with a hangover."

No, she certainly couldn't. But she'd like him to stay right where he was for a while longer, thank you very much. Since she had a life-changing job offer in hand—a dream job worthy of closing down the business she'd spent seven years building and keeping only a handful of clients—she and her girlfriends had decided it was time for Amy to take a chance and lay her feelings on the line with Tony. She picked up her glass and ran her finger around the rim, hoping she looked sexy doing it. Then she sucked that finger into her mouth, feeling a little silly.

I suck at this whole seduction thing.

"I'm a big girl, Tony. I think I know what I can

handle." *And I don't want to handle my liquor tonight. I have plans. Big plans.*

Tony rose to his feet with a perturbed look on his face and rubbed his stubbly jaw. "You sure?"

"Mm-hm." Even as she said it, she considered saying, *Water's good. Just get me water.* She watched him walk up to the bar. At heart, Amy was a good girl. Her courage faltered and she tried to hang on to a shred of it. She needed to know if there was even the slightest chance that she and Tony might end up together. The problem was, she wasn't a seductress. She didn't even know where to begin. That was Jenna's forte, with her hourglass figure and sassy personality. Even Bella, who was as brash as she was loving, had pulled off being seductive with Caden. The sexy-kitten pictures on Amy's pajamas were more seductive than she was.

"Oh my God. I thought he'd never leave the table." Jenna glanced at Caden, Kurt, and Jamie, still enthralled with their fiancées at the other end of the table. She pulled Amy across the table and whispered, "This is your night. I can feel it!" She sat back and swayed to the music in her tight green spaghetti-strap dress with a neckline cut so low Pete could probably get lost in there.

Amy looked down at the slinky black dress the girls had put her in earlier that evening. They were always trying to sex her up. *One look at you in this dress with these fuck-me heels and Tony's gonna be all over you,* Jenna had said while Jessica and Bella shimmied the dress down Amy's pin-thin body. *Fits like a glove. A sexy, slither-me-out-of-this glove,* Leanna had added. They'd pushed her into a chair, plied her with wine, and sometime later—Amy had no idea how long, because the alcohol had not only made her body go all loose and soft, but it had turned her brain to mush—they were in the bar with the men, and with her friends' confidence, she'd actually begun to believe that she might be able to pull off being übersexy for a night. Her mind might be foggy, but she'd caught a few words while the girls primped her into a hot, racy woman she didn't recognize. Her friends had thrown out words like *sexy, hot, take him* as if they were handing out doses of confidence.

Now she tugged at the hemline of the dress that barely covered the thong they'd also bought for her and insisted she wear. She wiggled in her seat, uncomfortable in the lacy butt floss. She should probably give up even trying and just let the new job change her life. Move to Australia, where she'd be too far for any relationship with Tony, and be done with it, but every time she looked at Tony, her stomach got all fluttery. It had done that since she was six years old, so she was pretty sure it wasn't going to change.

Caden, Pete, Jamie, and Kurt must have taken Jenna's whispers and hot stares as a cue, because they headed up to the bar, and Jessica, Bella, and Leanna scooted closer to Amy and Jenna.

"How about you put those puppies away before the guys over at that table drool into their drinks," Leanna said to Jenna while glaring at the three handsome, leering men sitting at the next table. They finally looked away when Bella shot them a threatening stare.

Jenna wrestled her boobs into submission with an annoyed look on her face. She always acted annoyed about her boobs, but Amy knew it was a love-hate annoyance. Jenna wouldn't be Jenna without her boobs always trying to break free.

"Look at our men up there at the bar." Bella wiggled her fingers at Caden. "Pete has his eyes on the drooling men. Kurt and Jamie are eyeing Leanna and

Jessica like they're on the menu, and Tony..."

"*Your* men," Amy corrected her. "Tony's not mine, and he looks mad, doesn't he?"

"Sexually frustrated, maybe. Not mad." Bella took a sip of her drink. "But you'll fix that tonight. I mean, be real, Amy. Who tells a girl to *behave and be careful* whenever she goes out if he's not interested? Why would he care? And not just that—he always adds that you can text him if you need him and he'll come running. Just. Like. Always."

Amy couldn't stop the exasperated sound that left her lips. "You read my texts?" That was the only way she could have known that Tony always offered to be there if she needed him.

"Duh. Of course I did. Consider it a recon mission. I had to know what we were dealing with here from his side." Bella had been pulling for Amy and Tony to get together as long as Amy had been in love with him, which was just about forever. She stood and dragged Amy toward the dance floor. "Come on, sweetie. Time to have some fun."

The other girls jumped up and followed them. Amy sensed Tony's eyes on her before she caught sight of him watching them. It made her nervous and excited at once. The music blared with a fast beat. Amy's head was spinning from the alcohol, and as Bella and Jenna dirty danced up and down her body, gyrating with their hands in the air, Amy tried to ignore the rush of anticipation mixing with nervous energy inside her. Leanna and Jessica danced beside them in a far less evocative fashion that was more Amy's speed, but she could no sooner disengage from being the target of Jenna's and Bella's sexual dancing then she could ignore Tony as he moved to the edge of the dance floor. His eyes raked slowly down her body, making her insides twist in delight. His jaw muscles bunched as he slid his eyes around the bar and leveled the leering men at the table a few feet away with a dark stare.

The sexy dancing, the alcohol, and the way Tony was guarding her like she was a precious treasure—his precious treasure?—boosted her confidence. Amy rocked her hips to the beat. She closed her eyes, lifted her hands above her head, and let the music carry her into what she hoped was a plethora of tempting moves.

"You go, girlfriend," Jenna encouraged her. "He's not going to be able to resist you. You're drunk, sexy, and ready for action. What man could resist that?" She wiggled her butt against Amy's hips.

"Oh, please. He'll probably *never* reciprocate my feelings, which is why I'm seriously considering the job offer from Duke Ryder." *Never again, anyway.* Her chest tightened with the thought.

"No, you are *not.*" Bella's eyes widened as she froze and pointed her finger at Amy, right there in the middle of the dance floor. "You are not going to move to Australia for two years. You'll never come back to Seaside in the summers if you're in *Australia*. Can't you tell Duke you'll consider nine months out of the year instead of twelve?"

Duke Ryder was a real estate investor who owned more than a hundred properties throughout the world. He was also Blue and Jake's older brother. Blue Ryder was a specialty carpenter who had renovated Kurt and Leanna's cottage and built an art studio for Jenna and Pete. He'd since become one of the gang and hung out with them often. Jake was an Army Ranger and mountain-rescue specialist. Amy had dated Jake briefly last summer, but he was younger and too wild for her. And...he wasn't Tony.

"No, I can't," Amy answered. "It's a full-time

position heading up the creation of the new Ryder Conference Center. The conference center is going to be the focus of international meetings with major corporations. I think I need to be on-site full-time." Amy had worked with Duke on a consulting basis for several years. When Jessica and Jamie had said they were getting married at the Ryder Resort in Boston, Amy had jumped at the chance to help plan the event and work with Duke and his staff again. Amy had known that Duke was negotiating on a property in Australia, but she hadn't realized he'd sealed the deal until she'd arrived at the resort two days ago and he'd offered her a full-time job as director of operations for the Conference Division Center. She'd never been to Australia, and between all of her friends getting engaged and summer after summer of wasted energy spent on a man who treated her more like an adoring brother than a potential love interest, she decided it was high time she made some changes in her life.

Amy tucked her straight blond hair behind her ears and moved her shoulders to the slow beat of the music. "I'm not sure being here for the summer is smart anyway. It's like torturing myself." She stopped dancing at the thought of not coming back to Seaside for the summers. Could she really do that? Would she even want to? Could she survive not seeing Tony even if she knew for sure he didn't want her?

This was why she had to figure out her life and make a change. She was becoming pathetic.

She sensed Tony's eyes on her again and forced her hips to find the beat as Bella and Leanna danced closer. "It might be time I move on," she said more confidently than she felt.

"Move on from Tony?" Bella took her hand and dragged her back toward the table with the others on their heels.

Amy saw Tony's eyes narrowing as they hurried past. Why was he so angry all of a sudden?

"He's so into you, he won't let you go." Bella elbowed her as they took their seats. "He texts you almost every day."

"Yeah, with stuff like, *Won another competition* and *Check me out in* Surfer Mag *next month!* He texts me when he's going to miss an event at Seaside. He doesn't text me because he misses me or wants to see me." Tony had started texting her during the summers when they were teenagers, because Amy was the only one who checked her cell phone when they were at the Cape, and at some point, those summer texts had turned into a year-round connection. He'd stopped texting her for a few years when she was in college and he was building his surfing and speaking careers, although she knew the real reason he'd stopped, and it had nothing to do with either. After she'd graduated from college, he'd begun texting again. She hadn't known why he started up again, and after losing that connection for so long, she didn't ask. She was just glad to have him back. Since then, she'd become his habit, but not exactly the type of habit she wanted to be.

"It's not like what each of you have. I want that, what you have. I want a guy who says I'm the only woman for him and that he can't live without me, like your guys say to you." *I want Tony to say that.*

Seeing her girlfriends so much in love was what really drove home how lonely Amy had become over the past few summers.

"I think he takes care of you like you're *his*. I mean, how many guys text to say they saw a kitty pajama top you'd look adorable in if they aren't gay or interested?" Bella shifted her shoulders in a *Yeah, that's right* way.

"I'm probably the only woman he knows who wears kitty pajamas. He was teasing me, not being flirty or boyfriendish." *Was he?* No, he definitely wasn't. There had been times when Amy had thought Tony was looking at her like he was interested in a more intimate way, but they were fleeting seconds, and they passed as quickly as he'd taken his next breath. She was probably seeing what she wanted to see, not what he really felt, and she'd begun to wonder if she'd really loved him for so long, or if he'd become *her* habit, too.

"You know, he's never brought another woman to Seaside." Leanna's loose dark mane was wavy and tousled. With her golden tan and simple summer dress, she looked like she'd just come from the beach. Her gaze softened in a way that made Amy feel like she wanted to fall into Leanna's arms and disappear. "And look how he treats you. He's always got an arm around you, and when you drink too much at our barbecues, he always carries you home."

Amy wanted to believe them and to see what they apparently saw when he looked at her, but she never had. It was the secret memories of being in Tony's strong arms that long-ago summer, feeling his heart beat against hers, feeling safe and loved, that made her hopeful there would come a day when they'd find themselves there again. But then her mind would travel to the *end* of those recent nights when she'd had too much to drink and he'd carried her home. When he tucked her into bed and went along his merry way back to his own cottage across the road, quickly dousing her hope for more with cold reality. Whatever they'd had that summer, she'd ruined.

"Exactly, Leanna. That's why she's not making a decision about Australia until *after* this weekend," Jenna said. "Right, Ames?"

"Yes. That's my plan. I'm going to talk to Tony, and if he looks me in the eye and says he has no interest in anything more than friendship, then I'm going to take the job. It's pretty stupid, really, because how many times has he had the opportunity to...you know?" She dropped her eyes to her glass and ran her finger along the rim. Amy was as sweet as Bella was brash, and even thinking about trying to seduce Tony and find out where his heart really stood had her stomach tied in knots. When her friends had come up with the idea of seducing Tony, she'd fought it, but they'd insisted that once he kissed her, he'd never look back, and she'd grabbed that shred of hope as if it were a brass ring. Now her fingers were slipping a little.

"Talk? That's not the plan," Jenna said.

Jessica shook her head. "So, seduction? You're going to try?"

"If I can muster the courage." Amy drew in a deep breath, hoping she wouldn't back out. As much as she wanted closure, the idea of actually hearing Tony tell her that he didn't see her as anything other than a friend made her almost chicken out. But she didn't want to chicken out. She had a great job opportunity, and at thirty-two, she was ready to settle down and maybe even start a family. But that thought was even more painful than Tony turning her away.

Tony set a disconcerting stare on Amy as he moved confidently across the floor with the other guys, heading for their table. Her pulse ratcheted up a notch, as his eyes went dark and narrow. She broke the connection, grazing over his low-slung jeans and short-sleeve button-down shirt, afraid to try to decipher if it was an angry or an interested look in his eyes. She'd probably see only what she really wanted to see anyway.

Big mistake. Now she was even more nervous.

Several women in the bar turned and watched the four gorgeous men crossing the floor, but Amy knew they had to be looking at Tony. She was held prisoner by his sun-drenched skin, sandy hair that brushed his devilishly long lashes, and squared-off features that amped up his ruggedness and made her pulse go a little crazy. She reached for a glass of liquid courage, having no idea whose it was, and drained it as Tony slid in beside her. His thighs met hers, and his goddamn scent made her hot all over again. She grabbed another glass and drained it, and another, until the glasses were all empty and the nervous stirrings in her stomach stilled.

"Since when did you become Beyoncé?" Tony grumbled.

Beyoncé? Was that good or bad? Amy couldn't form an answer. All she could think about was that no matter what the outcome, after tonight her life would never be the same.

TONY HAD SPENT the last three hours watching men ogle Amy in that damn skimpy dress of hers. What was she thinking, dressing like that? He worried about her when she drank. She was too small to protect herself against unwanted advances, and she exuded sweetness like she was made of sugar, making her an easy target for a savvy guy. And he knew for a fact that Amy Maples was made of sugar—and spice and all things in between that were delicious and worthy of being savored. But that was a long time ago, and he'd spent years making sure Amy was treated as she deserved to be and putting his own desires on the back burner. Or trying to, anyway. He didn't think anyone else noticed that he could barely hold his shit together when it came to Amy, and he was grateful for that.

She was looking at him in a way that was reminiscent of that summer years ago, and he assumed it was caused by the far-too-many drinks she'd consumed. She never could hold her alcohol. He ran his hand through his hair and ground his teeth together. Maybe he'd take a walk back up to the bar to get away from the assholes watching her. He'd seen Pete stare them down when they were leering at Jenna, but Pete was Jenna's fiancé. She was his to protect.

Well, he wasn't Amy's fiancé, but she needed protecting too.

She's with Bella and the girls. They'll protect her. He mulled that over for a minute or two. *Bella and the girls.* Yeah, they'd protect Amy. They were about as protective of Amy as he was, but the idea of moving from Amy's side and having some asshole saunter over and hit on her messed with his mind. She was so damn beautiful and way too naive for her own good. One of her gorgeous smiles could stop a man cold, and she was clueless to that fact. *Fuck.* It was so easy not to think about those things when they were in different states during the year, but summers? *Christ.* They were torture. And these last few summers, watching his summer friends fall in love, made this time with Amy even more difficult. But they'd crossed that line years ago, and not only had it not ended well, but Amy seemed to have moved on just fine, while Tony never really had.

He thought about all the summer nights since then that he'd spent checking up on her, making sure she got home safely. The summer she'd turned twenty-two and insisted on going out with that bastard Kevin Palish. What a prick. Tony'd stalked his window that night until she arrived home safely. Normally he tried to ignore the Seaside gossip about who Amy was dating, and she seemed to keep guys away from the complex, as far as he could see, but a few summers ago she'd dated that other guy who came around more than a handful of times. What was his name? Hell, Mr. Tall, Dark, and Annoying. Tony had waited up every night for a week to make sure Amy got home okay—and to make sure the dude left shortly after dropping her off at her cottage. Not that it was any of his business or that he could have done anything about it if they'd spent the night together. That was the problem. It wasn't his business. Luckily, Amy had come to her senses and broken up with the guy before Tony ever woke up to the guy's truck in her driveway.

Amy wiggled in the seat beside him, tugging at that way-too-fucking-short dress. Her thigh pressed against his, and it suddenly got way too hot in there. He unbuttoned another button of his shirt and exhaled loudly, trying to talk himself out of going up to the bar. He should stay right there to ward off looks, like the one the dark-haired guy from the table of oglers was giving her. Amy smiled and fidgeted with the hem of her dress again. *Goddamn it.* Tony's thoughts drifted to last summer when she'd dated bad-boy, mountain-rescuer, handsome-as-Brad-Fucking-Pitt Jake Ryder. Tony had seen all the women at the beach party eyeing Jake, and Amy had acted the same adorably nervous way around him. Jake was younger than Amy, too, which pissed Tony off even more, and he was friends with Jake. He actually liked the guy. But she needed a man, not a boy.

Fuck it. If he couldn't be the man she deserved, he could at least make sure no other jackass treated her badly. He laced his fingers with hers and set their hands on her thigh.

"What?" Amy asked.

Tony nodded at the guy at the next table. "No need

to flirt with a guy like that. He'll only hurt you."

"Then maybe you should take me back to my room." She said it with wide, innocent eyes that tore right through him like lightning.

He rose to his feet and pulled Amy up with him.

"We're calling it a night," he said to their friends. He needed to get her to her room before she got herself into trouble—or before he got himself into trouble. "I'm going to walk Amy back to her hotel room. Jamie, Jessica, enjoy your last night of freedom."

"You're kidding, right?" Jamie rubbed noses with Jessica. "Who needs freedom? All I want is to wake up with Jessica in my arms for the rest of my life."

Yeah, and all I want is to wake up with Amy in my arms.

He shifted his eyes to Amy, standing before him pink-cheeked, glassy-eyed, and sexier than hell in that skimpy little black number that looked painted on and high heels that did something amazing to her long, lean legs. He forced his eyes north, over her perfect small breasts to the sleek line of her collarbone, which he wanted to trace with his tongue. Her hair fell over one of her heavy-lidded green eyes, giving her a sultry look that sent heat to his groin. When she trapped her lower lip between her teeth, it took all his effort to force something other than, *Damn, you look hot,* from his lips. Well...how was he supposed to resist her now?

She slid her arm around his waist and leaned her head against his chest.

"Okay, big guy. Take me home."

If she only knew what those words coming from her while dressed in that outfit did to him. As he'd done for too many years to count, he bit back his desires and walked her back to her room. He pulled her room card from his pocket, and it dawned on him that he always carried Amy's stuff. Her keys, her wallet, her phone. At some point, his pockets had become her pocketbook.

Tony held the door open for Amy and kept one hand on her hip as she walked unsteadily past him.

He closed the door and took in her hotel room. Standard upscale fare, it looked like his room, with a king-size bed, a long dresser and mirror, and a decent-size sitting area. Amy's perfume and lotions were lined up neatly on the dresser, along with her birth control pills, which made his gut twist a little. He didn't want to think about Amy having sex with anyone. Well, except maybe him, but—

"Hey." Amy reeled around on him, stepping forward in those sky-high heels. He didn't need to inhale to know that she smelled like warm vanilla, a scent that haunted him at night.

She wobbled a little, and instinct brought his hand to her waist. He'd held Amy in his arms a million times, comforting her when she was sad, carrying her when she was a little too drunk to be steady on her feet. He'd cared for her when she was sick and sat up with her after each of her girlfriends had fallen in love, when she simply couldn't handle being alone. He had a feeling those nights were their little secrets, because he'd never heard Bella, Jenna, or Leanna ever make reference to them, and those girls talked about everything. Now, as she stepped closer and touched his stomach with one finger and looked at him like she had years ago, not like the sweet, too-good-to-be-true Amy that she never strayed from around him unless she was drinking, he found himself struggling to remain detached enough to keep his feelings in check.

He forced himself to act casual. "What's up, Ames?"

She trapped that lower lip of hers again, and his

body warmed.

Amy stumbled on her heels and caught herself against his chest. She slid her hands up the front of his shirt, and his body responded like Pavlov's dog. Amy had that effect on him, but he'd always been good about keeping it under wraps. What was happening to him? Was it the romance of the impending wedding? Watching his best buddies whisper and nuzzle their fiancées while he had walls so thick around his heart that he didn't know if he'd ever be able to move forward and love anyone else again?

She gazed up at him with naive curiosity in her eyes, and it was that innocence that threatened his steely resolve. It almost did him in every time they were alone together. Only this time she had the whole hips-swaying, breasts-pushing-against-him thing going on.

Christ. He covered her hands with his and breathed deeply. With those heels, they were much closer in height. A bow of his head and he could finally taste her sweet mouth again.

With that selfish thought, he pressed her hands to his chest to keep them from roaming and to keep himself from becoming any more aroused. She gazed up at him, looking a little confused and so damn sexy it was all he could do to squelch his desire to take her in his arms and devour her.

"What do you need, Ames?"

"I'm pretty sure you know what I need," she said in a husky voice as she pressed her hips to his.

You don't mean that. You're just drunk. He clenched his jaw against his mounting desire. She was all he ever wanted, and she was the one person he knew he should walk away from.

"Amy."

"Tony." Her voice was thin and shaky.

"You're drunk." He peeled her hands from his chest. She got like this when she was drunk: sultry, sexier, eager. As adults, she'd never taken it this far. She'd made innuendos over the years, but more in jest than anything else. He wasn't an idiot. He knew Amy cared about him, but he also knew she sometimes forgot things. Important things. Life-altering events that were less painful if forgotten. He was certain it was why she drank when they were together and why he'd spent years protecting her. Not that she needed protecting often. Drinking was a summer thing for Amy, and really, she rarely drank too much. She didn't drink when she wasn't at the Cape. He knew this because over recent years, after Amy had graduated from college and settled into her business, he'd begun texting her more often. He'd been unable to ignore his need for a connection to her any longer. He could count on one hand how many times she'd made reference to drinking.

"I might be a little drunk." Her sweet lips curved into a nervous smile. "But I think I know what *you* want."

What I want and what I'll let myself have are two very different things.

He exhaled, took her hand, and turned toward the bed. "Sit down and let me help you get out of your heels and then I'll go back to my room. I don't want you to break your ankle."

She swayed on her heels and attached herself to his side again. "I don't want you to go to your room."

Tony stepped back. The back of his legs met the dresser. "Amy—"

"Tony," she said huskily, taking him by surprise.

"Ames," he whispered. She was killing him. Any other man would have silenced her with a kiss, carried her to the bed, pushed that damn sexy-ass dress up to her neck, and given her what she wanted. But Tony had made a career out of resisting Amy, protecting her. He respected her too damn much to let her make a mistake she would only regret when she sobered up.

He gripped her forearms and held her at a safe distance.

She narrowed her eyes and reached for his crotch.

For a breath he closed his eyes and let himself enjoy the feel of her stroking him in ways he'd only dreamed of. Every muscle in his body corded tight as he reluctantly gripped her wrist.

"Amy, stop." He'd learned his lesson with her when he was a teenager, and he was never letting either of them go back to that well of hurt. "We're not doing this."

The dark seductiveness that had filled her eyes when she was touching him was gone as quickly as it had appeared. Her shoulders rounded forward, and hurt filled her eyes.

"Why?"

He felt like a heel. A prick. A guy who *should* have taken her to bed, if only to love her as she deserved to be loved. Even if she might not remember or appreciate it in the morning. He draped an arm over her shoulder and pulled her into a hug.

"Come on, Amy. You're drunk and you won't remember any of this tomorrow. Let me help you get ready for bed."

"Don't you want me?"

Her broken voice nearly did him in, and when her arms went limp, he tightened his grip on her. "Amy," he whispered again.

In the space of a few seconds she pushed away from him, determination written in the tension around her mouth and the fisting of her hands.

"Tell me why you don't want me. What is it? Am I

too flat-chested? Too unattractive?"

"No." *Fuck. You're the sexiest woman I know.* Anger felt so wrong coming from her that it momentarily numbed him.

"I know I suck at seduction, but don't these fuck-me heels or this stupid dress turn you on? Even a little?"

"Your fuck-me heels? Boy, you are drunk. You don't realize what you're saying. Come on." He reached for her hand and she shrugged him off again.

"Goddamn it, Amy. Let me help you." *Before I give in to what I really want and lay your vulnerable, gorgeous, sexy body beneath me and devour you.*

"So that's it. I don't turn you on." She paced the room on wobbly ankles, looking like she was playing dress up in her mother's high heels—and it did crazy things to Tony's body. He followed beside her in case she stumbled, fighting the urge to give in and show her just how much she turned him on.

"Maybe if I had bigger boobs, or if I were better at acting sexy, or if I were smarter, you'd want me."

It surprised him that she avoided the secret they'd buried so long ago, but then again, after that summer, she'd never said another word about it. And he'd let her get away with that, believing it was the only way she could survive what had happened. Just like him.

"Amy, it's none of those things." He did *not* want to have this conversation with her. He wanted to fold her in his arms and kiss the worry away.

Tears slipped down her cheeks.

Hell. Tony could handle a lot of things, but Amy's tears melted his heart, and that he'd caused them was further proof he wasn't the right guy for her.

"Then why, Tony? Just tell me once and for all. Why don't you want me? I need to know so I can decide about taking this job in Australia."

Tony opened his mouth to answer, but his thoughts were jumbled as he processed what she'd said. "Australia? I thought you said you weren't taking it."

She crossed her arms, and he hated knowing it was to protect herself from his rejection. Tony felt like an asshole, but he knew that taking Amy up on her seduction would only dredge up bad memories and lead to hurting her. They'd spent a lifetime denying the past between them existed, even to themselves.

"I said I wasn't sure what I was going to do." She dropped her eyes to the floor, and he slid a hand in hers, as he'd done a million times before. It was a natural reaction. Taking care of her. Protecting her. Helping her feel safe. He knew it could send her mixed messages, but he just couldn't help himself. His hand had already claimed its spot with hers.

"You'd give up everything you've built to run Duke's resort? You'd move to Australia?" He had nothing against Duke Ryder. But the idea that Amy would change her life to help him just pissed Tony off.

She sank down onto the bed and buried her face in her hands.

He wrapped an arm around her shoulder, and when she tried to pull away, he tightened his grip and kissed the top of her head.

"Amy, you're sexy, smart, and everything a guy could want."

She cocked her head to the side and narrowed her damp eyes. He felt like the biggest prick on earth, and at the same time, his own heart was fighting tooth and nail against the space he was trying to maintain between them.

"Christ." He scrubbed his hand down his face. "You are all those things, Amy, and so much more, but..."

"But you like me as a friend."

He'd never seen so much hurt concentrated in one person's eyes, and even if he had, it wouldn't have compared to seeing it in Amy's. He touched his forehead to hers, and he did the only thing he knew how to do without doing irreparable damage to their friendship.

His lie came in a whisper. "No. I *love* you as a friend."

He loved Bella, Caden, and the others, goddamn it. What he felt for Amy was so much bigger than friendship, it threatened to stop his fucking heart.

She didn't say a word, just nodded, and Tony knew in that moment that she wasn't drunk enough to forget what he'd said by the morning—and he almost wished she were.

(End of Sneak Peek)
To continue reading, be sure to purchase
SEASIDE SECRETS, Seaside Summers, Book Four

Please enjoy a preview of the next
Love in Bloom novel

Dreaming of Love

The Bradens

Love in Bloom Series

Melissa Foster

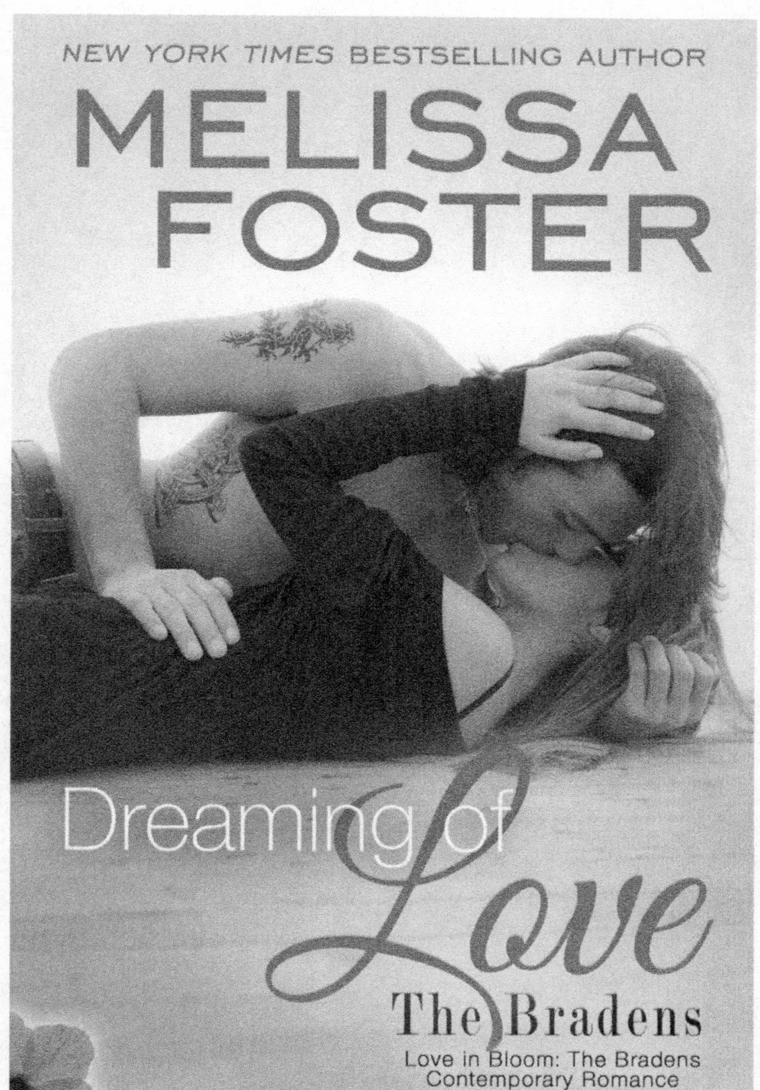
NEW YORK TIMES BESTSELLING AUTHOR
MELISSA
FOSTER
Dreaming of
Love
The Bradens
Love in Bloom: The Bradens
Contemporary Romance

Chapter One

LUSH. VERDANT. HILLY…Amazing. Emily stood on the covered balcony of the villa where she'd rented a room just outside of Florence, Italy, overlooking rolling countryside and the spectacular city below. The sun was kissing the last light of day goodbye, leaving chilled air in its wake. She sighed at the magnificent view, wrapped her arms around her body, and gave herself a big hug. She couldn't believe she was finally here, staying at the villa that her favorite architect, Gabriela Bocelli, built.

Gabriela Bocelli wasn't a very well-known architect, but her designs exuded simplicity and grace, which Emily had admired ever since she'd first come across this villa during her architecture studies. That felt like a hundred years ago. She'd dreamed of visiting Tuscany throughout school, but in the years since, she'd been too busy building her architecture business, which specialized in passive-house design, to take time off. If it weren't for one of her older brothers, she might still be back in Trusty, Colorado, dreaming of Tuscany instead of standing on this loggia, losing her breath to the hilly terrain below.

She pulled her cell phone from the back pocket of her jeans and texted Wes.

You're the best brother EVER! So happy to be here. Thank you! Xox.

Emily had five brothers, each of whom had hounded her about her safety while she was traveling. Or really, *whenever* they didn't have their eyes on her. Pierce, her eldest brother, had wanted to use his own phone plan to buy her a second cell phone with international access. *Just in case*. She'd put her foot down. At thirty-one years old, she could handle a ten-day trip without needing her brothers to rescue her. It wasn't like she ever needed saving, but her brothers had a thing about scrutinizing every man who came near her. Yet another reason why she didn't date very often.

Still, she was glad they cared, because she adored each and every one of their overprotective asses.

Adelina Ambrosi appeared at the entrance to the balcony with a slightly less energetic smile than had been present throughout the day. Adelina had run the resort villa with her husband, Marcello, for more than twenty years. She was a short, stout woman with a friendly smile, eyes as blue-gray as a winter's storm, and wiry gray hair that was currently pinned up in a messy bun. She must have mastered the art of walking quietly to keep from disturbing the guests.

"Good evening, Emily." Adelina brushed lint from the curtains hanging beside the glass doors. Emily was glad they loved the property as much as she did. They rented out only two rooms of the six-bedroom villa in order to always have space available for family and friends. The villa was a home to them, not just a business, as was evident in the warm guest rooms.

"Good evening, Adelina. Any news on Serafina's

husband?"

Serafina was Adelina and Marcello's daughter, who had recently moved back home with her eight-month-old son. They'd been living in the States when her husband, Dante, a United States Marine, had gone missing in Afghanistan while out on tour almost three months ago. Adelina had told Emily that she'd begged Serafina to come home and let her take care of her and baby Luca until her husband returned—and Adelina was adamant that he *would* return. Emily, on the other hand, wasn't quite so sure.

"Not yet, but I have faith." Adelina lowered her eyes, and with a friendly nod, she disappeared down the hall in the direction of her bedroom.

Emily turned back toward the evening sky, sending a silent prayer that Serafina's husband would return unharmed.

"It's a beautiful view, isn't it?"

The rich, deep voice sent a shiver down Emily's spine. She turned, and—*holy smokes.* Standing before her was more than six feet of deeply tanned, deliciously muscled male. His hair was the color of warm mocha and spilled over his eyes, hanging just an inch above the collar of his tight black T-shirt. She opened her mouth to greet him, but her mouth went dry and no words came. She reached for the stone rail of the archway she'd been gazing through and managed a smile.

His full lips quirked up, filling his deep brown eyes with amusement as he stepped closer.

"The view," he repeated as his eyes swept over her, causing her insides to do a nervous dance. The amusement in his eyes gave way to something dark and sensual.

It had been so long since Emily had seen that look directed at her that it took her by surprise. She cleared her throat and reluctantly dragged her gaze back to the view below, which paled in comparison to the one right next to her.

Holy crap. Get a grip. It must be the Italian air or the evening sky that had her heart racing like she'd just run a marathon.

Or the fact that I haven't had sex in...

"Awestruck. I hear Italy has that effect on people." He leaned his forearms on the thick stone rail and bent over, clasping his large hands together.

"Yeah, right. Italy." Emily's eyes widened at the sarcasm in her voice. She clenched her mouth shut. She hadn't meant to say that out loud. He probably had this crazy effect on all women, and here she was gushing over him. She didn't gush. *Ever*. What the hell?

He cocked his head to the side and smiled up at her. Emily saw the spark of something wicked and playful in his eyes, like he could be either in a heartbeat. A hint of danger that Emily thought maybe he knew he possessed. A low laugh rumbled from his chest as he arched a brow.

Oh God. She felt her chest and face flush with heat and crossed her arms. A barrier between them. Yes, that's what she needed, since apparently she couldn't control her own freaking hormones.

"I'm sorry. I just got in this evening and it was a long trip. Eye fatigue." *Eye fatigue?* She held her breath, hoping he'd pretend, as she was, that that was the real reason she was ogling him.

"I just arrived myself." He held a hand out. "Dae Bray. Nice to meet you."

Emily felt the tension in her neck ease as he accepted her explanation. "Emily Braden. Day? That's an interesting name." She shook his strong, warm hand, and he held hers a beat too long, bringing that tension right back to her body—and an entirely different type of tension to her lower belly.

"Maybe I'm an interesting guy. Dae. D. A. E.," he said, as if he had to spell it often, which she imagined he did. "Is this your first time in Tuscany?"

How could he be so casual, speak so easily, when her heart was doing flips in her chest? He didn't have an ounce of tension anywhere in his body. He was all ease and comfort, his body moving fluidly as he shifted his position and leaned his sexy hip, clad in low-slung jeans, against the rail. When he crossed one ankle over the other and set his palms on the stone, his T-shirt clung to his wide chest, then followed his rippled abs in a sexy vee and disappeared beneath the waist of his jeans. Her eyes lingered there, desperately fighting to drop a little lower. It took all of her focus to ignore the heat spreading through her limbs and drag her eyes away.

"Yes." *Why does my voice sound breathy?* She drew her shoulders back and met his gaze, forcing a modicum of control into her voice. "How about you?"

He shook his head, and his shiny dark hair fell in front of his eyes. One quick flick of his chin sent it off his face, giving her another brief look at his deep-set eyes, his rugged features, and the peppering of whiskers on his square jaw.

"It's the first for me, too."

Emily's phone vibrated and Wes's name flashed on the screen. She reached for it and read Wes's message, desperately needing a distraction.

So glad. Be safe and have fun. You deserve it.

"Probably your husband wondering what you're doing talking to some dude instead of taking a romantic stroll through the vineyards with him." His eyes narrowed a hair, but that easy smile remained on his lips.

Emily met his gaze. "That would be a feat,

considering I'm not married." Not that she wouldn't like to be. Recently, she'd watched four of her brothers fall head over heels in love. They hadn't even been looking for love, and there she was, waiting to love and be loved and trying to keep the green-eyed monster inside her at bay. She was happy for them. She really was. But she couldn't deny her desire to find that special someone who would cherish her for more than the Braden wealth. She'd come to accept that she wouldn't find that in her small hometown. She'd buried herself in building a successful business to fill those lonely hours.

"Well, in that case, would you care to join me for a glass of wine?"

Before Emily could answer, another text came through from Wes.

Not TOO much fun! I'd hate to have to come all the way to Tuscany to pound some guy for taking advantage of my little sister.

Emily laughed, taking comfort in Wes's overprotective nature. Somehow, it put her at ease. She slid her phone into her jeans pocket and smiled up at the gorgeous man beside her. She was thousands of miles from home in the most romantic place on earth. Why shouldn't she have *too much* fun? She wondered what Wes considered too much fun and decided that, knowing her brother, holding hands with a guy was too much fun for his little sister. Maybe, just maybe, it was her turn to have fun.

Feeling emboldened, and a little rebellious, she lifted her chin and gave her best narrow-eyed gaze, which she hoped looked seductive, but she was sure it fell short. She didn't have much practice at being a temptress. But a girl could try, couldn't she?

"Sure. That sounds great."

Dae pushed from the rail and reached for her

hand. "Shall we?"

"Um..." Was that too familiar of a gesture? Had she given him too *good* of a look?

"I'm harmless. Just ask my sisters. But I'm also affectionate, so it's a hand or an arm. Take your pick."

"You have sisters?" Why did that make him seem safer? He reached for her hand, and damn if their palms didn't fit together perfectly. His hand was warm and big, a little rough and calloused.

"Two. And two brothers. You?" He led her through the villa toward the kitchen. She was glad he didn't release her hand when they reached the high-ceilinged kitchen, which smelled of fresh-baked bread. He surveyed the bottles in the built-in wine rack that was artfully nestled into the wall, pulling out one bottle after another and scrutinizing the labels until he found one he approved of.

"Five brothers. Um...Are we allowed to just take a bottle of wine?" Emily looked around the pristine kitchen. Colorful bricks formed an arch over recessed ovens and cooktops. A copper kettle sat atop one burner, and on either side of the ovens were built-in pantries in deep mahogany.

"They said to make myself at home." Dae handed her a bottle, then led her past the large table that seated eight and an island equally as large. He reached into a glass cabinet on the far wall and retrieved two wineglasses.

He smiled a mischievous smile. "So...You're a rule follower?" He narrowed his eyes as he opened the bottle of wine.

A rule follower? Am I? She had no idea if she was or wasn't. She liked to joke and tease. Did that make her a rule breaker? Were there rules for thirtysomethings? A fleeting worry rose in her chest. What if he was a *major* rule breaker? What if he wanted her to do things she shouldn't? She was a Braden, and her family was very well respected, and no matter where she was, she had a reputation to uphold, which somehow made the whole situation a little more tempting.

"Emily?"

Oh no. What if—

His hands on her upper arms pulled her from her thoughts, which were quickly spiraling out of control.

"Emily. Relax." His hair curtained his eyes, but she caught a glimpse of his smile. "I was kidding."

Now I look like a boring Goody-Two shoes. She rolled her eyes—more at herself than at him. Wes's text must have subconsciously made her worry. *Or maybe I really am a Goody-Two shoes who can take banter but not rule breaking. Boring with a capital* B.

"Adelina told me to help myself to anything in the kitchen, including the wine. Day or night."

He snatched her hand again and led her out a heavy wooden door and across the lawn.

"I'm sorry, Dae. I didn't mean to seem like a buzzkill."

"It's okay. If you were my sister, I'd have hoped for that same careful reaction. You had the am-I-with-a-serial-killer look in your eyes." He glanced at her and smiled.

"Yikes. That's not very nice, is it?" She walked quickly in her heeled boots to keep up. Her eyes remained trained on the thick grass to keep from ogling Dae.

"I'm guessing that it has less to do with *nice* than to do with *safety*. Safety's always a good thing." He stopped short, and Emily bumped right into his side.

Their hips collided. Her hand instinctively rose to brace herself from falling, and the bottle of wine smacked against his chest, splashing wine on his T-shirt. He wrapped an arm around her back, bracing her against him.

"Oh my gosh. I'm so sorry." *Crap, crap, crap*. She swiped at the wine on his shirt as she tried to ignore how good his impressive muscles felt.

"I've been impaled by worse." He flashed that easy smile again, but his eyes darkened and filled with heat, and just like that, her knees weakened.

Damned knees. He tightened his grip on her. *Damned smart knees.*

Just when Emily was sure she'd stop breathing, he dropped his eyes to her boots. "Heels and grass don't mix."

She was still stuck on the feel of his arm around her and the quickening of her pulse.

"You okay?" he asked.

I don't know. "Yes. Fine. Yes."

He ran his thumb along her cheek, then licked a dash of wine that he'd wiped off with his thumb. "Mm. Good year."

Holy crap.

His eyes went smoky and dark. She liked smoky and dark. A lot.

"Let's sit. It's safer." He nodded toward his right.

Emily blinked away the crazy unfamiliar desire that had butterflies nesting in her belly and followed his eyes to an intimate stone patio built at the edge of the hill. Her eyes danced over the wisteria-laced trellis. Purple tendrils of flowers hung over the edges, and leaf-laden vines snaked up the columns.

"This is incredible." Tree branches reached like long, arthritic fingers from the far side of a path at the top of the hill to the wisteria, creating a natural archway. Rustic planters spilled over with lush flowers, lining a low stone wall that bordered the patio.

Holding the wine and the glasses, Dae crooked out his elbow. "Hold on tight. Wouldn't want you to stumble."

She had the strange desire to press her body against his and let him wrap his safe, strong arm around her. Instead, she slipped her hand into the crook of his elbow and wrapped it around his muscular forearm, wondering how a man could make her hot all over after only a few minutes.

DAE COULD PRACTICALLY see the gears turning in Emily's head, and even in her befuddled state, she was sexier than any woman he'd ever met. She was slender, with gentle curves accentuated by her designer jeans and the tight white V-neck she wore under an open black cardigan. He stole a glance at her profile as she took in the patio. She had a cute upturned nose, high cheekbones, and long hair the same dark color as his, which he'd like to feel brushing his bare chest. She wore nearly no makeup, and as his eyes lingered on the sweet bow of her lips, the word *stunning* sailed into his mind. He had a feeling that when Emily Braden wasn't caught off guard by an aggressive demolition expert who rarely gave people time to think things through, she was probably feisty as hell.

He'd felt her body tense when she'd run into him, and unstoppable heat had flared between them. She'd melted a little right there in his arms. *Melted*. That was the only way to describe the way the tension drained from her shoulders and back and brought all her soft curves against him. If he were the type of guy who was into casual sex, she'd be ripe for the taking. But Dae had left casual sex behind and had grown a conscience a few years back.

As he poured them each a glass of wine, he

wondered who had texted her earlier and caused her to laugh.

Dae handed her a glass of wine and held it up in a toast. “To Tuscany.”

Emily smiled as they clinked glasses, then took a sip of her wine. “Oh, that’s really good. It’s just what I needed.”

Dae watched her as she forwent the long wooden bench and sat atop the wide table.

“I can see better from here,” she explained. “I don’t want to miss a second of this incredible view.”

She could have no way of knowing that Dae almost always preferred to sit atop tables rather than on benches or chairs. Always had.

“A woman after my own heart. I always prefer tabletops to chairs.” He sat beside her and rested his elbows on his knees. “So, Emily Braden, what brings you to Tuscany?”

“My brother gave me this trip as a gift for helping him arrange a special night for his girlfriend.” She smiled as she spoke of her brother, and he liked that she seemed to like her family. Family was important to Dae. He’d found that he could tell a lot about the generosity and loyalty of a person by how they spoke of and treated their family.

“That’s a hell of a gift.” Her thigh brushed his, and when their eyes met and she didn’t move hers away, he realized she’d done it on purpose, causing a stirring in his groin. *Down, boy.* Emily was just beginning to relax, and the last thing he wanted to do was to scare her off.

“Yes. It was. He knew I’ve been dying to see Tuscany, and this villa in particular. Gabriela Bocelli is one of my favorite architects. But if it had been left up to me, I’d never have made it here. Between work and my family, well, I’m not really good about taking time for myself." She finished her wine, and Dae refilled their glasses.

"Life's too short to miss out on the things you really want to do. I'm glad your brothers are looking out for you." Dae was a self-made man with enough money that he could buy all of his siblings trips to Tuscany, but while he and his sisters were close, buying them a trip to Tuscany was so far out of the realm of their relationships that he could barely comprehend the gesture. Leanna never planned a damn thing in her life, and Bailey, his youngest sister, was a musician with a concert schedule that rivaled the busiest of them. Even coordinating dinner with her was a massive undertaking. If he ever purchased a trip for them, Leanna would miss the flight and Bailey would probably have to cancel it. Their gifts to one another were typically as simple as making time to get together and enjoy one another's company.

"My brothers are good at taking care of me. Maybe a little too good." She sighed.

"Overprotective?" Why did he enjoy knowing that?

"Oh, you could say that. They're great, really. I adore them, but...yeah. They're overprotective." She met his gaze, and the air around them sizzled again. She looked away, pink-cheeked, and pressed her hands to her thighs. "To be honest, I don't hate the way they are. I mean, it probably sounds childish, but I feel the same way about them."

"Overprotective?" She couldn't weigh more than a buck twenty. What could she possibly do to protect a man?

She smiled, and it lit up her beautiful, dark eyes. Her voice softened, and she sat up a little straighter. "Yeah. I know it's weird, but like, when they started dating their girlfriends, I watched out for them. Made sure the girls weren't going to treat them badly, or...well...My brothers are the catch of our town, and girls can be fickle. I didn't want them to get hurt. But now the ones who live in town are all in relationships, so..." She shrugged.

Loyal. He liked that. He wondered if she was the catch of their town, too. "Do you live in the town where you grew up?"

"Yeah, in Trusty, Colorado. It's about as big as your fist. All of us live there except Pierce, my oldest brother, and Jake, my youngest brother. Pierce is in Reno, and Jake is in LA. But they visit a lot. We're all really close. I can't imagine living anywhere else—or living far away from my family. Being away for college was enough. I'm glad to be back in my hometown." She finished her wine and set the glass beside her.

Dae held up the bottle. "More?"

"In a few minutes. I'm a lightweight. I wouldn't want you to have to carry me back up to my room."

Now, there's an idea. "Fair enough." He paused, pushing the thought of Emily in his arms to the back of his mind. "So, what do you do for a living?"

"I'm an architect. I specialize in passive houses, green building." She gazed out over the hillside, and her features softened again.

"Really? The passive-house movement is a good one, but it seems like builders don't understand it well enough to make headway."

Her eyes widened, and he felt the press of her leg against his. "You know about passive houses? Usually when I bring it up, people look all deer in the headlights at me."

"That doesn't surprise me. Most people don't understand heating by passive solar gain and energy gains from people and appliances. It's a concept they just aren't familiar with, so it sounds space-agey to them." Passive houses were the wave of the future, as far as Dae was concerned, and not just houses, but schools and office buildings, too. The technology may seem space-agey, but then again, so had electric cars and cell phones twenty years ago.

"Exactly." She smacked his thigh, and both of their eyes dropped to her hand.

He lifted his eyes to hers, and she swallowed hard. In the short time they'd been talking, he'd seen a handful of looks pass through her eyes: embarrassment, arousal, worry. She had to feel the way the air zapped between them. Her eyes darkened, and her lips parted.

Oh yeah, she feels it.

She licked her lips, and it just about killed him.

"What about you?" she asked, visibly more relaxed now as she leaned back on one hand and turned her body toward him. "Where do you live? What do you do?"

Her question made him think a little deeper about the two of them. *A sexy architect into green building. Figures.* It had been his experience that tree huggers rarely held much respect for demolition experts. He sucked down his wine and went with an evasive answer in hopes of postponing any negative discussion.

"Depends on the week. I don't like to be tied to one place for too long. I get itchy." He'd always been that way. Spending too much time alone in any one of the houses he owned made him edgy. He'd never met anyone he'd liked enough to spend a few weeks with, much less settle down with.

Emily's finely manicured brows furrowed. Clearly he wasn't going to get off that easily.

"So..."

"I'm into construction. I go where the jobs take me."

"Oh. I thought construction workers usually worked around where they lived."

"Some do. I work with larger projects, which means that I travel a lot." He didn't want to talk about his job. Especially not the demolition job he was assessing here in Tuscany. He was enjoying spending time with Emily, and the last thing he wanted to do was talk about why he blew up buildings for a living.

"How long are you here?" His feeble attempt at changing the subject.

"Nine days, and I have every day planned so I don't miss a thing." She held up her empty glass.

"No longer worried about me carrying you to your bedroom?" Their eyes locked, and he couldn't help but think, *Or mine,* as he filled her glass. Although he knew it was just his ego talking. He'd stopped having flings a few years ago—but they were still fun to think about.

"I can think of worse things." Her voice was quiet, seductive. She mindlessly twirled her finger in her hair and lowered her eyes. When she raised them again, she said more confidently, "Besides, you have sisters. I think you'll take care of me."

"That's a lot of trust in a guy you've known for only a little while." He refilled their glasses.

"If you were a serial killer, you'd have stabbed me and hidden my body by now. And if you were going to make a move, I think you'd have done more than talk about family." She moved her fingers over so they were touching his. "Like I said, you have sisters. I think the big brother in you will keep me safe."

Damn. Talk about conflicting signals. The hand. The brother talk. A guy could get whiplash trying to keep up.

An hour and an empty bottle of wine later, they were standing in front of the door to Emily's room. She was tucked beneath his arm, her cheeks flushed, her eyes glassy, and her head nestled against his chest.

Lightweight, indeed. Cute-as-hell lightweight. Dae took a step back, leaned his hip against the doorframe, and crossed his arms, debating. He wanted to kiss her, to feel the soft press of her lips against his and taste the sweet wine on that sassy tongue of hers. *I think the big brother in you will keep me safe.*

"These five overprotective brothers of yours, would they mind if we spent tomorrow together?"

She took a step back and raked her eyes down his body. "That depends. Do serial killers ask women on dates?"

He laughed. "I don't have enough experience with serial killers to answer that."

Emily's phone vibrated in her pocket.

"Maybe that's one of them. You can ask."

Emily pulled her phone out of her pocket and read a text. She trapped her lower lip between her teeth and raised her eyes to his, then held up her index finger before responding.

"Christ, you're not really asking your brother—are you?"

She shook her head, and her hair tumbled forward. "Soon-to-be sister-in-law. Daisy. She's marrying my brother Luke the weekend after I go home."

Dae scrubbed his hand down his face at the prospect of her asking her soon-to-be sister-in-law about going on a date with him. "Great." He didn't even try to mask his sarcasm.

Her phone vibrated again, and her long lashes fluttered as she read the text.

"Well? What does Daisy say?"

"Um..." She lowered the phone and held it behind her back with a coy smile.

Dae rolled his eyes. So much for their date. The

words *stranger danger* came to mind. "It was nice getting to know you tonight, Emily."

Her smile was replaced with tight lips and a wrinkled brow as he took a step away. "What? That's it? I haven't answered you yet."

He closed the distance between them, so their thighs touched. Their lips were a breath apart, and her eyes held a seductive challenge. It took all of his focus for him not to lean down and wipe that smug look off her face with a kiss.

"I assumed..."

"Assumed?" Her voice turned low and sexy. "What happened to Mr. Hand or Arm? Wow, you're not quite the man I thought you were if you give up that easy." She touched his chest, nearly doing him in.

Dae clenched his jaw at the challenge. "I'm trying to be respectful. You're the one who gave me the big-brother lecture earlier."

"Oh, yeah." She wrinkled her nose, and her eyes held a hint of regret.

She was so damn cute that he wanted to take care of her as much as he wanted to kiss her. "Yeah." He leaned down and pressed his cheek to hers, then wrapped an arm around her waist, holding her against him. "I honestly don't give a rat's ass what Daisy said," he whispered.

Emily nibbled on her lower lip.

Their bedrooms were located on more of a balcony than a hallway, with wrought-iron railings overlooking the great room below. The villa was silent, save for the sound of their heavy breathing.

"It's your answer I want, not hers."

He leaned back and gazed into her eyes, hoping she'd take a chance on the desire he could see lingering in them.

"Okay," she whispered.

"Great, and just for the record, I'd have kept you safe even if I didn't have sisters, but I can assure you that my feelings toward you are not brotherly."

Emily's eyes widened.

"And I wouldn't mind if you didn't act sisterly toward me, either."

"I—"

"Good night, Emily."

(End of Sneak Peek)
To continue reading, be sure to purchase
DREAMING OF LOVE, The Bradens

Strawberry Spice Jam
1 cup water
1–1.75-ounce package Sure-Jell pectin
750 ml strawberry wine
4 whole habanero peppers
5 1/2 cups sugar
8 eight-ounce mason jars

Add water to a large sauce pan and mix in the pectin slowly, bringing it to a boil. Add the wine, then remove the stems from the peppers and add them in to soak as you bring everything back to a boil. Now add sugar and return to a boil for three minutes. Let it sit for one minute, then remove the peppers and any seeds that are left and fill the jars.

Recipe fills 7 to 8 eight-ounce mason jars

Available on Amazon.com or
http://www.alsbackwoodsberrie.com

BECOME ONE OF
MELISSA'S
MOST TRUSTED FANS!

• Chat with Melissa

• Get Exclusive Sneak Peeks

• Win Fabulous Swag

JOIN MELISSA'S
STREET TEAM
TO JOIN VISIT
WWW.FACEBOOK.COM/GROUPS/MELISSAFOSTERFANS/

Complete LOVE IN BLOOM SERIES

SNOW SISTERS
Sisters in Love
Sisters in Bloom
Sisters in White

THE BRADENS
Lovers at Heart
Destined for Love
Friendship on Fire
Sea of Love
Bursting with Love
Hearts at Play
Taken by Love
Fated for Love
Romancing my Love
Flirting with Love
Dreaming of Love
Crashing into Love

THE REMINGTONS
Game of Love
Stroke of Love
Flames of Love
Slope of Love
Read, Write, Love

SEASIDE SUMMERS
Seaside Dreams
Seaside Hearts
Seaside Sunsets
Seaside Secrets
Seaside Nights
Seaside Whispers
Seaside Lovers
Seaside Embrace

HARBORSIDE NIGHTS SERIES
Includes characters from
Love in Bloom series

Catching Cassidy
Discovering Delilah
Chasing Charley
Tempting Tristan
Embracing Evan
Reaching Rusty
Loving Livi

More Books by Melissa

Chasing Amanda (mystery/suspense)
Come Back to Me (mystery/suspense)
Have No Shame (historical fiction/romance)
Love, Lies & Mystery (3-book bundle)
Megan's Way (literary fiction)
Traces of Kara (psychological thriller)
Where Petals Fall (suspense)

SIGN UP for MELISSA'S NEWSLETTER to stay up to date with new releases, giveaways, and events

NEWSLETTER:
http://www.melissafoster.com/newsletter

CONNECT WITH MELISSA

TWITTER:
https://twitter.com/Melissa_Foster

FACEBOOK:
https://www.facebook.com/MelissaFosterAuthor

WEBSITE:
http://www.melissafoster.com

STREET TEAM:
http://www.facebook.com/groups/melissafosterfans

Acknowledgments

Writing the Love in Bloom series has expanded my world in so many wonderful ways, the best of which is how often I get to interact with readers. Thank you for reaching out and letting me know how much you enjoy the characters and stories, for sharing my books with your friends, and for pitching in and helping with names, locations, and other fun facts on my Facebook fan page. I truly appreciate each and every one of you and hope you will continue to reach out.

I'd like to thank Chelsea Monte' Falin-Hammond for referring Cecily Smith and Janet Matthews Waring for referring Chris Perdue to help me with cello research. I owe much gratitude to Cecily and Chris, professional cellists, for answering my questions and filling me in on all things cello related. I have taken fictional liberties for the story. Any and all errors are my own and not a reflection of their knowledge. Thank you all for your generosity and kindness. I hope I've done your profession justice.

My brother Jon Cohen will probably cringe when he realizes he's mentioned in the acknowledgments of a romance book and that the book is dedicated to him, but he gave me the drone in *Seaside Sunsets,* and for that I am very grateful. Jon, you have an amazing brain. Thanks for sharing it!

And to my editorial team, Kristen, Penina, Jenna, Juliette, Marlene, and Lynn, thank you for your meticulous attention to detail.

I wish I could reach out and hug every one of the bloggers, reviewers, readers, and members of Team Pay-It-Forward, for their support and encouragement. Thank you for inspiring me on a daily basis.

To my husband and children…you know the drill. I love you more than ice cream, but I'm on the fence with chocolate. Xox.

Melissa Foster is a *New York Times* and *USA Today* bestselling and award-winning author. Her books have been recommended by *USA Today's* book blog, *Hagerstown* magazine, *The Patriot*, and several other print venues. She is the founder of the World Literary Café, and when she's not writing, Melissa helps authors navigate the publishing industry through her author training programs on Fostering Success. Melissa also hosts Aspiring Authors contests for children and has painted and donated several murals to the Hospital for Sick Children in Washington, DC.

Visit Melissa on her website or chat with her on social media. Melissa enjoys discussing her books with book clubs and reader groups and welcomes an invitation to your event.

Melissa's books are available through most online retailers in paperback and digital formats.

www.MelissaFoster.com

CPSIA information can be obtained
at www.ICGtesting.com
Printed in the USA
BVOW08s1644190717
489750BV00001B/37/P